# BRUTAL SAVAGE

## LILIAN HARRIS

# TRANSLATIONS AND PRONUNCIATIONS

- Eriu – "Air-ooh"
- Iseult – "Ee-salt"
- Tynan – "Tie-nan"
- Cillian – "KILL-ee-in."
- Fionn – "Fee-yun"
- Bratva – Russian organized crime or Russian Mafia
- Mo chuisle – my pulse
- Is pian i mo thóin tú. – You're a pain in my ass.
- Ná caoin a stór. Tá tú ag briseadh mo chroí. – Don't cry darling. You're breaking my heart.
- Go sábhála mac Dé sinn. – God give me strength.
- Nozh – knife
- Blyat – fuck
- Horosho – good
- Suka – bitch
- Pashli – Let's go.

HUGE THANK YOU TO CHRISTIANA FOR ALPHA READING
THIS BOOK AND MAKING IT THE BEST IT COULD BE.

SO HAPPY WE MET!

# ONE

## ELARA

**M**y fingers feather over my abdomen, my heart racing.

I wish it would all stop.

I need it to stop.

Because it hurts.

It hurts so much I can't breathe.

I often wonder when it'll actually stop hurting. When I'll finally be able to breathe again.

Except that'll never happen.

I'll always live this way: in fear. Looking over my shoulder. Wondering when he'll come back and finish what he started.

I'm in a constant loop of the past. Stuck in cement. Unable to climb out.

I want to.

I've tried.

Yet I still see his face.

Both of their faces.

My life has never been the same since I found out.

Since I was forced to do things no one should be forced to do.

So I knew I had to go.

And I made a plan to run.

When that day finally came, I did.

I left it all behind.

My life.

My past.

I tore off the woman I used to be, and in her place, I became Elara Hill.

Evelyn Connors was someone else. She had to be. I couldn't be her anymore.

Foolishly, I thought leaving it all behind would be enough. But it wasn't. Because I'm still here, reminded of what was.

Reminded of the betrayals.

The lies.

The pain.

I didn't think I could get away. But I made a friend, Derek, who set me up with a whole new identity.

I didn't come alone, though. I had to take my grandparents with me, or the people who were after me would've killed them. They knew about my father's death. They knew the people coming after me were the ones who killed him and got rid of the body.

That was only half the truth, though.

Because they didn't kill him.

*I* did.

# TWO

## ELARA

I know teachers aren't supposed to have a favorite student. Yet we do. We all do.

And mine is Brody Quinn.

The sweet eight-year-old boy who never smiles.

Never laughs.

Never even likes to be hugged.

Not anymore. Not since he lost both of his parents last year, I'm told.

He barely even looks at anyone. Like he's afraid even that would be too much communication, and it breaks my damn heart.

I adore him, and I wish there was something more I could do.

But I try. I talk to him during snack time or lunch, when he's sitting alone or next to people who are talking. While he's just there, existing in his own head. In his own pain.

I know all about that too.

Closing my eyes, I see her.

*Nonono! Mom! No!*

I remember my screams. The blood. So much blood.

I can't unsee it. Her body contorted on the shower floor. Her eyes lifeless.

I blink away the tears.

*Don't go back there. Don't you dare go back there.*

Losing my mom almost killed me. But losing the people you love at a young age is cruel and unfair, and Brody lost his mother right after his father was killed.

The school counselor told me his mom committed suicide after his dad died from a boat accident.

He found her.

His own mother.

A pang hits my chest, and I pinch the bridge of my nose to stop from crying.

Tears swim in my eyes anyway as I stare at him, quietly eating his pretzels at his desk while others are chatting with one another.

Gathering my bag of popcorn and Oreos, I get to my feet and grab a chair, placing it beside him. A movie plays for the kids to enjoy as they eat, and it's the screen that has his attention.

"Hey, Brody," I whisper. "Whatcha got there?"

I peek over at his pretzels as though I don't know, and he tilts up the bag so I can see the front.

"Ah, pretzels. I love pretzels."

He throws one into his mouth, not looking at me. Then, slowly, he moves the bag in my direction and jerks his hand like he wants me to take one.

My mouth presses tightly, and I fight not to cry because it's the most he's done since I joined the class.

"I can have one? Thank you! That's so nice of you." Reaching in, I catch one and toss it into my mouth. "How about we share? Maybe you want some of this popcorn?"

I know popcorn is one of his favorites. It's why I brought it today.

The bag crinkles as I pull it open and move it toward him.

At first, it doesn't appear as though he'll actually accept my offer. Then his hand moves just a little until he's reaching inside.

Silently, I do a happy dance. This is progress. This is something to be excited about.

Glancing at him, I wonder what he's thinking right now. Does he wish he could talk? Is he afraid to? I can't imagine that kind of trauma on any person, let alone a child.

I should call and make an appointment with his father's cousin, the man who adopted him. It'd be good to discuss what steps he's taking to help Brody.

I don't know much about him. Never even met the man.

But maybe it's time that I did.

# TYNAN

I make it a point to pick him up every day after school. His mother or father would be there every single day, and I want him to know that'll never change with me.

The therapist said Brody needs consistency and trust, and I'm doing everything in my damn power to give him that. I have to.

His father, Aiden, and I were close. Hell, he was more like a brother than a cousin. We grew up together, along with his brother, Ryan.

Brody was supposed to go to Ryan, except Aiden left a will, and he wanted me to have him.

Fuck if I know why. Maybe because Ryan has been to prison more times than I can count. Maybe it's because he's not really into kids.

Then again, what the hell do I know about them? Never had any.

I think Ryan was relieved when he found out Brody wouldn't go to him. Not because he doesn't love his nephew. He does. Though he'd rather do work for my father than do things like this: pick up Brody, do homework with him, or cook him a meal.

I could let Ruby take care of all that—she already does a lot—but I want to show Brody I'm in it. That I'm here. That I'm not going anywhere.

Ruby has been invaluable, though. She cooks for us when I can't. She does everything around here. A live-in housekeeper. Sitter too. I wouldn't be able to work and raise Brody if it wasn't for her.

Standing outside on the grass, right across from the school building, I wait for Brody to get out.

When I see him, he's the first in line, walking out with *her*.

Long black hair is coiled up in a classy bun, a few strands falling across her right cheek, those crystalline blue eyes twinkling like damn stars when she whispers to Brody.

And I hate that I notice.

That I see how beautiful she is.

Yet I've started to notice other things too. Little things when Brody's around her. Like the way he doesn't recoil when she puts her arm around him. Or the way he stands just a little closer every time he's beside her, waiting for her to let him cross over to me.

He never does that with me. He pushes me away like he despises me.

I know he doesn't. I know he's hurting. I'm hurting for him.

But this new substitute teacher, she's good for him. I can see that already.

She doesn't know what I look like. A pair of sunglasses fixes that. I don't want her to. It'd be harder to keep tabs on her that way. However, as Brody's adoptive father, it's my job to vet everyone he comes into contact with.

Including the alluring Ms. Hill.

My brother Fionn did some digging on her too. Her social media accounts were nonexistent. No trail to go on. She's a ghost by all accounts, and that has my radar up even more.

What the hell could she be hiding?

Fionn did discover she was once engaged, though. I don't know who the hell the guy is or why the engagement ended. Said he heard from one of the old ladies in town who knows her grandma. But that's all she'd tell them. The rest, she kept quiet, and it makes me wonder why.

Is she hiding from him? Is he after her?

Peering at her, I don't sense danger. I don't think she'd hurt Brody.

Yet in our lives, no one is to be trusted.

Not even her.

When it's Brody's turn for dismissal, she smiles at him one last time as she points to me, her full pink lips moving as she talks to him, probably asking if I'm the one who's picking him up.

He nods once, looks up at her for a moment, then stoically walks over. Like he's making his way to the devil from just being with an angel.

He wouldn't be wrong.

My damn chest squeezes. He doesn't deserve this. No kid deserves to lose his dad and then come home to his mom's fucking brain splattered on the wall.

She didn't even have the decency to swallow some pills. She had to blow her damn brains out in her bedroom while he was at school.

When the teacher called telling me Willow hadn't shown up to pick him up, I rushed to get him. Once we got to his house, he went calling for her, trying to find her.

Then he did.

My eyelids slam closed. I hate myself for not finding her first. Hate that I'm thinking ill of Willow. She was a good woman. Aiden loved her with everything he had, and look where that got them.

Marriage is nothing but a useless commitment made by fools who don't realize the mistake they're making until it's too late.

My father, unfortunately, doesn't agree with that. As the head of the family, he gets to make up the rules, like forcing me to find a wife within two months so I can take over as the new head of the Quinn family.

He wants heirs. Lots of them.

It's not enough that my eldest sister, Iseult, is already married to Gio Marino, or that my younger one, Eriu, recently got married too.

As the oldest, my father's seat is mine, and he won't let me officially have it until I have a wife of my own.

That's going to be a problem since I have no plans to get married.

If I'm lucky, he'll forget about this bullshit and let me run things like I want to run them.

He's got two of my brothers and my two sisters who'll give him all the heirs in the world, so why the hell is he bothering me about it?

Brody heads in my direction, brushing right past me as though I don't exist. I follow him, glancing at her from over my shoulder.

She pauses, catching my eye for a mere moment, then smiles at the next child.

*I'm going to find out everything about you, Ms. Hill. We're going to become* really *good friends.*

I catch up with Brody as he treads toward my black SUV. Opening the backseat door, he hops into the booster, strapping himself in.

I swear the kid will always hate me. No matter what I try, he doesn't open up. He doesn't even look at me. If it ever happens, it's 'cause of necessity. I hate it.

We got along when his parents were alive. Aiden and I would play ball with him, take him bowling.

He's good at baseball. It's why I made sure he didn't drop out of the team once his parents were gone. It's good for him to have that.

"How was your day?" I settle onto the driver's seat, taking the car on the road.

He stares out the window and doesn't say a word.

My fingers curl on the top of my thigh. "That new teacher seems nice. What's her name again?"

He snaps his eyes to the rearview. And my fucking heart right about stills when he finally looks at me. Then it's gone as soon as it came. Yet it still happened. Even if it only lasted a few seconds.

And it was all because of her.

"It's Ms. Hill, right? That's her name? Is she better than the last teacher? Mrs. S was tougher, I think."

I mutter a curse under my breath. I'm always talking to myself. But the damn therapist said this is what I have to do. To treat him as though he does talk back.

Yet it's been around a year and he still hasn't spoken a word. I fear this is it. That he'll never talk. Even the doctors can't tell me anything definitive. No one has answers, except to give it time.

I never much liked time. Time passes, but it's not always a good thing. Sometimes with time, all you're waiting for is more shit to fuck up your life.

Like the fact that I only have a couple months to find a wife, or my father will force a marriage on me.

Over my dead body.

I have to figure this out on my own. If there was a woman I could pay to marry me, I would. We wouldn't need to love each other. Fuck each other, sure, but one doesn't need love for that.

I don't even know anyone I *like* enough to even consider it.

We arrive at my gated estate, my home built on parcels of land we all own. My father has built each one of us a house here. My sisters no longer live on the grounds; however, my brothers, Fionn and Cillian, and I still do.

We own a large farm as well. It's one way we're able to clean our money.

My father also built Caellach Academy. It's not just any kind of school, though. It's the place where the next generation learns how to become killers—assassins for the Mob. It's where I taught for a while. It's where my brothers and Iseult taught too. Combat and tactical skills, amongst many other things they need for the work they will be doing.

We recruit them young. Sixteen, seventeen. And we build them up. Not everyone is allowed to join. They have to be connected to my family to get an invite.

Brody jumps out just as I shut the car off. Together, we head up the cobblestone steps, and the doors immediately open, two of my men stationed inside.

He's used to that, having security everywhere. It's how he lived with his parents too. Round-the-clock security. Bulletproof vehicles. It has to be this way.

"Go wash your hands and start on homework," I tell him.

He marches to the bathroom, brushing right past Ruby, who laughs as she pats him on the head.

"Careful there, sweetheart. Almost knocked right into me."

He gives her an apologetic glance before he's out of the room.

She comes over to me as I swipe a hand down my face.

"What the hell am I doing?" I ask her, yet it's not even a question. "Maybe I'm not right for this." My tone drops so Brody doesn't overhear. "He hasn't made progress. Maybe I'm the problem."

"Oh, Tynan." She tilts her face sideways, sympathy playing in her brows. "Don't do that. You're doing everything you can." She lays a wrinkled hand on my forearm. "Trust me. I see it. Everyone does. You're a darling man, and you try. That's what anyone would do. Now…" She removes her hand. "How about you go rest, and I'll make dinner?"

I shake my head. "No. I'll do it. I told him I would. I don't want him thinking I break my promises."

Her smile stretches. "See? You're a good dad."

"I'm not his dad." My words swell with tension.

I don't want him to think he ever has to call me that.

"But you are, Tynan. You're the only parent he has now."

A labored sigh makes it out of my chest. "I didn't want to be. Not like this."

Her eyes gleam with emotion. "I know that. I loved them too. But this is where we are now, and you're doing right by that boy." Her shoulders sag. "Let me go help him with homework while you cook."

I nod and head for the kitchen, planning to make his favorite: mac and cheese with bits of bacon.

At least I can do that right.

# THREE

## ELARA

The following day, on the way to my Saturday morning run, I stop by the local coffee shop so I can grab my grandma some breakfast.

As soon as I enter, someone I know waves me over.

"Elara! Oh my God! Hi!" Alice, a fellow teacher at the school, calls.

She's about my age: twenty-three. I think she wants us to be friends. She's nice and all, but unfortunately, my trust issues run deep.

Not surprised to see her here. She *is* here, like, every weekend. Though I swear she acts surprised every time she sees me, like it's kismet.

Her eyes round with excitement when I start toward her, but she's not alone. A guy I don't know is with her.

"Hey, Alice." My vision bounces between them.

"Oh…" Her face lights up. "This is my boyfriend, Chris. It's kinda new." Her cheeks grow with color.

"Nice to meet you." I extend a hand, and he shakes it.

"You too. Alice has told me so much about you." He glances at her and smiles, his eyes filled with affection.

"She has?"

"Yeah…" He straightens in his seat. "She said you're her only friend at the school."

"Chris!" She giggles and smacks him on the arm with the back of her hand. "He's ridiculous."

"She's great." I smile tightly, unsure what to say.

I barely know her. Occasionally, we sit together at lunch or exchange some words when we see one another passing in the halls.

"Well, it was nice to see you, Alice, and good to meet you, Chris. I have to get my grandma some food or she'll get cranky."

"Of course! Oh my God, I *love* her grandma." Alice looks over at Chris. "She's hilarious. She plays bridge with my grandma, and she tells the raunchiest jokes," she whispers.

*Oh, no… That does sound like Gran.*

"This one time, I heard the funniest one." She laughs, her attention jumping between Chris and me. "Okay," she whispers. "So, how is sex like a game of bridge?"

"I don't know. How?" Chris grins.

"If you have a great hand, you don't need a partner." She bursts into a laugh. "Isn't that hilarious?"

"That's her: hilarious." *And mildly uncomfortable.* "Anyway, this was fun. I'll tell her you said hello. See you Monday, Alice."

"Okay, sure! I'll see you!"

I give her one last look, waving back and heading for the counter.

As I do, I run straight into a wall and all the air leaves my lungs.

"What the…" I stare up at said wall.

Well, not exactly a wall, it appears, but a man. A tall man with a body that may as well be made of bricks.

Not into bricks—or men, for that matter. Not anymore, anyway.

Not into women either. Kinda in my "not into adult humans" era.

I rub my shoulder as I mutter a curse, pain shooting down my arm.

He quirks a brow, his bright green eyes filled with mirth.

"You should probably watch where you're going next time," his deep, guttural voice reprimands, and I decide I already hate him.

Behind me, Alice gasps and the cashier stops moving, staring at the both of us like we've suddenly entered a very exciting TV show. And when I look around the café, I find the patrons all gaping at us too.

What the hell is this about?

He stares down at me with an amused expression.

Being five-two, I'm not exactly on the tall side, and standing next to this man, who's definitely over a foot taller, is making me feel even smaller.

Popping my chin, I zero an intense gaze at the man who has his eyes still set on mine. "Thank you *so* much. I'll be sure to take that under advisement."

"That's a good girl." His eyes play as he cracks a smirk.

I shift uncomfortably, his hypnotic tone dropping into my gut and spreading warmth throughout my limbs.

Never had a man say that to me.

Never even thought I'd like it.

Until now.

He meets my stare with equal fervor, like he won't be the first one to relent.

*Don't worry. I don't like to lose either.*

His smirk deepens, and I can't stop looking. I take in those vivid green eyes, the high cheekbones, and that hard, angled jaw with just the right amount of stubble I'd love to run my fingertips over.

His hair is combed back, and I bet it would look just as sexy if I ran my hands through the deep brown hue and messed it up a bit.

My stomach clenches at how attractive he actually is. How

21

dominating.

He commands a room just by entering it.

I try not to continue checking him out, but that's becoming quite impossible.

He's dressed like he's going to a business meeting on Wall Street. And something about those gray dress pants and the white button-down with that gray silk tie really turns me on. His shirt easily shows off every indent, every inch of muscle. His hard, defined chest jerks when he notices that my line of vision has inadvertently stopped there.

Okay, so maybe my "not into people" era has got a *teeny* dent.

His mouth twitches a fraction before it loses the amusement. And once his attention falls to my lips, his throat bobs.

My gut jolts hotly, the sudden electric energy between us making my heart skip right up my esophagus. And the more his penetrating gaze sears into mine, the more my skin grows prickly.

He stares like he knows me…or wants to.

Neither of which are good.

He stalks a step forward, and my breath hitches. His eyes bore deeper into mine, the air around us thicker with my undeniable urge to throttle him. Or have him return the favor. I'm not really being all that picky at the moment.

My pulse spikes from this pull between us. From this quiet, yet unnerving attraction I'm fighting like hell to pretend doesn't exist.

He doesn't appear like the type of man I need to be attracted to.

I've had my fill of dangerous men.

And this one? He even *smells* like danger.

Who even is he? I've never seen him before. I'd have instantly recognized him.

"I really should be going now…" I whisper, attempting to sound brave and totally unaffected, yet completely and utterly failing.

He doesn't say a word.

Instead, he drags in a slow breath, his fingers reaching for my face, stopping just short before he pushes a strand of my hair, tucking it behind my ear.

And just from that touch alone, I forget how to breathe.

I can't seem to look away, to move and walk out of this place. He keeps me rooted somehow, like he holds the key.

His mouth twitches as though he knows precisely what he's doing to me.

With gentle strokes, he smooths down his tie, the thick veins on top of his large hand snaking beneath his skin.

I hate that I want him.

That my body craves his.

My stomach drops from the exhilarating tension building inside me, like with one touch I'd fall apart.

The intoxicating scent of his cologne surrounds me—something masculine and expensive—making my heart beat faster while my mind conjures up thoughts of him and me ripping at each other's clothes.

Clearing my throat, I force myself to shake off the magnetic connection between us and head for the counter. But I can sense him behind me, feel the way his body almost brushes mine.

I take slow, shallow breaths, trying my best to forget that he exists, and order an egg burrito and coffee for Gran.

"Is that all?" the cashier asks, glancing behind me at *him*.

The room is still eerily quiet, making me shudder.

His hot breath creeps across the back of my neck, turning me to ash.

"No," that husky timbre drawls out, sending a shiver slinking up my spine. "She's going to order something for herself."

He outstretches his arm from behind me and hands her a card. And as he does, his fingers graze my arm like a slow-dancing flame, torching me where I stand.

I look over at him from behind my shoulder. "How do you know that—"

"That the food you ordered is for your grandmother and not you?" He hits me with a cocky, lopsided grin. "Heard you talking to your friends." He tilts his head toward an awestruck Alice. "So please order something for yourself. It's on me. You know…" His mouth descends across my ear, breath caressing down my neck. "…for running into you."

My inhales turn shaky, but he doesn't offer any reprieve. Instead, he moves in closer, until his front presses into my back just enough to make me feel it—his power.

And I don't mean the one in his pants. Or maybe I do…

I'm not entirely sure of anything at the present moment.

My nerves tingle through me, forcing me to pinch my thighs to satiate this pulsing need that has grown almost unmanageable.

This man, there's something about him—something I desire, yet fear—and he knows it too.

I've met men like this. I've looked them in the eyes as they hurt me and lived another day.

So with this man, I refuse to be like the rest. I won't cower in fear. I won't let another man hurt me like my father and Jerry did.

"It's awfully kind of you to offer to pay, but that's not necessary." Returning my attention to the cashier, I reach into the pouch around my waist and remove a twenty-dollar bill, holding it out for her. "Could you get my order, please?"

With his card in hand, she glances at him like she needs his permission.

"Run my card," he tells her.

She does so immediately, her fingers jittery as she hands him the card back, then gives me a receipt. She rushes off to get the stuff I ordered while I shake my head and turn around to face him.

"Does everyone just do whatever you want?"

"Usually. If they're smart, that is."

Something heavy sinks into my stomach. This man…he's definitely dangerous.

Yet utterly alluring.

"Here you go." The cashier hands me a brown bag and places the cup of coffee on the counter.

"Thanks," I tell her, turning to him. "Please take this."

His face hardens as I attempt to hand him the twenty.

"What are you doing? I'm not taking your money." He looks almost furious, yet it only lasts a moment. "It's my treat, Ms. Hill." His fingers trace up my elbow, and I inhale a sharp breath. "Don't fight it."

It hits me then.

He knows my name.

Panic creeps up my skin.

"Have we met before?" My words come out almost like a whisper as I stuff the twenty back into my pouch and close it.

His mouth bends into a quick grin. "I know everyone in this town."

I swallow down the fear those words just caused me. The last thing I want is for him to know who I am. Who I was before I became Elara.

I don't bother asking his name. I don't want to know it.

"Thanks for this." I grab the order. "Now, if you'll excuse me…"

I brush past him, hoping to make my escape, but his sudden grip on my wrist has me dead in my tracks.

My skin sears where he touches me. I glance back at him to find those eyes burning with a new flash of heat. The vein in his neck throbs.

"You dropped something, Ms. Hill." He accentuates my name like he's having sex with it.

This all becomes too much to bear.

Then he lets me go, kneeling to retrieve something, his eyes still on mine.

And I realize it's my driver's license.

*Oh God, how could I have been so reckless?*

"You can never be too careful." He slowly opens the pouch and places the license back inside.

And the way his fingers move, the veins atop his hand practically ripping through his skin, has a new murmur of desire breathing life between my thighs.

"Enjoy your run." That deep, raspy baritone turns my entire being into something warm and wanton.

Wait. How did he know I was going for a run?

Maybe he assumed because of how I'm dressed. I'm sure that's it.

With my heart hammering, I rush out the door, sucking in the cool air.

As I start toward Gran's, the doors open, and it's Alice, breathless as though she just ran a marathon.

"Oh my God!" she whispers, pulling me close and glancing sheepishly to her right at the café. "Do you have any idea who that was?"

"No." I shake my head. "I've never seen him before."

She swipes her forehead with the back of her hand. "He doesn't usually frequent this part of town."

"So who is he?" Now I'm really curious.

"His family's practically royalty here. Super wealthy. They own lots of land and property a few miles north. They own just about everything in this town too, including this café."

"What?" I can't help the shock in my tone.

"Yep." Her brows shoot up as she nods slowly. "And rumor is..." She leans in. "They're connected to the Mafia."

Before I even look, I feel his menacing green gaze on me—feel the burning intensity pulsating through me. I glance back and lock eyes with him through the window.

The hairs on my arms stand up.

I knew it. I knew he was someone to be feared.

What if he knows the people I was once connected to? What if he discovers my secrets and hands me to them?

And worse, what if he knows what I did…

The bodies I buried.

What if he uses that against me somehow?

Every molecule in me wants to pack my bags and run again. Everything about him makes me uneasy. Like my subconscious is telling me he's not safe.

But what if he wouldn't do that? What if I'm just scared?

I have to be sure. I don't want to leave my grandparents here alone unless it's for a good enough reason. I have to find out if he knows something about me.

"You okay?" Alice places a concerned hand on my forearm, and I accidentally fling it away.

"I'm fine. Sorry," I mutter. "I have to go, though. Have to get this food to my grandma before she sends a search party."

"Of course. Just be careful," she says softly.

I should go before the devil finds a way to unravel me more than he already has.

# FOUR

## ELARA

"I brought you breakfast, Gran." I knock on her door, waiting for her to answer.

Yet my mind is still on the mystery man.

I have to keep my distance from him. Being attracted to a man who might be in the Mafia is one of the worst things I could possibly do, especially if said man is somehow connected to my past.

"Coming, dear!" She shuffles around from behind the door before it opens. Her gray hair is in a short ponytail, her floral dress reminding me of a spring day. "You're so good to me."

Her arms come around me in the warmest hug before she takes the brown paper bag and coffee cup. "Do you wanna come in? We can watch some *Family Feud* like we did when you were little."

"Not right now, Gran. I wanna get my run in before we go see Grandpa."

"Of course, sweetheart. I understand." Her pale blue eyes shine brightly.

"I'll come pick you up in about an hour. Love you, Gran."

"Love you too, sweetheart." She smiles before closing the door behind her.

I slip my earbuds in and turn on some music.

Starting to jog, I head toward my usual spot: an open road, forests and mountains in the distance. It's scenic and peaceful, not too many cars passing by.

I like running. It helps clear my mind, like my own form of therapy. I try going whenever I can. On the weekends. After work. Sometimes more than once a day.

A mile into my run, and my mind is back on that awfully attractive stranger. No matter how hard I try to push him out of my head, he storms right back in.

His dark and dangerous aura commands my thoughts. But when he smirks, my heart grows weak. It's like I can still see him. Right in front of me.

Then, with a sudden shift, it's Jerry's hand around my throat… squeezing.

Tighter.

And tighter.

My breaths lurch out of me, my chest burning with every inhale.

"Fuck," I grit. "Get out of my head!"

It's then I see them together, prowling toward me. The stranger and the man my father sold me to.

I blink past the tears and fight them. Fight the pain and anger. Fight the reasons I'm still being hunted.

I focus on the present. On the fact that I'm still alive. On my job. The kids. On Brody. Sweet Brody, who always makes me happy even when he doesn't say a word.

Those things help me stay grounded. Because amidst the chaos, there's still a lot to be grateful for.

Once I hit three miles, I start heading back to town so I can get my grandma.

But suddenly, I feel something behind me. It's like my body knows someone's there before my mind does.

I lower the music, registering the roaring of an engine.

Every hair on my body prickles across my skin as I slowly yank the earbuds out of my ears and stuff them into the pouch.

My pulse ricochets in my throat as I glance behind my shoulder, finding a black SUV slowly following me.

*Fuck.*

Could it be them?

It has to be.

If I run, they'll just shoot me down. If I stay, maybe I can talk my way out of this.

A ball of nerves rides up my throat. I wish I had my gun on me. If it's Jerry or one of his people, I want to be ready.

I won't go down like a coward. I'll fight him until my last breath.

Frozen on the road, I wait for the car to come to a full stop, my chest heavy as the passenger side window rolls down.

And when I see who's inside, I realize it's not Jerry or his people.

It's *him*.

The man from the café.

A whoosh of a breath leaves my lungs, but the instant relief is only momentary.

"Ms. Hill." He greets me in a soft, yet rough tone, and I hate the way I take in those cunning green eyes, murky and full of secrets.

"Are you stalking me?" I arch a brow and his mouth lifts a fraction.

"Just out for a drive. How's your run?" His gaze laces down my body, and my breathing grows labored, every part of me aware of where his eyes have been.

"Fine. Until now. Anything I can do for you?"

Without a word, he opens the passenger side door. "Get in, Ms. Hill."

Okay, so he's clearly a lunatic too. Great... Why else would he want me to just jump into his car for no apparent reason?

"No, thanks." My features upturn with annoyance.

"It wasn't a request." His eyes narrow in challenge.

I scoff and start jogging.

Sure, pissing off a supposed Mafia man is probably not the smartest of choices this morning, but here we are.

I register the growl as he sends the car rolling down the road to catch up with me, the door still open.

"You need to leave me alone." I stop moving and send a hard stare his way. "This is getting borderline criminal."

He chuckles, and I hate to admit the way my stomach dips when I hear it.

I brush off the feeling and continue glaring. "What's so funny?"

"You." That one word, rough and gravelly, sends a tremor down my body. "Now, be a good girl and get in so I can give you a ride back into town. You never know who you'll find driving down this road."

"I do now."

His lips form a thin line. "Come on, Ms. Hill. Don't make me wait any longer. I'm not a very patient man."

I have two options: fight him or give in.

Thinking through it, I'm not sure running would get me very far. Because a man like this always gets what he wants.

What's the worst that can happen?

He could kill me...

Discreetly, I slip my hand into my pouch to retrieve my keys. They're the only weapon I have handy, and one could do lots of damage with them.

Stabbing him in the throat comes to mind.

My fingers close in around them as I nervously start toward the SUV.

Everything about him screams death and destruction, and I wonder if I'm headed toward my own grave.

He looks satisfied with himself when I hop in beside him, while every molecule in me begs to get out.

When I try to fasten my seat belt, he grabs it from me. "Let me."

His eyes snap to mine as he buckles me in. And when his knuckles accidentally brush my arm, my body crackles like fireworks.

I inhale sharply, his eyes hooded as they drop to my mouth, then back up, gaze sinking deeper, like he wants to devour me.

But the devil won't be able to. I won't let him.

He straightens his spine and starts the car, moving it slowly—like he wants to keep me here for as long as possible.

"Do you normally pick up random women on the side of the road? You should know that's how some creepy movies start."

That mouth, it twitches like he wants to laugh. "Do you think I'm creepy?"

"Will it get me killed if I answer truthfully?"

He tilts his penetrating gaze to mine. "Why would I kill you?"

I shrug. "Because you're you."

"What do you know about me? What did your friend tell you?" His voice simmers, and my stomach tightens.

"Nothing?"

"Come on, Ms. Hill." His palm drops to the top of my thigh right above my kneecap, and I instantly shiver, biting my lip to stop myself from groaning, my nails digging into my palm.

This is embarrassing at this point. How can a man affect me this much?

A tattoo snakes around the top of his hand, a lion with cold, discerning eyes, like it's watching me.

"What do they say about me in these parts?"

My breaths grow ragged when he squeezes his fingers a little.

I tremble in my seat, unable to withstand the strange creeping of need slinking down my body. Unable to shake off how much I like the way he's touching me right now. His hands—large and rough and masculine—like he'd throw me around with ease even if I fight him.

"Nothing. I swear." The words choke out of me, and that causes a harsh, short chuckle to break through his lungs.

"You're a bad liar." His touch leaves me, and the spot where his palm was feels instantly barren.

"I just heard you're dangerous. That's all." I stick with honesty because I'm sure he knows exactly what people say about him.

"Hmm. That wouldn't be a lie. And what about you, Ms. Hill? Are *you* dangerous?"

My eyes grow, and I quickly look out the window, trying to find a reply that won't get me a bullet in my temple. "Me? No. I'm just a teacher. I'm not the one who's supposedly connected to the Mafia."

Crap. Maybe I shouldn't have said *that*.

"You think I'm connected to the Mafia and you just freely offer up that knowledge?"

"I guess I'm not that smart."

It's back. His touch… A single finger crawling up my thigh.

My pulse throbs in my neck as I wait to see where it lands.

"I find that very hard to believe." His voice oozes with prowess, and I ache for him to do more.

I imagine myself touching the stubble riding up his angular jawline, while his eyes drift to a close, enjoying it as he holds me on his lap. Those big hands on my hips, keeping me just where he wants me.

I shift uncomfortably in my seat.

My God, when was the last time I was this attracted to a man? Much less this brazenly.

His hand disappears, and I'm both relieved and sad. It's been so long since I've been touched. Since I've wanted to be touched.

That's what this is. Lust. Pure, undulated lust.

"How do you like it? Teaching."

His question has me clearing my throat. Definitely need to keep the conversation on normal things like my job. That's safe.

His hands on me, on the other hand? Not very safe.

My smile widens when I think about the kids. "I love it. It's what I've always wanted to do. I love helping them, getting through to them. It fulfills me."

He nods. "And is that what you did back where you moved from?"

Shit. I don't want to give anything away, yet I have to give him something. There's no way he knows where I'm from or that we've been moving from place to place for the past year. This town is the longest we've lived somewhere.

"Yes."

"Commendable. We need more teachers like you, who care."

"Thanks." I stare at the empty road ahead. "Wish I could do more, though. You know, for the kids who need it."

"Oh?"

"Yeah, it's hard. Some kids come from heartbreaking situations and need extra love."

"Someone in class is being hurt?" He looks in my direction, and his icy glare makes him appear almost human. It nearly looks like he'd care if a child was being mistreated.

"Oh, nothing like that."

We continue to lock eyes, and I instantly regret it. He makes me feel things. Bad things. Or good. Depends on how you look at it, I guess.

"Then what, Ms. Hill?"

*Can he stop saying my name like he's constantly flirting with me?*

As though hearing my thoughts, that sinful mouth curls on one side.

"There's a boy in my class. He's…"

"He's what?" His jaw clenches.

"He's sweet and kind and he…he stopped talking about a year

35

ago. And it breaks my heart that I can't do anything for him."

I don't miss the way his hand tightens around the wheel, knuckles turning white, and I wonder if I made a mistake by saying something.

"You know why?" he asks.

"Why what?" My heartbeats speed up, fear of this man returning.

"Why he stopped talking."

"His parents died. That would do it. Trauma does a lot to a person, especially one so young."

His body turns visibly rigid, the vein in his neck twitching. He barely looks at me anymore as he drives us back to town. And before I can tell him my address, he's on my street.

A chill creeps up my arms.

He knows where I live.

The devil knows where I live.

He stops right in front of my home. "Have a good day, Ms. Hill."

His demeanor is no longer friendly. Those eyes darkening. His facial expression cold.

I stuff down my anxiety and hop out.

Closing the door behind me, I vow to get as far away from him as possible.

# FIVE

## TYNAN

After dropping her off, I continue to follow her, trailing behind her in my SUV.

I've been following Ms. Hill for a few weeks now. Tailed her to the café too. Ran into her on purpose. Even went to her place once while she was sleeping, just to see if I could find anything when she was at her most vulnerable.

I need to know who's teaching Brody. If he's safe around her. I'm still unsure. Neither my brothers nor I could find shit on her. She's like a ghost, and that doesn't smell right.

Hate that I've become a man who follows a woman around. I have people for that. Yet with her, I need to do it myself. I don't know why, but the thought of one of my men following her made me lose it.

I've been to her place when she wasn't home too. Saw the gun she keeps hidden in her nightstand.

And sure, that alone wouldn't mean much, but I've noticed the way she's always looking over her shoulder, like someone's after her.

She was afraid of me too.

I saw it in her eyes.

I can't lie and say it doesn't excite me.

Though what excited me most was that she wanted me. I could practically feel her shiver the closer I got. Almost heard her moan in the car when I touched her.

But she's guarded. And I need to know why.

What could a woman like that be hiding?

When I asked if she was dangerous, I noticed the jolt in her body. The way her eyes expanded for a brief second.

Why would she consider herself a danger? What has she done? And to whom?

She arrives at her grandma's house, helping her into the white sedan she drives. I like that she cares about her grandparents. It shows who she really is.

And everything I've learned so far points to her being a good teacher too. Don't want to lose her to whatever brought her here in the first place.

I know enough about people to know when they're running, and Elara Hill? She's running from something...or someone.

I need to find her ex-fiancé and figure out if he needs to be eliminated. Maybe he's hurt her and that's why she ran.

The thought of her being smacked around has my hands balling, heart fucking racing like I've gone mad.

I hope it's not true. He won't survive the day if I find him and learn he did something to her.

From the corner of the road, where she can't see me, I watch her as she smiles at her grandma.

And I wonder what it'd feel like to have her smile at me like that.

# ELARA

We arrive at Grandpa's home and check in at the front.

"Hi, Nora. Elara," the nurse greets us as we walk into his room.

"Hey, Paige." I hand her a box of candy I picked up at the store.

She treats my grandpa nicely, and I like doing little things for her to show I appreciate it.

"Oh, you're so sweet." She takes the box from me.

My attention jumps to my grandpa, who sits in a chair, staring out the window. Gran heads toward him, settling across and fighting her emotions as he stares at her blankly.

"I don't want a bath today," he tells her.

"Alright, Aaron. No bath, it is."

That makes him smile. I miss his smiles.

My face falls, and when Paige notices, she gives me a sympathetic look.

"He's actually doing better today. He knew who I was."

I let out a sigh. "Thanks, Paige."

Though we both know with Grandpa's dementia, things can change from hour to hour.

It breaks my heart to see him this way. He was fine when we first moved here six months ago. But soon after, Gran and I realized something was wrong.

Then he got his diagnosis.

Gran was able to take care of him at first. Until it got harder and we had no choice except to put him in a home. I wish I didn't have to, but I can't afford a live-in aide. I can barely afford to pay for the home.

So I have to keep my job. I can't let anyone find out I'm a fraud.

"I'll be right outside if you need me." Paige squeezes my hand before heading out, giving us privacy.

"Hi, Grandpa. It's me, Evelyn." I move toward him cautiously so as not to overwhelm him. Grabbing a chair, I sit beside Gran.

His mouth thins, and for a moment, he looks at me as though he knows me. Hope springs in my heart.

"Paige?"

Instantly, I deflate, and Gran's eyes shine with moisture. I take her hand in mine.

"It's Evelyn, remember? I'm your granddaughter. And this is Judith, your wife."

His brows knit, and he looks between us, panic setting in his eyes. "I—I…"

"It's okay." I fight my emotions. "It's okay. Just rest."

He nods, swallowing hard as he leans into the brown leather armchair. Lifting up his throw blanket, I tuck it around him.

"Paige?" he calls to me, and I blink back tears.

"Yes?"

"Could you get me some orange juice? I would really like some orange juice."

"Mm-hmm. Sure."

Tears roll down my cheeks, but I brush them away as I give him my back, heading for the fridge in his room. Grabbing the juice I bought for him last week, I pour some into a plastic cup.

How can life be so unfair? He was always strong and capable; now he's a shell of a man.

It feels like I'm losing everyone. Who's next?

My mind drifts to the happier moments from my past, when my friend Kennedy and I would go to the beach, laughing as the waves rolled over our heads. Meeting her was one of the best things that ever happened to me.

Yet also one of the worst.

Because we were both victims. Both used and abused and made to do awful things. But we had each other.

Until we didn't.

I press my eyes closed, my pulse speeding up as I recall her last few moments. The final time I saw her alive.

*"Hurry up!" I scream from the back seat. "She's losing too much blood!"*

*Kennedy's in my lap, blood leaking out of her stomach even through my torn t-shirt tied around her.*

*"Come on, stay with me! Don't close your eyes. Please!" I wail, as the car honks, zooming past other vehicles.*

*"We're gonna drop her off at the hospital. You can't go with her. You hear?"*

*I make eye contact with Jerry through the mirror, and my anger simmers. "Fuck you! You did this to her."*

*He laughs humorlessly. "The bitch did this to herself."*

*"Don't fucking talk about her like that!"*

*Kennedy groans. "I...I'm cold. Just wanna sleep."*

*"No. No, please stay awake. We're almost there." Tears bathe my eyes until I'm one with them, my heart aching.*

*I can't lose her. I just can't.*

*"Remember the time we went to Joe's Pizza and found the spider in your drink?" A mournful smile slips out of me. "The way you screamed and jumped out of your chair, almost knocking into the waiter?"*

*She tries to laugh, her eyes on mine as I stare down at her. "You—you..."*

*"Don't try to talk. It's okay." I slide my hand down the top of her head, trying not to sob.*

*There's so much blood. I don't know how much more she can lose before she's gone.*

"Hurry up!" I scream out at Jerry.

"Shut up. Going as fast as I can. Unless you want the cops to stop us. Is that your plan? To get me in trouble?" he seethes. "Remember, I can get you in worse trouble."

How could I forget?

"Asshole."

"What was that, bitch?"

*I hate him. The only reason we're still engaged is because of the blackmail. I have to find a way to get the proof and destroy it. But he always has his men around. No way I could break into his house and take his laptop. That's where he keeps it.*

*Kennedy starts to cough, gagging on her blood.*

"Oh my God!" I cry. "Nono! Please, don't die!"

"She's not gonna make it. We've gotta leave her in the woods."

"What? No! I won't let you do that to her."

*Tires screech as he stops the car on the side of an empty road.*

"Get her out," he tells Fred, one of his many henchmen.

*Kennedy's skin grows cold. I won't let her die alone like garbage.*

"Please, Jerry! Don't do this!" I plead with every ounce of my being. "We can help her. We can—"

*Fred opens the back of the SUV and roughly grabs her, lifting her in his arms.*

"No! Don't touch her!"

*Jerry jumps out of the car, rushing for me, holding me down as I fight him while Fred carries Kennedy out into the woods.*

"Let me go! I need to be with her. I can't let her die alone!"

"There's nothing you can do for her. Now get the fuck back inside so we can get you cleaned up."

"Get your filthy hands off of me!"

*He grunts, and in a snap, he grabs a chunk of my hair.* "Now, is that a way to treat your fiancé? Your father wouldn't be too happy to *see you behaving this way. Remember...I own you."*

*"Fuck you! He isn't here. Whatever deal you made with him no longer exists."*

*He chuckles, turning me around as his hand painfully grips my jaw, his face nearing mine. "That's not how it works. He gave you to me as payment. So now you're mine. That will never change. You'll never get rid of me." His mouth stretches into a sinister smile. "When I say jump, you jump. Do we understand each other?"*

*With rage seeping through my veins, I fling his hand off me, and he lets me go just as Fred returns empty-handed.*

*A sob wracks me. I can't leave her here.*

*Jerry lifts me up and throws me onto the back seat. And her blood? It's everywhere.*

*They start the car as my body shakes, my soul in pieces as my friend is there, dying alone.*

*The car speeds farther away, and before I can think better of it, I open the door and jump out, my body rolling onto the side of the road and hitting a tree.*

*"Ow, fuck!" I wince, just as tires shriek.*

*I jump to my feet and look back at the car, expecting Fred to chase me. Instead, Jerry stares with dark, soulless eyes and laughs before the vehicle speeds away.*

*With relief, I rush for Kennedy. My one friend in the world. And when I find her, I drop to my knees.*

*"I'm sorry. I'm so, so sorry! I can get you help."*

*I swipe under my lower lashes, hoping to find a car and ask the driver to take us to the hospital. Or even call the cops. I don't care what happens to me. I just need to save her.*

*I touch her skin...her cold, pale skin. And when I press two fingers into her pulse, I find it still. No life inside her.*

*"NO!" I wail. "No! You can't be gone!" My snivels choke out of me as I scoop her up into my lap and rock her. "Please come back.*

*Please!"*

*But she never does.*

*I remain there, holding her for hours until the darkness calls.*

*And I fall asleep beside her, wishing like hell I could undo it all.*

"Are you okay, sweetheart?" my grandma's voice calls to me.

I gasp, jumping back, and the cup of orange juice spills all over. "Ugh. Yeah, sorry. I'm fine."

"Didn't seem like it to me."

I ignore the concern in her voice, hurrying off to grab some napkins. "Just worried about Grandpa, that's all."

I wipe my white tank top, now stained. Fabulous.

"He had a good life," she muses, tentatively patting his hand. "He would hate to live like this." Emotions hit her tone.

I know she's right. What else can we do for him, though?

"I'll stay with him for a little while. You go, sweetheart."

"Are you sure? How will you get back?"

"I'll call Lucy and she'll pick me up." She waves off my concern. "She wanted to get some lunch anyway."

"Alright." I nod, knowing Gran likes to have her time alone with Grandpa. I understand completely. "If you need me to come back and pick you up, please call, okay?"

"Of course I will. But I'll be fine." She grabs the remote and turns on the game show network.

"Oh, *Family Feud*. I like *Family Feud*." Grandpa smiles, and my grandmother's face brightens.

"We'll be fine, sweetie. You go. Maybe meet a nice man, hmm?"

I roll my eyes. "Yeah, no. I'm good."

"Can't be alone forever, darling."

"Watch me." I wink. "I love you."

"Love you more." She tsks as I head out. "Those young people," she says to Grandpa. "They think they know everything."

I definitely don't.

Though I know one thing: I don't need a man in my life.

Especially not someone like the handsome stranger from the café.

# SIX

## TYNAN
### ONE WEEK LATER

The past week, I've been watching her more than usual, unable to stop myself.

I know when she gets home from work.

When she eats dinner.

The exact time she goes for her runs.

I'm always there, watching like a fucking psycho.

I've become obsessed with knowing everything about her, and I won't rest until I uncover what she's hiding.

Brody has warmed up to her even more these past several days. She's the only one he allows to be near him. He doesn't like to be around anyone anymore. It's like he doesn't want to feel shit after his parents. Like it hurts too much, and he just doesn't know how to say it—that he's in pain.

I swear I'd do anything to take it away. But I can't.

Maybe she can.

Maybe Elara is the key.

I should hire her to watch him after school or do his homework with him. Anything to get her to give him more attention. To allow him to open up to her. The therapist he sees hasn't been able to get him to do that. I'm losing hope.

She still has no idea that I'm his caregiver. Whenever I get him from school, she's too busy with all the kids; she barely pays attention to me.

Although I make sure to have my sunglasses on, so it'd be harder for her to realize we've met before.

That I've had my hands on her.

That I've thought about doing much more than that.

But I think it's time Ms. Hill and I had a proper introduction.

Arriving at my father's home, I enter past the guards at the door, already hearing voices. He asked me to come by today, and I don't know why.

Fuck me. If he starts on the whole "get married" shit, I'm gonna walk right out.

When I step into the den, I find him and his wife, Fernanda, along with both of my brothers and my younger sister, Eriu, with her new husband, Devlin.

Devlin is an enforcer for my father, and he was once Eriu's bodyguard. But he had a thing for my sister before he ever admitted it to himself. We all knew it, though. Glad he realized it sooner than later. Devlin is good for her. He believes in the sanctity of marriage and all that horseshit.

Not me, though.

It's all bull.

"Hello, son." Dad nods in greeting, and everyone else follows suit.

"Why am I here?"

My father chuckles. "Can't a father want to see his son?"

"You saw me two days ago."

Cillian laughs, whispering, "He's gonna harass you again."

Fitting him with a glare, I clench my jaw.

"What?" He throws his palms in the air. "It's not my fault."

"You go get married and get some girl knocked up so he can leave me the hell alone."

"I heard that," my father says in his thick Irish brogue. "Now, you listen, son. You're thirty-eight, you're not getting any younger, and the women are sure as bloody hell not waiting around for you to smarten up. So you better get yourself a good one or I'll do it for you."

"Not happening. You're not setting me up." The words are etched with my obvious disdain.

"Well, then you don't have much time to find yourself a suitable bride who'll put up with ya."

"I'd rather suck on a cactus than get married."

Everyone laughs, while I'm seething.

*This can't be happening.*

I groan internally at the thought of having someone in my space, taking over my time, wanting things from me I have no desire to give.

Falling in love, being vulnerable like that, makes you a target in my world. Makes you and those you love prey. I would think my father of all people could understand that after what happened to Mom.

"I told you," he goes on. "Two months is all you have. Less now, actually."

"Oh, Pat!" Fernanda shakes her head. "I'm sorry your father is such a pain in the ass." She hits him with a disapproving look.

I hate to admit it, but she's good for him. Fernanda and my father were high school sweethearts, and because she was Italian and he was Irish, their families didn't allow them to get married. So he married my mother. And though he loved her, he loved Fernanda too. I don't envy them.

Being alone is better.

Less hassle.

Less pain.

Less everything I don't want.

All I care about is Brody. He's my one and only priority. Assuming I find some random woman willing to marry me for money, how do I even know she'd be a good mother figure to him?

And if she's not? I divorce her and throw her out and start at the beginning? And if we have kids, then what? I'm stuck with her for the rest of my life, divorced or not.

I can't even think about that. Sounds like a fucking nightmare.

"Fine," I tell my father just to appease him. "I'll find someone."

"Glad you've come to your senses." He grabs Fernanda's hand, kissing the top of it.

I mutter a curse to myself, heading for the bar at the corner, then remembering I can't fucking drink because I've gotta get Brody from school in a bit. But at least I can hide here.

"That's rough." Devlin slaps a palm to my back.

*Clearly, I can't escape everyone.*

"Don't look so smug."

He huffs with a short breath of laughter. "I think it's funny you thought you had a bloody choice in the matter."

His Irish accent is as thick as my father's. He was in his twenties when he came to the States, so I'm not at all surprised he hasn't lost it.

"You just want your million." I fold my arms over my chest.

"Doesn't hurt, does it?" He grins.

"The bet was I pay you a million if I fall in love, not get married."

"I remember. And I have a feeling you're gonna lose. Hard."

"Is that right?" I let out a bitter chuckle.

"Bloody right. I saw the way you were following that teacher the other day when she was running. I was in town doing work for your da when I saw you lurking in your SUV like a stalker. She get a restraining order against you yet?"

Everyone is really starting to piss me off.

"I'm just looking out for Brody."

"Is that what you were doing?" He snickers. "Didn't know that's what we call it these days."

"I'm not marrying her. Plus, she's too young. She's only twenty-three."

"I didn't say you should." He shrugs. "Didn't say you shouldn't either."

He tries not to laugh. I swear he's having fun with this.

"What happened? You married my kid sister, and you're now an expert on marriage?"

"No. But I think you like her." He grins.

"She's the boy's teacher, and I'm pretty sure she doesn't like *me*."

"Maybe you can get her to like you. Throw on the charm." He laughs at my glare. "On the other hand…I can see where you'd have a problem."

I let out a grumble.

"If not her, then who?"

It's a fair question. "I'll figure it out. Need someone decent and desperate. I'll offer to pay her. That should be enticing enough."

He shakes his head. "Don't you want to find something real? Not a woman who just wants you for your money?"

"I don't want anything real."

He scoffs. "And they say I'm the stubborn arse."

"I'm not you. I don't want what you and my sister have." I grip his shoulder and look him right in the eyes. "But I'm happy you have each other. I mean that."

"Thanks, brother. One day, maybe you'll realize having someone love you, no matter what you've done, is beautiful, you know."

"Shut up, will ya? You're starting to sound like a damn Hallmark card. It's creeping the fuck out of me."

He pours himself a glass of whiskey. "Maybe it's your sister's writing rubbing off on me."

"Not sure if that's a good thing…"

My sister's hoping to become an author one day, writing romance books and stuff like that. Our father didn't originally approve of her career path, but he does now. Glad my sister can do what she loves.

Devlin's eyes go to her, and she somehow notices it while talking to Fernanda and mouths *I love you*. They're damn cute together. Nauseatingly so.

Too bad for me, I'm not looking for cute.

I'm not looking for anything except a transaction.

And I'd like to keep it that way.

# SEVEN

## TYNAN

Arriving at the school on time, I wait for Brody as Elara dismisses other kids.

I stare at her sunny expression as she approaches him next, and when she gives him a hug, he doesn't even flinch. Can't believe my damn eyes.

He points to me, and as he does, she gives me a double take, her brows furrowing like she recognizes me—or at least thinks she does.

Finally, she's paying attention.

A smirk tugs at my lips, then it quickly disappears when Brody heads toward me, brushing right past, all glum and expressionless.

I glance back at her, but she's already dismissing other kids.

"Hey, buddy." I attempt to kiss the top of his head, but he walks right past me. I try not to take the rejection personally and fail. "How was your day? Good, I hope."

Of course he doesn't answer back. Doesn't even look at me. Instead, he starts toward my SUV.

"Can you wait a minute, buddy? I want to talk to Ms. Hill."

At that, his face jolts up to mine and his eyes round.

"It's nothing bad. I just want to ask her something."

We return and wait until she's done with the class. Then I'm crossing toward her with him. Her back is to me, and a smirk falls to my mouth at the thought of her finding out who I am.

"Ms. Hill."

She gasps in a sudden breath as she whirls toward me, her eyes expanding with every second, fingers feathering over her very fuckable mouth.

I slip off my sunglasses, and my smirk widens. "It's a pleasure to be seeing you again." I lean in real close and whisper, "You look beautiful. I especially love how pink your cheeks get when you're around me."

She sucks in a wild inhale, her warm breath scattering across the side of my neck, and my cock throbs at the attention. I move back, gazing down her body, covered in a tight white blouse, black trousers, and small kitten heels.

Sexy as hell.

"Wh-what? You're…" She bounces back a step.

"Let's go inside so we can talk. In private."

The other teachers murmur amongst each other. I know I have a reputation. The people in town suspect what we do, but they're all too afraid to say a word about it.

Kind of entertaining to see them all whispering.

If they're wondering whether I wanna fuck her, they'd be right.

She peers down at Brody and nervously smiles, then clears her throat as our eyes lock. "Sure. I've been meaning to…uh, call his adoptive parent and discuss some things. I just…"

There's a tremor to her words, and the way her pretty pink lips quiver…fuck, it does something to me.

Thoughts of pinning her to the hood of my car consume me. My hand wrapped around her throat, my fingers inside her as she fights the desire building within her.

I brush off those thoughts.

Fucking Ms. Hill is the last thing I should be thinking of. Then again…

I chuckle.

"What's so funny?" Her brows knit.

"Nothing at all. Now, may we go inside?"

"Mm-hmm." She tightens her mouth before she gives me her back, leading me into the building.

We follow her, entering the first door to the right. Desks sit in the center of the room, the left side with some age-appropriate games and toys.

She kneels to Brody's height and grabs his hands, and he lets her. Doesn't even try to pry them off like he does with me. It shocks me every single time.

"How about you go and play while I talk to your…cousin?" She glances at me questioningly.

"Cousin is fine."

"Okay, Brody, you go." She brushes a hand down the back of his head.

For a moment, I think he'll just run off, but instead…he smiles at her.

My inhale freezes in my lungs.

He. Fucking. Smiled.

Her eyes fill with tears, a palm pressing to the center of her chest. She blinks faster, past those emotions she can't seem to hide.

Brody, though? He scurries off to look at some books while I stare at him, unable to fathom what just happened.

He smiled for the first time in a year.

And it was for her.

"Has he ever done that since…" she whispers. "He never smiles in class, or anywhere that I've seen."

"No." I return my attention to the alluring Ms. Hill and the magic she carries. "He must really like you."

"Well…" Her grin is shy. "I like him too. And now I'm completely embarrassed because I talked about him when you gave me that ride."

"Don't be," I say dryly. "I omitted that information."

"Why did you?" Her eyes dart to the ground before finding mine again, fingers slipping a loose strand of hair behind her ear that I'd very much like to do myself again.

Touching her in any damn way is all I can think about lately.

It's killing me.

*She's* killing me.

I need it to stop.

"I didn't think it mattered."

*Or because I have been watching you and didn't want you to know exactly who I was.*

I follow her to her desk, and she settles across from me, nervously clearing her throat.

I like it. I like making her nervous and uncomfortable around me.

"I see." She sighs and sits up straighter, that blouse stretching across her full breasts.

My God, what the hell is going on with me and this woman? My attraction for her has no bounds. I need it to end. It won't do me any good.

She notices where my eyes have just been, and those cheeks get even pinker. Wonder how pink her pussy is and how much of me she can fit.

There I fucking go again.

"I'm Tynan Quinn, by the way."

"Nice to officially meet you." She absently plays with the ends of her hair. "So what did you want to speak to me about?"

"I wanted to see how Brody was doing in your class since you've taken over."

"Yes, right. I was sorry to hear about Mrs. S's car accident, but Brody has adjusted very well. In fact, he's been great since I took over. He pays attention and does his work on time."

Her kindness and adoration for Brody shines in her eyes as she looks past me at him.

"I can definitely see that. It's also why I was wondering if you'd be willing to see him after class at my home, maybe for an hour or two a day. I'd pay you well, of course."

She scoots the chair closer to her desk. "Like extra help?"

"Yeah, sure. Homework, maybe talk to him, get him to open up to you." I run a hand down my face. "Look, I'll be honest. I haven't seen him the way he is with you, not since before his parents died, so I need your help."

My shoulders sag. I'm so damn tired. Just need him to be okay.

"He hasn't talked in a year, and I don't know if he ever will. But seeing the way he just smiled at you, the way he doesn't mind when you get close, it gives me hope. And that's more than I've ever had before."

Her eyes grow soft and her gaze drops to her lap. She's considering it.

"This isn't exactly typical, and I'd need to check with the school if it's allowed."

"I won't tell if you won't." I hit her with the best damn smile I've got.

"May I think about it?"

*Fuck.*

"Sure. Let me give you my personal cell, and you can call me if you decide to take me up on it. I'd pay a thousand an hour for your services."

"What?! One thousand dollars for an hour?" She stares at me open-mouthed. "Are you that rich?" A hand falls to her chest. "Oh

God, sorry. That was *so* not appropriate."

Her flustering is damn cute.

"That's quite alright, Ms. Hill." The corner of my mouth tips up.

What is she doing to me? When the hell did I ever smile this much? When did I want to?

I grab a notepad from her desk and write down my number.

"Could you stop saying my name like that?" She leans in with a whispered shout.

"Like what?" Of course I know exactly what I'm doing.

"Like you're, uh…flirting with me?"

"What if I was? Would that be so bad?"

I don't miss the way the skin peeking through the top of her blouse prickles.

"Yes, it would be bad. People would get the wrong impression. You're a parent of a child in my class, and we cannot have an inappropriate relationship. Not that I'm saying you're interested in being inappropriate with me." She scratches the side of her neck. "But flirting or perceived flirting is just not allowed."

My jaw tightens.

*Being inappropriate with you is exactly what I want right now. Want to throw you up on your desk and shut your pretty mouth with mine.*

"Noted, Elara," I say instead.

Her eyes flare when she realizes I know her full name. Doesn't she realize I know everything about everyone?

Ms. Hill may not want to like me, but her body does. And I wouldn't be a Quinn if I didn't use that to my advantage.

I start to get to my feet. "It was nice to see you again, *Ms. Hill.*" I give her a crooked grin, and her face flushes. "I'm sure we will be seeing a lot of each other. Let me know soon about the extra services."

"Sure. Yeah…uh, no problem."

She makes no attempts to stand, and I know her eyes are on me as

I loop my attention to Brody.

"Come on, buddy. We're going now."

He drops the book he was reading and heads in my direction, giving her a long look. When I peek over at her, she's got her focus on him as she gets up.

"I almost forgot!" She reaches into her desk drawer, a book in her hand. "I was at the bookstore the other day…" She approaches him. "And I saw this new graphic novel I thought you would like."

Her mouth pinches into the sweetest smile. Like it could light up the world.

She hands him the book.

And as though this meeting couldn't get any better, Brody smiles for her again.

For a moment, it feels like he's the same boy he was back then, and I start to relive one of the last days I spent with him and Aiden. When everything wasn't such a mess.

I want things to be good for Brody again, and I know I need Elara to make that happen.

I just need her to agree to my proposition first.

# A LITTLE OVER A YEAR AGO

*"Come on, Brody! Throw the ball just like I showed you," I call over as he holds the football in both hands—getting ready to chuck it at my head, most likely.*

*He's a funny kid like that. Takes after his father.*

*"You know he's gonna aim that thing at your head, right?" Aiden chuckles.*

*"Yeah, was just thinking the same. Just like you as a kid."*

*He sighs. "We had some good times when we were growing up, didn't we?"*

*"We sure as hell did."*

*Brody tosses the ball, and sure enough, he does aim it right at my head. I immediately catch it. He comes running toward me with a huge laugh.*

*"I throw better than you," he giggles.*

*"Oh, you little fucker." I start to chase him, and he runs away, laughing as he zigzags in front of me.*

*Then, at the last minute, I manage to grab him and throw him over my shoulder, flipping him upside down.*

*He continues with his laughter. "Save me, Dad! He's killing me!"*

*"You look alright to me." Aiden grins. "I will say, though, you do toss way better than he ever did at your age."*

*I snicker and drop Brody back on his feet. "Fine, but I did play better than your father."*

*"Oh, yeah?" Aiden grabs the ball and runs back. "Let's see how good you are now."*

*"Daddy is not the best." Brody giggles, and I can't help my laugh.*

*"Guess what Brody just told me?" I holler at Aiden.*

*"What?"*

*"Hey!" Brody smacks my thigh.*

*"Fine, I won't tell him." I wink, grabbing Brody and placing him on my shoulders, my palms out for the ball Aiden's about to throw. "He said you can toss the ball better than I can."*

*"That's my boy!" Aiden sends it flying, but it barely comes close to me.*

*The kid and I laugh, and I lift a hand to high-five him.*

*"I think we're done for today." Aiden grumbles playfully, coming toward us. "Buddy, go see if Mom's done making lunch and help her bring it out for us."*

*Brody nods, grinning as he starts back into the house while Aiden stares fondly as he runs inside.*

*"You ever thought about having kids?"*

*"Me?" I grimace. "Hell no."*

*He laughs, reverting his attention to me. "Why not? You're great with him."*

*"Yeah, that's because it's Brody. I wouldn't be good with my own kids. I know nothing about them."*

*He shrugs. "Neither did I. You learn with them."*

*"Nah." I shake my head. "I like being the uncle. Or cousin. Whatever the hell you wanna call me."*

*He hits me with a contemplative expression. "Look, I did wanna ask you something. Willow and I talked about this the other day." Concern grows in his tone.*

*"What is it?" I stalk a step closer.*

*"We want to put you in the will as his guardian in case something happens to us."*

*"Oh fuck, Aiden. Come on. Nothing is gonna happen to you guys."*

*Yet we both know that in the kind of life we live, that isn't true.*

*"I know Ryan won't be able to handle a kid." He laughs. "My brother isn't cut out for it. But you are. You've got patience. You're good with him."*

*Brody and I have a bond. I love the kid, and he adores me. But actually being his parent? That thought never crossed my mind in a million fucking years.*

*"Promise me you'll take care of him if something happens." Aiden's voice grows tight. "I need to know my boy will be okay without us."*

*Pain clogs my throat. I hate thinking about this. Hate imagining Brody hurting without his parents here. How would I manage it? Am I even capable of that?*

*Except what choice is there? Aiden and Brody are my blood, and I'd do anything for family.*

*"Okay. I'll do it. You guys will be fine, though. So let's go eat and forget about this damn conversation."*

*I throw an arm around his shoulders. By his laugh, it feels like a weight has been lifted.*

*But me? I'm still haunted by his words long after the day ends.*

# EIGHT

## ELARA

I still can't get over the fact that he's Brody's adoptive parent. I knew there was something familiar about him when I saw him after school the other day, but he was surrounded by other parents and I was too busy to really pay attention.

Lying in my bed, I replay his job offer in my head. Can't believe I'm even considering it.

How can I do this and possibly risk my job? What if the school uses that as a reason to let me go? I'm only a sub. I'm replaceable. Then I'd lose the only source of income and fulfillment that I have.

How will I pay my rent or pay for my grandpa's home then? Though a thousand an hour is a lot. It's more than I make, that's for sure.

Yet can I accept dirty money? Can I work for a dangerous guy?

For men like Tynan, nothing is ever enough. You give them a little, and they demand more.

Then what? I do what he says or die? Where will it end?

I can't put myself in that situation.

I wish I had someone to talk to about this.

My grandma isn't an option. I love her, but the woman has a big mouth. If I tell her, the whole town will know, and so will the school.

Groaning, I throw a pillow over my face, and when I close my eyes, it's him I see. That vivid hue of his green eyes, the way he smiles. And when he does, it's like a meteor shower, rare and beautiful.

Scolding myself, I focus on what matters: my grandparents, keeping my past in the past. I can't think about the attractive dad of the boy in my class.

But when I tell myself not to, all I do is think about him even more.

Remembering the way he put his large, heavy hand on my thigh in the car, how good it felt to be touched again…

Jesus. I should just fuck someone to get it out of my system. It's been too long. And now that my body has clearly decided it wants Tynan Quinn, I'm afraid my needs will not relent.

A pulsing sensation hits between my thighs, the desire coiling and wanton until my hand languidly slinks beneath my yoga shorts. I slip a finger inside me, sliding it in and out, swirling it around my clit while images of Tynan serve to inspire.

Him ripping my blouse open, buttons scattering across the floor as he spreads my legs on the edge of the desk. His face drops between my thighs, his tongue swirling, mouth sucking me where I touch. Those fingers, thick and hard, thrust inside me until stars erupt before my eyes.

"Oh God, Tynan, yes!" I moan, knowing he can't hear me. No one can.

The release comes fast and hard, and I ache for him to take me harder, bent over my desk, my hair in his fist, his cock driving deeper into me.

"Yes…" I continue circling my fingers around my already sensitive flesh.

I can't seem to stop, my need climbing again until I spiral into another orgasm, harder and faster, making every inch of me convulse.

Images of his muscled, naked flesh, him pounding inside me like he's lost his mind for me play on repeat. It's what I want, even though I'll never admit that to him.

My body sags, and I groan at what I've just done. I can't believe I was thinking about him while I did that. I've gone insane.

This is why I can't accept his job offer. Tynan enjoys toying with me too much, and I'm only human. A lot can happen when you're stuck in a house with someone you're attracted to. Even when that person is the last thing you should want.

On the other hand, I can't in good conscience pass up a thousand dollars an hour. That money could do me so much good.

I slap a hand over my eyes.

How do I continue to get drawn to men who are bad for me? I liked Jerry when I met him. He was always nice to me every time I saw him with my father over the years. I thought he worked for my dad, crunching numbers in his restaurant business.

But I was very wrong.

What I didn't know was that my father wasn't just a restaurant owner. He was a criminal, and Jerry wasn't exactly working for my dad. He was working for an organization who was in competition with my father, someone my father owed lots of money to. Money he couldn't pay back.

In exchange, he sold me to Jerry's father, the head of the gang, and Jerry forced me to work for their organization, doing horrible things.

And there was nothing my piece-of-shit dad could do about it. Unless he was willing to die for me, which he wasn't.

No one but Jerry knows I killed him. That asshole helped me bury the bodies. I had no one else to call except him.

Of course, he swore that if I tried something, if I didn't continue working for the gang, he'd make sure I rotted in prison.

So I had to run. If I hadn't, I'd have ended up dead, and so would my grandparents.

I can't go back, and I can't end up in prison.

I still remember the day I realized I was engaged to Jerry and who he really was.

I always knew my father didn't love me.

But to do *that*?

It was unforgivable.

# TWO YEARS AGO

*From my handbag, I retrieve the keys to my parents' home, wondering why my father asked me here today. He doesn't care much about spending time with me. Never has. This must be important.*

*Two cars are parked in the driveway.*

*Cars I don't recognize.*

*A chill creeps up the back of my neck. I don't know why, but it's there, like it's warning me of something I don't yet understand.*

*My father has always had people by the house, though. Even when I was younger and lived here. He'd say they were there to help him run the numbers for his business or deal with orders for the restaurant. He's made a good living doing it for over fifteen years. It's honestly all he ever cares about.*

*The door screeches as I start to open it.*

*"Hey, Dad, I'm—" The words die in my throat.*

*Three men I've never seen before—scary-looking men—stand around the foyer. Black shirts, tall, tattoos on their necks. They give me hard stares, and I gulp down my own fear.*

*"Um, do you know where—"*

*One of the men cuts me off and points to his left, toward the* kitchen. *Muffled voices grow louder as I head in that direction.*

*"Whatever you want!" my father tells someone.*

*My stomach knots from the fear in his voice.*

*As soon as I appear, a man in a suit, about the same age as my dad, stands behind him, lowering his gun out of view. But I saw it, and it was pointing at my father's head.*

*Every limb on my body trembles. Dread like I've never known zaps through me.*

*My eyes land on my father's. He's just as scared.*

*I want to run. I want to get help.*

*This man is either robbing us or something else is going on.*

*"Sweetheart!" My father attempts to jump from his seat, but the man shoves him back down by his shoulders.*

*"You stay here," he tells him, cunning dark eyes landing on me, a devious grin on his face.*

*Footfalls from the adjacent living room grow nearer, and from the side of my vision, I find Jerry walking into the room. His face is unreadable at first…until a touch of smugness crosses his eyes.*

*A heavy feeling sinks into the pit of my stomach.*

*I don't understand what's happening.*

*What the hell is Jerry doing here? It's been maybe a year since I saw him last at my father's restaurant, and as far as I know, he still works there.*

*"What's going on? Why am I here?" I ask Jerry.*

*His response is nothing but a glare.*

*My pounding heart raps across my ribs.*

*"That is a good question," the man in the suit says. "I'm Isaac. I've heard a lot about you from my son, Jerry."*

His son? Oh no…

*Terror prances across my skin. I'm unsure if I'm going to live through whatever is happening.*

*My eyes connect with my father's, and in them, I witness shame.*

*He did something. He had to have. It's why they're here, isn't it? I've seen enough movies to know how this plays out.*

*They're here to kill us.*

*But what could he have done? Does Jerry even work for him at the restaurant? Did my dad borrow money from them he couldn't pay back?*

"I know you must be afraid," the man goes on. "But I promise you have nothing to fear, Evelyn."

*He starts to approach, and I back up a step, glancing behind me to find two more men closing in on me.*

*I'm surrounded.*

*There's nowhere to go.*

*My heart pounds so loud, I'm afraid it'll rip out of my chest.*

"What do you want from us?"

*He chuckles, taking another step toward me.* "Well, you see, your father and I had a business going, and he's failed his end of the deal. I do consider myself to be a fair man, but one thing I do not forgive is someone who can't pay their debts."

*I hold back a scream as another man shoves a gun to the back of my father's head.*

"I'm sorry it took us so long to meet." *He reaches his hand for mine, forcing me to shake it in my clammy palm.* "I do hate that you're being dragged into this, pretty thing like yourself."

*He gives my dad a passing glimpse over his shoulder.* "But your father? Well, he thought he could outsmart me. He promised to pay me for something I delivered, and he hasn't."

*Nono! I can't let them kill my father. No matter how he's treated me, he's still my dad.*

"Maybe I can help?" *I'm shaking, yet I can't just do nothing.* "Maybe I can pay you what he owes. How much is it?"

*I have ten grand saved up. Maybe that would be enough.*

*His laughter is as harsh as his eyes.* "You're a good daughter to *try to get your father out of this mess, even though he doesn't deserve it. You see, your father has already provided us with a workable solution. It's why you're here."*

*Goose bumps prickle my skin.*

*"Me? How would I be the solution?" Panic clutches my throat, choking me. "Dad?"*

*He doesn't say a word. Can barely look at me.*

*Jerry comes forward, throwing an arm around my shoulders.*

*My gut gnaws. I never disliked Jerry...until now.*

*"I've always had a thing for you, Evelyn," he drawls.*

*My lungs grow heavy with the weight of my frozen breaths.*

*"So when your father offered you as payment for the five hundred K he couldn't pay back, I couldn't say no."*

*"What?" A sudden weakness hits my knees and my head spins, but he holds me up. "No, please!" I shake my head, begging him not to do this to me. "I'm not some object you people can barter with!"*

*Do I mean so little to my father for him to offer me as payment?*

*"You don't have a choice in the matter," Isaac says. "The deal has been made. It's the only reason your useless father is still alive. You're leaving with us. So don't fight it."*

*He runs his knuckles down my cheek, and my insides curl.*

*"But don't you worry. Since I'm a good man, I'll let you continue working and become the teacher you've always dreamed of becoming. Nothing will change."*

*Yet that's a lie.*

*Everything already has.*

*The room spins, my heart physically hurting.*

*"We'll arrange for your things to be picked up from your apartment today."*

*"No! I won't go with you!" Unspeakable agony engulfs me, swallowing me whole.*

*This can't be happening. I look to my father for help, and he lowers his head instead.*

*"How can you do this?" I scream with a cry, but he continues to ignore me. "Do I truly mean so little to you?"*

*"He didn't even put up a fight," Isaac adds, digging the betrayal in deeper. "He offered you to us in whatever capacity we wanted to use you, just so we'd spare his life. And I am a man of my word, so I will let him live." He grabs my jaw and glares. "But one disobedience from you, and I will kill your entire family. Do you understand?"*

*I nod, tears dripping down my face, knowing I can't fight them.*

*Isaac palms my shoulder and squeezes. "My son has a gift for you."*

*I want nothing from them. Nothing except my freedom.*

*Jerry reaches into his pocket and retrieves a black jewelry box, and my eyes grow. When he opens it, a large solitaire diamond shines through.*

*"I don't understand…" I whisper.*

*"Oh, we forgot to mention the other part of your father's deal. In exchange for letting him live, my son will marry you."*

*He tugs my hand in his, and I wince.*

*"I can't wait to welcome you into the family."*

I hate reliving one of the worst days of my life.

Of course, marriage wasn't the only thing they wanted. They took more from me in that year I lived with them than I could've even imagined.

Jerry never loved me. I don't think he even liked me. I was just a toy to use for his own needs.

I want nothing to do with that world anymore. I want a normal life. A normal husband. A family. I want to be happy. And I can never be happy with men from the belly of the underworld.

Men just like Tynan…

Though marriage isn't even in the cards for me. If Jerry or his people ever find me, I'm fucked. They'll kill me for leaving, and they'll kill my family too just because they can.

Staying single and on the run is what I have to do.

But accepting Tynan's job offer doesn't mean I'll have to stay here in Massachusetts. If I have to go, then I will. Tynan won't be able to stop me.

Leaving my grandparents worries me, though.

But Jerry would think they went with me. He knows how close I am to them. I'd never leave them behind.

I reach into the drawer of my nightstand and pick up the gun I left home with. Untraceable and mine.

Well, not mine. Jerry's.

If it ever came down to it, I'd give up my life in exchange for my grandparents.

I'm *not* my father's daughter. I protect those I love.

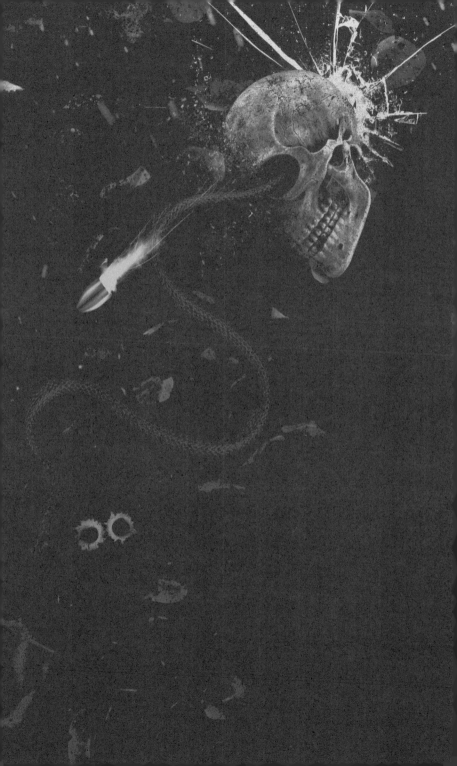

# NINE

## TYNAN

"**I** have a surprise for you," I tell Brody the following day after school, but he doesn't even look up from his book. I don't even know if this is a good idea. Pretty sure it's the worst one I've ever had.

Just thinking about the mess. The chaos. All the cleaning…

But if it helps him talk or finally be happy here, I'll try anything.

"I thought we could go to the shelter and you can maybe choose a dog."

That gets him looking up at me from below his long dark lashes, and I swear there's a glimmer in his green eyes.

Wasn't my idea, though. It was the therapist's. He said Brody may benefit from a dog. So I thought I'd take him to the shelter and have him pick one. Maybe that'll make him smile again.

"So, you wanna go?"

He nods.

"Go get changed."

While he runs into his room, I stare at my phone, wondering if something is wrong with it.

Why the hell hasn't Elara called or texted me about the job offer? Doubt my cell is broken. I press a few keys, checking for issues. None that I can see.

Just to be sure, I call my brother Fionn.

"Hey, what's up?"

"Can you shoot me a text?"

"Something wrong with your phone?"

If I tell him the real reason, he won't get off my ass.

"Just want to make sure it's working right."

He laughs. "Why? Has a girl not called you back?"

"Shut up and do it."

"Oh, damn. Did she ghost you?" He keeps chuckling, and I'm about to strangle him through the phone.

"I'm hanging up now. Do what I said."

His laughter dies when I end the call, and seconds later, my cell pings with a text.

**FIONN**

Pretty sure your phone works just fine.

**TYNAN**

Fuck you.

**FIONN**

Buy her some diamonds. Women love them.

**TYNAN**

I don't need advice from you.

**FIONN**

I think you do. When women say they'll call me, they actually do.

**TYNAN**

It's not like that. Was hoping Brody's teacher could give him extra lessons after school and she still hasn't given me an answer.

**FIONN**

Ask her if she's available for some lessons for you. You need them more than Brody does.

**TYNAN**

Fuck off.

The phone rings a few seconds later, and it's him. Of course my phone's working.

"Don't say it."

He's laughing again. "Give her time to consider it. You're a lot to handle."

"I don't have time. *He* doesn't have time."

The air grows solemn. "He'll talk. You'll see. It's still hard on him. When we lost Ma, that was…"

"Yeah…"

"And he has had it ten times harder."

"I know, damn it. I just wanna help him. I just want him to be like he used to be. Just say one damn word. Give me something to hope for."

He sighs. "You did what I could never do. You took him in without hesitation. You love that kid. You're his father figure now, and you're wearing that badge like you were meant for it. Aiden would be proud."

"Yeah…" Pain bites at my center. "Anyway, gotta go get a dog today."

"Wait, did you say a dog? Since when do you want a dog?"

"Since now. Let's hope the kid picks a good one."

"This I've gotta see." He chuckles. "Meet you at the shelter."

Just then, Brody returns.

"See ya there." I stuff the phone into my pocket. "Alright, kid, let's go see what we can get."

Hopefully Elara likes dogs.

He strides ahead of me, glancing from crate to crate, and I'm close to giving up hope that he'll actually pick a dog.

I really thought he'd like this, yet he hasn't even wanted to hold a single puppy. Not even the damn cute beagles the woman from the shelter showed us.

She struts beside him, keeping a small distance between. "We just got three German shepherd puppies you might like."

He simply shrugs as she leads him toward the far end.

She peeks back at me with a sympathetic smile, and I want to punch the nearest fucking wall.

Why can't he just talk to me? Hell, even to curse me out. I'll take anything at this point.

As we pass the last crate on the left, he stops in place, glancing down in concentration at the small dog barking and wagging its tail at him. He kneels and sticks a finger into the slot, and the dog excitedly licks it.

It's easy to see there's something wrong with one of its eyes. The pup paws the crate, as though trying to find an escape. Don't blame him. A cage isn't a life.

Then again, we're all in a cage one way or another. Some of us just don't know it.

"That's Bubbles." The woman squats beside him and opens the door, and the pup doesn't retreat, practically jumping out.

"I know you're excited to meet my friend Brody here." She scratches the dog on the ear and gathers it in her arms. "She's a Havanese and only one year old. We got her when she was around six months."

I stand behind them, watching his eyes light up at the sight of this shaggy black-and-white dog, maybe weighing ten pounds.

"Did something happen to her?" I move in closer, taking a good look at the pup.

"Yeah, she had a rough start in life. Lost her vision in one eye, and unfortunately, she gets passed on a lot for that reason. But she's a great dog and very sweet and playful."

I'm waiting to see what Brody thinks.

"Wanna hold her?" She grins at him.

After spending forty-five minutes with us, I think she's relieved he's finally gravitating toward a dog.

He nods.

*Halle-fucking-lujah.*

Brody tentatively stretches his hands out for the dog, and the woman places her in his arms.

As soon as she does, the dog gets even more excited, licking his face, practically leaping all over him.

He doesn't smile, though something in his eyes says he wants this one.

I can tell.

*Bubbles.*

Shit.

I can't own a dog named Bubbles. Just imagining myself introducing a dog named Bubbles to the heads of the Mafia... We'll have to change her name.

"She's a very happy dog. Aren't you, Bubbles?" The lady scratches the pup's ears, and I groan internally at the name.

Brody runs a palm down its head, and the dog burrows her face into his chest. His eyes close, and I swear he smiles.

Fuck me.

Bubbles is coming home with us.

"We'll take her."

"Great! How about we head to my office so I can get the paperwork started?"

I motion for Brody to follow me, and as we start after her, another employee named Bill stops her.

"Uh, I'm so sorry." He grimaces, looking between me and the woman. "But someone actually just got approved for Bubbles an hour ago. I forgot to put it into the system."

"Oh, no!" Her brows rise as she smiles nervously at me. "I'm so sorry about the mix-up. I'm sure we can find another dog he loves just as much."

One look at Brody's eyes watering and his bottom lip jutting out with a pout, and I'm ready to do anything to make Bubbles ours.

I grind my molars. "A word. In private."

"Umm...sure."

Bill makes his escape, glancing behind his shoulder at her before he completely disappears.

"Brody, stay right here. I'm going to talk to the nice lady about Bubbles."

We move a little distance away, where I can still see Brody with stars in his eyes as he pets the dog and hugs it tight.

And the dog? Well, she no longer wants to escape. She found someone she wants to escape to, and I'll do everything to make that happen.

If she thinks someone else is going to get this dog, she doesn't know me.

"You're gonna make this right." My voice simmers, and she

scratches her neck.

"Look, sir, I can see you're in a difficult position, but—"

*I can't believe I'm about to fight for a dog with such a horrible name. Who picks these names?*

"How much?"

"What?"

"How much to make that dog ours? I'll write a check to the shelter right now."

"Uh, we don't do—"

"Everyone has a price, Miss…" I glance down at her name tag. "Nancy."

"We have never had someone offer money before. I…I just don't know."

She's considering it. Of course she is.

"How's one hundred thousand?"

Her eyes pop. I'm afraid they'll fall out. Nancy has never seen money like that. If she had any business sense, she would've countered. I was ready to offer a million if it went there.

"Are you sure?" she whispers.

"For him, yes. Now, do we have a deal?"

She nods. "I'll let the other family know after we're done."

"Great."

"You two may follow me so I can get the papers in order for you to sign."

"I'll go tell Brody the good news."

I head back to him, and he doesn't even look up at me.

"Hey, bud. Bubbles is coming home with us. But I have to sign some papers before we can take her home."

He starts walking beside me, holding on to the dog even tighter.

"I think we have to have a talk about that name, though," I tell him as we enter a small corridor.

With a sharp look, he eyes me and slowly shakes his head.

*Oh, hell no.*

"You mean you like the name?"

He nods.

Jesus Christ. I guess we're gonna have a dog named Bubbles.

We finish the paperwork while Brody kisses the top of the dog's head, and I know instantly I'm making the right decision.

After my check has been written, we are good to go.

The woman gives us a collar, a leash, and a small bag of puppy food.

I plan to head to the store and buy some toys and treats for her.

As we start toward my SUV, I take the dog from him so Brody can get into the booster, but when I do, the dog growls and barks at me.

I narrow a glare in her direction.

Really? The dog doesn't like me either?

Wonderful. What else is new?

"Okay, Bubbles, you can relax. I'll hand you right back to Brody in a second."

*You little shit.*

Her tail wags as soon as I say his name, like she committed it to memory the moment she heard it back at the shelter.

Brody straps himself in, and once he's good, I give the tiny terror right back to him and get in.

"You know, having a dog is a huge responsibility. You will have to make sure her water and food bowls are cleaned and filled, that she's brushed every day, and we have to take her on walks together. Think you're up for that?"

He nods, almost enthusiastically.

I hide my smile as I start the car, knowing that the therapist was right. This was a good idea.

Now I just have to figure out how to get the kid and the dog to like me.

Maybe Elara too.

We make it to the pet store in thirty minutes, and the cart is full of too much crap. Food, bowls, treats, a pink doggy bed Brody picked out, and a bright purple collar.

I strap it around the dog's neck to make sure it fits. "What do you think?"

Brody inspects her as I slip on the black leash. No way was I going to be caught dead walking her with a purple one he originally chose. Luckily, the kid didn't object.

He gives me a thumbs-up, and I swear this is the most he's communicated with me since I've adopted him. Maybe I should've gotten the dog sooner.

"Alright, let's go pay."

We head for the cashier, who starts scanning and bagging all of the stuff while I remove my black card and pass it to her.

She gives me a curious glance, then proceeds to hand me the bags. They all know my family in these towns. How could they not? We practically own it all. Restaurants, bars, stores. We have our hands in everything. Makes hiding the dirty money much easier.

"You're good with walking her to the car?"

The dog stares up at me and barks with her dissatisfaction. Like she's offended I've even spoken.

Kinda starting to regret this decision right about now.

But seeing how happy Brody is makes the dog hating me worth it.

# TEN

## ELARA

I've yet to decide on the job offer Tynan made a couple of days ago.

Just the thought of that man sends a shiver down my spine.

I can't be forced to see him every single day. The way he makes my body grow weak is too much for me to handle.

"What's on your mind, honey?" Grandma asks from the other side of the table at the café, the one *he* owns.

He's everywhere, even when he's not present. It's like I can feel him watching me, even when that makes no logical sense.

Gran eyes me speculatively. She's a shrewd woman. Definitely fools lots of people with her sweet act. Not to say she's not sweet, but she's tough when she has to be.

She used to run a company she started with Grandpa. Textiles, that's what they sold. Then when they got older, they handed it off to my dad to manage, on top of his restaurant.

He wasn't very good at it. That, of course, made Grandma pretty pissy. And who wouldn't be? But with her help, my father figured it out.

Then after his death, she sold it to someone else. She didn't have it in her to work anymore. Of course, being on the run, she would've had to sell it anyway or leave it all behind. I'm glad she got the money for it before we had to leave. It helps. Though after the debts she had to pay off, it didn't leave very much.

Between us both, we're barely making it work. His home costs ten thousand every month. Money we don't have.

"Nothing." I force a grin and pick up my coffee, taking a few sips.

She sighs, grabbing my hand and clutching it, her blue eyes glistening. "You're worried. I can see it." She leans in closer into the table. "Don't be. It will all work out. You'll see. They won't find us. Not here."

"It's not just that. It's everything, you know?" A whoosh of a breath leaves me, and my eyes pin shut for a moment. "I hate that we had to run." An ache hits the back of my throat.

"It's not your fault." Her face drops to the side. "None of it is. Your father made that mess."

She's right; it *is* my dad's fault.

But she doesn't have the full picture. About Dad's involvement with Jerry. What they made me do. She thinks Jerry was just a bad boyfriend. Yet she's never seen the scars I bear because of my so-called father. That he sold me for his sins.

The thought of it all makes my stomach turn.

I force all thoughts of him away.

Can't think about that now.

I desperately need to go on my run to clear my head.

"You ready to go?" I ask her.

She nods, grabbing her wallet while I leave some cash to pay for our tab. She rises, and I follow her out the door.

As we start back to her place, only a short walk away, I notice a small black-and-white dog running in our direction, her leash dragging behind her, a purple collar around her neck.

"Oh, goodness!" Gran gasps. "Someone must've run off."

"Hey!" I call to the pup, hoping the dog stops so I can help the owner find her. "Come here! Look what I have!"

Kneeling, I pretend I have a treat in my hand, and the dog jumps into my arms.

*Well, that was easy.*

She starts licking my face, and I laugh, unable to stop her. I can tell there's something wrong with one of her eyes, and I instantly feel sorry for her.

"You're excited, aren't you?" I pet the top of her head, and she won't stop.

It's pretty sweet how happy she is to see me. I don't remember the last time someone was this excited to have me around.

I've never owned a dog. My father hated them, said they're useless creatures. As a little girl, I always envied all my friends who had them. Then I got older and got a job and realized I had no time for one.

"Uh, Elara?" Grandma's voice drops.

"Yes?" I keep laughing as the dog licks my eyes, my nose.

My goodness, she's precious. I bet her owners miss her very much.

"Um—" she continues, but a deep voice cuts her off.

"Ms. Hill."

An inhale stills in my lungs.

Because there's only one man who can make my heart beat that way.

And I hate that he can. I hate that he has an invisible power over me already.

Gradually, I lower the dog and stare up into the eyes of the man I've spent my nights thinking about, imagining all the dirty things he could do to me.

"Mr. Quinn? What are you doing here?"

His mouth quirks only a fraction, like smiling is almost painful. His eyes take a dangerous turn as he marches a step forward.

"That's my dog."

I laugh. Him owning such an adorable dog, and one with a purple collar, no less? Unlikely.

His brooding gaze flays me open.

"Oh…you're serious."

He cocks a brow. "Hand her to me."

"Uh…"

I have no idea what to do. What if he's lying? I hold the dog to my chest, and as she looks at him, she growls. Pretty sure if he does own her, she doesn't exactly like him.

His chest rises and slowly falls, like he's trying to collect every ounce of patience. "The dog, Ms. Hill."

"Elara, just give him the dog." Grandma's tone strains.

I glance at her for a second before I peek at him again, and instantly regret it. He definitely looks like he's ready to dismember me limb from limb. Makes me wonder if he's actually done that.

Of course he has…

His eyes narrow, and my stomach drops.

But it's no longer just fear.

His intense gaze roves down my body, searing into me, scorching me where I stand.

Desire winds itself around me, every inch of my flesh begging to be his until it becomes unbearable. There's just something about him. He's all man, with those big hands that could do quite a lot to a woman's body. My stomach clenches at his rugged sex appeal.

*Geez, Elara! Concentrate on the problem at hand instead of picturing him eating you out 69-style.*

Okay.

The dog.

Right.

I definitely can't just give him the dog, not unless he can somehow prove it's his. How do I know she really belongs to him?

"Do you happen to have a photo of her?"

He sighs. "This isn't in your best interest, Ms. Hill." He moves up until the dog is sandwiched between us, until his mouth lowers to my ear, his breath tingling across my neck. "I don't like to be questioned. Even by someone as beautiful as you."

My sharp inhale has him chuckling low and menacingly.

"You didn't call me." His palm grips my hip, and I grow breathless.

"Was I supposed to?" I whisper, dizzy from the feeling of his body this close to mine, the smell of his expensive cologne that I've now decided is my favorite smell of all time.

"Did you forget about my job offer?"

I shake my head, trying to remember to inhale. My heart rattles within my ribs, like it's in a cage, needing to break free.

"Good. Because I'm expecting an answer soon. I've never been good with patience."

He moves back a breath, and when his eyes level to mine, I swear the earth shakes under my feet.

Tynan Quinn, he's not good for me. He makes me weak and vulnerable and scared. I hate feeling scared.

"The dog, Ms. Hill. I won't ask again."

I clear my throat and move back, holding to my convictions, refusing to give him the dog. That would be irresponsible.

"Unless you can prove that the dog is yours, I can't just give her to you. How do I know you won't kill her?"

"I don't kill dogs."

I pop a brow and whisper, "Just people, then?"

His inhale deepens, and his hand gently cups my jaw, his eyes wildly searching mine.

"You're lucky I'm not in the mood to kill *you*." His lips fall almost a breath away, stilling my heartbeats.

"What are you in the mood for, then?" My voice is almost lost to the magnetism between us.

He leans his mouth nearer until it feathers against my lips. "To strip you bare until you can't hide anymore."

My eyes pop and my pulse quickens, until all I hear is his words on repeat. What did they mean? Does he know what I'm running from?

No. No. He can't.

I move back, the dog letting out a bark as I raise my chin. "I'll be going now. You know where I live when you have that proof."

He shakes his head, his scowl making me shiver, and I know he won't just let me go.

"Who is that?" Grandma's hushed words have me glancing at her, remembering she's here and probably terrified. Though she really doesn't look to be.

Before I can answer, he does. "My name is Tynan Quinn. It's a pleasure to meet you, Nora."

He takes her hand and kisses the top of it. She instantly melts, forgetting the aura of danger he had just exuded.

Figures. Grandma already likes him.

"You too, young man." She looks over at me. "Are you single? My Elara is strong-willed and feisty, but she'd make a fine wife. For the right man, of course."

"Grandma!" My eyes grow and my cheeks heat up, and when he smirks, I want to die of mortification.

"I *am* single." His smoldering gaze locks with mine and my gut clenches. "Very much so. How about you, Elara? Have you ever had a husband? A fiancé?"

My eyes widen. Every instinct in me is begging to run.

"There was someone." Gran grabs my hand. "But he was an asshole."

Darkness crosses his pupils. "How's that?"

"He—"

"Shit! We've been looking all over for her, and you've got her and didn't call me?" Someone comes marching up behind him—a man who resembles Tynan—and…

"Brody?" My head jerks with confusion.

The man smiles at me, stalking closer and extending a hand. "I'm Fionn, this idiot's brother." He gestures with a tilt of his head. "I hope he wasn't being a complete you-know-what." He winks. "We've been looking for Bubbles for over an hour. She ran off while Tynan was putting all her new stuff into his car."

I glance between him and Brody, who looks up and gives me a big grin. And just like last time, I want to cry. It's so beautiful when he smiles. I never want him to stop smiling.

"Hey, buddy!" I kneel, and when I do, the dog starts licking his face, so I hand her to him, and he gives her a warm hug.

My heart melts at the sight of them.

And with all the emotions swimming in my chest, all I want to do is look at Tynan.

It's there I find his eyes already sinking into mine. His face is hard, yet something in it feels almost human, almost raw. His expression slowly softens, and that mouth…it gives me a tiny smile.

Just a minuscule curve of his lips is all it takes for my gut to flip, butterflies soaring within. And just like whenever he smiles like that, I lose all self-control.

I force my attention on Brody, ignoring Tynan and all the things he manages to make me feel.

"Is Bubbles your new dog?" I pet her one last time.

She jumps all over him, licking him like she did me, her leash dangling on the ground.

He nods, and his grin widens as he holds her tighter, his eyes closing as he lets her kiss him all over.

"So, did you just get her?" I ask Tynan, even though I should just walk away—far away from him.

There's no way I can agree to help Brody, not after today. Not after how good it feels when Tynan's near.

Fionn smirks as he assesses his brother's intensity, his eyes never leaving mine.

Tynan nods. "We were in the parking lot when she ran off."

"Oh." My face falls. "I'm glad I found her. She's beautiful."

"Yes, she is…" He sucks me into his deep and searching gaze, green like summer grass, that low and seductive voice sliding across my flesh like satin, wrapping itself around my skin.

With each passing moment, he doesn't relent. It's as though he's staring into my soul.

Heat rushes to my cheeks, and I start to wonder if he was even talking about the dog to begin with.

"Join us for lunch," he says, and I blink back, breaking our connection.

"No, thank you. We just—"

"We would love to," Grandma offers instead.

*What is she thinking?*

"You just ate, Gran." I smile politely, rolling an arm over her shoulders as I whisper, "What are you doing?"

She grins at them while leaning into my neck. "You need a man like that. Strong. Powerful. Trust me."

"You have no idea what you're saying. He's dangerous." From the corner of my vision, I peek up at him, hoping he didn't hear that.

"We'll see." She pulls my hand, her tone rising. "Come on, dear. I could use another coffee, and we know you like yours."

"Okay, uh, sure…"

She strides up beside Brody and Fionn, all three walking ahead of us, and somehow I'm stuck behind with Tynan.

He steps closer, his arm brushing mine, the smell of his woodsy cologne infecting my nostrils, corrupting every inch of my mind.

"Your grandmother seems nice." He holds the door open from me, waiting for me to enter first.

"She's nice, alright. If she likes you."

He chuckles. "Seems like that won't be much of a problem for me."

"Right. And about what she said—"

"About you making a fine wife?" He scoffs. "I find that hard to believe." His breath lands across the crook of my neck. "You're quite the little serpent."

My lips wind up. "You'd better remember that the next time you corner me, Mr. Quinn."

"Cornering you is my new favorite thing, Ms. Hill."

A shiver races up my spine.

Mine too…unfortunately.

His laughter rings behind me as I make it to the booth Grandma's already settled into. Brody's beside her, while Fionn is seated in a chair at the end of the table.

Which, of course, leaves Tynan no other spot but the one right next to me.

He slides in, getting too close.

The side of his thigh touches mine, and my pulse pumps louder in my ears.

The waitress returns, the one who served us earlier. "Hi again!" When her eyes land on the two brothers, they grow a fraction. "Oh, sirs, I didn't realize…I…"

"It's okay, Tina. No need to get nervous," Fionn tells her. "We're just here with friends."

"Okay, uh… Here are the menus." She hands them to us, her face growing crimson as she glances at Tynan.

He doesn't pay her any mind, though.

"Have you eaten?" he whispers into my ear, and my body grows taut.

I shake my head. "Not hungry."

"She barely eats these days," my grandma volunteers with a tsk. "Maybe you can talk some sense into her."

"I intend to." His voice rumbles, and I swallow the lump in my throat. "Tina, get us one of everything on the lunch menu."

"Everything?"

"That's what I said."

"Uh, okay. Coming right up, sir."

She skitters away while Fionn starts talking to my grandma like they're long-lost friends. Bubbles sits politely on Brody's lap, and he nuzzles her, causing my heart to swell with adoration.

"Why aren't you eating?" His question zaps me out of my thoughts.

"I eat." My face skewers. "She's exaggerating."

I brush off his concern and pick up the glass of water the waitress placed on the table before she left.

"I don't think so." He grasps my jaw and turns my face toward him. Eyes intense, he sets me aflame, exuding every bit of power he possesses. "From now on, I'll know if you're not eating."

"Oh, yeah? How's that? You're gonna watch me every day?"

His mouth slowly curves on one side and he drops his hand away. "Make sure you do, Ms. Hill. Wouldn't want you fainting on me."

His palm drops to the top of my thigh, and I feel it—heavy and strong, making my skin throb and tingle in its wake.

It remains there as the food comes. It only leaves for a moment as he places different items on my plate. Pasta and salad, and some chicken too.

His hand cups my knee, a finger drawing circles over my leggings. And those eyes...they watch me intently, waiting for me to eat.

His brow bows, and I pick up the fork and throw a piece of lettuce into my mouth.

Not hiding his dissatisfaction, he takes his own fork and picks up a piece of chicken. "Open your mouth."

And I realize everyone at the table is now quiet, their attention on us. But Grandma? She's trying and failing to hide her smile.

He drops his lips to my ear. "The more you resist, the more I'll keep pushing. So come on, open your mouth for me."

My heavy exhale causes my chest to rattle, and I find myself obeying.

He pops the fork into my mouth and watches me chew with a hardened expression.

"I—I've got the rest," I stammer and he grinds his jaw, refusing to lower the fork. "I don't see you eating."

He lowers his mouth to my ear once more, my skin warm and languid. "I won't be eating until you're done, so be a good girl and open that mouth every time I tell you."

My heartbeats tremble in my rib cage. I don't know why those words just affected me so much. And every time he brings that food to my mouth, I accept it without a fight.

Because in some crazy way, it feels like he's taking care of me, and I like that very much.

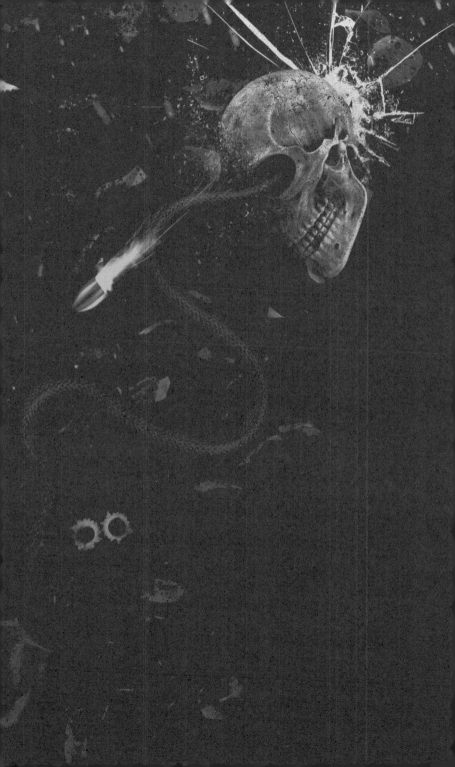

# ELEVEN

## TYNAN

"Can you take him back home?" I ask Fionn as soon as we've left the café, heading back to our cars. Brody holds the dog in his arms, afraid to put her down this time. I know how upset he was when she ran off. But it was my fault. I shouldn't have let him hold the leash. She got too excited when she saw a pigeon and pulled too hard and he couldn't hold on.

Tears filled his eyes, and I vowed to find that dog no matter how long it took.

I couldn't let him lose someone else. Not after everything.

"Why?" Fionn asks. "Where are you going?"

His amused expression makes it clear he thinks I'm going off to follow her. But he'd be wrong.

"None of your business." I kneel before Brody. "I'll be home soon."

He nods, and Fionn opens his car door for him before I get into mine.

I know where Elara is going now: on her run. She was already dressed for it—tight gray leggings that did nothing to hide her toned legs and round ass. One I'd very much enjoy.

Her sitting beside me that whole time had me wanting to do things I shouldn't want to do to her. I don't know what the hell she's doing to me and how, because I can't seem to stop thinking about her, no matter how hard I try.

She's a damn snake, wrapping herself around me until I can't so much as breathe without her permission.

I can't lie to myself anymore and pretend that I watch her for Brody's sake. This time it's all for me.

I've committed everything I can about her to memory. Like how she likes her coffee with only a splash of cream. And when she's out to dinner, she orders a glass of white wine instead of red. And when she's really nervous, she plays with her hair. There's nothing I haven't paid close attention to. Nothing at all, and that drives me crazy.

She's beautiful, though it's not just her beauty that entices me. It's her aura. The way she's afraid of me, yet speaks her mind and fights me with that sharp wit.

I want to feel her bare skin on my fingertips, want to expose every inch of her, in every way possible, until she trusts me enough to tell me what she's hiding.

When I mentioned a fiancé, I didn't miss the way her body visibly shuddered. He hurt her. That has to be it.

I need to know his name.

I need to find him.

Maybe her grandma will be more than happy to share that information.

But for now, I'll watch her and see what I can find on my own.

From a distance, her ponytail sways as she jogs up the path I saw her on the last time. I guess she didn't heed my warning.

Turning around, I roll my SUV the opposite way and head for her house, wanting to see what I can find. The last time I was there, I had to leave quickly when my father called. This time, I'll be taking my time.

Ten minutes later, I park behind her house. It's a small two-bedroom home, two stories, blue shutters. Perfect for her.

Opening the gate, I head toward the back door and easily pick the lock, strolling inside, right into the kitchen.

The smell of citrus drifts in the air from the bowl of oranges on her counter.

I run my fingers over the marble before heading for the fridge, not seeing anything there besides some magnets of animals. Dogs, cats, birds. She's an animal person. It's no wonder Bubbles was a fan.

I go through her cupboards. Every mug, every jar, every container. There's nothing in here that can give me answers.

There has to be something. Something right in front of my face.

Continuing past the kitchen and into the living room, I rummage through the sofa cushions, not finding a damn thing. Not even after looking through every inch of the first floor.

Taming my frustration, I head toward the end table, where photos of her and her family lie. There's one with her grandparents and another with two people I've never seen before.

Picking that photo up, I trace a finger down Elara's face—a few years younger, yet still as beautiful.

The couple's older, most likely her parents. She resembles the woman, same blue eyes, but Elara's hair is darker—her father's hair.

Where are they? Are they dead? She's like a damn puzzle.

I take out my phone and snap a picture of them. I'll run it through our facial recognition software to see if her parents get any hits.

Is she in witness protection? Is that what this is? We don't have contacts with them. Wouldn't be able to get those files.

I lower the photo back down, and as I do, it slips from my grasp. "Shit."

It can't break. I don't want her to know someone's been here. She'll think it's her ex. If she ran once, she's bound to do it again. Brody can't lose her.

The glass doesn't seem affected, but the back came undone. As I go to fix it, something slips from behind the velvet.

Tugging it out, I find a small, neatly-folded piece of paper.

What the fuck is this?

Opening it up, I read it. Just two letters and a phone number.

DK
732-555-6593

732. That's a New Jersey area code. Is that where she's from? Who the hell is DK?

Slipping my cell out again, I snap a photo of the info and return the paper back in the frame, placing it how it originally stood.

As I intend to head upstairs to her bedroom, soft footsteps pound across the ground before keys clink together.

Seems like she cut her run a little short today.

A smirk spreads across my face as I return to the kitchen and settle onto a stool, waiting for her to find me.

I think it's time we had a little discussion about how it isn't nice to keep someone waiting.

I want an answer about my job offer. And I want it today.

# ELARA

A chill creeps up the back of my neck, even as sweat beads across my forehead. I take in gasping breaths, but it isn't from the run. It's from something else entirely.

A car behind me slows.

A black sedan with no plates. The windows tinted.

My breaths rush out of me as I start to run faster, the engine roaring to life right before the vehicle speeds up.

Closer.

It gets closer.

Chasing me down the empty road.

Tynan was right. You never know who might find you here.

And this time, it isn't him.

My body prickles, the wheels burning across the concrete as the driver toys with me.

Is it Jerry? His father? One of their men?

No. I can't die. I can't give up.

*Run.*

*Keep running.*

But I'm no match.

It gains on me.

Faster.

Faster.

The horn beeps, but I keep going, my lungs burning like they're on fire.

Only a few yards remain between us. And as it comes up right behind me, I veer into the woods, rushing past the branches crunching beneath my feet, one slicing across my arm through my thin, hooded zip-up jacket.

I wince, yet keep running through the pain, unsure if the driver is still following me.

I can't look back. I must keep going. I know the way back home from here.

Only a couple miles remain until I'm safe.

Though that's a foolish thought.

Because whoever is behind that wheel must know where I live.

Maybe I should surrender. If I do, there's a chance they'll spare my grandparents' lives. I can't let them die.

I fight the tears filling my eyes. Staying strong and making it out of this is all I have left right now. There's no other choice. I have to make it home. I have to pack my bags and disappear.

Glancing behind me, I don't see or hear a sound.

*Just keep running.*

*Almost there.*

My heart is ready to rip right out of my chest.

Mindlessly, I hurry like hell until I make it back home, rushing to get my keys out and opening the door as quickly as possible.

"Oh, God…" I cry, the adrenaline leaving me, fear remaining.

My back hits the door, and I slither down to the floor, breathing heavy as I shut my eyes.

I need to figure out a plan. Maybe I can somehow find out who was chasing me before I do something rash like leave my grandparents behind.

But how? There were no cameras there, I don't think, and even if there were, how would I have access to the footage?

In that moment, Tynan comes to mind. He has connections. Maybe I could tell him what happened and he'd help me find the driver.

Brushing the back of my hand over my sweaty forehead, I start to rise, needing to clean my wound.

I grimace as I stare down at the blood already soaking the material.

My phone rings, and my pulse jumps in my temples.

Instant panic sets in when I retrieve it to find the nursing home calling. What if Jerry did something to him?

"H-h-hello?"

"Ms. Hill? Hi, it's Ms. Davis calling from Sunset Homes."

"Yes, i-is everything okay with my grandfather?" My breathing has yet to stabilize. I'm barely able to get the words out.

"Oh, yes, yes, of course. I was just calling about the outstanding bill we have on his account. I know you had asked for another week to pay the remaining six thousand for this month, but I'm afraid we still have not gotten a payment."

*Shit. I don't have enough.*

Pinching my eyes closed, I clear my throat. "Uh, right, yes. I'm so sorry about that. Is there any way you can give me another week? Please? I can pay two thousand today. I just need a little time."

She sighs. "Ms. Hill, have you thought about sending him to Care Park? It's a few thousand less a month and they have space for him."

No way. That place is awful. I personally toured it and read the terrible reviews. I'd never send him to that dump. I'll have to get another job.

*Tynan offered you one…*

My stomach clenches.

"Ms. Davis, I swear, I will have the money for you in a week. You won't have a problem again."

She releases an impatient exhale. "Alright. I'll speak to billing. But a week, Ms. Hill. That's all you have. There will be no other extensions."

"Understood."

"Have a good day."

"You too."

She drops the call, and I grip the phone in a tight grasp, my breath ravaging in my chest. I have to tell Tynan I want the job. That'd give me at least seven thousand a week. I'll have the rest of the money from my salary.

My arm stings, and I groan as I head toward the kitchen.

As I step inside, I gasp through my racing heart, jumping back and almost tripping over my own feet.

Because sitting there in my kitchen is none other than Tynan Quinn.

Wearing that same smirk I can't seem to get out of my head.

# TWELVE

## ELARA

"What the fuck!" I drop my palms on my knees, trying to quiet the pounding of my heartbeats. "What in the world are you doing in my house?"

He folds his arms over his chest with a menacing twist of his mouth. "Hello to you too, Ms. Hill. I think it's time we had a proper chat, don't you?"

"And you just break in? You're insane," I huff out, still frazzled. "You need to get the hell out of my house before I call the police."

He blows out a long breath, like he's bored. "And how do you expect that to go? I know every cop in this town."

His eyes dance over my frame, and heat blooms across the path of his gaze. Those green eyes snap back to mine.

"You're crazy!"

My body trembles with anger and frustration, with everything that just happened—the car, Grandpa's bill. I can't take another second of this! My emotions are in overdrive, and if he doesn't leave right now,

I'm gonna kill him or burst into tears.

"You need to go!" Rage simmers in my voice, but he doesn't so much as move, remaining seated like this is his home, not mine.

"Have a seat, Ms. Hill." He extends his hand and I laugh incredulously.

My head grows dizzy, and I'm about to scream.

"Get out!" I warn him one last time.

When his mouth twitches, I growl and lift the mug sitting on the counter, tossing it at his face. He jumps off the seat and watches it go flying straight into the wall, shattering into pieces.

"Wow. You have some balls." For a moment, he looks proud, then his face shifts to something scarier. He stalks toward me, grabbing my jaw in a tight grip. "Let this be your first and final warning, little serpent. You try that again, and I won't be so nice. Do we understand each other?"

My chin trembles, tears blurring my vision, and every strength in me fades. And I wish he would do it. I wish he'd just kill me.

My body rocks with heavy breathing as I fight not to cry, not to appear weak. I can't take any more of this. None of it. Maybe my grandparents would be better off without me.

His brows furrow and his grip loosens, concern fitting his features.

"What's wrong?" His thumb climbs up my cheek, wiping away the tears that happened to fall. "Did I hurt you?"

I shake my head, wincing from the pain in my arm, and then he sees it: the blood. With my black hoodie, it was easy to miss it at first.

"What is this?" he snaps, his nostrils flaring as he gently lifts my wrist to examine my arm. "Who did this to you?"

"I'm fine." I swipe at my eyes. "I fell during my run. That's all."

I try to walk away, but in an instant, his arm curls around my stomach and he turns me to him, my front landing right against his.

His eyes sink into mine, my lungs stilling, refusing to allow a breath.

In this moment, I almost forget everything that happened. Everything except the way he's looking at me, like he wants to keep me safe.

This sudden feeling comes over me, like if I were to fall, he'd be there to catch me.

And that's the scariest thought of all.

Because that means I'd have to trust him.

His palm cups my cheek, a gentle thumb stroking the corner of my mouth. "Who hurt you?"

"I...I..."

"Just give me a name, and you'll be reading his obituary."

My heart, it practically bursts. He sounds like he means it, and I wish it were that easy.

"It was no one. I fell." My emotions tighten in my throat as I meet his imperious gaze, not wanting to fight his hands on me anymore.

It feels too good to be touched by him, to be held this way.

"Elara, I know you didn't fall. I know you're scared of someone. Don't lie to me. All you need to do is give me a name."

My tears return, treacherous and wild, running down my cheeks. I want so badly to trust someone. To not be alone in this.

But I can't. I can't trust anyone with what I've done, the people I'm running from. Especially him. He'll either use it against me like Jerry did or turn me in to the police. I am Brody's teacher. He wouldn't want someone like that teaching his son.

"There is no name. I fell. I swear."

His eyes narrow and his thumb rolls across my lips. "It's only a matter of time until I get you to trust me enough to tell me who's hurting you, Ms. Hill."

Warmth cruises over my barren and hollow limbs, filling me with oxygen.

"Good luck with that, Mr. Quinn."

"Mm." He pulls his body even nearer, until I can feel how strong he is, how hard his muscles are.

I inhale sharply, a throbbing pulsing between my thighs. He must notice the change in me because his smirk widens and his mouth moves just a little closer, warm breaths twining with mine.

I want him—no, *need* him—to kiss me.

To make me forget.

"You're trouble," he whispers, his mouth stroking mine, a growl emanating from his rumbling chest.

"I thought a man like you liked a little trouble."

Deep, raspy laughter rolls out of him, the fingers of his other hand running up my spine before they get lost in my hair.

I moan low as he snaps a fist into my waves, tilting my head back. His lips land on my throat, kissing up to my jaw, teeth nipping and sucking along the curve.

Every inch of me aches for him, for this undeniable yearning coursing between us.

He yanks my head back even more, staring down into my eyes. "Who hurt you? Just tell me so I can help you."

I want to tell him, I do. But no good would come of it.

"No one."

"Fine. Have it your way." He drops his hands off of me and moves back a step. "Though I will find out and I will take care of it, whether you ask for my help or not."

Damn it. I don't want him to start digging and looking for Jerry. If the car that was following me wasn't actually the gang, then Tynan would just lead them to me without realizing it. I have to tell him something without giving much away.

"Fine. I'll tell you."

His eyes narrow as he leans against the counter.

I scratch at my temple, trying to find the right words. "I honestly don't know who it was. I was running, and a car came out of nowhere and started chasing me."

"What car?" An infinitesimal jerk hits the muscles of his neck, his stare explosive, like he's ready to tear the world apart and find the culprit.

"It was a Toyota Camry. Black. No plates, and the windows were tinted, even the front one."

"Fuck." He runs a hand through his thick brown hair. "I should've been there."

"What?" My features draw in confusion. "Why would you be there?"

His fingers curl into a white-knuckled fist. "Never mind that. What else do you remember?"

"That's all. I ran into the forest and got this cut from a tree branch."

"Take it off." He starts removing his own suit jacket, unbuttoning it and throwing it over the chair. "Your hoodie. Take it off so I can clean and bandage your wound."

Something in my heart squeezes and emotions pound in my eyes. This is the second time he's made an effort to take care of me.

Why would he want to? And why do I crave that so much?

*Because since your mother, no one truly has.*

"Come on, Elara. You don't want it to get infected."

I nod, blinking back tears as I start removing one sleeve. But when I try to get the other out, I grumble in pain.

"Let me."

Our eyes connect, and I almost forget the pain. Almost forget that I shouldn't be attracted to him.

He inhales long and deep, gently easing off the hoodie, his eyes still drowning in mine. And every time they do, something unnerving pummels in my stomach.

"Do you keep alcohol and bandages in the bathroom here or upstairs?"

"Here."

He heads toward it, like he knows my house already. Maybe he does because he knew the old couple who lived here before I moved in.

Seconds later, he returns, placing the alcohol, ointment, and gauze on the counter before he's undoing the buttons of his cuffs.

I know I shouldn't be staring the way I am, but I can't look away. The veins running up his thick forearms snake beneath his skin as he pulls the right sleeve to his elbow, exposing the rest of his tattoo, thorny vines and skulls leading up and around his entire arm. Heat zaps between my legs even as I try to fight it.

This attraction is otherworldly.

Sinful

Dark.

Ominous.

Downright wrong at the very core of it. Yet I can't stop it, no matter what I do.

He does the same to his other sleeve, dragging it up, that arm empty of tattoos, and I can't decide which one I like better.

He's all man—tall, rough, large hands, wide shoulders. He towers over me, yet I don't feel small in his presence anymore.

"Sit down."

He pulls the chair for me and lifts me onto it by my hips, and my skin tingles where he touched me.

He moves to my side and picks up the alcohol, holding my wrist above the sink. "This is gonna hurt."

I nod, and he's pouring the alcohol over the wound.

"Shit." I crush my teeth and shut my eyes as the most intense stinging hits my skin.

"I'm sorry."

"It's okay." I manage to look back at him, his expression tense as he glares down at my wound.

"This will never happen again."

"Okay." I laugh to myself.

He has no idea who I am and that this definitely won't be the last time.

If that was in fact Jerry after me, I'll have to leave, and soon. But at the thought, an ache beats in my heart.

For the first time, I don't want to go. I'll miss teaching. I'll miss Brody. I may even miss *him*.

That's ridiculous, I know it is, yet somehow it's also true.

He starts to bandage up my arm, glancing at me periodically, sending my heart spinning.

"Thanks," I whisper.

"I'm sorry this happened, Elara." My God, he sounds so sweet and sincere.

My eyes water.

"All done." He lowers his sleeves back down, and I really wish he wouldn't. "From now on, you'll have one of my men watching you at all times. His name is Rogue. He'll have an SUV just like mine. I'll text you the plates so you know it's him when you're followed."

*Oh, no.* As much as I need the protection, I can't afford Tynan finding out about my past.

"That's crazy! You can't do that."

"Watch me." Intensity brews in his gaze.

"You're infuriating! You think you can just waltz into my life and control everything?"

"That's right. And you won't do a thing about it."

I snicker.

"Someone is clearly after you and you won't tell me who you think it is, so it leaves me no options."

Something pulls at my heart, and I want to cry all over again. "Why do you even care what happens to me? You're not my boyfriend or my husband. We're not even friends."

He moves into my space, his hard body meeting my soft one. I look into his eyes as his knuckles brush down my cheek, and those treacherous tingles return.

I try to fight his touch, yet it just feels too good, like being pulled toward the fire, knowing you're about to burn. But the warmth is just too alluring.

His lips brush across my ear. "I'd like us to be friends."

"Please," I beg with a shameful groan. "Please don't do that."

"Don't do what, Ms. Hill?" He kisses the spot right below my ear, and I gasp in pleasure.

"That. I—I can't…I can't fight it."

"Then don't." He fists my hair. "Look at me."

I try not to. I can't stare at this man without crumbling.

"I said look at me."

And when I do, I find a man hungry and wanton.

"You're slowly turning into my obsession."

His confession causes my heartbeats to flutter even faster.

"I won't let anyone hurt you again." His baritone is smooth and rough, a concoction of everything forbidden. "Do you understand?"

*Why? Why do you care?* is what I desperately want to ask.

But instead I say, "Yes."

My breaths stutter as he sucks me further into his tempestuous gaze.

Stroking my jaw with the back of his hand, he lowers his face until only the breadth of a whisper remains between us.

Then his lips crash into mine, like a wild and vicious storm. His tongue roughly parts my mouth, invading me without a fight.

I'm weak for him, and he knows it.

My nails sink into his muscled back, his palm gripping my ass, while the other clutches my hair, deepening our connection.

I can't stop moaning as his wicked mouth peppers passionate kisses down my throat, biting the skin between my neck and shoulder.

"We can't…" My pulse beats like drums in my ears.

That kiss, it was everything I could've wanted. But it's not enough, and my body knows it.

"Why not?" He captures my lips again, kissing me slowly this time, like he wants to show me that he can be both men—the quiet and the loud, the gentleman and the beast.

"Because I could lose my job." I tug on his hair, groaning with unspeakable pleasure. "And I don't date."

"I wasn't looking to date you, Ms. Hill." His growling rumbles as he squeezes my ass, pressing me into his rock-hard erection.

My face instantly heats up from his words, and I push off of him. Of course a man like him doesn't date. He just fucks anything that walks.

"Great. Glad we're on the same page. Let's never do this again." I start toward my fridge, needing a bottle of water for my dry throat.

He prowls behind me, palms landing on my shoulders, fingers tracing up and down my arms. "Do you want to date me? Is that what has you so upset?"

I laugh and whip around to face him. "Wow. You're one smug jerk." Moving closer, I pop my chin and push my body against his. "I'm not looking to date you, nor am I looking for a quick fuck. From you or anyone."

That devilish mouth tips up and his eyes turn hooded as he tilts my chin up between two fingers. "You don't date and you don't fuck. So how do you get off, Ms. Hill?"

My shocked expression only makes his smirk grow.

"See, they actually invented toys for that, and they can get me off better than any man could."

He chuckles, gripping my chin tighter. "Any man you've fucked so far."

His eyes burn with meaning, and my stomach dips, my heart beating frantically.

"I'd love to watch you play with yourself. But see, no toy could ever replace the real thing." His thumb rolls across my mouth, and my body shivers, nipples pebbling and aching for his mouth. "The feeling of human skin, the sounds, the connection. A toy can't give you that."

Those words send a shockwave to my already-pulsing core.

"But you can?" Another laugh simmers out of me, though I try to sound like I'm not insanely turned on.

Knuckles drop to my jaw, stroking it, making me dizzy. His eyes burn into mine, and I want to rip off his shirt and experience everything he just described.

"It doesn't matter, does it? You're not interested, so you're right. This can't happen again." Mirth fills his gaze.

"Glad we're in agreement."

*Please get out of here so I can finally breathe…*

When I try to get him off of me, he curls his arm around the small of my back and tugs me nearer.

"Five thousand," he husks.

"What?"

"That's what I'm willing to offer you. Five thousand a day for helping Brody. It's my final offer. Then I'll be looking for someone else."

Okay. That's an insane amount of money. Money I desperately need.

"When do I have to let you know by?"

"In the next ten seconds."

My chest clenches. "What?"

"Time is ticking, Elara. You either say yes now or you don't."

"You…you have to promise you won't touch me like this again. I can't—"

"Can't what, baby?"

Jesus Christ. He's torturing me. He knows the effect he has on me, so he's doing this on purpose.

"Don't call me that, or little serpent, or whatever other nickname one would call their significant other. I'm not your girlfriend or your whore. So please, if I agree, you can't push this."

"When was the last time a man was inside you, Ms. Hill?" He arches his hips into me, and I feel it again: his thick, hard length pressing into my stomach.

"None of your business," I choke out, my arousal heating.

*Too damn long...*

He pushes his hot, muscled body into mine, driving me up against the wall.

Trapping me.

His lustful gaze entraps me further. "Your time is up. What will it be?"

"Okay, yes. I'll...I'll do it. I'll help Brody."

He groans, rolling his hips into me, his mouth against my throat. "Good girl."

And before I realize what's happening, his hand slides into the waistband of my pants, lowering between my thighs.

"No panties," he growls. "It's like you're asking me for it."

"Oh, fuck!" My head slams back, eyes closed as he fingers my clit, leaving a trail of waking heat prancing down my body.

"You're so wet already, little serpent. Is that all for me?"

I cry as he slips two fingers inside, thrusting them deeper and harder.

"You're an asshole," I moan, yanking his hair, gyrating my hips for more.

His laugh is dark and dirty. "Yet you're the one soaked for me. Maybe that's what you like." Another thrust. "Is that it?"

His gaze darkens as his fingers press deeper, curving and pushing into my G-spot.

I can't help the erotic sounds falling out of me in succession.

"You don't want to like me, but you like this, don't you?"

I hate that he's right.

Hate that I desperately want him.

"Have you touched this pussy thinking about me?" He pinches my clit, and my eyes roll back.

I can't admit to that. It would give him the upper hand. And if I am going to work for him, I can't let him know how attracted I am to him.

Though he probably knows by now. You know, considering how needy I sound.

With a frustrated growl, he stops his movements, grasping my jaw and forcing me to open my eyes. "Tell me the truth. I want to hear one fucking truth from your mouth." He gazes down at my lips, grinding his teeth. And I swear this man could eat me alive. "Have you thought about me, Elara?"

"Why does it even matter?" My tone is but a whisper, my chest falling with heavy gasps. "You don't date, I don't date, and I won't be your whore."

"But you'll let me finger-fuck you like one. Isn't that right?" A lazy half smile grows on his face, and as though sensing my incoming rage, he flicks my clit, and I release another moan. "Deep down, you wanna be my whore. There's nothing wrong with that, baby. You'd be my only one."

"Never." My lashes tremble, my core coiled with need, and he rams his fingers back inside me. "Oh, fuck… Please!"

"Tell me the truth and I'll let you come."

With a frustrated groan, I grab his shirt. "Fine! Yes, okay? Yes, I have. I've touched myself thinking about you."

"Shit," he hisses.

And when he slams his fingers back inside me, his mouth takes mine in a rough kiss.

His cock arches into my stomach while his thumb plays my clit, daring the orgasm out of me.

This kiss, it's carnal. Like he's claiming me and wants me to know it.

My body turns tight, hands trembling. And when he flicks my clit this time, I fall, screaming his name.

"Yes, Tynan, oh God!"

"You sound so good screaming my name like that."

He pummels deeper, faster, taking everything from me, leaving me breathless and hungry for more.

For him inside me.

For his bare skin against mine.

His fingers slide out of me before he sinks them into his mouth, sucking them clean. "I could get real used to the taste of you on my tongue."

My cheeks grow hot, and with a bend of his mouth, he leans down and kisses me again.

Slower, like he's savoring it. Savoring the taste of me.

His groans vibrate across my lips, his hands in my hair, pulling and fisting. My God, can this man kiss.

"Fucking hell," he mutters, drawing back, feathering his lips on mine like he's not ready to let me go. "You'll start on Monday. How's six?"

"Um…fine. Yeah." I swallow past my dry throat, ready to agree to just about anything for him to kiss me like that again.

"Good. I'm looking forward to it." He releases me and straightens out the collar of his shirt, leaving me unsatiated and barren. "Oh, and Rogue will be parked outside your home in less than an hour."

I can't seem to get a word out, unsure what to say or what to do, robbed speechless.

"I'll be seeing you soon, Ms. Hill."

When he starts for the door, I rush up a step.

"Tynan?"

"Hmm?" He looks back at me, eyeing the wound, and his anger appears again.

"Thank you."

"For what?"

"For caring." I shrug with a broken kind of smile. "I almost forgot what it felt like."

Something passes in his eyes, but it disappears just as quickly as it came.

Then he's out the door, and I wonder if I just made the biggest mistake of my life.

# THIRTEEN

## TYNAN

I can still smell her on my fingertips when I walk into my home.
Still hear the way she moaned for me, begging me to come.
I didn't think that would even happen. I didn't intend to do it,
yet I couldn't help myself. She ran her poison straight to my heart,
and all I could think of was kissing her and making her feel good.

I should've fucked her bent over against the wall. Yet I resisted.
I don't know why. Never had a problem taking what I wanted, and
she's exactly what I want. But she and I, it's destined to happen. It's
only a matter of time.

"Come on, Bubbles, drop the shoe!" Ruby calls.

When I stalk into the living room, I find her and Brody chasing
after the dog.

*Fuck*.

Bubbles has one of my loafers in her mouth. Italian fucking leather
destroyed.

"Oh, come on…" I groan.

They both look up at me, finally realizing I'm home.

"I'm so sorry!" Ruby's shoulders deflate. "She's relentless. And she seems to like your shoes more than anyone else's. This is the third one she's destroyed."

"Great." I clench my jaw, and when Brody catches my irritated look, his face falls.

Shit, I should relax. They're just shoes. The kid's happy; that's all that matters.

"It's okay, Ruby. I've got it from here."

"Are you sure?" She's visibly breathless, and I feel sorry for that.

"Yes, go relax. I've got the little monster."

"Okay." She shakes her head. "Puppies are tough."

"I can see that."

"Oh, and she peed in your office."

"Ugh, fuck…"

"Language," she tsks. She's the only one I'd let reprimand me. "I cleaned it already, but wanted to let you know. You may want to hire a trainer."

I shut my eyes, seriously regretting the decision to get Bubbles with each passing second.

She walks out of the room, leaving me with a pouting Brody and the dog running with a shoe in her mouth.

"It's okay, buddy. I'm not mad."

His mouth thins.

"Come on, Bubbles. Drop it."

She stands in front of me, growling, tail wagging, shoe still in her mouth as though taunting me.

Kinda reminds me of Elara. I laugh to myself at the thought of that feisty woman whenever she stands up to me. I like that very much.

I pounce toward the pup, but at the last second, she jumps out of my way and starts for the den.

Brody runs after her, grinning wide, and that has me smiling too.

She can destroy all the leather she wants if she can get him to smile like that.

"Maybe we should grab one of her treats to tempt her. Why don't you get the new bones we got her? They should be in the kitchen under the sink."

He nods and rushes out. Less than a minute later, he has one in his hand.

"Look what Brody has, Bubbles."

As soon as I say his name, she turns and sees it in his hand, and that's all it takes. She sprints toward him, dropping the shoe.

One look at it, and I groan, picking up the slobbery, torn-up loafer. Gonna have to hide all of my shoes from now on.

Brody brings Bubbles to her bed in the corner of the room, and she chews on her bone while I toss the shoe in the trash in the kitchen.

"Hello? Anyone home?" My father's voice carries from the foyer, and I go to see what he wants, hoping he hasn't come to pester me again.

"Hey, Dad." I incline my chin in greeting as soon as I see him. "What are you doing here?"

"You're always so pleasant." He chuckles. "I'm just here to say hello. Have a minute?"

I inhale sharply, knowing to expect the worst. "Let's go into my office."

"Alright." We pass Brody on the way, sitting beside the dog, and this is the first time my father has met her. "Hey!" He walks toward Bubbles, kneeling to pet her. "I've heard a lot about you. She's so cute," he tells Brody, who nods, refusing to smile.

Hopefully, once Elara is here, she can get this kid to smile for everyone.

The moment she comes to my mind, my cock twitches, still wanting inside her.

Scrubbing my face with a rough palm, I chase the scent of her away, needing to stop this madness.

"I'll see you in a bit, buddy," Dad tells Brody before we're marching down the hall and entering my office.

I shut the door while he settles on the sofa.

"So, I needed to talk to you about a possible marriage arrangement."

"Are you fucking kidding?" I run an irritated hand down my hair. "I told you last time I would never agree to that."

"Yes, but you should take a look at her. She's the daughter of one of our associates. Beautiful. Smart. Docile. Just the way you like them."

"You don't know what I like."

Docile is the last thing I want. I want her tempered and fierce. I want to see the flames in her eyes.

It's then I see Elara. And I hate it.

I can't marry her. That would never work. I crave her too much. Would be impossible to keep our marriage as merely a business arrangement. I need to marry someone I feel nothing for.

This thing with her and me is just attraction. Heavy, burdening attraction that weighs on my chest until I can't breathe. It's why she can't be the one I marry.

Yet who else is there?

My father ignores me and removes his phone, pressing a few buttons before he's shoving it into my hand.

I stare at a brunette with brown eyes. She's pretty. But she does nothing for me.

I hand him the cell back. "I don't want her."

He groans. "Look, son, you're making this more difficult than it needs to be. Find a wife, make sure she's what you want on paper, and get her pregnant. That's all."

"That's all?" I chuckle, then my face turns hard. "You're making me do something I never wanted to do."

"But you want to take over for me. Unless you want me to pass my seat to Iseult. Though do you really want your lineage to die with you? Don't you want children to pass along your wealth and your name to?"

"Maybe."

That thought isn't as bad as the thought of marriage, but I have Brody. However, for my father, that's not enough. He wants lots of grandkids.

"That seat is mine." I glare, and his mouth jerks.

"That's my boy. Now, if you don't agree to a wife on your own, you will marry Cassidy." He lifts his phone in the air.

*Fuck that.*

"Do you have anyone else in mind at all? Or are you buying time, thinking I'll bloody forget?"

"Maybe…"

Elara seems to be my only option. But she'll never agree. Not willingly, anyway.

Though I don't have to give her a choice. She needs money. I know the issues she's having with paying for her grandfather's care. I can pay for it and more. She'll never want for anything with me.

I'll have to think about it. Have to see what happens when she starts working with Brody.

"I've gotta go," I tell my father. "You can see yourself out."

"Love you too, son," he calls out with amusement while I storm upstairs to take a damn shower.

The water roars to life as soon as I have it running. I step out of my clothes and enter under the steam.

Liquid pours down over my head, my cock hard and throbbing as I grab it in my palm and stroke it. Images of her storm into my mind.

The feeling of her pussy, how wet and warm it was when I finger-fucked it. I can feel it now, stretching over my fingers. Want to watch her cunt stretch to fit me. Gonna make her take every single one of my piercings and beg for more.

Should've dropped to my knees and tasted her.

"Oh, fuck."

My head falls back against the tiled wall, and my balls ache as I imagine doing just that, throwing her leg on my shoulder and running my tongue over her wet cunt.

She bucks and groans, my name on her tongue as she yanks my hair and comes all over my mouth. And as she does, so do I, roaring as my cum shoots out, washed away by the water. Yet I'm still not satisfied, because I want the real thing.

I want *her*.

This is precisely why I can't marry her... Yet the thought of her taking someone else's last name makes my blood boil.

Elara Quinn. That sure has a nice ring to it.

When I'm done washing off, I get dressed and pick up the phone I left on my bed. Opening it, I find one of the photos I took. I need to know who this DK is. Grabbing my laptop from my dresser drawer, I enter our security system, hoping to find something on this person and how he knows Elara.

But I'm empty-handed. The number is encrypted at the highest level. Whoever she's connected to knows how to hide his tracks. I stare at the number, knowing I shouldn't call it.

To hell with that. I can't sit here and do nothing. I need to know who is on the other line.

I dial it before I change my mind, and it rings twice.

"Hello?" a man answers. "Hello? Evelyn? What are you doing calling me from this number?"

*Who the hell is Evelyn?*

The phone clicks, and I realize he hung up.

Shit.

Maybe I should just call back and scare the fuck out of him so he tells me who he is and how Evelyn is connected to Elara.

But when I do, I realize that the number is now disconnected.

"Damn it!" I squeeze the phone in my grasp.

What have I done?

Now I really have nothing to go on.

# FOURTEEN

## ELARA

Derek, the one who created my new identity, never calls my burner unless it's an emergency, so when I find that cell vibrating in my bag, my pulse spikes. Especially because I don't recognize the number. But he's the only one who has it.

Why would he have a new number?

Maybe it's not him…

Did he give me up to Jerry? Oh, no! They could've tortured him to talk. If they realize he's a rat, they'll feed him to the dogs. Literally.

I sling my work bag over my shoulder and head toward my car as I answer it, not saying a word just in case it isn't him.

"Evelyn?" he whispers.

"Derek? Are you okay?"

"Oh, thank fuck!" he exhales harshly. "I thought something happened to you."

"Why would something happen to me? Did you say something to

them?" Alarm rings in my voice.

"Of course not! I'd die before I gave you up. You know that."

I sag against the door of my car. "I don't expect you to die for me. But thank you."

"Look, I called because I had to get a new number. Two days ago, someone called the one I gave you. You're the only one who has it. I don't know what that means, Elara, but it's not good."

"Wait, what? Someone called you?"

"Yeah, and they didn't say anything, but…"

My stomach clenches. "But what?"

"I said your name. I called you Evelyn."

"Oh, no… Do you think it's Jerry or his father?"

"I don't think so. They would've killed me by now. I waited to call you just in case, but they haven't bugged my phones or my place. I don't think it was them. Has anyone had access to my number? Where do you keep it?"

"I—"

Then it hits me.

Tynan.

No…

Yet it makes sense. He was in my house. He broke in. He must've found it and called. Now he knows my name.

"I think I know who it was."

"Anyone I need to worry about?"

"No. I'll take care of it. I'll come up with something. Don't worry."

"Okay, but, Evelyn, watch your back. You can't trust anyone."

"I know that. You too."

"Bye." He drops the call and I stuff the phone in the zip pouch of my bag.

I start working for Tynan tonight. I'll have to confront him, and I'd better figure out what I'm gonna say about Derek.

Maybe I can give him a taste of the truth without giving much away. That has to work or I'm gonna end up dead, and I'm not sure if it'll be Jerry or Tynan who kills me.

After work, I make it home for a quick shower and a change of clothes before heading to Tynan's.

My stomach is in knots just thinking about what I'm going to say to him. He needs to believe it so he can let go of whatever suspicions he has.

Slipping into a pair of skin-tight jeans and a simple black tank top, I figure out what to do with my hair. Should I wear it down? In a ponytail? I have no idea.

Ugh! Why am I worrying about how I look anyway? I'm trying not to make him want me.

*Ha! Who are you lying to? You want him to eat his heart out just so you can tell him to get lost.*

I groan. Why am I like this?

Fuck it, hair down it is. Curling the ends a little, I run my fingers through them, then add some mascara and blush.

I look at my arm, the wound appearing much better. Retrieving a large Band-Aid from the bathroom, I stick it on the best way I can.

When I stroll out, I find Rogue, my new bodyguard, standing against the passenger side of his car.

"Ma'am." He nods in greeting.

"Hey. Do you want something to eat or drink? I feel bad having you out here every day."

"Not necessary, but thank you."

"Okay, well, if you change your mind…"

When I start toward my car, he interrupts me.

"Mr. Quinn instructed that I drive you to his estate."

"I can drive myself." I open the door just as he places a hand on it to stop me.

"He insisted. Should we call him?"

I drag in a long, annoyed inhale. "Fine. Let's go."

He heads back toward his SUV and opens it for me, helping me up before getting into his side.

Thirty minutes later, and we're pulling up into a massive gated estate, acres of land beyond, more than I can even see. There are some homes in the distance and a few towering mansions that come into view as we drive past.

These people are loaded. Rich is an understatement. I wonder how it feels to live like this, never worrying about money.

We pass another mansion—pale brick walls with black shutters, a terrace on the first floor—and this time, Rogue slides into the driveway. I can just imagine what the inside looks like.

Rogue exits first, and before I can open my door, he's doing it for me, helping me out and following me to the front.

Two guards stand on each side of the heavy double doors, and fear prickles across the back of my neck. They stare intensely, greeting me with curt nods before they're letting me through.

When I step into the foyer, a large crystal chandelier sparkles from the high cathedral ceiling. The pale gray and white marble flooring glistens below my feet. The place is immaculate.

From somewhere in the house, I register a dog barking and immediately smile.

Must be Bubbles.

"They're this way." Rogue leads me to the right, past a kitchen where a woman with her gray hair in a tight bun looks up from the tomatoes she's cutting.

As soon as she sees me, she grins, wiping her hands on her pink floral apron. "Hi! I'm Ruby. You must be Elara! Tynan's told me so much about you."

"He has?"

That doesn't sound like him. Then again, I don't know much about him, do I?

She wraps her arms around me, then pulls back. "Oh, yes. He says you're an amazing teacher and Brody adores you." Her expression grows sad at the child's name. "We'd do anything to have him talk again." Those brown eyes of hers glisten with pain, but she clears her throat and returns to her cooking. "Will you stay for dinner?"

"I—"

"Yes, she will."

My pulse wakes with a rapid beat when I hear his raspy voice behind me.

Turning toward him, I find those smoldering eyes zeroing in on me, his mouth set in a tight line.

"I really don't want to impose."

I can't help but wonder what he's thinking. Does he want me to stay so he can interrogate me? Torture information out of me? It's what people in the Mafia do, isn't it?

"It wouldn't be an imposition." He saunters closer, and my heart picks up speed. "I don't see a reason you couldn't join us for dinner."

His mouth drops nearer, until it's angled against my ear.

A pant rises out of me as he says, "If you want me to pay you for staying, just say the word, Ms. Hill. As you can see, money isn't an issue for me."

"Um…"

His lips skim right below my lobe, and I stifle a gasp from the sensation it brings in me, completely forgetting that Ruby is very much still here.

"I can still smell you on my fingers."

*Oh my God.*

My face flushes. An inhale traps in my lungs.

Desire winds tighter and tighter through me.

He chuckles all deep and low, straightening himself as he lifts the sleeves of his dress shirt, and those forearms do sinful things to me. They always do.

Ruby stares between us, fighting a smile, and that only makes my face grow hot with embarrassment.

I knew this was a bad idea. I can't even stand beside him without getting turned on.

Scratching my throat, I throw on a nervous smile. "Not necessary, Mr. Quinn. I'll accept your offer for dinner. Thank you, Ruby."

"Of course, dear."

Something passes between Tynan and Ruby, and his jaw clenches. *What was that about?*

"Come on," he says. "I'm sure Brody is very excited to see you."

At the thought of him, I forget how nervous I am and follow Tynan to the den. And as soon as Brody turns to me, he runs straight into my arms.

"Hey, sweetheart." I hold him close, shutting my eyes, my heart instantly breaking every time I think about his life. "So…" I perch back and clasp his face between my hands, staring down at him. "Are you done with homework?"

He nods.

"Good boy. Maybe we can go for a walk with Bubbles."

Seems like there's plenty of land to cover here. I glance at Tynan, who nods his approval.

"Great. Hi, Bubbles!"

And at her name, the dog rushes over and licks my hands, jumping up like she wants to lick my face too.

"Okay, okay." I laugh, picking her up, letting her do her worst.

She lets out a happy little sound, excited as ever.

"I like you too." I pet her, glancing at a brooding Tynan.

"Better watch out for her. She's trouble," he tosses out with a lopsided smirk that lands right in my gut.

"Are you talking about me or the dog?" I place Bubbles back down.

"Wouldn't you like to know?" That smirk deepens, and so does my attraction for him.

But it's all wrong. Everything about this is.

My teeth sink around the corner of my bottom lip, and at that, his eyes turn hooded, the muscle in his jaw twitching.

Dirty thoughts fill my mind.

Us together.

In his bed.

On the floor.

In the kitchen.

Those arms, those veins thick and throbbing as he tosses me around and plays with me like his personal fuck toy even while I refuse him. But resistance only emboldens a man like that, and I like it.

"You okay, Ms. Hill?" He steps closer until he's before me, his smirk widening. "You're blushing."

He runs his knuckles down my cheek, and the dog growls like it's warning him to stay away.

That'd be nice, because this is too much. The way he smells—all manly and expensive—and the way he forces himself into my space.

My pulse gallops in my throat. "I am *not* blushing."

His gruff laughter drapes around me, warm and enticing, calling to me like a familiar song.

Yet it's just an illusion. This man is nothing but a distraction, a drug I need to keep away from, no matter how much the devil calls to me.

I brush past him toward Brody, who's slipping on his sneakers. Yet I still feel Tynan's eyes on me from behind, my flesh prickling with awareness.

Glancing over my shoulder, I find him with his arms curled over his chest.

The memory of his fingers inside me floods my mind, and I desperately crave a repeat performance.

*Nope. We are not going there.*

Need to get out of here before I act on my feelings.

Brody runs out, probably to get the dog's leash, while I'm left alone with the man who has started to haunt my dreams.

It was him I dreamed about last night. It felt so real, it was like I felt him inside me, heard him say dirty things as he fucked me, heard him say that he loved me.

Insane what the mind can do when we're sleeping. But just look at him. All hard edges and calloused hands. How could I not want him? And Lord, would those hands feel good running up my body.

His mouth tilts like he can see inside my mind.

Am I that obvious? Am I blushing again?

"Come on, Brody!" I tell him, while Bubbles lets out a little yelp like she wants to get out of here just as much as I do.

Brody comes running in, attaching the leash on the pup and gripping it tightly, while I hold out a hand for his. He takes it without any hesitation, and that fills my heart with joy.

Tynan's brows knit as he stares down at our clasped hands, and his face softens. And though he's a hard man, I've seen glimpses of the softer side already, making me feel things I don't want to.

Brody leads me toward the back, opening the double glass doors and heading toward the lush garden.

Three benches sit on one side, overlooking a round pool with a swan statute in the middle, shooting out water. To the left is a huge rectangular pool, and a hot tub close behind. There is also a gazebo with chairs and beds that look comfortable enough to sleep in. We head past the pool and through the open land—green grass for what feels like miles.

*What a beautiful place to run every morning.*

I don't know why that thought just hit me. Not like I'll be waking up here every day to do that. Still, the place is scenic, and I can just imagine what the rest of the land looks like.

"It must be nice living here." I glance over at Brody. "Though I'm sure you miss your home too."

His face slants, and he stares down at his feet while the dog sniffs and wags her tail.

"I'm sorry, Brody." I squeeze his hand. "I can just imagine how hard this is for you. But if you ever want to talk to me—and it doesn't have to be with words, it can be a letter, anything really—I'm here to listen. I want you to know that I care very much about you, just like your cousin does."

He nods and doesn't look my way. I don't want to bring up anything painful, but I think it's good for him to embrace the pain and learn to heal from it instead of being afraid to face it. He just needs to feel safe enough to open up. To scream and cry and do all the things that he has to for as long as he needs.

"You know, I lost my parents too. I wasn't as young as you, but I really loved them. I was very close to my mom. She was my best friend."

He glances up, and his chin trembles, eyes filling with tears, and mine do too. I can feel his anguish like it's palpable.

"She was a good mom, just like yours was. Your mom loved you very much. I know that for certain. Your father too. I know wherever they are, they're watching you and they are so, so proud of you."

Tears drip from his eyes. Kneeling before him, I grab his face, letting my own tears fall freely.

"It's okay to cry, sweetheart." I wipe his tears with my thumb. "It's okay to miss them and wish they were here with you."

With a sniffle, he throws his arms around me and holds me tight as he sobs. And I clutch him, wanting to take his pain away and make it mine.

From a distance, I see *him*—watching us, like a shadow.

He stares intensely, and fear prickles up my spine. There's a part of me that's still afraid of him, even while my attraction for him grows.

He starts toward us just as Brody wipes his eyes with the back of his hand.

"You feel better?" I give him all of my attention.

He nods.

"Good. How about we get some ice cream after dinner? I'm sure there's some in the freezer."

His eyes pop with excitement.

"We can eat until we're too full to breathe. How does that sound?"

He hits me with a huge, toothy grin and a thumbs-up.

We start making our way toward Tynan, and when he's in front of us, he pats Brody's head.

"How about you go run with Bubbles a bit while Ms. Hill and I have a talk?"

*Here we go.*

Nervousness falls over me, and I shiver, knowing he's going to want to talk about Derek.

I'm ready for it. I have to be. I need him to stop chasing my demons before they take me with them.

Brody gives us both a curious glance before he marches away with the pup.

"Look, I—"

But he doesn't let me finish, cutting the distance between us until his front presses to mine. "Who's Evelyn?" He tilts my chin up with the back of his hand. "And don't you think about lying to me. You're around my kid. I need to know what you're involved in."

His eyes narrow, his expression harsh.

My lashes flutter to a brief close while my chest grows heavy. "Okay, I'll tell you. But promise me to let it go after that. I can't have you messing up my life more than it already is."

Though I hate thinking about my past, I gather the courage to tell him just enough so he'll stop asking questions.

"Start talking."

I blow out a breath and look up at the sky before my attention falls to him. "Look, you were right. There is an ex. I left him, and—"

"Why?" His demeanor instantly shifts to something darker. "What did he do?"

My brows pinch, and I fight the tears when they come, the scar on my abdomen burning at the thought of Jerry.

I shake it off. "He hurt me, okay? Until I couldn't take it anymore."

His Adam's apple bobs, and though his face hardens, his eyes grow tender. And it's then his thumb skirts up my cheek and wipes the remnants of my pain.

"Elara..." His tortured breath kills me a little.

"I don't want him to know where I am, so I changed my name. My real name is Evelyn Connors."

His jaw clenches.

I hope I didn't just make a mistake by telling him that, but I had to do something. He won't find much on me anyway.

"The number you called, he's a friend who still lives back home and keeps me in the loop if my ex goes sniffing. He's the one who set me up with a new identity. Same for my grandparents."

"Is your ex connected?"

"Please, Tynan." I grip his hard bicep and it jerks. "I'm begging you to please let this go. Let me live in peace. I want to stay here. I want to be happy. Let me be happy."

My vision blurs, and he inhales a long, deep breath.

"Was he your fiancé?"

I nod, shame filling my face.

"How long were you together?"

"Not long."

"How'd you meet?"

Why does he look so upset about it?

I release an exaggerated sigh. "It wasn't like that. My father arranged it for business purposes. I never loved him. In fact, I hated him."

"And he hit you?"

I nod. "He did a lot of things. So if there's any part of you that meant it when you said we're friends, let this go."

"You don't know me very well, Ms. Hill." His knuckles gently stroke my cheek, his eyes filling with the raw power of his emotions. "I do not let things like this go. If someone hurts a person I care about, I take care of it."

*Care about…*

*He cares about me?*

My stomach coils into knots, and my heart throbs to have that—to have a man care for me and mean it.

Those knuckles stroke my lips, and they tremble in the wake of his touch.

"If you don't want to give me his name, I will find it on my own, and I will kill him. And that's a promise."

Part of me wants that. I want to see that bastard and his father dead. But another part just wishes for it all to be over. Though can it ever be if they're still alive and looking for me?

"You don't know how to let things be, do you?"

"Not when it matters."

"And I matter?" I whisper, shuddering with anticipation, hoping to hear that I do. That I mean something.

His expression goes slack, a hint of a smirk appearing at the corner of his mouth. "I'll see you inside, Ms. Hill."

He lets me go, while all I want is for him to touch me again, craving for that warmth to return.

Yet most of all, I crave to hear him say that I matter.

But instead, he walks away.

I remain there long after, wondering how I went from wanting to keep my distance to wanting Tynan Quinn to admit he actually cares.

# FIFTEEN

## TYNAN

It took a lot for her to be honest yesterday. The way her pain seeped from her eyes, it haunts me. I hated knowing she was hurt by someone who thought he could treat her that way.

Staring at the computer in the underground tech office of our academy, I look up Evelyn Connors and find a photo of her staring back at me.

Her social media profile is inactive and from a few years ago, but it's her. There's nothing on the fiancé, though it's only a matter of time before I find him and who he works for. They're not in our circle, but there are many factions of gangs out there. He could be in any one of them.

I'll have to do more digging after Brody goes to bed. Elara should be here any minute. Shutting off the screen, I head up and out the door.

My home is a ten-minute walk from the academy, and I make it back in less, smelling the dinner Ruby has already started to prep.

As I start for the door, Rogue pulls up.

She's here.

Our eyes meet, and her mouth trembles into a small smile.

Before Rogue has a chance to touch her, I'm there, opening her door.

"Let me." I take her hand in mine.

Her long, dark lashes fan as she steps out, and when she tries to snap her hand from mine, I tighten my grasp.

"It's nice to see you, *Elara*."

She clears her throat, glancing to the back of Rogue's head, who walks before us.

"Don't say my name like that!" Her voice is low and raspy.

"But you're so fun to toy with." My words rough across her ear.

She scratches there, and I chuckle. I don't know why I like setting her off as much as I do. Don't remember having this much fun with a woman before.

She pushes past me and heads toward the kitchen, greeting Ruby while I stand behind her, unable to stop my gaze from wandering down her sinful curves.

No matter what I told myself before, she has to be the one I marry. She's the perfect choice. She not only needs money, but protection too. I can offer her both in exchange for staying with me. Divorce wouldn't be an option.

The thought of getting her pregnant makes my cock throb. She'd object, but I'd make her fall in line. Just need to approach this delicately. Make her think this is a good idea for the both of us.

And if she doesn't agree…well, there are other ways.

She heads off with Brody, who brings over a board game for them to play in the dining room. I stare at them from the doorjamb. He looks genuinely happy with her being here, and it's only day two.

The puppy sleeps at their feet while they play Monopoly. When she looks up at me and gives me one of her real smiles, something in me snaps, coming undone until I'm lost to the feeling of her eyes on mine.

My hand curls, and I force myself to walk away. This isn't meant to be anything besides a mutually beneficial relationship.

I'll give her the chance to agree willingly. But if she doesn't... well, let's just say this woman's already my wife. She just doesn't know it yet.

But just because we're married doesn't mean we have to love each other. Plenty of loveless arranged marriages in my circle.

We'd just be one of many.

With great sex.

I know it will be.

Besides that, besides making a baby, I don't have to see her much or spend time with her. Not unless it's for Brody's sake.

We'll fuck enough to make children, then we'll live separate lives. Hope that works for her. Because it will for me. I told myself long ago I wouldn't get attached to a woman.

I won't let myself feel something real because that shit only leads to pain.

Images of my mother storm into my mind. Her body ignited by flames while she screamed tied to a chair as Sergey laughed until her voice died.

Until *she* died.

I suck in a rough breath.

No. I won't love her. I can't.

Love is something I can't afford.

Scrubbing my face, I settle onto the stool in the kitchen while Ruby cuts up some romaine lettuce for the salad she's prepping.

"She seems nice." She glances at me with a knowing smile. "Don't you agree?"

"Don't do that, Ruby."

"Do what, sir?" She gives me her back, grabbing some peppers, probably busting out a grin she doesn't want me to see.

"Don't call me 'sir.' And you know exactly what. I'm not interested in her."

She pops a brow once she peers at me again. "Did you tell your face that?" Her shoulders jump with a quick laugh. "You're starting to like her, and it's killing you, isn't it?"

I groan and pinch my temple. "I'm going now."

Rising to my feet, I start for the den, needing to avoid Elara.

"It's hard to hear the truth," Ruby calls after me. "But she's lovely."

Too lovely.

And beautiful.

And sweet.

Insufferably so.

I pass by the living room, needing to see her again.

It's like I'm infected. Can't just walk away in the opposite direction if I know she's right there.

Close enough to touch.

To taste.

To feel.

Fuck, she makes me feel everything, and that terrifies me.

When she finds me staring, her mouth curls on one side.

"Wanna play with us? Brody's in the bathroom and is about to come back."

I take in a long drag of an inhale.

*This is not a good idea.*

"Why would I do that?" Though my feet are already moving toward her.

Her face bends with a smile. "Uh, so I can beat you?"

I chuckle dryly. "Fine. But you won't beat me."

"We'll see." She tips her chin. "You should know, though. I'm very competitive."

I pull the chair beside hers, my palm landing on the inside of her thigh.

Her eyes widen.

She's so small. So fierce. So beautiful.

"I am too, Ms. Hill. I won't let you win."

"I'd be offended if you did."

She's enjoying this, the gleam in her eyes brightening, and something in me likes it. Her playfulness. Want to see more of it. More of her smiling and happy.

Thoughts of her ex fill my mind, and I can't stop picturing what he could've done to her. I want to ask for every detail, because I need to know. I want to rip him apart for every single transgression. But I won't make her relive that.

He touched her.

He hurt her.

And that's enough.

Brody rushes back excitedly, and when he sees me, he stops in place, his gloom returning, his vision jumping between the two of us.

I fucking hate this. What did I do to make him hate me? I try to think back to before his parents died. We always got along. Things changed after they died. Like he hates me for it. I don't know what the hell to do to fix this. To bring back the relationship we once had.

She must notice, because she grabs my hand and holds it tight, looking my way for a moment. But I hide the way the rejection affects me. I have to. I have to focus on helping him.

"Tynan is gonna play with us. Isn't that awesome?"

Brody shrugs.

"Maybe I should go?" I whisper into her ear.

"No." Her voice is just as low. "He needs this. You have to understand that you probably remind him of his parents, his dad, and it hurts. That's all this is. Pain." Her eyes lock with mine.

*I wanna kiss you...*

"I didn't think of it that way."

"I know. That's why you have me." She winks. "Now, let's play!"

She rubs her palms, and Brody finally sits down on her opposite side.

We play for over thirty minutes, having too much fun. I don't think I've played a board game since I was really young, when Iseult would beat me every time and gloat about it. Not much has changed with her. She still gloats, and she can still kick my ass.

"Dinner, guys!" Ruby calls.

Brody helps us clean up and puts away the game, leaving us standing alone for a minute.

"That was nice. Thanks for asking me." My hand reaches for hers and our fingertips brush, jolting all the molecules in my limbs.

"You're very welcome. Maybe we can do that again sometime. It's good for Brody."

"I'd love that." I run my fingers up her arm and enjoy the way every tiny hair rises.

She grows visibly uncomfortable from our proximity and pushes her chair all the way into the table before she walks past me with a quick glance.

I keep the laugh to myself, though I savor the reaction I bring out in her when I touch her. It's like an aphrodisiac.

I follow her into the kitchen, the smell of chicken and garlic wafting in the air.

We all settle around the table and start to eat. Ruby asks about the game and who won, and of course, we both let Brody win. But I know she would've beat me if it came to it. I grin internally at the thought.

"That was delicious. Thank you, Ruby." Elara smiles at her, taking her plate and Brody's to the sink, where she proceeds to wash them.

With mine in hand, I walk up behind her, pushing her into the counter.

She gasps, and I let out a low groan, almost forgetting about Ruby or Brody or anyone except this woman. This damn woman who's turned my mind upside down. I drop my plate into the sink and take her soapy hands in mine, washing Brody's plate with her, running my wet fingertips in and around her fingers.

"Tynan," she whispers, all low and throaty, and my cock instantly hardens.

I know she can feel it.

I want more. I want her bare and begging and—

A sudden noise catches our attention, ripping us from the trance.

She pushes off me as we both turn to find Brody staring hard with a glass cup in hand.

"Hey, buddy!" Elara marches toward him, ignoring me while kneeling before him.

When she whispers something in his ear, he eagerly nods, grinning at her with excitement.

I happen behind her and Brody gives me a tight look.

"What are you two up to?" My eyes connect with hers, and it's like the world shifts all over again. Every single time she looks at me.

I can't stop myself from touching her, the molecules in my veins pulling to hers. My hand caresses up and down her shoulder, feeling her quiver.

"We're gonna go watch a movie and eat ice cream. Wanna come?" She plays with her hair.

I'm making her nervous.

"Yes." No hesitation.

"Great." She clears her throat and grabs a carton of ice cream from the freezer while Brody retrieves three spoons.

*Maybe he doesn't hate me* that *much.*

Who am I kidding?

He leaves us for the den while Elara fidgets, holding tight to the ice cream.

"So, we're eating right out of this thing?" I ask.

"Have a problem with that?" There's a twinkle in those beautiful eyes.

"None. Just checking what the rules are."

She laughs, like a real laugh. And I vow to make her do that again.

"I promised him, and I keep my promises."

"That's a good trait to have." I feather my thumb over her bottom lip as soon as Ruby disappears. "You're driving me crazy," I growl, pushing her body up against the wall, my hand tangled in her hair.

"We talked about this, Tynan," she moans, grabbing my wrist, yet not even attempting to push me off.

My skin instantly warms at her touch.

"I can't help myself." My mouth descends to her throat, tempting her with hurried kisses.

In the background, the noise of the television comes to life, and she releases a heavy groan.

"Please…" She tugs my hair, pushing my mouth even deeper. "Please stop."

I chuckle against her beating pulse, kissing there, inhaling her floral scent. One I wanna get lost in.

"Only 'cause you asked nicely." I smirk against her throat, leaving one last kiss on the spot where her shoulder and neck meet.

Reluctantly, I let her go before she ends up getting fucked against the wall. Running a frustrated hand down my face, I promise myself to behave the rest of the day.

"Ready?" I ask her.

She nods, clearing her throat and rushing out of the room.

A crooked smile falls to my face as I follow her into the den, where Brody waits on the sofa. She settles beside him, while I take the other side of her. I have no idea what movie is playing, nor do I care.

She dips the spoon into the chocolate ice cream and sucks on it, staring at the screen, while I stare at her. And all I can think about is kissing her.

My eyes fall to the top of her breasts, full and enticing through the pink blouse she wears, the first two buttons popped open. Takes me back to when I was in her classroom, wanting to rip her shirt open and have her right on her desk.

I curl my hand at my side to quiet the need for this woman.

"You're not eating any?" she whispers, shoving the carton toward me.

I could use something cold. I take a spoonful into my mouth, and she watches me from her periphery.

Filling up the spoon, I drag it to her lips this time. "Open your mouth."

Her eyes glisten as she locks them on mine, parting those gorgeous lips. Sucking on the spoon, she makes me groan.

My mouth lowers to her ear. "You probably shouldn't look that good doing something so innocent if you want me to behave."

She stares at me all open-mouthed, face flushed, and fuck, does she turn me on.

Brody scoots closer to her, eagerly watching the screen, and I force myself to be on my best behavior.

Again.

"He's having fun," she murmurs, clearly needing the change of topic as badly as I do.

"You're good for him, just like I thought you would be."

"So are you." She places her palm on top of my thigh, and my muscles ripple.

Her hand jolts back, like she just realized what she did.

I grab her wrist and return her palm to where it was.

"Leave it," I whisper into the shell of her ear. "I like it there."

She visibly swallows while the spoon in her hand jitters. Taking it from her, I start to feed her, realizing I very much enjoy it.

She doesn't take her eyes off of me as I part her lips with the cold metal and watch her mouth move. Even the way she eats is attractive.

I know marrying her will be a mistake. But right now, it's a mistake

I'm willing to make.
Because I want her.
And that's the end of it.

# SIXTEEN

## ELARA
### ONE WEEK LATER

The days bleed into one another, and with all the time we've been spending together, my heart only softens for the man I vowed not to get close to.

He pays me for the days in cash. I can't believe I have this much money. I can actually save some in case I have to run again.

The nursing home stopped bothering me for payments too, which is a huge relief.

"Right hand on red," Ruby announces as Brody and I figure out which one of us will win this round of Twister.

He places his hand on the spot, grinning as he almost falls.

Ruby spins the wheel again. "Left foot on yellow."

"Oh, boy." I grimace, trying to figure out how to do that when my hand is too far away from my foot.

As I somehow maneuver my foot, my head down, I try not to fall.

From between the split of my thighs, I find Tynan moving up behind me, his body coming closer. Black loafers and gray dress pants. My knees grow weak from how insanely hot he looks. He's always in a suit of some kind, probably costing more than a down payment on a home.

He comes to stand right behind my ass. "Need help, Ms. Hill?" His voice is like a soft, caressing touch. "Seems like you've got yourself all twisted up."

"Nope." I fight not to fall. "Just need you to stay far away from me before you make me lose."

Ruby laughs.

While I shiver as his fingers run up the small of my back and I feel it everywhere.

"Once you're done here, meet me in my office. I have something important to discuss."

My stomach dips. "Okay."

What in the world could he have to talk to me about? He hasn't brought up Jerry or anything he's learned about me. But maybe he finally found him somehow. Maybe he already killed him and wants to give me the good news.

We play for a few more minutes before I fall on my behind.

Brody grins.

"You win again, kid. I'm no match for you." I shake my head. "I'll be right back, okay?"

I kiss the top of his head, and his small arms curl around my hips, holding me tight as I return the embrace. I love this little boy so much.

He lets me go and treads to Bubbles, who's currently ripping up a sock she found. I'm pretty sure it's Tynan's.

Walking nervously out of the room and through the narrow corridor, I knock on his door, the first one on the left.

"Come in, Ms. Hill," his irresistible voice calls, and I rub at my collarbone from fear of what he's about to tell me.

The door parts and he's there, jacket slung over a black leather chair, his cuffs undone, sleeves tight around the crooks of his arms.

Even through my nerves, I grow warm at the sight of him.

"Close the door and have a seat." He leans back, swallowing up all the air in the room with his presence.

My heart batters in my chest, the beats unsteady as I take the empty chair across from him.

"So, why am I here?" I brave the question, ignoring the fluttery feeling in my chest.

His eyes concentrate on mine, and for a moment, I wonder if he'll even talk.

"I have another proposition for you."

My brows hit my hairline. I knew he'd want more from me. Nothing is ever enough for men like him.

"And what's that?"

"Marry me."

I burst out laughing. I can't seem to stop.

But the more I look at him, the more I realize…

"Oh, you're not joking."

"Not even a little." He folds his arms over his chest.

Oh my God. I can't believe he just asked me to marry him.

"You're clearly insane. We don't even know each other. Hell, we haven't even gone on a date, and you're asking me to marry you?"

"I am. And I can. Ask you on a date. Would you like that?"

Shivers run down my arms.

*Yes. No. Maybe?*

I stare incredulously at this lunatic, my pulse drumming in my temples. How do I get out of this conversation?

"That's not what we're talking about." I shake my head with derision curling through my features. "I don't know what game you're playing, but I won't stand for it. I'm here for Brody. That's it. If you're looking for a wife, find someone else. I'm sure you'd find many willing participants."

*Please let him find someone else!*

"I could do that. But I'm choosing not to." His gaze narrows. "I want *you*, Elara Hill, and you *will* say yes."

Another swell of laughter escapes me, yet a sinking feeling drops to the base of my gut. Like there's no getting out of this. Fear crawls up my spine.

"You're a presumptuous, conceited—"

"Go ahead. Finish that sentence." His lips thin, like he's daring me.

"Asshole." My face heats up from my irritation.

He chuckles. "As long as you get soaking wet for assholes, I'm happy to stay one."

I shake my head at his brash behavior, though he only finds it amusing.

I should never have agreed to work for him.

"I won't marry you, Tynan."

Why he'd want that in the first place is the question. Makes no sense. What does he get out of it?

"Hear me out first."

I huff a sigh. "Fine. But it won't change my mind. So you're wasting your time."

"I need a wife for business purposes, and you very much need protection and money."

"Oh my God…" My jaw goes slack. "You've got to be kidding me."

He ignores me as he continues. "I can give you both. You'll never struggle again. You'll have everything. Money, power. I will take care of you and your grandparents. Isn't that what you need?"

I tug back, unable to comprehend what he's actually saying. He's treating marriage like a chess game. Yet…other thoughts start to play in my head too.

Crazy thoughts.

Like the fact that he can actually protect me and my grandparents from Jerry, long enough for me to figure out my next move.

"For how long?"

"What do you mean?"

"How long will I have to remain your wife?"

His mouth dances with a wry smirk. "For the rest of your life, Ms. Hill. This arrangement will be permanent. I have no intention of letting you go."

My pulse quickens, and I shudder at being his for the rest of my life.

"So you mean to tell me I'd have to be your wife forever just so you can get some deal?" I stare at him in disgust. "You have some nerve!"

He leans closer to the desk, dropping his elbows over it and staring intently at me. "I'm not him, Elara. I won't hurt you. And you'll get a large check for every year we're married, and a bigger one for every child we make together. And at all other times, I'll leave you alone if that's what you want."

"How romantic." My stomach churns. "I hope you know I'd never sleep with you."

He coughs a laugh. "That'd be difficult, since having a child is the point of all of this."

I stare wide-eyed at this delusional man. "You're clearly crazy. I won't let you touch me or treat me like some vessel to create your future generation." I jump to my feet. "No, Mr. Quinn, absolutely not. And don't you dare ask me again, or I'll stop working for you. And I don't want to do that to Brody."

His nostrils expand and his irises narrow.

I turn and start to walk away, not caring how angry he is. *I'm* the one who should be angry.

His voice looms behind me. "You're making a very big mistake,

Ms. Hill."

Fear drips down my body. Rearing around to face him, I spring forward and grip the edge of his desk.

"Maybe you're not used to hearing no. But I'll gladly be the first person to tell you. *No*, Mr. Quinn. And that's final." My brow hikes in challenge. "Now, excuse me. I have to get back to Brody."

With my body buzzing, I storm out of there and shut the door behind me with a bang, hoping that's the end of it.

But with men like Tynan, I know better.

A couple of hours later, and I can't get over what happened. He didn't say a word to me while I was with Brody, which was a good thing. I was bound to make a scene.

How dare he? I'd never marry a stranger, let alone a man like him. A dangerous man. No matter how much money he throws at me.

I know the Mafia isn't made up of nice guys. They're brutal. I won't be stuck to one for the rest of my life.

How did this even happen to me? First, my father's betrayals, then being forced to get engaged to Jerry. Now this? What the hell did I ever do to deserve any of it?

"You okay, sweetheart?" Grandma asks from across the table.

She came for dinner after we visited Grandpa, but I could barely eat. I was already struggling with my appetite, though after today, it's gone. Being on the run, constantly glancing over your shoulder, makes it hard to stomach anything.

Grandma keeps staring at me curiously, and I release a sigh, needing to talk to someone, and she's all I have.

"What's troubling you?" She tucks my fingers into her palm while I stare up at the ceiling for a brief second before peering at her.

"Do you remember the guy from the café?"

"Of course. Who could forget him?" She looks at me flirtatiously, and I roll my eyes.

"I'd personally love to."

"Oh, come on. I saw the way you were checking him out. He's a good-looking man."

"Seriously?"

"What?" She throws her hands in the air. "I may be old, but I'm not blind. So, what about him? Did he do something?" She instantly grows concerned.

"No, nothing like that."

"Oh, good. I was ready to shoot the bastard."

I release a laugh. "Oh, Gran, I love you."

She pats my hand as I go on.

"Okay, so don't laugh, but today after work, he…uh…" I don't even know how to say this out loud without it sounding ridiculous.

"Yes?"

"He asked me to marry him."

"What?" She rolls back into the chair, her eyes flaring.

"I know, right? He's insane. Clearly needs some heavy medication."

"Why would he do that?"

I shrug. "He didn't give me too much detail except that he needs a wife for some business deal. If he thinks I would accept such a ludicrous proposal, he's out of his mind."

She stares silently, scratching the side of her gray hair.

"I told him about Jerry, saying I had to leave because of the abuse. So he used that against me, telling me he'd offer protection and money in exchange, like I'm some desperate little girl who needs him to save her."

"Hmm." That's all she says.

"What?" My voice turns irritated.

"Nothing." She clears her throat, though I can tell she wants to say more, and I know I'm not going to like it.

"Oh my God. You're crazy too!"

"Just hear me out for a moment."

I drop my face into my palms, shaking my head. "Unbelievable."

"Look, sweetheart, I've heard about his connections. And, well, I think he may not be so bad for you, considering our situation."

I narrow my gaze as she goes on.

"I told you. You need a strong man to stand up to the likes of the people we ran from. Throw Jerry on top of that, and…" She sighs. "What kind of man do you think could do that? Some random fella? They'd run before they'd save you."

It's like she's repeating the same thoughts I had when he offered the marriage proposal. But I didn't want her to actually agree with that rationale!

"So I marry a stranger? Give up my life to be a mobster's wife? Is that what you're proposing?"

"Your grandpa was a stranger to me when I married him."

"What?" I settle deeper into my chair.

That's news to me.

"Yes. We were arranged to marry, and look at us!" Affection grows in her eyes. "That man is my whole world. So the truth is, sweetheart, you never know what will work out in the end."

"This is crazy." I laugh incredulously. "The fact that you're telling me to consider it is unbelievable. He's dangerous."

"Look at the life we're living! We've been running from those people who will probably never stop chasing us. Don't you remember what they did to your father and your mother?" She shuts her eyes for a second before she's looking at me again. "So you have to decide what's better. That, or marrying a man who could keep you safe."

"But who will keep me safe from him…?" My voice drifts, and his face appears before me.

My skin prickles when I feel his hands on me, his body pressed up against mine.

*I'm not him, Elara. I won't hurt you*, his sinful voice whispers against my ear.

And I want to believe him. I want to believe he's different.

"You like him."

My fingers feather across my throat. I can still feel the warmth of his breath as though he's right here.

"I can see it in your eyes," Gran goes on. "That's enough to start a marriage."

"No way, Gran. I'd rather keep running than marry that awful man."

*Oh, Elara. You're not even cute when you lie. There's nothing awful about him, except maybe how awfully handsome he is.*

She shakes her head. "You're just as stubborn as your father."

I grind my molars, not wanting to be associated with him. "Let's just eat. I don't want to talk about this anymore."

"Alright." Her mouth twists, but she respects my wishes and continues with her stir-fry.

I'd hate to lose Brody, though if it comes down to it, I'll quit.

I'll have to.

There's no way in hell I'll ever become Tynan Quinn's wife.

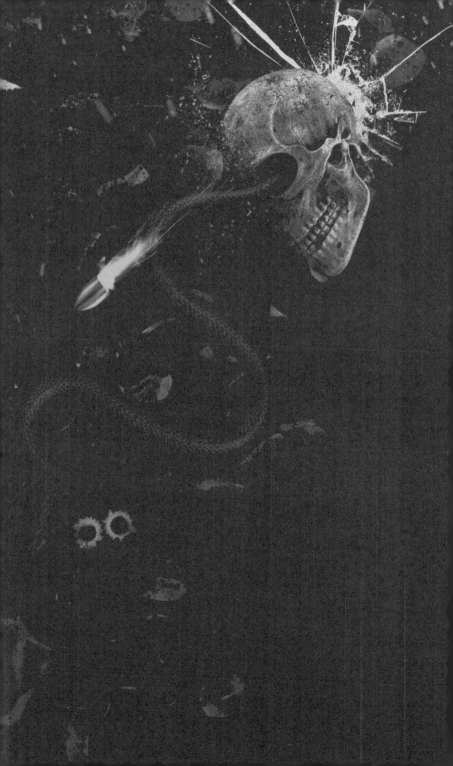

# SEVENTEEN

## TYNAN

I can't get her eyes out of my head the following day, the anger within them.

She doesn't want this.

*Neither do I, Elara. But sometimes we have to do the things we don't want to do.*

And she's going to realize soon enough that she has no say in this. Not with me.

She *will* be my wife.

She *will* wear my ring.

And she will *not* refuse me.

There's a knock on my office door at the house. My brothers, Fionn and Cillian strut in and settle on the sofa, tipping their heads up in greeting. Cillian is three years younger than me, while Fionn and I have seven years between us.

"You ready?" Fionn leans back.

"Yeah. They should be here any minute."

We execute most of our deals here on the estate. And the latest is with the Russians to secure a weapons agreement.

The Marinov family is powerful and has deep connections in the drug and arms world.

They have access to some of the most quality weapons out there. Working with them may not be my favorite, but we need firepower.

Konstantin Marinov runs the Bratva. He's unhinged, and so are his remaining brothers, Aleksei, Anton, and Kirill.

We know the kind of shit they've done, ripping people apart with their teeth.

Their father, Sergey, was the worst of them. He was the one who killed our mother.

Her screams as her body burned alive still haunt me, and it's been about fourteen years since it happened.

He did it all because he and my father had a dispute over property. My mother was just revenge. Then my father killed one of his sons. Blood was spilled on both sides until Konstantin made a truce and banished his father, who returned to Russia.

But three years after that, he came for Iseult.

My blood simmers remembering how she looked after she escaped. Bloody and bruised, but in her face was the fury she still carries.

She took one of his eyes before she escaped, and the bastard just wouldn't go away.

He came after Eriu not long ago, and that was the nail in his coffin. Now he's rotting in the ground.

We've existed with the Russians without any war for a long time, and we'd all like to keep it that way. Yet if the need comes, we will be ready. We always are.

My cell rings, and I answer it when I see it's one of my men. "Yeah?"

"They're here."

"Send them in."

My brothers sit up straighter.

From the distance, heavy footfalls pound closer until the door opens and Konstantin walks in first.

"Konstantin." I rise, and my brothers follow.

I slap his hand with mine, all of us greeting one another. He's damn huge, probably over six-seven. Big bastard with an even bigger ego.

"Please sit down," I tell them as they move toward the two unoccupied leather sofas while my brothers take the other. "Thanks for coming. I know it's a trip for you."

"Eh." Konstantin waves off the concern, his accent heavy. "We took my jet. Was a quick ride."

Of course he did. He's in New Jersey. Would be too long to drive.

The thought instantly makes me think of Elara and the number for DK that I found. She gave a reasonable explanation of who he is, and that could all be true, but I have a feeling there's a lot more to it. Once we're married, she *will* tell me everything.

"How about we get down to business?" Konstantin's voice snaps me back to the present.

He leans back against the leather, his dark, cunning eyes assessing me.

Aleksei leans forward, running a hand through his black hair. "We have the supplies and the means to get them here to the States." His accent as thick as his brother's. In fact, they all have it. "We just need to know you're good with the asking price."

"What's that?"

The Russians don't negotiate. The price is the price. And we need their weapons.

"Three million."

It's not unreasonable.

"Ammunition?"

"Everything, my friend." Konstantin's mouth twitches. "Five

hundred companions."

I know what he means. Firearms. Five hundred of them, just like we asked for.

"That's fair." I nod. "How will you get it to the States?"

He runs his fingers over his trimmed goatee. "Don't you worry about that." His grin grows. "All you need to know is we have a system that's been working, and we don't disclose it to anyone outside the family. Question is, will you be ready for the shipment when it comes?"

"Our land is secure. We can do it here, no problem."

"Good." He glances around my office. "I will say I am very impressed by your land and the way you run everything. It almost rivals our process."

Guess that was supposed to be a compliment.

"When will the shipment arrive?"

"Two weeks' time. I will let you know once it reaches the States so you can make the proper arrangements."

"Alright. My father will be happy to hear that."

"Where is your father?"

"He's out, though as you know, I will be heading the family very soon."

"Ah, yes." Konstantin stretches his arms. "I heard about your father wanting you to marry. How is that going?"

Fionn chuckles. "He's got someone in mind."

I shoot him a glare, and he shrugs.

"What? They'll all know soon enough."

"And who is that?" Kirill narrows his eyes, the tattoos on his neck twitching as he does. "You know, if it doesn't work out, we have plenty of beautiful women in the family."

"Ah, my brother does make a valid point. That may be a good idea." Konstantin thoughtfully glances between my brothers and me. "It's always best to form alliances in our circles, don't you think?

And with all the bad blood we once shared—in the distant past, of course—I wonder if a marriage would prolong our mutually beneficial relationship."

"Thanks for the offer, but I'll pass."

The vein in Konstantin's neck jerks, his mouth curling at the corner. "Well, you're not the only Quinn." His attention snaps to my brothers.

Fionn grins. "I like myself a Russian woman. How about you, brother?"

He elbows Cillian, who doesn't look as pleased with the idea.

"Yeah, I mean…" He clears his throat. "I'll think about it."

Konstantin clenches his jaw. "Good."

"Yeah," Cillian mutters, not wanting to piss the fucker off any more.

Konstantin isn't wrong. May be something to consider. Just not for me. I have the wife I want. She's the perfect woman to get me what I need and help Brody.

"We have brought you a gift." Konstantin removes his cell, pressing a few keys. "One of my men will bring it in here."

"Sure."

Minutes later, one of his guys hands him a gold bottle of liquor. Konstantin places it on my desk.

"This is Russo-Baltique vodka. Have you heard of it?"

"Of course I have."

It costs 1.3 million dollars.

He laughs. "Then you know it comes in a bulletproof flask made from gold. Only the best for friends. And we are friends, are we not?"

It's either you're friends with the Russians or you're their enemy.

"We are." I pick up the heavy bottle and examine the diamond-encrusted cap, a replica of a Russian eagle. "This is generous."

"Well, I do what I can for friends." His brothers start to rise. "Now, I expect the money in my Cayman account by next week. That won't be a problem, will it?"

"Of course not."

"Very good." He starts for the door, but before he does, he glances at my brothers again. "You know, when you attend my next party, you can meet some of the very single women in my family."

"Sounds like a plan." Fionn slaps his palm with Kirill's, and we all exchange pleasantries before they get the fuck out of here.

I hate having them in our space. One wrong move and they could start another war. It doesn't take a lot to set them off, especially Konstantin. I once heard he feeds bodies to Calabrian black pigs he imported from Italy solely for that. I must admit that is a useful way to dispose of bodies. No evidence to clean up.

"Damn, imagine marrying into that family." Cillian whistles.

"That would make for some interesting family dinners." Fionn laughs, knowing how big my father is on them.

Glancing down at my phone, I realize I am running late to pick up Brody. Shit.

"I've gotta go." I gather my keys and phone and head for the door. "Brody is waiting for me. Probably angrier than he usually is."

"Yeah, the kid basically hates you." Fionn grins. "Who can blame him?"

"Fuck off." I glare at my youngest brother before heading out and into my car, getting the SUV on the road.

I hope she's still there. I hope Elara hasn't gone home yet like she normally does before Rogue brings her to me.

I see her then.

In my mind.

That body made for sin.

Every inch of her begs to be corrupted.

To be owned.

But that's all I want.

All I need.

She will be mine in every sense of the word.

Twenty minutes later, and I'm pulling up at the school. The place is empty, no parents gathered outside waiting for their kids. Just a few exiting the building to get their children after running late like me.

As soon as I'm buzzed in, the security officer greets me. "Mr. Quinn, how you doin'?"

"I'm doing well, Phil. How's your family?"

The ex-cop shrugs. "Good as ever. Kids are in college now."

"Wish them well for me." I turn to the secretary, seated in an office separated by a plastic partition right past the main entrance doors. "Sorry I ran late."

"It's no trouble. Brody will be out any minute."

"Thank you."

Impatiently, I glance through the glass door leading farther into the school, wanting to get Brody and Elara and get out of here so I can talk to her again. Make her see reason before I have to resort to drastic measures.

Just then, Elara appears in the hall, talking to someone.

Not just someone.

A man.

He's staring at her, discreetly glancing at her mouth and other parts of her body.

Hot rage boils my blood.

She doesn't see me. Not yet.

The bastard doesn't seem much older than me, and when he places a palm on her shoulder, I lose all self-control.

"Could you buzz me in?" I tell the secretary. "I want to have a word with Ms. Hill about Brody."

"Of course."

No one gets to touch her. Or look at her like that. No one but me.

I try to contain the adrenaline coursing through me as I slowly approach. She's yet to look at me. Yet to catch the evidence of my unfathomable jealousy.

"I would love to take you out sometime," he tells her.

*Got a death wish?*

She laughs nervously, shifting on her nude stilettos. The black pencil skirt, so damn sexy on her—tight and classy—makes me want to bend her over my knee and watch her ass get pink from my hand.

"That is so sweet of you, Vincent, but I—"

That's when her attention lands on me and her pretty mouth parts, eyes lost to mine, shock and arousal growing within them.

A miniscule smirk tilts up my mouth.

*Vincent* glances between us, his eyes expanding. Because, of course, he knows who I am. Everyone in this town does.

*I'm gonna be watching you now, Vincent. Bad move to try to hit on my future wife.*

"What are you doing here?" she asks, trying to hide her shock.

"I'm here to get Brody and to pick you up. Figured I'd give you a ride since I'm here."

Her chest rises and falls, the swell of her breasts large enough for my hands.

I never cared much about the specifics of a woman's chest size or the type of body she had. I've always found all kinds of bodies beautiful.

But with Elara, I now have a type.

What's-His-Name clears his throat. "Mr. Quinn, uh, hello. I'm—"

"I don't care who you are."

The cockroach stares up at me with just the right amount of fear.

"I've missed you." I kiss her temple, and she jerks beside me.

I don't overlook the way the asshole's face goes white.

Curling an arm around the small of her back, I drag her right up against me, leaning my lips down across her ear. "Better behave and go along with it, Ms. Hill."

She elbows me in the ribs, the pain radiating down my torso. This feisty little serpent needs to be tamed.

He stares uncomfortably between us.

"Are you ready to go?" I ask her. "I made us dinner plans."

She narrows her eyes at me, her features tightening.

I can't hide my satisfaction.

"Great." She grins, attempting to push me away.

He clears his throat. "Well, I'll leave you to it. I'll see you tomorrow, Elara."

His smile disappears as soon as he looks at my face.

*If you don't keep your dick away from her, you may not live to see tomorrow.*

"Come on, let's go." I pull her toward the exit.

"I'm not ready to go yet."

"Don't make a scene and follow me. I'll be taking you to my place personally so you can get started with Brody early today."

*Shit. Brody.*

"You are unbelievable! I told you not to flirt with me. I can't lose my job, and here you are, acting like we're together. What the hell?"

With a growl, I grab a fistful of her ass.

"What are you doing?" Her voice is pitched low, irritation marking each syllable.

Stopping in place, I press the front of her body up against mine.

"He wants to fuck you, and he's still watching us, so I'm telling him rather nicely that you're mine." I brush my lips with hers, unable to stop myself. "Would you prefer it if I killed him instead?"

Her breathing turns heavy, fanning across my mouth. "I'm not yours. I can fuck anyone I want."

Her croaky timbre shoots right down to my cock. I bet she's soaking those panties right now.

"We are not together," she continues, failing to sound convincing as she does a shit job of pushing me off with her palms against my chest. "We're not dating, and we sure as hell will never get married. Get it through your obviously thick head."

I chuckle coldly.

My thumb slowly rolls over her lips, my eyes following its path. "Such a dirty mouth. Makes me wonder what else it can do."

Her face flushes, and the tension in my jaw radiates through me.

My lips drop lower, almost meeting hers again. "No one will fuck you, Ms. Hill. No one but me."

My thumb strokes across her chin and she sucks in a breath. I bet she can feel how hard I am for her.

"This is my town, Elara. My rules. Everyone obeys them, and soon you will too. It's best you remember that."

"You need to stop," she whispers, though her voice is full of obvious arousal.

"But you don't want me to stop, do you? You like this." I fist her hair with my other palm.

"Yes…"

The admission emboldens me. "This is only the beginning. The things I'm gonna make you do…"

Need to get us home as quickly as possible.

Someone clears their throat, and she jumps from my grasp like a bomb exploded between us. The older nurse stands there with Brody, staring at us disapprovingly.

"Mr. Quinn." Her stern tone only makes me grow more irritated.

She's never liked me. I don't know who this woman thinks she is. "Gretchen."

I don't miss the way her face tenses when I call her by her first name.

"Come on, Brody. Let's go," I tell him.

He pouts, and instead of coming to my side, he moves toward Elara's.

"Hey, buddy," she greets him.

With my arm around her, I lead them out of the building, not missing the wide-eyed looks from the secretary and the security guard.

I just staked my claim, and there's nothing Elara can do about it. She's mine, whether she wants to be or not.

Now everyone in this town will know it too.

Rogue's waiting for us by the SUV parked behind mine. He nods in greeting when he sees us.

"Brody, why don't you ride with Rogue? Ms. Hill and I have some things to discuss. Don't we, baby?"

Brody doesn't seem pleased with the idea, sulking before he stomps over to Rogue.

Elara's disdain for me shines on her face as she glances my way.

"Don't call me baby," she whispers.

The back of my hand strokes the outline of her jaw before I grab her delicate throat and stare into her eyes with promise. "I will call you anything I damn well please."

She cracks a cold smile before it disappears like quicksand. Her mouth rises to my ear. "You'll never own me like those shiny cars you drive."

My fingers squeeze around her throat as I let out a low growl. "Get in the car, Elara."

"Let me go," she hisses between clenched teeth.

My smirk only makes her angrier.

But I drop my hand before I give the school any more to talk about.

Her fingertips run across her throat, and in her eyes there's something other than hate. Her attraction to me is obvious.

This is what I need in a wife. Someone I'll enjoy fucking. Someone who wants to throw me through the wall before I put her up against one and take everything she fights not to give.

She walks over to Rogue's car, and at first I expect her to jump in, but she talks to Brody instead while I discreetly rearrange my slacks, needing to tame this massive hard-on.

"I can't wait to get home and play Monopoly!" she tells him as I appear behind her.

He grins, and I swear every time he does, it's something I can't explain in words.

"Okay, buckle yourself in." She pats his knee. "I'll be right behind you."

He nods and does as he's told.

She ignores me as I walk back to the car with her by my side.

"It never ceases to amaze me how good you are with him."

"He makes it easy." She opens the car door, her back to me, but I register the smile in her voice and it sets my heart ablaze.

I wrap my arm around her front and kiss her shoulder. She inhales sharply and stays in my embrace, unable to move or do much of anything.

And neither can I.

Why is it so easy with her when I barely even know her? Why does it feel like everything is possible when I'm this close to her?

She turns in my arms, her brows furrowed as she scans my lips before staring up at me. "You really shouldn't be touching me like this in front of Brody. It will give him the wrong idea."

With a ragged sigh, I let her go. She's right; I should keep my hands off her. Though not because of Brody.

She brings things out in me I have no interest in.

A business arrangement. That's all this will be.

Marrying her.

Fucking her.

Getting her pregnant.

Rinse and repeat.

No feelings.

No attachments.

That's all.

"You coming?" Those eyes call to me, and this fierce instantaneous possessiveness latches on to me.

*Shit. I'm so fucked.*

"Get in." I help her inside, grabbing the seat belt and securing it around her.

She doesn't protest. What a fast learner. My mouth tugs at the corner.

Making it to my side, I turn the car on, getting us on the road and following Rogue.

Her eyes drift to my groin, my cock thick and hard.

She fights not to stare, squeezing her knees tight and shifting uncomfortably in her seat. But she just can't help herself.

Thoughts of prying her thighs apart and tasting her overtake me until I'm the one shifting in my seat.

I glance down at my erection. "Bad wife. Look what you did."

Her throat bobs as she clears it. "I'm not your wife."

"But you will be."

"I'm serious, Tynan. You need to get over yourself and your convoluted idea that we're getting married. I will never accept your proposal."

"I don't remember asking for your permission." I clasp the top of her thigh, and her tongue slips out to wet her lips.

"What the hell does that mean?" She fights her nerves and keeps her tone steady.

"It means this is gonna happen whether you want it to or not." I massage her skin with my thumb, pushing the skirt up to her mid-thigh. "And just so you know, if I find out you've fucked anyone, they won't survive the night."

"You're insane!" she scoffs.

"Certifiable." My mouth forms a thin line.

She has no idea how serious I am.

"I'm so done talking to you for the rest of the day."

I let out a low chuckle. "We're not done talking yet, Ms. Hill. Now sit there and behave."

Her nails dig into the leather.

"I don't know why you're fighting it. It's obvious you wanna fuck me as much as I wanna fuck you." My fingers slide up a little higher, right over her inner thigh. "We'd have fun. It doesn't have to be unpleasant for either one of us." From the corner of my eye, my gaze roves down her body. "I would very much enjoy waking up next to you every morning and devouring you for breakfast."

A visible tremor rolls through her.

"I would take care of you, Elara. Your enemies would be my enemies. Your problems would be my problems. Anything you wanted or needed, I would make it happen."

She sits up straighter, finally listening even while staring out the front of the car.

"You are who I need for Brody," I explain further, rubbing my palm up and down her leg, feeling her skin prickle beneath my hand. "I don't want to force you. I want you to say yes of your own free will."

"That's never gonna happen, Mr. Quinn. You're a criminal. I'll never marry you. So if you wanna kill me, go ahead."

I hate that she called me by my last name. I like hearing her say my name.

"I have no plans to hurt you, Elara. I don't hurt women. No matter how badly they get under my skin. And you, Ms. Hill, have dug so deep…" I squeeze her inner thigh. "I don't ever want to get rid of you. And that's a first."

I don't know where that confession came from or why I said it out loud, but it's like when I'm near her, my heart does all the talking.

Her chest rises faster and faster, and I just want to hear her admit that she wants me. That she feels what I'm feeling when I'm with her.

But she's too stubborn for that. She's made up her mind about me, and it'll take a lot to destroy that notion.

Doesn't matter either way.

Because I take what I want.

And it's too bad for Ms. Hill, I've decided I want her.

# EIGHTEEN

## ELARA

I don't see much of Tynan while I'm with Brody, running around with the dog and spending the time playing games.

I don't know if I'm close to getting him to talk, though the fact that he has fun? That's important to his healing. Hopefully one day when I'm gone, he's talking again and he's okay.

But I know I can't stay here. Not after everything Tynan said.

He won't let me go. I'll have to take matters into my own hands. There's no other choice.

"I'll see you tomorrow, buddy."

Before I can head to the car, he squeezes his arms around my hips.

"I love you too." My hand brushes over his head, and I kiss the top of it, my heart squeezing so painfully I might cry.

But this is for the best.

I have to leave.

As I glance up, Tynan is there leaning against the doorframe, face haunted by demons, the same ones that live in his heart.

He's not a good man, no matter how he treats this little boy. No matter how safe I feel when I'm around him. It's all a well-crafted lie.

He lives a life of crime. He murders people. I won't become his wife, a mere puppet for him to command at his whim. Someone he can abuse and cheat on and throw away like trash when his needs aren't met.

An ache pushes up my throat, and instead I smile at Brody, refusing to look at the beautifully harsh man staring at me. He's in a simple white t-shirt now, gray sweats hung low on his well-built hips. Shameful heat pulses in my core, knowing I have to leave before I fall into temptation.

Sleeping with him is the last thing I should do.

Yet the one thing I want.

"I'll walk you to the car," he says.

A chill sways over my limbs, like a premonition of what's to come if I remain here.

"Okay." I say goodbye to Brody one last time before Tynan is beside me, standing too close.

He turns to me. "See you tomorrow, Ms. Hill."

"Yes." My smile fades as soon as we make eye contact.

Knots tighten in my stomach.

His fingertips brush faintly over mine, and tingles erupt over my skin. Treacherous things. Reminding me that my body craves him more than my mind ever could.

"Ready to go?" Rogue asks, already waiting in the spacious driveway.

"I am." I get in the passenger side. "Goodbye, Tynan." I give him one last glance.

Something curious crosses over his face, but it only lasts a second.

Shutting the door behind me, I find him watching intently, as though he can see me through the tinted window.

Does he suspect I'm planning to leave?

No, of course not. I haven't even figured out where I'll go or how I'll do it.

I have the money he's given me so far. I can pay for my grandfather's home for a few months, and the rest I can use. That'll give me enough time to find a place to live and get a job so I can send more money for him.

Sorrow builds in my chest. I hate leaving my grandparents. I can't tell Grandma anything. Not until I'm long gone. It's better that way. I don't want her to try to convince me to stay. She's already told me she thought marriage to Tynan was a good idea.

As soon as I get home, anxiety builds. I have to go. Tonight. Tynan will make me marry him if I don't. I'm not sure how he'll do it, but he will. He's said it in so many words, and I refuse to be his pawn.

Locking the door, I peek out the curtain, seeing Rogue sitting in his car. He'll be here all night. But around four a.m., he leaves and returns an hour later. That's when I'll go.

I head upstairs and take out one piece of luggage, the largest I have, and start adding my clothes, shoes, and anything else I need into it until it's completely full.

I'll sleep for a few hours, and wake up at three in the morning. Then, as soon as Rogue's gone, I will be too.

If only I didn't have to go. I love this town and my job. And I love Brody too. I will miss him like crazy. And it breaks my heart to know he might be sad to know I'm gone.

I won't be able to work as a teacher anymore, will I? Tynan will find me easily that way. I'll need to keep a low profile.

Now I'll have to hide from both Jerry and Tynan. This is gonna be great.

Hours later, and I force myself to eat something before heading to bed, though I'm so scared and nervous, I can't stomach anything. The peanut butter and jelly sandwich tastes bitter, but I get it down.

There's so much I have to do while on the road. I'll have to tell the owner of this house that I won't be returning, then call the school and come up with some plausible excuse for my disappearance. A family emergency of some kind. It *is* partly the truth.

I settle on the sofa and turn on a random TV show, needing to distract myself from the fear of what will happen when Tynan realizes I've left for good.

"Shh…" a voice hums from beside me, caressing me out of deep sleep.

Or maybe I'm dreaming.

I groan, stretching my limbs and yawning, remembering why I have to be up.

Is it time already? My alarm didn't go off.

"Wake up, Elara."

The instant I hear his voice, I jolt up to a seated position, my heart racing uncontrollably.

And sitting beside me on the bed is the man I vowed to get away from.

*What is he doing here?!*

Oh, God. The luggage.

It's…it's in the corner of my bedroom.

Maybe he didn't see it.

Maybe he's just crazy and broke into my house again like the last time.

I drag my comforter over my chest, in nothing but a baggy sweatshirt and leggings, my hair disheveled too. I look like an absolute mess.

"What the hell are you doing here?"

"I'm disappointed, Ms. Hill." A venomous smile twists his lips. "I thought there was a chance that you'd actually come to your senses, but you haven't, have you?"

I gulp down the fear. "Wh-what do you mean?"

He casts a disdainful glance at my luggage. "You're leaving."

"I—"

"Don't you dare lie to me." He grabs my jaw, leaning his face close to mine.

I shut my eyes, tears filling them. I tried. I really tried, but he found out anyway.

"How?" I breathe.

"How did I know?" He barks a laugh. "It was the way you looked at me before you left. I could see it in your eyes. The wheels turning." His thumb rolls over my lips. "You have two options now, little serpent. Fall in line, or bite back. I suggest you choose wisely."

"I…I don't understand." My heart pounds.

Even in the dark, I don't miss the way his eyes flash. "We're getting married, Elara. Either you agree willingly or I make you."

I shake my head, fear clawing at my chest. "Please don't do this."

He shrugs. "Yet here we are. So tell me, what will it be?"

My eyes scan the place. Maybe I can run. Maybe I can hit him and get away from the back door. But where will I go with nothing except my clothes?

He gets to his feet, turning on my bedside lamp.

Before I can think, I grab my phone and jump off the other side of the bed, running out as his growl echoes through the room.

"You really shouldn't have done that." His voice thunders behind me as I rush down the stairs toward the back door.

Pushing it open, I run barefoot across the grass, the world silent and dark around me. Only my heartbeats echo. My exhales piercing through the air.

I can get away.

I can hide until someone brings me my stuff. Then I'll disappear.

I'll call my forger friend, Derek, to set me up with a new identity. Tynan is resourceful, a lot smarter than Jerry was. I'll be more careful this time.

Footfalls crunch behind me, a car roaring to life in the distance.

I'm only fooling myself, aren't I?

"Fuck!" Something pierces the heel of my foot, and I groan in pain, but I don't stop.

I can't stop. I know he's close behind.

*Just keep running.*

It's one thing I know how to do.

I head toward the road I always take my runs on, knowing both sides are covered with woods. Maybe I can find somewhere to hide.

As soon as I make it toward the edge of the road, an arm wraps around me as I fight it. Fight to get away.

But I can't.

He's too strong.

"You're making me do this." His voice crawls down my body—a silky, yet deadly mix of all my worst nightmares. "I promise to make you happy, Elara."

Before I can fight any more, he covers my nose and mouth with something.

My vision dims.

Then it all goes dark.

# NINETEEN

## TYNAN

I hated doing it. I didn't want it this way, but what did I actually expect? For her to give herself to me without fighting it? I was fooling myself into believing she would.

I warned her, though.

I gave her the option.

She didn't take it.

Gently, I lower her onto my bed so I can clean the cut on the sole of her foot. It isn't deep and should heal quickly. Still, I hate seeing it, knowing she's hurt because of me.

I pick up her foot and kiss the top of it, watching her face as it lies still on my pillow. "I'll take care of you from now on. You'll never have to be scared of anyone again."

*She's scared of you, especially after today.*

I'll have to change that if I want her to be happy. And she may not believe it, but I do want that.

This is our home. She will have to meet my family. Attend events

I'm forced to attend. I can't let the world think my own wife hates me.

Placing her leg back down on the bed, I head for the bathroom to get something to clean her wound with and wrap it.

Minutes later, it's clean and covered up as I sit beside her, stroking her cheek, waiting for her to wake up.

Any second now.

"Mm," she groans, stretching her limbs, her lashes fluttering.

But once her eyes fall on mine, they grow with horror.

"Get away from me!" She recoils, sounding weak from the drugs.

"Welcome home, Ms. Hill."

"Please!" She shakes her head, pain radiating in her eyes. "Don't do this to me. I can't marry you."

I release a disappointed exhale, reaching into my phone to type something before handing it to her.

"What's this?" She stares at the number.

Five million.

"The amount you will be paid every year for being my wife. I've already set up a bank account for you, and you will get your own card. No one will be able to touch that money. Not even the government."

She stares at me with tears filling her eyes, and I fight what those tears do to me. The way they undo me.

"You'll find that I've already deposited one million into it to get you started."

When she glances down at her quivering hands, she gasps. "Oh my God. What the hell is this, Tynan?"

A large solitaire diamond glistens on her finger.

I pick up her hand and kiss the top of it, staring into her wild blue eyes. "It's your engagement ring. You were asleep when you said yes."

My mouth spreads into a smirk, but her face only carries disdain.

A tightness hits my chest. "Can you walk? Or should I carry you?"

"Carry me where?" Fresh tears build in her eyes, turning my heart to stone.

"We're getting married, Elara. Right now."

"WHAT? You…you can't do this!" The words tremble out of her. "You won't get away with it!"

Scooting my arms under her, I lift her up against my chest.

"I already have." My lips drop to the corner of hers. "'Til death do us part."

# ELARA

I cry at my own wedding.

The priest stares between us, me in Tynan's arms, him looking as rigid and displeased as ever.

His two brothers, Fionn and Cillian, stand as witnesses, just as cold and unmoving as he is. They don't say a word. No one does. No one except the priest.

"Uh, are you sure about this?" he asks Tynan, who appears ready to shoot the man to death.

I let out a sniffle, and when he peers down at me, his features soften and he almost appears kind.

What a stupid thought.

The back of his hand softly caresses my cheek, and I hate them. Hate those butterflies that seem to soar every time he touches me. I don't want them. Not after today.

He stares deeply and his mouth drops to mine as he whispers, "Ná caoin a stór. Tá tú ag briseadh mo chroí."

Those words pour out of him.

I can feel them, even though I have no clue what they mean. But for some strange reason, they bring me comfort even while every part of me fights what's happening.

"You speak Gaelic?"

He nods with a tiny hint of a smile. "We all do. Our father has taught us the language, and I'll teach our child too."

*Child. He wants a child. Oh, God. I forgot.*

He wipes my tears away and drops a kiss to my forehead. "I'm sorry, Elara." His voice hums across my ear. "Please don't cry. You're breaking my heart."

I didn't even know he had one.

The tip of my nose stings as I accept my fate.

At least for now.

As I throw my arms around his neck, all the fight in me washes away. I don't have any strength to fight right now.

His brows gather, intensity flashing through his eyes, like he realizes what that means. That I'm ready.

"Start," he tells the priest. "And just get to the good part. I want it done."

The priest nods nervously, holding the Bible tighter in his grasp.

"Repeat after me," he tells Tynan. "I, Tynan Donal Quinn, take you, Elara Rain Hill, as my wife, for better, for worse, for richer, for poorer, in sickness and in health, 'til death do us part."

I swallow the lump in my throat as I wait for Tynan to recite his portion of the vows. I'm glad he knew to use my new name. I don't want to give Jerry any chance of finding me.

Tynan repeats the words. Then it's my turn, swearing to be the wife of a man I don't want.

The priest finishes off the rest, reciting blessings before he says, "Lord, bless Tynan Donal Quinn and Elara Rain Hill and consecrate their married life."

One of Tynan's brothers hands him two rings, and Tynan slips a diamond-encrusted band over my engagement ring and gives the other to me.

"Place it on my finger." He pushes his hand up from under me so I can slip it on.

"May these rings be a symbol of your faith in each other and a reminder to you of your love. Through Christ our Lord. Amen. You may kiss the bride."

At that, Tynan's eyes darken, his chest rising with each deep breath. He cups my cheek and stares into my eyes, and it's like I'm frozen, unable to look away. Not wanting to.

And as he captures my lips and groans, I almost forget I'm supposed to hate him.

# TWENTY

## ELARA

I'm still in shock when the priest leaves. It's like a bad dream. But when I stare down at my finger, I realize this is reality.

"I don't want this."

His eyes scan mine when I look into them. I hate him right now. Hate what he's forced me into. Tears prickle within my eyes, and he's there, cupping my face and looking at me like I matter.

But he's a monster.

And monsters don't care.

"I don't want this to be bad for you, Elara. I know you don't believe me, but your happiness matters to me."

His thumb brushes over my lips, and my lashes flutter. I hate that his hands on me make me feel this damn good.

"My happiness matters so much that you take me against my will?" I scoff.

He drags in a long breath. "I'm not your ex. I won't hurt you."

"Yet you forced me to marry you." My laugh is short and dry.

"You're a real gentleman."

I push off his hand, and he releases me, walking back a few steps and running his hand down his face.

I shake my head. "What the hell will I tell people at school once they find out? I could lose my job. Do you even care, or will you stop me from working too? Because I swear, Tynan…" I walk up to him and dig an index finger into his hard chest. "If you assume I'll quit, you have another think coming."

He grabs my wrist and brings my knuckles to his lips, kissing them slowly as he gazes down at me through hooded eyes. "I don't expect you to quit, and if you're worried about being let go, don't be. I know the superintendent of the district well. He wouldn't wanna piss me off by firing my wife."

*His wife.*

I shake off the warmth those words just brought me, and relief washes over me instead. At least I won't lose my job.

Except, you know, I'll be married to a Mafia man. And he intends to get me pregnant. Will he force me? Oh, God…

"Just tell me why you're doing this. Why me?"

He releases a heavy sigh. "Come sit with me."

He moves toward the sofa. The house is dark, no one awake at this late hour. When I lower to the opposite corner from him, he shakes his head and pats the space right beside him.

"Better get used to being close to me."

A lopsided smirk lifts his lips, and it settles in my gut, reminding me that beneath the hate, there's insufferable attraction waiting to consume us both.

I scoot closer, yet keeping a little distance. But he curls an arm around my back and brings me up against him, uncomfortably so. Our outer thighs meet, and my heart gallops in my throat.

"Now that we're married, I'll tell you what you need to know."

He takes my hand in his and holds it in his lap, rubbing circles over my skin, making me warm. It's what he does to me, and there's nothing I can do about it, no matter how hard I try.

"My father is the head of the Irish Mob. He plans to retire soon, and I'm next in line."

I cup my mouth, realizing what he's trying to tell me. "And you needed to get married to do that…"

"Yes. My father is big on continuing our family line, and I had two months to find a wife. Then I met you and saw how good you are for Brody, and he's the one person in my life who matters most to me."

His eyes fall to a brief close, and when he looks back at me, my heart swells. Because I can see it…the way he loves Brody. Really loves him. His anguish, it's there too.

"So instead of finding some random woman, I chose you."

"I'm so lucky." Sarcasm drips from my tone.

He exhales a short breath of laughter. "I get it. This wasn't how you envisioned your marriage. You probably wanted to fall in love and have a big wedding." He stares contemplatively. "And I can give you that—a wedding, a dress, anything you want. But I will never love you. It's my one stipulation. That this thing between us remain… friendly." His eyes dance over my lips, and my skin rises with goose bumps.

"So you wanna fuck me. Get me preg—"

"More than once." A smirk flits across his face.

"Right. More than once," I repeat with a roll of my eyes. "And not fall in love with me. So we'd be what? Friends with benefits?"

"I guess so."

"How sweet."

"I like you, Elara. Isn't that enough?"

Pain throbs at the back of my throat, and I fight not to cry. I fight to keep it together because after Jerry, falling in love and marriage wasn't in the cards.

And now to know that this man, who's intending to spend the rest of his life with me, refuses to love me? It hurts.

I should be thankful. I don't want his love. Or his affection. I don't want anything from him. I just want my freedom.

But in the back of my mind, that little girl I once was, who saw a bright future, she wants to be loved. She wants a man who would lay down his life for her, who cares for her. Who *wants* to love her. And that'll never be him.

"I have no plans on falling in love with you either, Tynan Quinn, so don't you worry about it."

Something crosses his eyes, something that resembles heartbreak. But that's a ridiculous thought.

"We should go over the rules," he continues.

"There are rules?"

"There are, Ms. Hill…" He smiles, catching himself. "I mean Mrs. Quinn."

I hate how good that just sounded. "What are they? These rules."

"For starters, Rogue will continue to follow you wherever you go. If your plans change, you have to let him know."

"Okay. Anything else?"

He reaches into his pocket and retrieves a jewelry box. My eyes expand, wondering what's inside. When he opens it, he reveals a thin gold tennis bracelet. Picking up my arm, he secures it around my wrist.

"You're never to take it off."

My brows knit. "Why?"

"It has a tracker."

"What?" My brows shoot up.

"If you take it off, I will know. It's waterproof, so you can wear it in the shower too."

"You're planning on *tracking* me?"

"You're now the wife of the head of the Mob. Yes, I'm tracking you. My enemies are also yours now, and they won't care that you're a woman. So this is for your protection, Elara." He tucks my chin in his palm. "If you disobey, I'll have to put a tracker *in* you. It's up to you which you'd prefer."

Staring at this man, I'm unable to believe how insane he truly is. I shove his hand off of me and try to control my rage. At least he won't do what Jerry did to me. At least there's that.

But I'll find a way to get away from him.

He might think this is forever, yet I have other plans. When the right opportunity comes, I'll disappear for good.

"How about I give you a tour of the house before I show you to our bedroom?"

He starts to rise, and I follow him, knowing I don't have much of a choice.

"Our bedroom? We can't sleep separately?"

"You're my wife, Elara. I want you in my bed." His arm winds around me, pressing me up against his body.

Those eyes align with mine, and as soon as they do, that shift in the air…it returns. Slams into my chest and makes me feel it. I feel everything when he touches me and looks into my eyes like that.

Like I matter.

"If you don't plan on falling in love with me, it's better if we spend as little time together as possible."

He flings a loose strand of hair away from my face, his mouth dropping across my ear and making me shiver.

Heavy, warm breaths skate against my skin. "You think you're that easy to fall in love with?"

I swallow down the thick taste of arousal tickling across my flesh.

His deep, rumbling chuckle sends my pulse into overdrive.

He straightens himself, slipping my hand into his. "Come on, let me show you your new home, Mrs. Quinn. This is just the beginning of all the things I plan to give you."

*I could get used to that…*

No. No. I absolutely cannot.

He takes me all throughout the house, showing me the many bedrooms. A game room and a theater, even a library. This place has it all.

Then we get to the bedroom.

The one I'll be forced to share with him.

Every night.

He opens the door, inviting me into the large space. My heart beats faster the farther I step into it. And that black upholstered bed in the center of the room somehow appears bigger.

"Do you like it?" he rasps behind me, and a chill scurries down my arms.

"It's okay," I lie, because clearly it's a lot more than okay. His home is beautiful.

Trying to ignore these feelings, I glance around the rest of the place. A white chaise with a shaggy rug beneath stands at the foot of the bed. A large fireplace is centered against the wall. It's probably cozy in the winter.

His big, strong palms lower to my arms, stroking up and down, making me molten lava.

"Well, I hope you do like our bedroom, Mrs. Quinn." He lowers his wicked mouth to the space behind my ear. "Because this is where I intend to fuck you every single moment that I can get my hands on you."

I visibly quiver, wanting him in every crevice.

"I will not sleep with you," I whisper, wanting it to be true. Despising myself for even thinking about him throwing me around and taking me roughly in this very bed.

I shouldn't want him in any capacity. But my body and my mind are at war, and my body is currently winning.

"You're my wife. My property." A single finger traces up my sternum, causing a breathy sigh to escape. "You *will* share my bed.

You *will* share your body. And I will own every inch of you."

I shouldn't like his words, yet all I want is to hear them again.

How is he doing this to me?

"I want an heir, and you will give me one. That's all I need to make my father happy."

"That's all you want? One child?" I breathe, still not turning toward him, afraid of the feelings he elicits from me.

"That's all." His mouth drops to the crook of my throat, and my head falls against his chest.

"And our child has two parents who don't even love each other?"

"No," he husks. "Our child will have parents who love him."

"Or her."

"Yes…or her. But we don't have to love each other to have a child."

"And you're gonna wanna…"

"Fuck?" he grunts, rolling a thumb over a pebbled nipple. "Yes. A lot." His teeth nip my earlobe, and I let out an illicit moan. "I thought we established all this earlier. How quickly you forget."

"Mm…" I can't help how amazing this feels.

"You keep sounding so good, and I might start trying early."

"Oh, God… After the baby, you…you won't touch me anymore, right?"

*Please touch me again…*

"Well, you will be my wife, and a man does have his needs. Do you suggest I go elsewhere?"

"No." The answer is instant.

"Good girl."

I want him so badly, I can't even comprehend feeling this way for a man. Never been this way for anyone.

"I'll not only pay you for every year we remain married, but I will also pay you to have my children."

"You mean *our* children, and you said you only needed one."

"Yes, Mrs. Quinn." He spins me around until my body is pressed up against his. "But with all our fucking, we may end up with more than one child."

His words flit down my skin, causing every inch to wake.

"You understand how crazy this is, right? Please tell me you understand."

He nods. "I never wanted a wife. It was never in the cards for me, but my father had other plans."

"It wasn't in the cards for me either." I glance at my feet right before he takes my chin firmly in his hand.

"Why not?"

The way he looks at me, it's like he wants to see me. Like he wants to know everything about me. It's almost enough to tell him everything.

Almost.

"My ex. He's taken a lot away from me."

His eyes turn to slits, quiet rage within them.

"I'm sorry he hurt you. I'll make him pay. I promise, Elara." His thumb gently strokes the underside of my jaw.

My gut swirls with emotions, with nerves he put there.

I grab his wrist. "Thanks for saying that, but I'd rather he never found me. I don't want anyone else getting hurt."

A yawn escapes me.

"How about we get some rest? It's late." He lifts the covers for me and I slide in.

"Which side do you sleep on?" I ask.

"The one closer to the door."

He starts to remove his shoes, placing them in the closet, unbuttoning his shirt next, until he's pulling the sleeves off. The sight of shirtless Tynan is making me thankful I'm already in bed. My thighs squeeze into one another when his solid eight-pack of muscles jerks at the attention I give it.

I glance at the window, and he lets out a chuckle.

"No, please, keep looking. I like your eyes on me."

"I wasn't looking. I mean, I was, but not in that way."

He chuckles. "You're cute when you lie."

Swallowing thickly, I return to ogling my husband, and the outline of his thick cock is hard to miss.

Okay, we definitely have a problem.

How am I supposed to share a bed with this man and pretend I won't let him fuck me? And the more I look at him, the more I accept that fate. I mean, sleeping with him wouldn't be the worst idea. I have an itch to scratch, and he's a very willing participant.

*But he wants to get you pregnant, you idiot.*

Right. Okay. Maybe I forgot about that part.

He rummages through his dresser drawer, then he's tossing a white t-shirt at me. "Put this on."

I pick it up and give him a puzzling look. "I'm already in my PJs."

"And as adorable as they are, I want you in my clothes moving forward. And make sure you're not wearing anything underneath."

Nerves skitter up my throat. "Um…"

He starts toward me, his knuckles falling across the side of my throat. "I'll never force you, if that's what you're afraid of. But I think it's good for us to start getting comfortable with one another, don't you?"

*No. I prefer to keep my distance.*

"I'll go change in the bathroom."

He releases me, and I feel bare without his touch.

Rushing up, I enter the bathroom and drag in a long, shallow breath, my pulse skipping in my throat. I married the head of the Mob. I'm a mobster's wife now. That's going to take quite some time to sink in.

Maybe this will scare Jerry and his father. Maybe they'll avoid a war with the Quinns once they find out I married him. Or maybe they'll get cocky and think they can take on the Mob. Isaac always thought highly of himself, and so did his son.

Running away is probably the best option.

I start removing my clothes, and I realize I haven't closed the door all the way.

From the crack, I see him watching me.

He doesn't turn away when our eyes meet. Instead, his gaze cruises down my naked form, and in it I find deep desire.

It's then I remember the scar on my stomach. The one Jerry gave me.

I'm careful to hide it with his shirt, but he'll see it sooner or later. I should tell him about it so he's prepared.

His throat bobs, and I realize I enjoy the attention he gives me. He likes what he sees…but will he like me with the scar, or will it repulse him?

I cut our connection, slipping the shirt over my body and open the door. "Pretty sure it's impolite to peep at a woman while she's naked."

A small smile plays on his face. "You're not just any woman. You're my wife, Elara. And you don't get to hide from me."

He grabs the back of my neck, forcing me up against him until I register every solid muscle on his body.

"You're beautiful." His thumb traces my jaw. "You should hear it every day, and I plan to tell you that every chance I get."

My face heats up, and the thought of the scar comes crashing down. "You should know…"

"What is it?" He tugs my face up to his.

"I have a scar. On my stomach. It's pretty bad, so if you think it's ugly and want to…you know, keep the lights off when we have to—"

"Show me." His angered voice makes my throat go dry.

My face flushes. "I…uh…don't have anything under here, and—"

"I don't care. I want to see it."

I pinch my eyes closed, and when he moves back, I start lifting my shirt. I refuse to look at him as I drag it up, revealing the thick vertical scar starting from the right of my belly button all the way to my lower abdomen near my hip.

His audible breath fills me with shame.

"He did that to you?" he spits out through clenched teeth.

When I lower my shirt, I dare to look at him as I nod.

"Fuck, Elara!" The pained way he says my name…

Oh God, it's like he wants to undo all that's been done to me.

He grabs a fistful of his hair, pinching his eyes tight. And when he looks back at me, it's softer.

He cups my face between two hands. "I need his name, baby. Please…" His forehead drops to mine, and he kisses the tip of my nose. "I can't survive another day knowing that the person who hurt you this way is still breathing."

I clasp his forearms, tears prickling. "I want to tell you, I do, but I don't want him to know where I am. You just don't understand how much it took to get away. I'm finally free of him and his family, and I'd like to keep it that way. Please respect that."

"I'm not used to feeling useless, Elara." He pitches back and sighs.

"You're not being useless. You're giving me what I need, and that's what a good husband does."

"Is that what I'm being?" A melancholy smile falls over him. "Somehow it feels like I'm failing you already."

"I promise you're not. Let's get some rest. I have work tomorrow." Then it hits me. "Oh my God. My clothes!"

"My men are already at your place, bringing everything over. You will have it all when you wake up."

He removes his pants until he's in nothing but a pair of boxers.

"These are for your benefit." He tugs the waistband. "I normally sleep naked."

Then he's pulling me back to bed and sliding in behind me. And instead of letting me go, he holds me tighter, until we're spooning.

"Goodnight." He shuts off the lamp and kisses my shoulder.

I register him blowing a series of short breaths, like he's trying to calm himself.

"Tynan?"

"Hmm?" He burrows closer to me.

"I'm okay."

He releases a rough exhale, holding me even closer. "Tell me about that tattoo on your hip, the one of the flower."

A sad smile paints my lips. "My mother loved poppies. She'd fill our home with them." I laugh mournfully. "Those flowers made her happy, and as much as I miss her, I miss those flowers too. They were like a part of her."

He holds me tighter as I go on.

"One day she asked if I wanted to get a tattoo with her, and of course, I said yes. So we both got the small red poppy on our hips."

"I'm sorry." He kisses the back of my head, and my lashes fall to a close, feeling that kiss drown my body in warmth.

"Me too. This tattoo is the one thing I have left of my mother. One last thing we did together." Tears sting my eyes.

I hate that the tattoo is right next to my scar, though it offers me some comfort in some weird way. Because I could've died that day, yet I'm still alive, and maybe that's all because of her. Maybe she was watching over me that day. Maybe there's a reason I'm still here.

He doesn't say another word, but he lets out a heavy breath, as though he understands my pain all too well.

Yet how could he?

His palm splays across my abdomen and his lips softly land on the back of my head yet again.

And for once, I feel calm, like this is where I belong.

With this man.

In his arms, holding me until I close my eyes.

Until it's safe to fall asleep because maybe, for once, I've found a man who'll protect me.

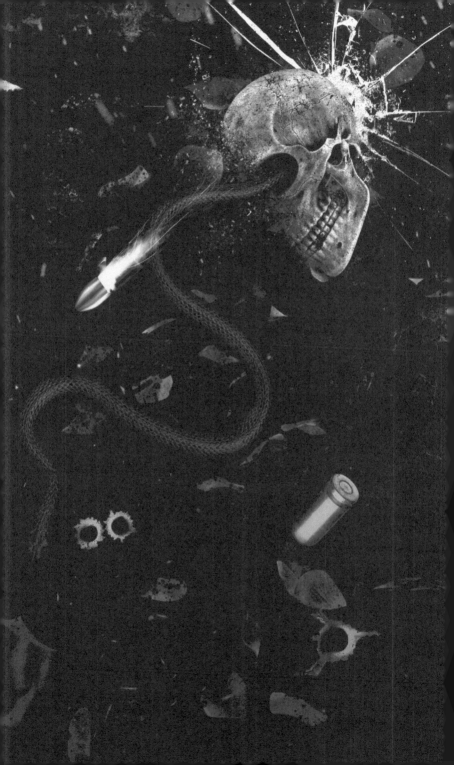

# TWENTY-ONE

## ELARA

An alarm rings beside me, and I peel my eyes open, lids heavy, stretching my limbs over the silky soft sheets. By the time we went to bed, I barely got any sleep.

Exhaustion hits me like a truck, though I can't skip work. Groaning, I look over to find the space beside me empty.

I guess he left already. What does a Mob boss even do every day?

It's six in the morning, according to the clock on the wall, and I have to be at school in an hour and a half.

When I get up, I notice a small vase on the nightstand that wasn't there before, and inside it is a bouquet of red poppies.

Tears fill my eyes, a trembling hand rushing up to my quivering mouth.

I can't seem to catch my breath from my soft cries.

He got me poppies.

Somehow, before I woke up, he managed to get them and made sure I saw them first thing in the morning.

What is he trying to do to me? I want to run and find him, to throw my arms around him and thank him. Because this was really sweet.

Brushing my tears away, I head for the door, and it's then I notice my luggage in the far corner of the room.

He made sure my things were here for me too, just as he promised.

I move toward his closet, opening the door to find a large walk-in space. My hand falls across my chest when I notice that all my clothes have already been hung, with my shoes neatly lined up on one side, not that I have that many. I didn't want too much to run with.

I don't have as many clothes as he does either. Suits and pants and t-shirts are organized by color.

How in the world did he get all this in here without waking me? Were his men in the bedroom while we slept?

I don't like that. I need to ask him about it. But first, I really want to thank him for the flowers.

Rummaging for an outfit, I settle on a pair of black dress pants and a baby-blue blouse. Putting on a light touch of makeup and running my fingers through my hair, I'm finally ready. Heading down the stairs, I hear Ruby.

"Come on, Bubbles. Be a good girl and drop my apron."

I stifle a laugh just as I make it the last step, and from my right, I see him strutting over to me.

"How'd you sleep?"

When we lock eyes, my heart gives a little leap. And all these thoughts instantly rush into my head. Remembering the way he held me last night, how good it felt.

Yet I can't forget why I'm here to begin with.

Because no matter how sweet his gestures have been, he still kidnapped me. He still forced me to marry him. How do I forget that?

I refuse to let him think I'll fall in line and pretend this is okay.

No matter how good it feels when he's touching me.

"I slept like shit. Your mattress is terrible."

A lie. A complete and utter lie. The mattress was heavenly. I wish I could go back and sleep on it some more.

"I'm sorry about that." His jaw tenses.

"It's fine." Clearing my throat, I push my hair back with a finger, moving the strands away from my eye. "Thanks for the flowers. They're beautiful."

"It's not a problem. I know your mother felt like home. I wanted to bring a piece of her here to you. So that maybe one day this house can feel like a home too."

"Tynan…" Emotions well in my chest.

I can't handle him being this nice to me. I want him to be what I would expect from someone in the Mafia: someone cruel and heartless.

But Tynan Quinn? He's shattering every perceived notion I held about him.

I shove down the emotions stitching up my throat. "Thank you for having all my clothing when I woke up too. But, uh…" My face flushes.

"What is it?" He cups my cheek.

I instantly close my eyes, and somewhere inside me, I want to believe that this—whatever this is—could be something real.

"I wanted to ask if maybe the next time your men are in our bedroom while I'm sleeping, you wake me up first?"

Confusion settles in his brows. "What do you mean?"

"Well, that's how my clothes got here, right? You said your people packed my stuff from the house?"

"They did, but I'm the one who brought them to our bedroom." He tucks his other palm across my face, his eyes staring intensely. "You think I'd allow other men into our space while you're asleep? I'd burn their eyes before they'd be allowed to see my wife lying in our bed, looking as good as you did when I woke up this morning."

His thumb brushes over my lower lip, his eyes following its

movement.

A heady pulsating need burns between my thighs.

*My wife.*

It sounds so good when he says it.

"You mean you did all that?" My lips part.

And my heart? It beats against my ribs, waiting for his answer.

He nods. "I woke up a few hours before you to make sure it was done as promised. I tried to be as quiet as possible. I hope I didn't wake you."

"No, you didn't," I whisper. "Thank you."

He did that…for me.

Why is he such a complicated man? How does he go from the man who chased me down and drugged me just to marry him to a man who would get my mother's favorite flowers, who'd wake up early just to make sure I had all my stuff ready when I woke up?

He lowers his arms and slides a hand through mine. "Let's go get breakfast before you have to leave for work. I have a meeting I need to get to shortly, but I want us to all eat together before I do."

As soon as Brody sees me, his eyes light up. Ruby looks questioningly between us.

Tynan pulls a stool for me and helps me up, clearing his throat. "Elara and I are married. She's going to be living here."

*Way to drop the bomb, husband.*

Ruby jerks back, while Brody's little mouth pops open, staring between us with bewilderment. And I'm not quite sure if that's good or bad.

"Congratulations, you two!" Ruby's shocked expression transforms to a happy one as she embraces us both. "I'm so thrilled to have you here." She pats my hand, her kindness radiating through her eyes. "If you don't like how I do things around here, you just let me know and we can fix that right up."

"Oh…" I throw a hand in the air. "I'm not hard to please. Don't worry about me."

"You're the woman of the house now, Mrs. Quinn. Whatever you say goes."

From the corner of my eye, Tynan's mouth twitches, and I try to control the butterflies soaring in my gut.

He heads for the coffee machine, making two cups, while I stare at all the breakfast options: bacon, eggs, crepes, and muffins.

So this is how the rich live.

"Now, you guys enjoy your breakfast," Ruby says. "If you need me, I'll be down the hall in the laundry room."

"You're not eating with us?"

"Oh, no. I ate while I was cooking. But you all enjoy."

She darts out of the room while Tynan makes me a plate, dropping it in front of me just before sitting beside me with his own. "She lives here, so you'll be seeing a lot of her."

"She seems nice. How does she have the misfortune of working for you?"

"You're funny." He hikes a brow. "I met her when I was doing a deal at a hotel and saw how badly she was being treated. So I offered her a job, and she took it. That was five years ago."

"Does she have family?"

He shakes his head. "Her only son died in the Army, and her husband passed away years before."

"That's so sad," I whisper.

"We're her family now."

"I can see that."

Brody continues to stare at us with bulging eyes, like he really can't believe this. I don't blame him, because neither can I.

"This must be confusing for you," I tell him. "But I promise, I'm still going to be your teacher. I'll just be living here."

"Right," Tynan throws in. "I'm sure you'll like having Ms.—" He chuckles. "I mean Mrs. Quinn all to yourself after school."

"But…" I turn toward him and narrow my eyes before looking back at poor—probably confused—Brody. "I'll still be Ms. Hill at school."

"For now," he says, and I swear I'm about to take a fork to his eye.

"Do you have any questions?" I ask Brody.

He shakes his head.

"Great. Let's all eat now," Tynan adds.

I force myself to pop some bacon into my mouth, and as soon as it hits my tongue, I groan slightly. I must admit this is the best piece of bacon I have ever tasted.

"Good, I know. Ruby is the best cook around." He takes a sip of his coffee before he reaches into his pants pocket. "I almost forgot to give you this before I go."

He hands me a credit card.

I stare blankly at it.

"It's a credit card. Not a bomb."

"Why are you giving it to me?"

"To use?"

"You already set up that account for me. I don't want any more of your money, Tynan." I peek at a curious Brody before I continue with a whisper. "I appreciate the flowers, the clothes, and the cards. But you can't just buy me with money. It's not gonna work. I'm not that woman."

Am I being ungrateful?

*He forced you to marry him! Of course you're not!*

He groans. "For fuck's sake, Elara. I'm trying, okay? I want you to be happy. Just because I told you I won't love you doesn't mean I don't want to take care of you, and this is just one way I can do that." He roughs a hand through his hair. "Just take the damn card. That money I set up in your account is for you to save."

He places it in front of me. "There's no limit on it. Unless you spend over five hundred in one day, my bank doesn't even call me, so buy whatever you want for you, your grandparents. Whatever you need."

"Five hundred dollars? Why would I need to spend that much?"

He's already giving me enough to cover my grandfather's housing costs. And I can pay for Gran's place easily now too. I don't need his credit card.

He laughs. "Five hundred thousand, babe."

My eyes almost fall out. "Uh, I'm pretty sure I'll never need to spend *that* much. Ever."

"Well, if you do, I'll know about it." His mouth curves, and my God, he's so sexy. Especially when he smiles like that.

I take the card just to get him off my back and place it in my wallet. Releasing a sigh, I glance down at my plate, before leaning into him, lowering my tone so that Brody doesn't overhear.

"Is there any chance you would reconsider?"

"Reconsider what?"

"This!" I gesture between us with a hand. "Please, Tynan," I implore with every ounce of my being, dropping my mouth closer to his ear. "I can't be your wife. I can't do this."

He cuts a piece of bacon and places it into his mouth, staring at me with indifference. I know I shouldn't talk about any of this in front of Brody at all, but I'm desperate. I need him to let me go. To stop this madness once and for all.

"Eat before your food gets cold." He continues to act as though I've said nothing at all, and that only enrages me further.

Pushing his plate back, he rises, giving Brody a kiss on top of his head. "I'll see you after school, buddy." He gives me a quick glance. "Can you take him to school with you?"

I nod.

"Thanks. And, Elara?"

"Yeah?"

"I know this seems like the end of the world right now, but you'll see. It won't be so bad."

Then he's walking away, leaving my soul aching and bruised. Because this is not what I want, and he doesn't seem to give a shit. And for that, I can't forgive him.

# TWENTY-TWO

## TYNAN

I didn't expect Elara not to fight this. Anyone in her position would. I need to give her time. I know that. And luckily, we have all the time in the world. All I needed was to get married, and now my father's seat will be mine.

I don't even know why I care about her or why I'm trying so hard to ensure her happiness. When the hell did a woman's happiness ever matter to me? Yeah, she's my wife, but not because I want her to be.

She's a means to an end.

That's all.

Picking up the phone, I call my personal shopper.

She answers on the first ring. "Sir? How may I help you?"

"I need a new mattress. Top of the line. Soft. Comfortable."

"But, sir, you already have that."

"Then get me another. And make it today. Do you understand?"

"Uh, yeah, of course. Whatever you need."

I hang up and run a hand down my face. I didn't like Elara telling me she wasn't comfortable in our bed. Hopefully she sleeps better tonight.

I make another call, this time to my sister Iseult for advice. Not how I wanted to begin my day, but I have to start telling the rest of my family that I'm married.

"Hey, big bro. What can I do for you?"

Blowing out an exhale, I know I'm about to regret asking her. Yet she's the one person I can go to for this.

"What are the best high-end clothing stores for women in Boston?"

We know many people in the fashion world, but I can't keep track of what women wear these days.

She bursts out in a laugh. "Now, that is one question I never thought I'd ever hear from your mouth."

"Just shut it and tell me, will you?"

"Why?" Her voice quirks. "Have a secret girlfriend you're keeping from me?"

I groan in frustration. "No."

"I figured."

"I've got a wife."

Silence. Complete and utter silence.

"Um, what? Are you pranking me? Because that's a stupid joke."

"Not a prank. Got married last night."

She exhales a laugh. "I'm sorry. Back up a second. You married someone and I wasn't invited? Does Dad know? And who the *hell* is she?"

I pinch the bridge of my nose. "He doesn't know. Yet. But he will tonight. I messaged him earlier to come over for dinner. Planned on texting Eriu next. Your text probably got lost."

"Ha-ha," she scoffs. "So, who is this woman?"

"Brody's teacher."

"Shit… She married you? Willingly?"

"Mmm. Not exactly. I kinda broke in, kidnapped her, and forced her to marry me. I did get a priest, though."

"Aww," she gushes sarcastically. "You're *so* romantic."

"Shut up, Iz."

"I'm surprised she hasn't killed you yet. I would've by now."

"She's not you."

"I can change that. Just give me five minutes with her."

I can just see a grin on her face.

"She hates me, understandably, but we both needed this."

"Are you sure about that? Seems like you're the one who needed it and you're just using her. Not cool, bro. Not cool."

"Well, it's done, so…" I let out a sigh, knowing she's right about it all. I needed Elara more than she needed me. "I didn't do it just for me. It was for Brody too. He likes her. She's got him smiling, Iseult. Can you even imagine that? What if she's the key to get him to talk?"

Her silence returns, yet only for a moment. "You can't have a marriage like that and expect her to be happy."

"I wanna try."

"You're so fucked. But I love you anyway." She laughs. "As far as stores, tell me about her style first."

"I don't fucking know. She dresses classy. You know, blouses and knee-length skirts. I mean, she works at a school. I've seen her in jeans and tanks when she's not working. She's not flashy or anything like that."

"Okay, so I'd try Carolina Herrera. Call Vera."

"Thanks. I'll arrange an appointment."

"I can't wait to meet her tonight. We'll drive in with Eriu and Devlin."

"Just don't embarrass me."

"That's what sisters are for. Oh, and congratulations. Don't fuck it up."

She ends the call while I'm already dreading being around my entire family and all the questions they're gonna have.

# ELARA

All day while here at school, all I can think about is this ring on my hand and what it means for my future.

How will I get away from a man like Tynan, especially with Rogue trailing me?

Staying isn't an option, but I can't leave right away either. I need him to think I've accepted this life. Until he lets his guard down.

Because someone like that assumes he always has the upper hand. Though I've escaped men just as bad and lived to tell about it.

When I've dismissed all of the kids, I take Brody with me, strapping him into the car seat Tynan already installed in my sedan.

I had a talk with the principal about my marriage, and he was happy for me, which was strange, because I swear I thought I was walking into my last day here at school.

Rogue approaches my vehicle, his expression tight as always. "Ma'am, Mr. Quinn called and said I am to take you shopping today."

"He what? Why?"

I already have all my things. What else do I need? Maybe some more underwear…

"I don't know. Should we call him?"

I release a frustrated sigh. "No, it's fine." I look down at Brody. "We're going shopping, bud. Isn't that exciting?"

He shrugs. Basically how I feel about shopping. I much prefer to buy things online and return what I don't like.

"You can follow me, ma'am."

"Okay. Yeah, sure."

I head to the driver's side, securing my seat belt and fixing my mirror before I start after Rogue. I probably should've asked him where we're going, but it doesn't matter to me. I'll just grab a few things and be done with it.

When he stops at an unmarked warehouse building, I grow concerned. What the hell is this? It's not a store. That's obvious.

He gets out first, and I roll my window open.

"Where are we, Rogue?"

"This is a commercial building owned by Mr. Quinn. He asked the owner of the store to bring all of their clothes here for you to try on."

"Oh… Did he say which store?"

"Carolina Herrera, I think. Hope I pronounced it right."

My mouth goes slack and I swallow down my shock. "Could you give me a minute to speak with him, please?"

"Take your time, ma'am."

I call him immediately, and he answers right away.

"Have you gotten to the store yet?"

"You mean some shady-looking warehouse? Yes, I'm here."

"Why do you sound mad?"

"Because," I whisper-shout. "I told you I don't need things, Tynan. I have everything I need already. I can just imagine how much this stuff costs."

He blows out a frustrated breath. "You don't seem to get it. You're my wife now. That means something not only to me, but to the outside world as well."

"What does that mean?"

"It means you have to dress the part and act the part. Do you understand?"

I glance down at myself. "Is there something wrong with my clothes?"

"No, babe. I like your clothes. In fact, after what I saw, I much prefer you out of them, though when we're in public or social events, when other women are wearing designer shit, I don't want them thinking I'm not taking care of you."

I scoff. "I don't care what they think. But fine, I'll play your game, since I don't have much say in anything, it seems."

He groans. "Of course you do, Elara. But you have to give a little. It's just how it is now."

"Fine. I'll go spend a ton of your money."

"*Our* money. How's Brody?"

"He's absolutely fine. Just as excited about shopping as I am."

He chuckles, knowing I'm being sarcastic. "Alright, well, try to enjoy yourself. I'll see you at home. Oh, and before I forget, you're meeting my family tonight."

"Great! One big, happy family. How exciting."

"There's that feisty mouth I enjoy. They're gonna love you, don't worry."

"I'm not worried about them loving me. Will I love them is the question."

"Guess we'll find out. Have a good time shopping." His tone turns husky. "Can't wait to see what you get."

And when we're talking this way, it almost feels as though this is an actual relationship.

"I've gotta go." I shut my eyes and breathe in slowly, overwhelmed by all my emotions: hating him, liking him, wanting him.

"Call if you need me. Anytime." Then the line goes dead.

"Okay, Brody, seems like we'll be going inside."

He undoes his seat belt and jumps out, while I get out and shut my door.

"Thanks for coming with me. I definitely wouldn't have fun if you weren't here."

His small smile grows.

"Come on, let's go." I grin, grabbing his hand and walking over to Rogue, who takes us inside the building.

"Hello there!" An older woman, maybe in her fifties, greets me.

She looks like one of those highbrow kinds of women, dressed in a white blouse that probably cost more than my weekly paycheck, her blonde hair coiled up in a perfect bun.

"I'm Vera, and you must be Mrs. Quinn. It's a pleasure!" She takes my hands in hers and air-kisses both sides of my face.

"Thanks. Nice to meet you too." I glance around the large space with shiny marble flooring, a glistening chandelier overhead, and racks of clothes, bags, and shoes all around us.

"We have arranged a wide variety of items, per Mr. Quinn's request. You may follow me so I can show you some of the pieces we have waiting for you in the dressing room."

"Sure." I glance back at Brody, sitting near Rogue.

"I'll watch him, ma'am. Don't worry."

"I'll be out in a sec, okay, buddy?"

Brody nods, looking a little sad.

My heart sinks. I hate leaving him, but it's Rogue and he works for Tynan, so I know he's in good hands.

When she takes me back there, I expect to find a tiny dressing room; instead it's huge, with so many outfits waiting for me.

"Mr. Quinn mentioned you would need not only work attire, but casual and evening wear as well." She picks up a long black silk gown.

I don't even want to look at the price tag, yet I find myself grabbing it.

*Holy fucking shit.*

$9,990.

I mean they could've just rounded up. Ten thousand dollars for a single dress? I can't even fathom that sort of money.

She gives me a concerned look. "If you don't like anything in this assortment, I have plenty more for you to try on."

"Oh…" I laugh nervously. "It's not that. I'm just not used to all of this."

Her mouth forms a tight line. "Understandable, but you're a lucky girl. Now why don't you start trying things on, hmm?"

"Okay, sure. Thanks."

She exits and shuts the door while I look around at all these clothes hanging around me.

My mother never wore designer, and neither have I. I've always felt it was crazy to spend so much on something you wear, but now, looking at the beautiful pieces, I can't help wanting them. What does that make me?

I start removing my clothes and slide into a black pencil dress that would be perfect for work. When I look at the price tag, my pulse spikes. Two grand. For one dress. I mean, better than ten, but still…

So much good could be done with this kind of money. I feel almost selfish for buying this stuff.

Except when I put it on and look at myself in the mirror…it's beautiful. A pair of nude pumps lies on the floor beside ten other pairs of shoes, and I slip into them before exiting the dressing room.

"Wow!" Vera gushes. "Look at you!"

She's not alone this time. Two other store reps stand beside her. One, though…she doesn't seem to like me, unless that scowl is just her face.

"Thank you." I run my hands down the soft material. "I'll definitely take this one."

"Great!"

"Will you actually show me where the bathroom is?"

Probably should take this dress off first before I dirty it, but I don't think I can wait.

"Of course! Just go past the room and turn right."

"Thanks." I start toward that direction while the women enter the dressing room beside mine.

Realizing I forgot my handbag, I take a step backward when I hear them talking.

"I have no idea what he sees in her," one of the women says to the other. "I mean, she's not even that pretty."

Another one laughs. "You're just jealous he turned you down."

"Now, ladies, it isn't our business who he chose to marry," Vera says. "Though I do agree with you, darling. I don't think she's anything special. Not for someone like Tynan, anyway. Clearly, she married him for money, but why he chose her, I can't possibly understand."

"Maybe she's good in the bedroom."

They all laugh, and my face heats up.

One of the women snickers. "Or maybe he's an idiot. He could've had me, and he settled for her? God!"

"Well, sweetheart, I doubt it will last long between them. Then you can have your chance. We're always attending many of the same events. I'm sure you can seduce him."

Anger radiates within me, and I force my feet to move, wanting them to hear me approaching. I'm no longer interested in this dress or anything they have to offer.

When they register my footsteps, they dart out of the room. Vera's face turns as red as the lipstick she's wearing. She clears her throat while I try to control the tremble in my hands.

How dare they speak about Tynan and me that way?

"There you are." Vera scratches her temple. "We'll be right here when you need us."

My mouth lifts at the corner, my eyes narrowing. "Actually, I've decided I no longer like any of these clothes. But I will be keeping this dress, and the shoes too."

Vera's brows shoot up. "Uh, that's all you want? B-but we have all these fabulous items lined up for you to try on."

I step up to her, almost face-to-face, and that younger woman who was scowling earlier, the one who wants my husband…well, she looks terrified now.

I stare at Vera with a tight glare. "I wouldn't want someone like me tarnishing your wonderful clothing." Her face pales. "It seems like you ladies had a lot to discuss when you thought I couldn't hear you."

"I…ugh, I'm…I'm so sorry, Mrs. Quinn! Please forgive us. My daughter, she's just jealous that Mr. Quinn didn't want her and—"

"Mom!"

"You hush. You've done enough damage."

"I'm not interested in your fake apologies," I tell her. "I'll be going now, and you won't be charging me a dime."

She grabs my arm. "Please don't tell Mr. Quinn about this!"

I laugh, throwing her hand off of me.

"Please. I'll do anything you want."

"How about go to hell?" I take my things from the dressing room and head toward Rogue and Brody, my heartbeats exploding in my chest.

Once Rogue sees my expression, he straightens his back, his eyes narrowing, staring behind me at the women. "What happened?"

"Nothing much." I raise my chin and pretend their words hold no power, yet that's a lie. "They were insulting me while they thought I was in the bathroom. I just wanna leave."

A muscle flexes in his jaw. "Let's go."

I grab Brody's hand, who glares at them, and if my heart didn't love him already, this just did it.

I know I shouldn't let those women get to me, but is that how they see me? Some ugly gold-digger? Not that I think I'm ugly, but their words still hurt.

The whole ride back, I try to get what they said out of my head and focus on preparing to meet Tynan's family tonight.

Is that how they're gonna see me too?

# TWENTY-THREE

## TYNAN

Rogue just texted me that they've arrived at the warehouse. I drop the phone on my desk just as my brothers walk in. "Hey. What's up?" Fionn settles on the sofa.

"What are we doing here?" Cillian takes a spot beside him.

"I need you to do a deeper dive into Elara."

"Why?" Fionn asks.

"Elara isn't her real name. It's Evelyn Connors. I need to know what she's been running from and why. Look up her parents, grandparents, friends. Anyone you can find. She's from New Jersey, I think. So start there."

"You think she's involved with something?" Cillian drops his elbows on his knees.

"I hope not." I spin my gold band on my ring finger. "By the way, you're coming over for dinner tonight."

"We are?" Fionn leans back into the leather.

"I've gotta tell everyone else that I'm married," I mutter.

Cillian chuckles. "Don't look so excited about it. It's a good thing. Now Dad can leave you the fuck alone."

"Right…until he starts pestering me about something else."

"Well, I, for one, can't wait to get to know my sister-in-law." Fionn grins. "Feels like I already know her from all the photos and shit we've gathered on her so far."

"Yeah, and make sure she never finds out."

"She won't. But listen, why don't you also ask Grant to look into her? He can find anything."

I consider that. Grant Westfield is a friend of Gio Marino, Iseult's husband. He's the best hacker around. It also doesn't hurt that he owns Westfield Enterprises, which created the most popular cellphone currently on the market, and some other tech shit like memory chips. His company is also very heavily involved in AI. He has access to everything. And not all of it is legal. Rumor is when he was in high school, he hacked the CIA database. He's a damn genius. I hate getting someone outside the family involved, but it could help.

"That's a good idea. I'll do that. Though I want you guys looking into her too. Don't pass it on to our IT guys. I don't want anyone knowing anything about her."

They both nod just as my phone rings, and I find Rogue on the caller ID.

"Yeah? Everything okay?"

"No, sir. We just left the store. Apparently, the women were insulting her while they didn't think she heard. She's very upset."

"They *what*?" My fingers curl at my side. "What did they say?"

"She wouldn't tell me."

"I'm on my way home." I hang up the phone, ready to rip those women's throats out.

Vera owns the Carolina Herrera store in Boston. She's known my family for years. And she has the audacity to insult my wife?

"I need you to do something for me," I immediately tell my

brothers, knowing that woman will regret what she did.

I write down the address and give them the instructions.

Fionn grins. He lives for this.

"What did she do?"

"Hurt my wife."

"Should it look like an accident?'"'

I nod.

"We'll get it done." Cillian starts to rise.

Vera's about to learn a very hard lesson about what happens when you fuck with what's mine.

# ELARA

When we pull up to the driveway, I find Tynan's SUV already there. He's home? That's odd.

With Brody beside me, I step inside the foyer and find him pacing. As soon as he sees us, he rushes forward.

"Are you okay?" He clutches the side of my neck, his thumb tilting up my chin. Concern fills every inch of his face.

"Yeah, I'm fine. Why?" My pulse thumps louder at his touch.

"Rogue told me."

"Oh, that." I wave off his concern, while my heart twists as though their words put a knife into it. But I don't want him to know it hurt me. "I'm fine. I just didn't want to give them any business if that's how they treat their customers."

"Brody…" He roughs his hair. "Why don't you go see Ruby in the kitchen? She made you a snack before dinner."

He nods and gives me one last long look before he rushes away, leaving me alone with my concerned husband.

That's a strange feeling, to have him act as though he cares. Never had a man do that before.

"Elara, look at me." He nestles my face in both hands. "What did they say? I need to know."

I shut my eyes for a moment, grabbing on to his wrist. "Just that they don't know what you see in me, that I'm probably a gold-digger and too unattractive for you. That you must be blind and how Vera's daughter should seduce you."

"Her daughter? What a joke." His wrath sparks in his irises, simmering and deadly. "You do realize you're the most beautiful woman that I've ever laid eyes on, right? I'm not just saying that."

My stomach clenches, but I shrug in response, emotions coating my eyes.

"Say it, Elara." His thumbs glide across my cheeks. "Because I need you to know that and accept it. You're beautiful."

A faint smile paints my lips. "Okay, yes, I'm beautiful."

My heart thuds faster when his mouth nears mine.

"You're *so* damn beautiful." His body moves closer, pushing me up against the door. "I could never do better than you."

Lips fall to my throat, latching on as I gasp, my fingers raking through his hair as he lays kisses over my raging pulse.

"Tynan…we shouldn't, not when someone could walk in."

A growl permeates through the room. "Let them." He grabs the hem of my dress and starts dragging it up. "I like this. We need to get more."

"It's the only one I got before I left. And I didn't pay a dime." I grin with a moan as his finger snaps into my cotton thong and he shoves it to the side.

He hungrily peers down at me with a proud smirk as he eases a finger inside me, causing my eyes to roll back. "That's it, baby. Let me touch you."

Then he's thrusting inside me, deeper and deeper, yet slow enough for me to feel everything.

"I love how wet you get for me, little serpent. I can't wait to watch you lose yourself when I'm inside you."

Those words, they send a pulse throbbing to my achy center.

On instinct, my hand wraps around his thick length, and I feel something through his trousers…

"Are those…" My eyes expand.

"If you're wondering if I'm pierced, yes, I am." He chuckles huskily. "And I'm gonna enjoy watching you take each one."

"Oh, God…"

His fingers slide in and out in a hurried rhythm, while his other palm snaps around my throat, squeezing until every bit of air I take is with his permission.

"You drive me crazy, Elara. So fucking insane," he growls against my ear, and I combust into flames.

His grunts, the way he thrusts into me, the feeling he gives me when he owns me and controls my body the way only he can…I can't get enough of it.

That hand wrapped around my throat only intensifies it all.

"I want to flip you over and fuck you up against this wall. But I won't." The pads of his fingers squeeze deeper into my neck. "Not until you ask for it."

"And what if I never do?" I'm barely able to get the words out.

His chuckle is rough, coated with his own arousal. "Oh, you will, babe. And I can't wait for that day."

When his thumb plays with my clit, the pleasure becomes too strong, and I'm unable to stop myself from moaning, the air filling with my desire.

I can register Rogue talking to one of the guards right outside the door, can hear Ruby saying something to Brody in the kitchen. Anyone could walk in and find us like this.

Except I can't stop myself, my groans dripping in ecstasy. He eases his fingers out, then back in halfway, edging me in the most torturous way.

When the sounds I make start getting louder, he clasps a palm around my mouth and smirks.

"When we're in our bedroom, I'll let you scream my name as loud as you want, but right now, be a good girl and keep quiet."

With his gaze aligned with mine, he pistons inside me, hard and deep, until I'm shaking and whimpering, biting his palm to stop myself from screaming his name.

He doesn't stop, keeping me prisoner against the door as he shatters me to pieces, my unending release washing over me until it ebbs and flows to a steadier rhythm.

My exhales scatter in waves as he slides out of me, filling my mouth with his fingers, forcing me to suck them as he watches with intensity.

"Fucking gorgeous," he grits, his own desire evident in his tone.

He removes his fingers and I can't seem to catch my breath.

Dragging my dress down, he takes my hand in his, bringing the top of it to his lips. "Come on, take your shoes off and relax for a bit before my family arrives and drives you insane."

I let out a weak laugh, still dizzy from that orgasm. "I have to call my grandma and tell her the delightful news. I haven't told her yet."

"I think she'll be happy. Oh, and I already called her earlier and invited her over." He looks smugly at me. "Unlike you, she actually likes me."

"Yeah, that's what I'm afraid of." Then it hits me. "Wait, did you tell her we were married?"

"Nah." He shakes his head. "I figured I'd leave that to you."

"And what do you suppose I tell her? 'Hey, Gran, remember that scary man from the café? Well, he kidnapped me and made me marry him. Surprise!'"

"I'm sure you'll come up with something a bit more romantic."

"How about, 'I woke up in his bed wearing a four-carat ring.'"

"Hmm." He considers it, a playful look on his face. "Now we're getting somewhere."

I roll my eyes. "You're annoying."

"Wasn't annoying a second ago." He runs the fingers that were just inside me over his nose.

My face turns crimson.

This is gonna be a long night.

Hopefully Gran doesn't say anything too embarrassing.

# TWENTY-FOUR

## ELARA

The doorbell rings, and my eyes round. The first of the Quinn family have just arrived.

Tynan looks over at me, reaching his hand for mine. "Come on. Don't be shy now."

"I'm not shy." My fingers slip through his, and I grow warm all over. "Just never met a bunch of mobsters before."

"You met the worst there is." His mouth twitches. "The rest are not so bad. Except Iseult. She's…well, an acquired taste."

"And that's…"

"My sister. I have two. She's the older one."

"Gotcha."

Hopefully she isn't as bad as he's making her sound.

Together we head for the door. When he opens it, I find an older man with Tynan's eyes and a woman, not much younger, fixing her shoulder-length brown hair.

They both stare at me inquisitively. Did he not tell them who I am?

Oh my God…

"Come in." Tynan moves aside to let them in before he shuts the door. "Let me introduce you to my wife, Elara."

I think their eyes are about to fall out of their sockets. Don't blame them. Who doesn't tell his family he got married?

Oh, right.

A man who forced a woman to do it.

In the middle of the night.

In a pair of sweats and messy hair.

The only thing we were missing was a photographer to capture the lovely moment.

"Elara, this is my father, Patrick, and his wife, Fernanda."

*His wife.*

So that's not his mother. I wonder where his mom is…

"Wife? You two got married? Without us?" His dad can't seem to erase the shock on his face. "You must excuse me." He coughs a laugh, his Irish accent hard to miss. "My son doesn't tell his old man anything. Feels like I just saw him, and he didn't tell me at all about his plans."

"It happened quickly," Tynan mutters, clearly wanting this conversation to end. "We didn't have time to invite anyone."

Fernanda's shrewd, dark eyes connect with mine. I force a smile, hoping she believes this is real. Or doesn't assume I'm pregnant or something.

"Well, congratulations, son." Patrick palms his shoulder before he and Fernanda both hug me, congratulating me too.

"So, how long have you two known each other?" Fernanda asks, looking between us.

*Crap. Crap. Think!*

"Umm…" I peek at Tynan for help, expanding my eyes a bit so he gets the hint. "How long would you say, honey?"

I hook my arm through his, tugging him to me, grinning at him like a complete idiot. A completely in love idiot. Or that's the story we're selling.

"Give or take, three weeks, right?" A slow smirk spreads across his face as he gazes at me. "I guess when you know, you know."

His father chuckles. "That's right, son. I'm glad you've finally come to your senses. Time was ticking."

Right. He needed this to secure his position, so of course his father is pleased. I'm sure he doesn't care how Tynan found me as long as he did.

"How did you two meet?" He raises his brows, shooting us both with a confrontational stare.

"Um…" I don't know if I'm allowed to tell them who I am or how I knew Tynan before he stuck a ring on my finger.

"She's Brody's teacher."

"Wow!" Fernanda looks over at her husband. "How crazy is that? Right, Pat?"

"Well, I definitely never expected that." He takes my hand in both of his. "But I've heard about you through my other boys, and I know how good you are to our Brody. I'm thankful that he has you."

My cheeks heat up. "I adore Brody. He's just so easy to love."

His mouth quirks, his gaze filling with affection before he's peering at his son. "She's a keeper." He gestures to me with a tilt of his head.

"Yeah…" He kisses my temple. "It's why I married her."

"Aww, this is so beautiful." Fernanda pats under her eyes. "You remember us like this back then, Pat? How in love we were?"

He wraps her in his arms and gazes deep into her eyes. "And how in love we still are, lass."

My heart melts at the sight of them. There's clearly history here I don't know.

Tynan releases a dramatic exhale, causing me to laugh.

"Stop it." I swat his chest. "They're cute."

"See, son? We're cute. Listen to your lady." He tugs Fernanda to his side and kisses her temple, just like Tynan did to me.

And it wasn't the first time either. I remember he kissed me that way when he was intimidating Vincent at my school. Is that where he learned it? From his father?

I hold him just a bit tighter, causing him to look down at me with a puzzled expression.

"So, lovebirds, will there be a wedding?" Fernanda asks.

"Only if that's what Elara wants." Tynan's eyes go to mine, and images of me in a white dress, him in a tux waiting for me at the altar, make my pulse quicken.

But I can't. It would be another sham.

"I'm not much of a wedding girl." I grimace. "I'm sorry."

"Oh." Fernanda almost pouts. "That's okay."

"You have to excuse my beautiful wife," Patrick says. "She loves a good party."

"Can you blame me? There's just something so beautiful about weddings…" She sighs. "If you change your mind, please let me know. I would be happy to plan it all."

"Thank you, we will." I smile politely, feeling bad about disappointing her.

I like them. They seem normal. Definitely don't give me the "we're in the Mafia" vibes. Then again, you never really know anyone.

The doorbell rings again.

"We'll go inside while you two greet everyone," Patrick says, taking Fernanda with him.

This time, when Tynan opens the door, there are four people I've never seen before.

A beautiful, tall redhead is holding a cactus, smirking at Tynan, while beside her stands an even taller man with dark eyes and even darker hair. He looks a lot like Fernanda…

Could it be?

"I'm Gio Marino, and this is Iseult, my absolutely beautiful wife."

She rolls her eyes and elbows him, strutting past us. Everyone follows her before Tynan shuts the door.

"Shouldn't I be introducing us since this is *my* family?" She twists her face at him playfully before zeroing her attention on me while shoving the cactus at Tynan.

He takes it with a scowl.

She stretches her hand for mine. "Hey. I'm Tynan's sister, and this is my insufferable husband."

I laugh at their exchange, shaking both their hands.

"This is my other sister, Eriu, and her husband, Devlin." Tynan finally introduces the other couple.

"Nice to meet you guys. I'm Elara."

"Really happy to meet you." Devlin nods in greeting.

"We both are." Eriu grins, her irises just as green as her brother's.

There's an obvious age difference between her and Devlin. She's much younger, while Devlin is definitely around Tynan's age. I wonder if she was forced too. But from the way her face glows, I'd say she's very much in love.

Jealous.

"I really never thought my brother would get married. Right, Devlin?" She gazes up at her husband.

"That's right, mo stoirín. Guess he proved us wrong." He hides his smirk when he catches Tynan's irate gaze.

"Maybe it was a big mistake having you all here for dinner."

Iseult pats his back. "There, there, brother."

He shoves her hand away, causing her to chuckle. "Why the hell did you bring me a cactus?"

"Oh…" Her lips tilt up. "That's your wedding present."

"That's sweet," I offer.

"She's never sweet." Tynan glares at her.

"Well…" She tilts her chin. "On the way here, Eriu told me that just the other day you said, and I quote, 'I'd rather suck on a cactus than get married.' Well, here you are. Enjoy it."

She winks while he shakes his head with complete irritation.

"You did *not* say that!" I stare at him with my mouth wide open. "And here I thought you were in love with me the moment you met me. I may have to file for an annulment now." I feign being insulted, and Gio chuckles.

Tynan, though? He's not laughing. In fact, he looks like he's about ready to kill us all for torturing him. He deserves it, though.

Before we can torture him some more, the bell rings again. Tynan practically runs to open it, causing me and Iseult to fall in a fit of laughter.

She moves over to me, whispering, "I enjoy torturing him."

I stare at his ass as he opens the door. "I think I'm gonna enjoy torturing him too."

"Oh, we're gonna get along so well."

"I think you're right." My mouth curls as I glance at her before heading toward Tynan, finding Gran there with Fionn and Cillian.

Though I have met his two brothers when they stood as witnesses at our ceremony, I don't exactly know them at all.

"Elara, sweetheart!" Gran gives me a big hug, whispering in my ear. "Is that a ring on your finger?"

"Yes?"

"Oh my goodness!" she exclaims. "Congratulations, you two!" She hugs me tightly before embracing Tynan. "You take care of my girl, you hear? She's special."

"I will." He nods. "I promise."

Her eyes fill with moisture. "Such great news!"

The rest of the family greet her before Tynan says, "How about we head to the dining room? Dad and Fernanda are already there."

We shuffle after one another while Gran slides her arm through mine, both of us the last to go.

"You were smart to marry him." She glances around the foyer, beautiful paintings of mountains and nature on both sides.

"If you say so." When my eyes wander toward the far left corner, something magnificent catches my eye.

A large vase with red poppies stands at the center of a side table.

I stare at it, my heart filling with so many emotions, I can't contain it.

"Weren't those your mom's favorite?" Gran whispers.

"They were." I sniffle.

He must've had them put here today. My heart warms at the care and thought he put into this. It may seem simple, but it means so much to me.

"Isn't that sweet? I knew he'd take care of you. I knew it from the moment I met him."

My lashes flutter as a smile stretches to my face. "I'm sorry I couldn't invite you to the ceremony. It was sudden and it was just us."

She throws a dismissive hand in the air. "As long as you're happy and he's good to you, then I'm happy."

I hate keeping things from Gran. I want to tell her the whole truth of how I really got married. But telling her wouldn't help matters. It would just make her worry that he's going to be cruel. Yet so far he's been…well, good to me.

"Would you look at the size of this place?" she gushes. "You did well, Elara."

"Gran. Hush. I'm not like that."

"I know you're not, but I am." She winks. "You needed a win in your life, and whatever the case may be, he's your husband now."

"I'm just scared that the people who hurt Dad will come after Brody or Tynan."

She squeezes my fingers. "Tynan is a big boy. They don't stand a chance against him. I wouldn't worry, sweetheart. Now let's go and have fun. I want to get to know your new family!"

I groan. "Please don't say anything embarrassing."

She tips up her chin. "I would never."

Minutes later, and she's already chatting up Fionn, telling him her latest raunchy joke.

As I watch them, my arms suddenly start to prickle, every molecule in my body lighting up. I can sense him drawing near, and I don't even have to look to know he's standing right behind me.

It's like my body has made him its home and I'm just playing catch-up.

"Your grandma seems like she fits right in," Tynan whispers into my ear, stroking my arms with his palms.

"It sure seems that way."

He circles his arms around me and pins my back to his front while we watch everyone.

I glance over at Brody, sitting on the sofa with a book in hand, completely enthralled. I love that he gets lost in his books. Reminds me of myself when I was a child. Getting so drawn into the world, I'd lose all track of time until Mom would be telling me to turn my lamp off or I'd never wake up for school.

The thought of Mom instantly takes me back to the day I found her dead. My heart starts to race.

I can't let this touch Brody. I can't let anyone in this family get hurt because of me. I know for people like them, danger is probably at every corner, but I can't add my own to it. That wouldn't be right.

Jerry and his family are vicious. They would kill Brody. They have killed children before just to get to their parents. The thought makes my stomach turn.

I want to tell Tynan everything in hopes he'll let me leave. But I know to him, it won't matter. He won't let me go. He'll want to fight Jerry. Then what? Brody loses the only parent figure he has left?

Iseult catches my eye, saying something to Eriu before she separates from her little sister and heads our way.

"So…" She pops a hand on her hip. "I hope my brother has been treating you well…considering." She gives him a stern look that could cut glass.

I choke on my words, unsure how to answer that. Does she know he forced me? She must.

He groans and tugs an arm around my hips, bringing me to his side. "Treating her just fine, see?"

"Right. Well…" She leans in toward me. "If he requires a good kick in the ass, just call me. I always beat him in a fight."

Her wink makes him grunt in irritation. The sibling bickering is kinda cute. They're obviously close and she likes getting under his skin, which doesn't seem all that hard.

"We're happy to have you in the family." She definitely seems sincere, and it makes me feel just a bit better about being here.

I don't know, maybe because I don't have much family left and he's got a lot of that, I kinda wish they really were my family.

"Thank you," I tell her.

From behind her, I find Gio talking to Patrick before he slaps a hand on his back, rising to grab his wife around the waist.

She jumps in surprise before a touch of a smile makes it to her lips.

"My God, I love this woman," he groans, grabbing her jaw and kissing her hard.

"Lord, can you not maul me in public?" She rolls her eyes, but her mouth curls just a little.

He adjusts his tie and releases a weighty exhale, his dark eyes locked on his wife. "She likes to pretend she doesn't like me when others are around because she knows how much it turns me on."

"Gio!" She smacks him on the chest. "I'm sorry about him." She stares at the ceiling, shaking her head for a moment. "Every time I think I can take him out in public, he reminds me I can't." She narrows her eyes at him and tugs his wrist. "Come on, let's go before you say anything else obnoxious."

As they walk away, I whisper to Tynan, "Your sister seems nicer than you described."

"Yeah, she is. When she's not killing a man."

"Oh…" My eyes gape as she continues strutting away.

Of course she kills people for a living.

Eriu and Devlin move toward us. Devlin chuckles, slapping a hand on Tynan's back.

"So, how long until you owe me that million?"

Tynan suddenly fuses his gaze to mine, and my body shivers from the intensity.

But then he sharply turns back to Devlin, leaving me wondering what that look was about or what they're even discussing.

"Just shut up," he tells Devlin, who laughs in response.

"I find it funny that you think you have a choice."

Tynan visibly grows tense, so I decide to change the subject.

"So, Eriu, how did you and Devlin meet?" I'm actually genuinely curious.

She stares up at her husband. "Well, he used to be my bodyguard."

"Oh." I can't hide the shock on my face.

"Aye." He rounds an arm around her and pulls her in, kissing the top of her head. "She had a little crush on me."

"And by little, he means so big I wouldn't take no for an answer."

"It's what I needed." His eyes go to hers, and they're full of love. He tilts her chin up with a finger and kisses her.

Just then, Patrick clanks his glass, silencing the room as everyone's attention goes to him. "I'm so happy to have all my children here. And I'm especially happy that Tynan finally decided to settle down with such a lovely woman."

Everyone claps, and my whole face flushes.

"You've got your work cut out for ya, darling," Patrick says. "But don't worry, you've got all of us on your side. So if he needs a good kick in the arse, you just tell us."

"I already told her that." Iseult looks proud of herself.

Tynan lets out a groan, and I can't help finding it all amusing. They seem like a normal family. Not at all who they actually are.

Though, as we know, looks can be deceiving.

# TWENTY-FIVE

## TYNAN

After the night has wound down and my family has gone home, we get ready for bed. It was no surprise that everyone adored her. What's not to like about Elara? I can't think of a single thing.

My eyes drift down her body, draped in one of my t-shirts, the size practically devouring her. It's damn cute seeing her this way. Hair in a messy bun. Face bare from her makeup.

So beautiful.

My pulse grows wild.

How the hell do I stop myself from catching feelings when all I want to do is hold her?

"Why are you looking at me like that?" She clears her throat and nervously moves a piece of her loose hair behind her ear, shifting her gaze down for a moment.

"No reason." I shuffle toward the bed, foregoing my t-shirt, and fling the comforter over for her to enter first.

As she does, her shirt rides up her thighs, almost revealing her ass, and I let out an unintentional groan.

Her breath hitches, and she glances at me over her shoulder, biting her lip.

"If you're gonna keep looking at me like that, then ask me to fuck you."

My nostrils flare as she gets on top of the mattress and moves all the way to the edge, like she wants to get as far away from me as possible. Not because she's scared or repulsed, but because she feels the lust growing between us.

She sits up, gripping the comforter against her chest, her cheeks flushed. Her sweet cunt is probably already wet and begging me to taste it.

I crawl into the bed, wrapping my arm around the small of her back until her front meets mine. And I know she can feel how hard I am. I don't give a shit if she knows what she does to me. I want her to.

"Tynan…" Her breathing turns shallow, fingernails clawing my shoulders.

"I can give you what we both need, wife." I grab her jaw, leaning in until I feel her hot gasps. "I know you want me as much as I want you. You just hate to admit it."

I sink my hand into her hair, wrapping her strands around my wrist. Her chest rises, eyes searching my gaze, and my cock throbs to be inside her.

"Stubborn fucking woman." I drop my mouth even nearer, until it's just brushing hers, until every last restraint untethers and I crash her lips to mine.

Her soft feminine sounds vibrate through me until I feel them in my balls. My tongue invades between her parted lips as I suck hers into my mouth, desperately needing every inch of her.

I slide on top of her, pinning her to the bed with my weight, grinding my hips between her thighs. Our kiss turns deeper and eager, her hands everywhere, clawing into my flesh.

Want to lay claim to every cell on her body.

Want her to know she's mine.

What the hell is happening to me?

Her nails rake up my back, her shirt rising as the crown of my erection rubs against her clit. Fucking hell, I don't know how much more I can take before I own every gorgeous inch of her.

The way she's soaked for me, the way she's kissing me back…

Never felt a thing like this.

Never will.

Never want to with anyone else.

I know that to be true, no matter how much I want to deny it. It's like the walls are closing in and I can't do a thing to stop them.

I'm crazy about her. I was the moment I saw her and began to follow her. I was fooling myself into believing otherwise.

My hand slides between us, two fingers stroking her clit. Those eyes connect with mine, brows drawn in pleasure, back bowing, legs trembling. There's never been a sight more beautiful.

"Please," she begs, writhing in pleasure.

"Please who?"

I want to hear her say it. I want her to know who she belongs to.

"Tell me who I am." I push my fingers inside her, stretching her, wanting her until the need for her taste consumes me. "Say it and I'll let you come."

I piston deeper until she's a shaky mess, needing the release as badly as I do.

"H-husband…you're my husband."

"Yes…" I hiss, thrusting deeper, wishing it was my cock instead. "That's right. I'm your husband, and this is mine."

My thumb rolls over her clit as I fuck her with my fingers, her sweet pussy sucking me in deeper until she's screaming my name.

And this time I let her.

I capture her mouth, kissing her like this is the last day I'll ever get to have her. The air in my lungs fills with the taste and smell of this woman.

My wife.

My possession.

Absolutely maddening, that's what she is.

Maneuvering myself lower, I grab under her knees and bend her legs toward her stomach and her eyes grow wild.

"What are you—oh, God…" Her voice is lost to her pleasure, body twitching when my tongue takes a swipe over her clit before nudging inside her.

"Again…"

Her body bows, hands fisting the sheets while I hold her thighs flat on each side.

"You're gonna come again for me." I roll an index finger through her wetness. "So pretty and pink."

She bucks when I suck her clit into my mouth, growling with the need seeping through my veins.

She's mine.

Will always be mine.

This is forever.

"Tynan! I'm gonna come."

My groans roar through my chest, and the more she fights my hold on her, the harder I clasp her thighs apart, until a scream dies in her throat and her body jolts.

Jerking and crying out, she gives it to me, her nails scraping and digging into my scalp as she continues to come, forcing my mouth deeper into her pussy.

I let out a small chuckle, working her with my tongue until she whimpers and her body stops convulsing.

"So sexy…" I pepper kisses up her thigh, to the underside of her knee, my mouth tracing up to her scar, kissing every centimeter before I go higher.

My hand yanks up the shirt, exposing her breasts, needing to taste them too.

"Take it off," my rough voice demands as I slide over to her side.

Breathlessly, she obeys, haphazardly trying to shove it off her head, and I help her the rest of the way.

"Much better…" My gaze drinks in her wild curves, not believing that this woman is all mine. My index finger traces her sternum until she shivers. "My wife likes when I taste her, doesn't she?"

My fingertip rolls around her clit, and she pants, trying to push me off.

Fuck, my dick throbs like hell. The animal in me wants to take her. Fuck her until she's full of me.

But I won't do that. I want her to give in to me.

Her eyes land on my jutting erection, and she swallows hard.

"That's only for good girls who ask nicely. Are you gonna ask for it?"

I know she wants to. I can see it, though she refuses to say the words I desperately want to hear.

*Fine, baby. We can play this game.*

I kiss her slowly before I pin my forehead to hers. "Goodnight."

Shutting off the bedside lamp, I spoon her, wanting her skin against mine. But there's no way in hell I'll be sleeping tonight, not while my cock is begging to be inside her.

*Fuck.*

Tossing and turning, I wonder if I should go into one of the spare bedrooms and take care of my raging hard-on. I can't sleep beside her knowing she's right there, damn naked like a personal offering.

When I start to quietly get out of bed, her voice stops me.

"Tynan," she moans, thrashing her legs a little, sliding the comforter down to expose her breasts.

A brow arches when I find her calling for me in her dreams.

"Mm…" she goes on, making it harder for me to leave.

I don't want to go. I want to be right here beside her. Fucking her senseless.

"Shit," I grumble, grabbing my cock through my boxers, stroking myself to her bare body.

To the sounds she makes.

So damn crazed for her, I can't stop myself from gently dragging the comforter lower, until she's completely exposed.

She's damn right sinful.

And all mine.

The desire to worship her, to wake her up with my cock buried deep inside her, takes over until my fingertips trace up her inner thigh.

She releases a raspy cry and her head turns my way, her eyes still fastened. Carefully, I stroke a finger along her warm slit, pretty and wet.

Needing more, I open her up, shifting her legs to the sides to maneuver myself between them, until I find her pretty clit staring at me.

With my cock in a tight grip, I rub the tip against her pussy, biting my damn lip from the sensation it brings. I stroke faster through her wetness, pushing the crown inside her just a little.

"Tynan…" she cries. "Please."

But she's still asleep, wanting me even in her subconscious.

Squeezing my shaft in a tight grip, I let myself enjoy her body for a little longer, knowing that I'm gonna need the release before I grow insane.

Though not like this. No matter how good that would be.

Yet I can't stop myself.

"Fuck…." My head falls back.

This is heaven. I'd take a bullet right now and die happy if this is the last thing I feel. The last sight I see.

She continues to thrash and moan, continues to sound like a piece of heaven wrapped in the form of my wife.

My wife.

Those two words…I never needed them. Never wanted them. Now…

I'm not sure of anything anymore.

She consumes me. And that no longer scares me the way it once did.

Her body quivers when I press my cock against her clit before slowing and forcing the tip into her entrance again.

Her bottom lip trembles, her gasps louder until…

"What are you—" Her eyes pop open, words caught in her throat, gaze wandering down to where my body meets hers.

She rises on her elbows, but makes no attempt to shove me away.

All good signs.

And I can't help my wicked smirk.

"I was enjoying you while you were asleep, calling my name while you dreamed of…" I groan, stroking her clit, and her eyes roll back. "What exactly *were* you dreaming about, mo chuisle?"

"I—"

"Was it this?" I line the crown of my erection against her entrance, rubbing it there as she cries out. "Did you dream of my cock inside you, stretching this perfect pink pussy?"

"Tynan… Please, this isn't fair."

She gasps when I thrust into her just a little more.

"Never pretended to be a fair man, Elara."

She grabs my wrist, trying to pull me deeper.

"Fucking hell, what are you doing to me?"

"What do you mean?" Her eyes snap to mine, chest heaving, nipples beaded and begging for my tongue.

"What do I mean?" I lower my body on top of hers, grabbing her jaw in a tight grasp, my mouth hovering above hers. "I mean I can't get you out of my head. I can't sleep or eat or breathe without you on my mind, without needing the taste of you on my tongue and your voice in my head. You're always there, Elara. You're all I think about. Tell me how to stop it."

I force the head of my cock inside, and she tightens around me like a vise.

"Tell me how to end this torture once and for all." My mouth brushes against hers.

"Tynan…" Her needy voice only continues to set me off.

"It was never supposed to be like this, not for me."

"Please…"

"Ask your husband for his cock. I want you begging."

"It—it won't mean anything…" The spark in her eyes returns, my little serpent making an appearance.

"Ask me anyway."

Her eyes soften, her walls just starting to stretch to accommodate my thick size.

"I want to feel you," she cries. "Want to feel those piercings inside me."

"Shit." I capture her lips, kissing her roughly, her fingernails clawing up my back.

I want her to feel them too, want to feel all nine of those barbells sink inside her.

Drawing back a fraction away, I stare down at her with a maddening obsession. "I need you to know that you're mine. You'll always be mine, no matter how hard you fight it. I own you, Elara Quinn, and it's time I remind you of that."

Growling, I thrust an inch until she feels the cold sensation of the first piercing against her.

"Oh, God!" Her nails dig in deeper, and I savor the pain.

"Count them as they go inside you." I wrap my palm around my hard-on and start to push the first one in.

Her eyes grow, mouth wide open. "Oh...my God!"

"Count."

"How many?" She can barely speak, and I can't wait to watch her scream.

"Nine."

"What?" Crystal-blue eyes stare at me in shock, and a chuckle rumbles.

"Count, Elara."

She squeezes her eyes shut for a second, teeth nipping at her bottom lip. "One."

"Good girl. Keep going."

I force myself deeper, wanting to go slow so she can feel each one enter her.

"Two."

"Mm. Look how good you take it."

Her warm exhales escape in waves, her breaths catching in her throat. "So good."

"Not even close to being done with you yet."

My hips arch, and another one enters her.

"Three." Her thighs clamp around my hips. "Four... Oh God, Tynan."

She's breathless and needy, desperate to be filled and fucked.

"I'll never get the sound of you moaning my name like that out of my head." Unable to stop myself, I thrust all the way in, not giving her a second to breathe.

Her back bows, her mouth parted, a scream dying off in her throat. *So fucking hot.*

"You okay?" I seat myself inside her and stay there, needing to move so goddamn bad.

Her gaze seizes mine. "Don't stop."

*Thank fuck.*

I start to move, rolling my hips, dragging my cock all the way out, then entering harder and deeper each time.

The feeling of her—all wet and warm, the way she clings to me, gazes at me—it's more than I even imagined it would be.

It's everything.

"Yes, yes, yes, please!"

My pace increases as I lift one of her legs and drape it over my shoulder to take her even deeper.

Fuck. She feels so damn good.

Her walls close in around me, convulsing with little tremors. Bet I can make her squirt.

"Tynan, I'm…I'm coming!"

Just as I thought, her pussy spills all over, soaking the sheets like the hot fucking mess she is. She gasps, crying out in pleasure, unable to stop.

And as she does, I take in every damn moment of it, savoring the very first time I made her come on my dick. Nothing can top this.

With a growl, I capture her mouth and thrust all the way, unable to stop my beastly movements, wanting to coat her walls with my cum.

Needing to own her.

To mark her as mine.

Elara will have my baby.

And fuck, I want it now.

I fist her hair, deepening our kiss, sucking her tongue into my mouth as I release into her wet and warm cunt, grunting until she's filled to capacity.

My movements slow, and she's staring back at me with equal parts want and confusion.

"I…" Her mouth closes, and she pinches her eyes shut. "That was just sex."

But she doesn't sound all that convinced.

"Yeah, baby." My mouth curls into a smirk, my cock still inside her warmth, not wanting to leave. "Just sex."

Then I take her mouth slow, and she falls in line, hands clutching my shoulders, kissing me back with fervor.

I drop my lips to the curve of her jaw, kissing down her neck, between her breasts, as I part her legs and get to where I want to go.

With our eyes fastened, I lick her up from entrance to clit, tasting her just the way I promised I'd do. She lurches, grabbing the back of my head.

The bed beneath is soaked, and I can't help my laughter.

She groans, covering her face.

"You taste so good. You ever done that before?"

She shakes her head, refusing to look at me. It's cute how embarrassed she is. I continue to laugh, licking up the insides of her thighs, insane for this woman.

"Haven't you had enough yet?" She lowers her arm from her face and grimaces.

"Not even a little." I suck her clit into my mouth, and her back jolts up. "I rather enjoy making you come."

"Oh, God!"

I hum over her pulsing flesh. "Need it again, don't you?"

Then it's all mouth and fingers, working her as I let my tongue do all the talking. Until she's crying out and thrashing and begging.

And fuck, does she sound good begging.

"Please, please, just like that!" She yanks a fistful of my hair, dragging her hips up into my mouth.

A growl rumbles from within my chest, and I add a third finger, curling them, slamming them into that spot inside her until she's falling again, squirting all over. And this time, I taste it all, wanting her with a desperation I can't describe.

Right now, I don't care about the bet I made with Devlin.

I don't care about what I swore to myself I'd never do.

That I'd never fall in love.

Because for the first time in my life, I want to.

# TWENTY-SIX

## ELARA

I'm alone in the kitchen the following morning after just finishing my run around the property. Definitely plan to do that whenever I can. It's just so beautiful here. The smell of freshly cut grass, the view of the mountains.

Ruby already made breakfast, leaving some bacon and waffles on my plate.

I didn't see Tynan when I woke up and wondered where he had gone so early. It's only six thirty, but he's probably at work already. Seems like he's always working.

I'm thankful for some alone time, though. Time to process what happened between Tynan and me last night.

Magical, earth-shattering things…

I can't believe I let him fuck me. But I can't get it out of my mind, and how much I want it to happen again.

How much I crave him in my bones.

It should repulse me that he was touching me while I was asleep, yet it only turned me on. Is that what I'm into?

I don't even know the things I like. Jerry was revolting. And the guy before him was very straightlaced. He never even went down on me.

But Tynan? Well, he clearly has no problems with that.

The way his tongue moved…I've never felt anything like it. I was tired when he carried me to another bedroom, vowing to get our bed cleaned tomorrow. I had never squirted before. Never even realized I could, but wow. There's no going back after that, because it was truly amazing.

"Good morning." His voice booms behind me, hands on my shoulders, startling me with a jolt. "Did you sleep better last night?"

"Mm-hmm." My face flushes as I glance back, my body prickling when those large palms caress up and down my arms.

He's dressed in a dove-gray suit, and I'm unsure if he's been home the whole time or just got in.

"Good." He presses a kiss behind my ear, and I swear I melt.

I shouldn't be melting. Yet here I am, feeling things for him. Dangerous things.

He pours himself a cup of coffee and takes my empty mug and adds more into it. "I have to run to the office today for a little bit, but I should be back later." He drags in a slow sip, eyes burning into mine. "I also arranged for you to shop somewhere else tomorrow. I promise they will take care of you. I'll make sure of that."

"Thanks. But it's really not necessary."

"It is. Also, they will be dropping off some evening gowns later today for you to try on."

"Why? Are we going somewhere?"

"Yes. We have a charity event tonight at six. I completely forgot about it."

"Oh. What charity?"

"It's one I started years ago. For childhood cancer research."

My eyes widen.

"You look surprised." He laughs dryly.

"I just…"

"Didn't think someone in the Mob gave a shit about a bunch of sick kids?"

I nod.

"Well, this one does."

My husband has a heart.

"Uh…" My face grows hot at what I want to bring up, but it feels like an elephant in the room.

"What is it, Elara?"

"Um…" I pick up the mug, my hands growing warm around it. "About last night. It was nice, but…"

*But I'm terrified of how good it was.*

He drops his coffee on the counter and comes over to me, cupping my face in his hands. "I'm not here to push or make you uncomfortable. I just got distracted by how gorgeous you looked in our bed. It won't happen again unless you want it to."

*I want it to…*

"Okay."

He removes his hands from me, and I want them to return so badly, I ache. He starts to head out instead.

"Tynan…"

"Yes, babe?"

"Where do you work?"

"We own a corporation, which handles all our business. I run it. Lots of paperwork." He hits me with a lopsided grin.

I'm sure it's more than just paperwork, but I don't say it aloud. I don't want to know what he actually does. The people he certainly kills.

"Have a good day at work, then."

He nods. "Enjoy your day too."

Then he's walking away, and when the door shuts, I kinda wish I'd kissed him goodbye.

Hours later, after Brody and I have had a fun day swimming in the biggest pool I've ever seen, we decide to watch a movie. He chooses *Toy Story*, which was always a favorite for Mom and me.

At the thought of her, tears brim in my eyes. I miss her so much. I wish she was still here to talk to. With a sniffle, I wipe under my lashes, and Brody's alarmed expression turns to me. He places a palm on my cheek, and when those sweet eyes land on mine, all it does is make me cry even more.

I hug him tight to me. "I'm okay. Just thinking about my mom. I miss her very much."

It's then I sense him crying too, harder with every breath he takes.

"It's okay, sweetheart. You can miss them with me."

For minutes, we remain each other's lifeline, feeling these emotions that sit dormant inside us. I'm glad he feels comfortable enough to cry with me.

"Maybe one day, you can tell me all about your parents."

Teary eyes look up at me as he nods.

"I bet they were special and you miss them very much."

He pouts, tears leaking down his cheeks.

"I love you, Brody."

That makes his eyes fill with fresh tears. His arms jump around me, and he hugs me with all his might. I know this is his way of telling me he loves me right back.

Minutes pass when we finally put on the TV, and before I can turn on the movie, a news broadcast catches my eye.

"What the…"

A newscaster stands before a charred store, and it's the name that makes my heart beat faster.

"The owner of the Carolina Herrera store in Boston says she's completely distraught that the space burned to the ground late last night and into the morning hours. The fire marshal does not have an official cause yet, but he has told us they suspect it was bad wiring."

I don't hear the rest of it.

What are the chances? Maybe it's karma? Though I didn't want *that* to happen. That's her livelihood.

Tynan appears in my thoughts.

Could he have…

No. He wouldn't.

*Your husband is in the Mob. Of course he would.*

Oh, crap.

# TYNAN

I have no idea if she knows I ordered Vera's store to go up in flames, nor do I need her to know.

Whether she's aware or not, I'll always be there to protect her. Make all her wrongs right.

It's what a husband does.

Vera's lucky her store was all I took. She was close to losing her life, although I figured Elara might object to that line of justice.

The day drags, but thinking about my wife makes it tolerable. I hope I didn't scare her off with what I did. Because that's the last thing I want.

Images of us from last night fill my mind. The way she took my cock. How hard she came. The way it felt to wake up beside her this morning.

I watched her sleeping for a while before I got out of bed. My hand stroked her face, and I swear she smiled in her sleep.

I groan. I'd rather be with her and Brody instead of here in the office.

But there's work to be done. The deal with the Russians had a little hiccup. One of their suppliers ended up dead, so they're in the process of working with another. That may cause a delay in shipment, however, and my father isn't too happy about it.

Once I'm finally done for the day and out of the office, I text Elara so she knows I'll be home soon.

Our charity event is in three hours. I cannot wait to see her in a dress I bought her, which I'm gonna enjoy ripping off her after we get home.

Getting into my car, I make it home in forty minutes, pulling into the driveway and parking the SUV next to my Ferrari.

Stepping out, I greet my men at the front before making my way inside.

As soon as I enter the foyer, Bubbles comes bouncing up, growling at me as she normally does. We still have a love/hate relationship going on, like with every other person in my life apparently. Why would the dog be any different?

"Hi to you too, yappy." I move past her just as Brody comes running with a squeaky toy.

"Hey, buddy. You have a good day?"

I don't expect a response. I know better than to expect anything at this point.

Then, out of nowhere, he looks up at me and nods with the biggest smile.

A flush of adrenaline hits my center, my heart racing.

Glancing behind me, I wonder if there's someone else there.

He has never done that with me before.

For the first time, I'm speechless.

Before I can say anything else, he gathers Bubbles in his arms and scurries out of the room.

Immediately, the first thing I want to do is tell Elara all about it.

She's probably upstairs getting ready for the evening. I should let her finish instead of distracting her, but damn, do I wanna see her.

I start for the kitchen, knowing Ruby is probably finishing dinner for Brody. When I walk in, she's wiping her hands by the counter.

"Wait until you see her!"

Well, now I have to go and take a look for myself.

"Is she almost ready?"

"I think so." Her eyes gleam. "You look happy, you know that?"

My mouth forms a thin line. "What gave that away?"

She waves off my tight expression. "You're not fooling anyone. I've never seen you this happy, not until you met her, so stop lying to yourself."

"Yeah, yeah." I start heading out. "I'll see you later, Ruby."

Her laugh echoes as I rush for the stairs, taking two at a time, needing to see my wife.

As soon as I open the bedroom door, the sight of her stops me dead in my tracks. My gaze roves down her body, attempting to simultaneously cling to every stunning inch of her, unsure where to look first.

"Wow." My voice goes low, my heart close to giving out.

She's in a long silver dress with a glistening belt around the middle. The straps are thin, dipping to a V to show off her full chest.

May wanna consider keeping her home tonight. Not sure what I'm bound to do if someone looks at her like they shouldn't.

"Good?" A smile tugs at her lips, bright red lipstick making them extra kissable. And definitely extra fuckable.

My cock swells to the point of pain.

*Hell. I should fuck her before we go.*

I force my legs to move. "Good? I'm speechless."

As I grasp her nape, my lips hover until I can almost kiss her.

Her long lashes flutter, and she stares at me, all shy and sexy as hell.

"You look insanely gorgeous. Jesus, Elara." My mouth drops closer, a groan escaping from my chest when her lips brush mine. "Fuck, I wanna kiss you."

"You'd ruin my lipstick." Her breathless tone has my jaw tightening, my fingers spreading in her hair.

"That'd be a shame." I can't help my deep grunt. "I'd at least like to wait until the plane ride to fuck your pretty mouth."

"Jesus, Tynan," she pants.

I can't be an asshole. I can't ruin how beautiful she looks.

*You could just bend her over and lift her dress…*

"Go sábhála mac Dé sinn," I mutter, and her brows snap.

"What does that mean?"

I let out a sardonic chuckle. "I'm asking for divine intervention to stop me from fucking you senseless right now, babe."

She beams at me, her shy, sexy smile not helping matters.

I grab her jaw, grinding my teeth. "We need to get the hell out of here."

I force my hand off of her. The more I touch her, the more volatile this situation is gonna get.

The sass returns to her gaze, and she's running her hands down her hips, grinning salaciously. "I really like this dress."

I'm on her before she can take her next breath.

Rolling her long hair around my wrist and yanking her head back, I bring her ear to my lips. "You're going to be a huge distraction for everyone tonight, especially me."

I run my nose down her neck, nipping her shoulder as she whimpers.

"You're going to have to forgive all the dead bodies tonight, Mrs. Quinn. 'Cause anyone who looks at you will find themselves no longer breathing."

"Maybe I should change, then," she whispers. "Wouldn't want to be responsible for your murderous escapades."

"Fuck," I growl, licking along her jaw, needing a taste. "You're such a little cocktease." With a jerk of my hand, I'm roughly dragging up her dress, my fingers tracing between her thighs. "No panties, huh?"

"Tynan!" she cries when two fingers thrust inside her, fucking her just a little bit, just enough to satiate my need for her.

She gasps and cries, clawing my bicep, begging me for it. But when her walls start to clench, I release her.

Grinning like a motherfucker at her hooded expression, I bring the fingers that were inside her to my mouth. Our gazes align as I suck her taste onto my tongue.

"So fucking good. Now, you wait here until I finish taking a shower, and you'd better behave while I get dressed. Because I swear, Elara…" I grab the back of her neck. "Tease me again, and I'm gonna rip this dress to shreds. Understand?"

She nods, her chest flying up and down.

"Good girl." I lean in and kiss the corner of her mouth. "I'll be quick, I promise."

I start to reluctantly head to the master bath.

"Tynan?"

I turn to her, admiring her flushed and sexy appearance.

"Can I ask you something? And please promise to tell me the truth." Worry grows in her eyes, and that has me standing straighter.

"What is it?"

"Well, I caught the news today, and I saw something. I don't know if it was you or…"

*Ah, so she did see that. Good. Now she knows.*

"You want to know if I burned down the store."

She nods.

"Yes, Elara…" I stalk toward her, clasping the back of her head. "It was my doing. I ordered it."

Her mouth parts, and her eyes enlarge.

"And I'd do it again. I'll hurt anyone who hurts you."

"Why?" Tears appear in her eyes.

"Because you're mine, Elara Quinn. And no one hurts my wife. Does that answer your question?"

She swallows thickly and nods.

"Glad we worked that out." I kiss the tip of her nose.

She stands there, awestruck, while I head for the bathroom, hoping she realizes I meant every damn word.

# TWENTY-SEVEN

## ELARA

We arrived by private jet to an airport twenty miles outside of Boston before a limo took us to a luxurious hotel in the heart of the city.

Of course a man like him has his own plane.

Music plays in the background as we walk into the grand ballroom. Gold ornate ceiling, a white marble floor, and tables with gold Chiavari chairs are set for at least three hundred guests.

The décor is the epitome of class. Wouldn't expect anything less.

Tynan's hand clasps mine as we make our way toward the bar, women ogling him at every turn. I tug him closer, and he glances down at me with a smirk.

My belly flip-flops. It's not enough how handsome he looks in that black tux, but he has to smile at me like that too? My God, this is going to be a torturous night.

Images of him yanking my dress up and fingering me flood my mind until I'm clearing my throat, trying to move toward the bar as fast as I can.

But right before we get there, an elderly couple approaches us.

*Of course…*

"Tynan," the woman gushes, grabbing his forearm and kissing the side of his face. "We're so pleased to be here. You always manage to pull off such a beautiful event."

"Yes, this event is my favorite every year," the man says, his eyes darting to me. "And who might this be?"

Tynan tugs me closer to his side. "Bernard, Camila, I want you to meet my wife, Elara."

"Wife?" Camila stares at him open-mouthed right before shooting him a playful glare and slapping him on the shoulder. "And you didn't invite us?"

"We didn't actually have a wedding. It was family only." He snaps his eyes to mine with a chuckle. "Isn't that right, baby?"

"Mm-hmm." I play with the ends of my hair.

"It's a pleasure, darling!" Camila moves over to hug me.

But when her husband kisses the top of my hand, I don't miss the way Tynan's jaw flexes. I bite back a smile.

Seems like he has a bit of a jealous streak, and I kinda like it.

"Thank you," I tell them. "It's great to meet you both."

"You as well! I must say I've never seen you around. How quick was this wedding?" Then she gasps. "Are you pregnant?" Her voice grows low.

"Camila!" Her husband shakes his head.

"What! I'm just asking." She rolls her eyes, giving me a little discreet wink.

"Not yet." Tynan's arm wraps around my hips, pulling me into his side, his mouth dropping to my temple.

My God, I love when he kisses me that way. Makes me feel so cherished.

"But we can't wait to have children," he says. "Right, babe?"

Right. Children. The real reason he wanted me.

"Yes, that's right." Anxiety roils in my gut, making me wonder if I truly matter or if I'm just a means to an end.

"Well, I'm so glad to see you finally settle down." Camila grins. "I was worried for a moment. You're too good of a man to be alone forever."

"You sound like my father."

"Well, you know us parents. We worry. We want our kids to settle down and have lives of their own."

The more she talks about kids, the more uncomfortable I become.

This isn't real. He doesn't really care about me. He just needed me. That's all.

But the way he touches me. Holds me. Is it just all lust?

Or could there be a chance for more for the both of us?

And is it wrong for me to want that with him? To want this to be real? Because I do. I want it badly.

I want to be loved. I want a man who cares for me. And Tynan makes that all feel possible.

With a sigh, I glance around the room, suddenly freezing in place. He must notice my change in mood, and once he follows my line of vision, he realizes exactly who I'm looking at.

"Would you two excuse us?" he tells the couple. "There's someone here I need to speak to before they get away."

"Oh, yes, of course," Camila says. "You two go have fun!"

"Enjoy yourselves," he tells them, pulling me toward Vera and her daughter, Stephanie.

"Tynan, I really don't want to see them again." My heart races uncontrollably, hands growing clammy.

I don't know why I'm acting like this. They mean nothing. I shouldn't care. But something in me still does.

"I've got you," he whispers, eyes lingering on mine. "You have nothing to worry about when I'm with you."

And my heart somehow stops and skips a beat all at once.

I nod, and he lifts my hand to his mouth, kissing my knuckles without even so much as looking away.

How can this not be real? He can't possibly fake this…can he? Or does he act this way with all the women he sleeps with?

I don't have long to wonder, because he's pulling me toward those bitches again.

I almost feel sorry for Vera. When she sees us approaching, her face goes white. She's whispering something to Stephanie, who looks even more nervous.

"Ladies. It's so good of you to make it." He holds my hand tighter—squeezing it for reassurance, I imagine.

Vera laughs nervously. "We wouldn't miss it. It's such a worthy cause. Isn't that right, honey?"

She peers over at Stephanie, who feigns a smile.

"I'm sorry to hear about your store," he tells Vera, but he doesn't sound sorry at all. "It's a shame what happens when we're not careful."

Her mouth spasms. "Tynan, I'm sorry."

She knows.

Oh my God…

"For what?" Keeping our hands clasped, he brings his face closer to hers. "For insulting *my* wife and thinking you could get away with it?"

Her lower lashes brim with tears. "We didn't mean to offend her, I swear!"

He chuckles and there's nothing pleasant in it. "You did mean to. You just didn't think you'd get caught." His arm curls around my hips as he narrows his glare at the women. "And I just want you to know no matter how hard you try, you'll never come close to being as perfect as my wife."

His eyes go to mine for a moment, lingering there before he's staring hard at her again. "I won't tolerate anyone disrespecting her.

So I suggest you both learn to keep your mouths shut before you lose more than just your store. Hope we understand each other."

He doesn't give her a chance to reply, pulling us away.

Emotions weave through my heart until it feels as though it's weeping—not from sadness, but from happiness.

He stood up for me. He defended me.

He just proved to me that I mean something.

That being happy with him could be possible.

"Thank you," I whisper, stopping in place and cupping his cheek in my palm.

His brows furrow, eyes searching mine. "Anything for you, Elara."

My gut dips, and with a clench of his jaw, his mouth is on mine, hungrily devouring me.

My hands slide into his hair.

Tugging.

Pulling.

Feeling...*everything*. Wanting it too.

His teeth nip on my lower lip as he sucks it into his mouth, his hard chest pressed against my soft one.

I don't know if they're all watching.

I don't care.

Because nothing else matters right now except the way he kisses me.

Like this is the only thing he ever wants to do.

The night turns more enjoyable after that. He introduces me as his wife to just about everyone who approaches us, and there have been many of them.

A song I know starts playing, and I find myself swaying a little.

He doesn't miss it, his lips landing on the crook of my neck as he whispers, "Dance with me."

My head whips back. "You dance?"

"I dance." He grins, making my heart stop.

He leads me to the dance floor, people parting for us. And the way they look at him… It's with fear.

He slides his arms around the small of my back as the music continues, our eyes locked, my breath catching as he spins me on the dance floor, pulling me in close.

His lips whisper and tease.

Just a little more and I'd feel them.

He groans as he spins me again, pulling my back to his front.

"Where did you learn how to dance like this?" I ask, my pulse beating wildly, his fingers clasping my hips.

"My mother." He turns me to him, jaw clenched, green eyes dark and warm, like a fire burning brightly. Enticing and furious all at once.

"Where is your mother?"

"She died a long time ago." His sad smile breaks my heart.

"Oh. I'm so sorry." I hurt for him because I know that pain.

"Me too. I wish she'd had a chance to meet you."

Emotions burn in my throat. "I wish I could've met her too."

His gaze pierces into mine, and I can feel him deep in my soul. It's unsettling, yet I crave it.

Glancing behind him, I find the guests staring.

"You know they're all watching us, right?"

"Think they'll be watching this?"

Before I can wonder, his mouth crashes into mine.

Consuming me where I stand.

This kiss is slow and filled with passion. With yearning. With unbending need.

His body presses to mine.

Heart to heart.

Two shapes that shouldn't quite fit, yet somehow they do.

A thumb strokes my jawline while his tongue invades without

mercy. Without permission.

And my world only knows one thing right now: how good it is to be Tynan Quinn's wife.

# TYNAN

We make it home close to two in the morning, and I don't remember having such a good time at any of the past fundraisers.

I glance at her, sitting on the edge of the bed, ready to undo the straps of her shoes.

"Let me." I walk over, grabbing under her knee, lifting her foot up to my chest.

I stare into her eyes as I grab her ankle, slowly slipping off the high heel and rubbing the sole of her foot as she groans.

"Feel good?"

"So good. My feet have been hurting all night."

"Why didn't you tell me?" I massage her foot, doing the same to the other. "I would've taken you up to my suite at the hotel and let you rest."

"Mm," she groans, closing her eyes, her body falling backward against the bed.

Fuck, she looks so sexy.

"Keep doing that…" She bites her bottom lip, her face contorting in pleasure as I suck her toes into my mouth.

She sighs, eyes heavy. "That feels so good."

"I like making you feel good, mo chuisle."

"Mo chuisle. What does it mean?" she whispers.

I want to tell her. I should. But a part of me feels as though I'm giving something to her, something I've never been ready to give anyone.

But it's just words. That's all.

"My pulse."

"Why?" Her brows knit, those eyes lighting up, waiting for me to tell her.

"Because…you've made my heart beat like it never has before."

"Tynan…" Her voice cracks, a breath catching in her throat.

Carefully I lower her foot onto the floor and start dragging up her gown. "This dress, it's beautiful on you."

"Thank you." Her chest rises and falls desperately like she needs it.

And I need her too.

Right now.

Right here.

I need my wife.

"Take it off. Unless you're not all that attached to it. Then I'll gladly rip it off."

"You're quite fond of threatening to rip up my clothes." She runs a finger in between her breasts.

"I'm quite fond of seeing you naked." I smirk. "Now, stand up."

I grab her hand, pulling her to her feet and turning her around.

Her audible breaths only swell my insatiable need for her. Gathering her hair, I slide it over her shoulder, and her skin prickles. Her soft, slender throat begs for my mouth.

I want inside her. In every way. Want to seep into her veins. Want her to taste me in her marrow, until she wants me just as much.

The sound of the zipper reverberates through the room, goose bumps rising at the back of her neck. As a finger traces down her spine, her shoulders rattle, exhales scattered and heavy. I slip the straps of her dress down her arms, taking my time, enjoying the feel of her skin.

"Tynan…" My name is a frantic plea for me to give her what she craves.

I pull the dress lower until it pools at her feet.

"Say my name like that again." I cup her tits and pinch both nipples, eliciting a moan.

"Tynan…" Her hands find my thighs, and she squeezes them when my lips drop to her throat.

My cock throbs to feel her again, to make her feel me too. Grabbing her delicate throat, I let my other hand slip between her thighs. Two fingers thrust inside her, my thumb playing her clit as she bucks, crying out in pleasure.

"Already soaked for me. What a good girl."

"Tynan, I need—"

"I know exactly what my wife needs."

Sliding my fingers out of her, I spin her around and push her roughly down onto the bed. With her pretty mouth parted, she waits for my next move, obediently lying there with those perfect rose-colored nipples I need to taste again.

"You're so goddamn sexy."

She stretches her body, pressing her knees together, making it impossible to think of anything but fucking her. I take her legs in the air and over my shoulders before I'm kneeling on the floor, spreading her wide, exposing her glistening cunt.

Her eyes pinch closed, teeth sinking into her lip.

"Look at me." The tip of my tongue teases her slit.

"Oh my God!" she cries, eyes locked with mine.

"That's it, keep looking at me." My tongue takes a leisurely swipe up from her entrance to her clit, and she jolts, snapping her thighs around my face.

I only grip her tighter and spread her wider, holding her thighs prisoner as my tongue rams inside her tight hole before swirling around her core.

She snatches a fistful of my hair, and I chuckle, grunting as she yanks harder.

Fuck. She's perfect.

"Don't stop. I'm…I'm…close."

"Mm," I growl, sucking her deeper into my mouth, feeling those small tremors around my tongue.

But I don't end the sweet torture. Not until she's screaming and begging.

"Oh God, I'm coming! Don't stop!"

My teeth graze. My mouth sucks and nibbles while my tongue rolls until she's there, writhing and coming all over my damn face.

I can't help my groan of satisfaction.

She lets out a breathless little laugh, shyly peering at me. "Wow…"

"That's right. It's only the beginning." My erection straining in my trousers as I stand, slowly undoing my bow tie, staring at her.

Her face flushes even more, teeth nipping her bottom lip as she watches me strip for her. I take my time, undoing my cuffs, grinding my molars, needing inside her so damn bad.

My shirt comes off.

The clack of the buckle drifts in the air as I undo my belt.

Then the zipper.

And through it all, she watches me. Her eyes grow with her arousal, and they fall to my obvious hard-on.

"Show me," she strains.

"Really wanna see it?" I smirk.

She nods.

"I didn't hear you ask nicely."

She shuts her eyes and shakes her head with a playful smile.

When she looks back at me, there's renewed heat in her eyes. "Show me your cock. Pretty please."

She gives each word a feisty emphasis, and I don't have it in me to play with her anymore. I just need her.

With a groan, I drag my pants and boxers down, and my dick juts out.

"Just sex, right?" I stroke myself, gaze raking down her body right before I start to crawl over her.

"That's right. That is all this is. Just sex." Her irises gleam with tortured passion.

"Good." I grab her jaw tight and kiss her hard, searching her hungered gaze. "Then I won't have an ounce of guilt for what I'm about to do."

Before she can question it, I'm clutching her hips, flipping her over onto her front and forcing her on all fours. With a palm, I push the side of her face into the mattress, her ass in the air.

"What a beautiful sight you are," I growl, lining my cock at her entrance, and without giving her any warning, I slam inside her all the way.

"Oh, God!" Her moans come in fragmented waves.

"God has nothing to do with us. This is all you and me."

Spanking her ass, I pound into her, wanting to go as deep as I can, making her scream and claw the sheets beneath. Her eyes roll and latch on to mine, and it only makes me increase my tempo, my dick throbbing and pulsing inside her.

Her walls start to tighten, and I slow my movements, dropping my body weight over her flesh.

"Don't stop. Keep going," she pants, looking at me from over her shoulder.

"You're so needy for it." I circle my hips, and she whimpers.

"Please, Tynan. Please…"

"Please what?" I slide out and rise to my knees, teasing her with the tip, rolling it up to her ass, and pressing it into the hole there, needing that too.

But I don't have the strength to take my time and stretch it out right now. That will have to wait.

"You like me using your body?" I slide my hand around her throat and squeeze, hissing between my teeth at the feeling of her unsteady pulse. "You look so good. Eyes red, makeup a mess. All mine to use."

I piston into her, propelling her body farther up on the bed. Slipping out, I circle her wetness around her clit with the crown of my erection.

"Who do you belong to?"

Her mouth quivers, legs trembling.

I spank her ass hard. "I asked you a question."

"I belong to you," she cries.

"Good girl. Now say that with my cock inside you."

And I ram all the way back in, over and over until she can't catch her breath.

"Yes, yes, yours. Tynan…please!"

A smirk flits through my mouth. "I'm gonna fuck you senseless all night long. Wanna see how many times I can make you scream for me."

Then I keep my promise, taking her deeper, faster, her hair in my fist as I release all of my pent-up need. All the reasons why I shouldn't be falling for my own wife.

"How dare you make me want you this badly?" I groan, rolling her long hair around my wrist, bending her head backward. "You make me fucking desperate."

My voice is pained, my pulse battering, and my heart… It's never felt anything like this before. Now I don't know how I'm supposed to live without it.

Without *her*.

She's embedded herself into my bloodstream, and now I'd die for her. Live for her. I'm hers to command. She holds the power, and she doesn't even know it.

"Tynan!" she screams as she squirts all over the bed.

"Hottest damn thing, every time," I grit, unable to stop myself from continuing to fuck her. "You're gonna do that again."

She squirms, trying to fight it, but I drop my body over hers and take her harder, keeping her hair locked in my palm.

"I want you sore tomorrow. Want you unable to walk for days."

"Don't stop! Just keep fucking me!"

Her arousal twines in that shaky voice, and I know this time she's only going to come harder. I slip a hand under her and find her clit, rubbing it in hurried circles, making her scream my name until the walls shatter.

Until my own hollow heart fills with all things Elara.

My hips pound against her, and the sound of skin on skin, her gasping moans echoing…it makes this all even better. Her release shatters through her limbs, and I savor every moment, never wanting it to end.

When it's over, she's finally still, turning over while I'm still on top of her.

She feathers her fingers across my jaw, her eyes fixed to mine, slowly drinking me in.

Until I start to unravel.

"You're beautiful," she tells me.

And as I draw in a breath, holding it in my unsteady lungs, I realize right here, in this moment, that I'm starting to fall for my wife.

And there's not a goddamn thing I can do about it.

I may have stormed into her life, but Elara Hill? She stormed into my heart, and now I'm left with the aftermath.

# TWENTY-EIGHT

## ELARA

Tynan stares at me from across the counter in the kitchen the next morning, sucking me into his gaze, and every cell in my body pulses.

I try not to react, especially with Brody right next to me.

Yet as his eyes continue to hold mine in that deep and searching way, my face heats up.

I force myself to look away, unable to handle the way he gazes at me. My gut tightens as thoughts of us from last night replay in my mind.

The things that man did to me.

Unspeakable things.

Twisting my body in ways I didn't know I was capable of. I've never come that many times in one night before.

I would very much like to request a repeat.

His dark gray dress shirt stretches and conforms to his muscled chest, making my throat go dry. But that man could wear a garbage bag over his body and still look good. It's seriously unfair.

He roughs a hand through his hair and messes it up a bit.

*Jesus Christ.*

I squeeze my thighs on the stool.

"Your grandma called while you were sleeping." He drags a sip of his coffee, his heavily hooded gaze falling to my lips, and I shiver from the sultry attention.

"Oh? And you two had a nice chat, I assume?" A smile plays on my lips.

"We did, in fact."

He fixes his navy silk tie, the muscle in his neck popping like he's having a hard time being around me too. Like he wants to bring me back upstairs and remind me how good we are together.

My heartbeats stutter as the veins of his hand jerk when he runs it down his tie.

*Yes, Elara. He's hot. Time to get over that now.*

I groan internally at myself. This is *so* not like me. I'm never this pathetic with men.

"She wanted to get lunch with you," he interrupts my self-scolding. "So I told her that sounded like a good idea. I did also ask if she was interested in going shopping with you, which she was very eager about."

My pulse gives a little thump as I gaze back at him.

His actions render me speechless.

I completely forgot that he mentioned I was going shopping today. But the fact that he planned a day for me and Gran really nudges at my heart.

"You okay?"

I nod, unable to hide my grin. "It's just…that was sweet of you."

Brody smiles as he bites into his bagel, and seeing this boy smiling so freely with each passing day brings me immense joy.

"It's not a big deal." He adds a few pieces of bacon to his plate.

"Told her Rogue would pick her up in an hour."

"Thank you." I reach my hand for his and hold it tight, running my thumb over his knuckles.

His eyes close for a moment, like he's savoring my touch. When our gazes connect this time, I find warmth.

"I don't think you've ever told me what's wrong with your grandfather. Anything I can do?"

As though my heart didn't already beat for him, he just made it hammer even faster.

"No." I shake my head. "You've done enough. The money helps. He has severe dementia, so he needs round-the-clock help. And neither Gran nor I can do it on our own." My shoulders sag, and his brows instantly furrow. "Makes me feel so guilty because he's my grandpa, you know? I should take care of him. He was always there for me growing up, and I feel as though I'm abandoning him by leaving him there."

He tugs my hand into both of his. "No, babe, don't do that. You can't expect to do everything yourself."

I shrug. But I want to. I should be able to do more for my grandfather.

"Anyway, thank you. Like I said, the money helps. I was drowning with having to pay for that place on my teacher's salary."

"If you need more, you just tell me."

I nod.

He releases my hand, and tingles remain there. I don't expect them to go away anytime soon.

"Brody has a baseball game later, by the way," he says. "You don't have to come if you're too tired after your day out, but if you do, you're more than welcome."

"Of course I'll be there." I peek over at Brody, whose eyes twinkle with excitement. "I'd never miss Brody playing! When is the game?"

"You have time. The game is at four." Something passes in his eyes—something like concern. "Make sure you stay close to Rogue."

"Of course."

He's worried about me. And here come the tears I won't shed.

With Jerry still being out there, I'm worried too. I just really hope whoever chased me wasn't him. Though I know I'm just fooling myself.

"You have the credit card I gave you, right?"

"I do."

"Good. Make sure you actually spend our money this time."

"It's not our money. It's yours."

He releases an exasperated sigh as he rises over to me. He grasps my jaw, his thumb brushing over my lips.

"It's *ours*, Elara. You're my wife." His mouth descends toward my ear, lips lingering, breaths warm. "Didn't I remind you of that last night, or do you need me to do it again this morning?"

I clear my throat, shivers running through my entire body as he rights himself, arousal growing in his gaze.

"I'll be sure to spend as much as I can."

He kisses the corner of my mouth. "Good." His heavenly lips lower to my ear once again. "Think I got you pregnant yet?"

I don't know why, but that made my breath still in my lungs. "I…I don't know."

"Then we should keep trying." His voice—rough, yet smooth—is a deadly concoction of sin.

"I…uh…should go get ready if I want to make that game."

*Yes, talk about anything else just so you can stop being so turned on by the idea of him getting you pregnant.*

"It won't be a far drive. The store will bring items to the same warehouse for you to try on."

"What store this time?"

"Valentino."

I breathe a laugh. "Way to spoil a girl."

Will I ever get used to this lifestyle?

"It's what I'm here for." His knuckles feather down my cheek, leaving goose bumps behind. He kisses my temple before returning to his breakfast. "I'm happy to see you eating so well now."

He glances down at my bare plate, the crepes he made long gone.

"It's kinda hard not to when you're such a good cook."

He shoots me a lopsided grin.

I vow to make him do that as much as possible.

I take Gran's bags and place them in the trunk, helping her up into the SUV before sliding in beside her.

"This was so much fun!" She grins. "I really adore that man. Don't you? I mean, he was so generous with me when he didn't have to be."

She fastens her seat belt as Rogue takes us on the road.

Tynan not only arranged clothes for me, but Gran too. I really almost burst into tears when I realized that. To have someone not only take care of me, but my grandparents too? That's special. How can I run from it?

Yet how can I risk something happening to him or Brody?

"Yeah, it was really sweet of him to do this for us."

I reach inside one of my paper bags, wanting to make sure the receipt is in there just in case I change my mind about some of the items. They were expensive. It took some convincing from Gran for me to even be okay with buying them.

But instead of a receipt, I find a simple folded white paper.

I don't think much of it.

"What's that?" Gran asks.

"I don't know." I glance at her, brows knitting in confusion as I start to unfold it. "Maybe the cashier dropped it accidenta—"

All the words escape when I look down at it.

I drag in a long, shallow inhale, fear clawing its way up my throat.

"Elara?" Gran calls, yet her voice is distant, like she's not right beside me.

My head spins and my pulse spikes when I read the words again.

*No, no, no.*

*Can't breathe. Can't breathe.*

"Elara! What's going on?"

I knew it was him. I knew Jerry would come for me.

*Can't hide from me, Ev. I'll always find you.*

Tears fill my eyes.

With a shaky hand, I crumble up the paper and toss it right out the window.

"Elara!" Her hand snaps around my forearm.

That's when I finally look at her, trying to keep it together.

"What did you just throw out?"

I take a deep breath. "N-n-nothing. Nothing at all. I…uh, don't wanna talk about it."

She shakes her head. "If it was them, you need to tell Tynan. No one can do everything by themselves all the time. We all need help sometimes."

I stare out the window, wondering if she's right and I should tell Tynan about this. I don't know what the right decision is. Telling him could help, or it could only make him worry more.

He's already doing everything he can to find Jerry. Adding to his stress wouldn't do either of us any good.

# TWENTY-NINE

## TYNAN

While she's out shopping and Brody's with Ruby and Bubbles, I head for my study, returning a call from Grant. Hopefully this means he found something. I need to find her ex, and I need to get rid of him once and for all.

As soon as I dial his cell, he answers.

"Hey, I've got some info. May wanna sit down for this."

*Fuck.*

"Just tell me."

"Alright, so her ex's name is Jerry Baker. His father runs a gang called the Eights in New Jersey. Super small, though they've been making a name for themselves. They're heavy into drugs and prostitution. With the Marinovs also being in Jersey, they've been careful where they sell, but they're growing and they've been getting cocky, killing off their competition one by one. They play real dirty too. Killing off women and kids when they need to send a message."

My fingers curl, anger splitting through my limbs. What did that son of a bitch do to my Elara?

"What else?"

"Jerry isn't in Jersey right now, and neither is his father."

"So where the fuck are they?"

"Jerry was in Vegas about a month ago, looking for a girl. Your girl. After that, he just disappeared. His father too. I haven't been able to spot them anywhere since."

They're hiding on purpose. They want the element of surprise. Jerry probably already knows I married her.

"Do you know what she was involved in?"

If I find out he was selling her, his father won't have a corpse to bury.

"I don't know. Not yet."

"Keep me apprised of any developments."

"I will."

I ball a hand on my desk. "Were you able to find Derek, that guy she said helped her?"

"No. He's skilled, though. He knows how to hide, but I'll keep looking for both of them."

"I owe you."

"Friends don't owe each other. I'll talk to you soon."

"I won't forget this."

"You take care."

He ends the call, and all I can see is that scar on Elara's stomach, wondering how the hell she got it.

Blood blisters in my veins.

I need to get rid of them all. It's the only way she'll feel safe.

And I won't rest until that happens.

# ELARA

After dropping Grandma back home, I bring my bags to our bedroom, trying to act as though nothing happened. Like Jerry or his people never got close enough to somehow slip a note in one of my bags.

I still don't understand how he could've done it. Unless he passed it to someone who works at the store, pretending he's a friend. He was always charming when he needed to be. I can see someone innocent falling for his bullshit like I did when I thought he worked for my father.

"How did it go?" Tynan appears behind me, strong masculine palms stroking my arms.

I grow rigid, swallowing harshly, nervous that he'll somehow find out I'm keeping a secret.

"It was fun. Gran had a great time too. She told me to thank you again."

"I like your grandma." He spins me around, tilting my chin with the back of his finger, and every nerve in my body explodes. "You ready for the game?"

*Shit. The game. I completely forgot.*

"Of course."

He takes a step back, gaze running down my body over the tight jeans and black tank top. My skin heats up from his perusal.

"I feel so tiny compared to you when I'm not wearing heels."

He examines my tennis shoes and shoots me a smirk. "I like you being short. Easier to toss you around and do with you as I please." His arm curls around my back until his body meets mine, and he kisses me. "You smell nice. We should go, though," he husks. "Or I'm bound to make us late."

His lips feather with mine, and I let out a little moan just as the door creaks and Brody is there, staring at us.

*Crap.*

"Hey, buddy!" I push Tynan off and rush over to him. "You look so great!"

He's adorable in his blue-and-white uniform and matching baseball cap.

"Ready to kick some butt?" Tynan asks.

He nods, grinning wide.

Together, we start heading out, Brody beating us down the stairs.

"I'll never get used to him smiling again." Tynan sighs, grabbing my hand. "Thank you, Elara." Emotions stitch up his voice, and my eyes get lost in his.

"He loves you, Tynan. I swear he does."

He nods, looking uncomfortable, and for the first time, I feel sorry for him. Truly sorry.

He releases a sigh and leads us out the door, locking it behind us.

After Brody hops into his booster and straps himself in, we're ready to take off. Tynan keeps his right palm on my thigh, using the other to maneuver the wheel, bringing us to the park about fifteen minutes later.

A large crowd of people is already seated in the stands, and we take Brody to join his team. As we do, he looks at a boy and immediately makes sure not to stand near him.

That has my radar up. What's going on there?

I want to ask him, but I'm distracted by Tynan talking to me.

"Wanna go get a seat while I get us something to eat?"

"Sure."

My attention remains on Brody as Tynan heads for the food truck, and when that sweet boy turns toward me, there's fear in his eyes.

*What the hell?*

Maybe he's just nervous.

"Good luck, sweetie," I whisper so as not to embarrass him in front of his teammates. I know how kids can be.

I move to the side of the fenced enclosure, wanting to make sure everything is okay. Maybe mention it to Tynan when he returns.

Brody remains standing at the end of the bench, and the boy he tried to avoid walks right over to him. This kid is bigger than Brody, maybe even a few years older.

I start closer as soon as he leans into Brody's space.

"Hey, dumbass." The kid laughs.

I gasp in shock, ready to rip his head off.

"Do you even hear me, or are you too stupid to understand what I'm saying?"

Brody's little body trembles.

*Oh, that's it.*

I'm rushing past some of the coaches on the team. They have to have heard. Yet they pretend not to.

Despicable.

"Excuse me. Where are you going?" one of them asks.

I give them a dirty look and rush past them just as I hear the little demon say, "Your daddy isn't here to protect you, is he? Oh, wait. He's dead. And your mommy hated you so much she killed herself."

"Hey, you little shit!" I snap as I appear right behind him.

At first, the boy doesn't realize I'm talking to him.

"I'm talking to you."

He finally turns to me. "Who the hell are you?"

Brody's eyes grow.

"I'm Brody's friend. And *you* are a little asshole. Who do you think you are, talking to Brody like that? What are you, ten?" My eyes narrow. "Haven't your parents taught you not to be a bully?"

"Hey!" A woman with long blonde hair rushes toward me. "Don't you talk to my son like that! Who even are you?"

Glaring at her for a moment, I glance around the stadium, realizing all eyes are on us. And I notice it's quieter than it was when we first got here.

The head coach approaches. "What's going on here?"

"This boy…" I point toward the kid. "…was tormenting Brody,

saying ugly things to him."

"Is she serious?" The mother snickers. "My son is an angel! You know this, Coach! He would *never* say anything mean to another child. Right, Jake?"

He pouts. "I didn't do anything. She's crazy, Mom. She called me an asshole." He starts to cry.

The mother appears horrified that I would call her demon spawn that.

But I don't miss the cunning tug of his mouth. No one else noticed because he did it so discreetly, wanting me to see it.

"She started yelling at me for no reason. Right, Brody?"

But he knows Brody won't say anything, since he can't.

Anger surges through me, my breaths shallower.

"What's going on here?" Tynan's gruff voice booms behind me.

Relieved, I turn toward him. "That kid was bullying Brody." I look at Brody. "May I tell Tynan what he said?"

He nods, his pain swathing through his features. He's trying like hell not to cry.

I tell Tynan everything, saying it out loud so they all hear. His face upturns with so much fury, even I cower.

"I want that kid off the team," he tells the coach, hitting him with a venomous look. "Now!"

"What?" the mom protests. "Absolutely not! Jake has a real shot at going pro! And this is the best team in the state. I won't ruin his chance because of this no one!" Her eyes squeeze into thin slits.

"I would suggest you watch how you speak to my wife." He spits the words through gritted teeth. He's close to losing his control completely.

"Wife?" The woman's face goes ashen.

"That's right, *Laura*. Now, get your fucking things and your shitty-ass kid and leave before I run you out of this town for good."

Her nose flares. "Come on, Jake. Let's go!"

He groans.

"Now!" She starts marching away—very dramatically, I might add.

Huffing, her evil spawn eventually follows her.

Once he's gone, we pull Brody to the side, and everyone goes back to what they were doing.

"Has this been happening a lot?" I ask him.

He nods, but avoids eye contact with us.

"He must do this when I'm not close enough to hear." Tynan inhales sharply.

Brody nods again.

"Buddy, if this ever happens again, promise me you'll tell us." Tynan tucks his chin in his palm. "We don't want anyone to think they can treat you this way. We'll always protect you."

My hearts swells from him saying *we*. Like we're a family.

I guess we are, aren't we?

"Yes, always." I smooth a hand down the back of his head. "Don't think you have to deal with anything by yourself. We love you, Brody."

Tynan glances at me with his own emotions wavering.

"Promise us," I tell him. "I need you to promise you'll tell us if someone bothers you again."

He nods.

"Good," Tynan says, fixing Brody's baseball cap. "Now go win that game."

That's all the encouragement Brody needs as he finally smiles and returns to his team. And when I see one of the boys giving him a high five, it melts my heart.

"I swear I didn't know." Tynan sighs, sounding distraught. "How the hell didn't I know?"

I grab his forearm, and through the pain seeping from his eyes, he stares at me.

"Parents aren't perfect," I remind him. "They don't always know everything. That would be impossible. But you're doing everything right. I need you to know that."

I place a palm against his cheek, and those eyes of his deepen into mine.

"You love him like he's your own, and he knows that."

"He *is* my own. He's my blood."

My heart clenches from the way he adores Brody. "He's lucky to have you."

"The way you stood up for him, Elara. I'll never forget it."

"I love him too."

"I know you do." His arm bands around me and he pulls me flush against him, his lips on my temple.

His mouth remains there, across my skin, making me feel things I've never felt before—like I'm floating.

"He and I are lucky to have you." His tone is deep and low, and I feel those words everywhere.

I press my cheek to his chest, holding him tight, waiting for Brody to start playing.

He looks over at us with a small smile right before he runs toward his coach.

It makes me feel better that he accepted that Tynan and I are married so well. The last thing I'd want is for Brody to be upset about it. That wouldn't help his healing.

*Neither would you running away.*

I force myself to ignore my thoughts and focus on the moments happening before my eyes.

We cheer and clap throughout the game, and the team ends up victorious.

As soon as we see him rushing to us, Tynan lifts him in the air, throwing him on top of his shoulders.

"That was some game!"

"Yeah, you're so good!" I peer up at his excited expression.

"How about we grab some dinner?" Tynan starts toward his car.

"And dessert." I wink at Brody, who nods ecstatically. I know how much this boy loves his dessert.

"Of course we'll get dessert. Maybe more for me later." He whispers that last part, sliding his palm across my ass and holding it possessively.

Pulling his wrist away, I whisper-shout, "Behave."

He only chuckles. "Don't look that good in jeans, then."

"Yeah, I'll take that under advisement," I tease just as we get to the car and he places Brody inside.

And as soon as we're all settled in the SUV, we're heading out of the parking lot and onto a two-way road.

We drive for a few miles, only a few cars on the street. But suddenly, one of them starts speeding behind us. Tynan stares at it through his rearview and switches lanes.

The car follows us.

"Fuck," he mutters.

My heart jumps, pumping frantically.

"Is he following us?" I whisper, unable to stop the air choking up my throat.

With a tight jaw, Tynan glances at the rearview again. "I'll get us out of here."

He accelerates, sending the car speeding, but the vehicle is still on our tail.

My stomach twists and turns, knowing that has to be Jerry or his people. I instantly hate myself. I should've told Tynan about the note. If I would've, he'd have made sure we had protection.

Glancing behind at Brody, I find his eyes growing with absolute fear. This is exactly what I wanted to avoid. I never wanted my past to hurt them, yet it's exactly what's happening.

"It's gonna be okay, buddy," Tynan tells him, veering into another lane. "I'll have us back home in no time."

"Yeah, it's just some silly driver. Nothing to worry about."

I stare at the black sedan, still tailing us, but I can't make out the driver.

"He's wearing a baseball cap and sunglasses," I whisper to Tynan.

"Does it resemble your ex?"

Turning back around, I zero my attention on the driver's face. He's about a quarter of a car length away, but it's hard to make out anything significant about him. I narrow my gaze, trying hard to make out the man's features.

"I can't tell." I straighten myself, my foot bouncing. "Oh God, this is all my fault."

"Once we're safe, you and I are gonna have a little talk. Do you understand me?" His intense voice only rattles my nerves further.

I nod, twirling my hair with a finger at a frantic pace. After this, I know it's time. He has to know what happened to me and what I ran from. He has to know everything if I want us all to be safe.

The black sedan increases its speed, almost reaching Tynan's bumper.

"Son of a…" Tynan presses his foot on the pedal, sending the car surging, and fear crawls up my spine.

Brody cries, and I immediately look back at him.

"It's gonna be okay, sweetheart. I promise."

I know that's not a promise I can keep. But right now, I have to lie to get him through this.

Tynan makes a sharp turn, sending the vehicle veering down the side of the road, through thick grass and gravel. "There's a clear path back to town this way. His car won't be able to handle the rough terrain."

He reaches into the cup holder and takes his cell, dialing a number and putting it on speaker.

"Hey, what's up?" a man answers.

"Cillian, listen. Someone is chasing us on the highway. I'm about fifteen to twenty minutes out. Call Grant and get satellite on this."

He shoots off a precise location.

Cillian mutters a curse. "Alright. Fionn is here too, and he's on it. I'm gonna send reinforcements."

"They won't get here in time." Tynan swerves down another narrow gravel road.

"I'll send them anyway. Call me as soon as you're at the gate."

Tynan drops the phone back into the cup holder.

The sedan still follows us, slower this time, like it's getting stuck. But until we can get rid of him, we aren't safe.

I shut my eyes tight and breathe heavily, talking myself out of the fear, wanting to believe that Tynan can protect us.

He clasps my thigh. "I won't let anything happen to either one of you. I swear I'll die before that happens."

At the thought of him dying, something inside me snaps and pain shoots into my chest cavity. "I don't want you to die."

My eyes fill with unshed tears, and I slip my hand into his, not wanting to let go. Not wanting to lose him. Emotions hit the back of my throat, and I kiss his knuckles, holding them against my chest.

He sucks in a breath as he increases the speed, taking one sharp turn, then another, causing my shoulder to roughly hit the door.

As he scans the rearview, his forehead creases when he finds the car still there, yet a good distance away now.

"We're gonna cut through another path, so hang on," he tells us.

Brody only cries harder, and my heart breaks into pieces. Tynan's expression turns darker, set with unmitigated fury.

Not that I can blame him. I want them all dead too for doing this to Brody.

"I'm gonna get us out of here soon, buddy. I promise." He takes a sudden left turn onto a tight uneven path before there's a clearing and we're on a main road.

Relief washes over me when I glance back and don't see the car anymore.

I reach for Brody, taking his little hand and squeezing it in mine.

"We're almost home," Tynan says, every line on his face tense.

His palm lands back on my thigh as he peers at me from the corner of his eyes.

"You okay?" he whispers.

I shake my head, wanting to throw my arms around him and hold on to him. Hold on to something that matters.

For the rest of the way, we don't say a word. Before I know it, we're pulling up to the security gate at his family's estate and driving up to the house.

As we pull up, I find his father and brothers there.

Fionn is the first to approach. "You guys alright?"

Tynan nods, climbing out before he gets Brody and lifts him in his arms.

Brody sniffles and blinks back tears.

"Oh God, I was worried!" Ruby comes rushing out, her eyes watery.

She grabs my hand and squeezes.

"Wanna go in and see if Ruby has those cookies you like?" Tynan asks Brody.

He nods, and Tynan kisses his forehead before he drops him to his feet.

Ruby immediately takes his hand and starts leading him inside, trying to change his mood. "They're nice and warm. I just got them out of the oven."

Once they're inside, Tynan turns to his brothers and father. "Did you get anything from Grant?"

"Yeah. He says the car was registered to a Jerry Baker."

I gasp, my heart hammering, eyes glossing over as I trip backward a step, unable to breathe.

He wanted me to know. It's why he made sure he drove a car he was tied to.

Jerry wanted me to know it was him.

He's taunting me.

"Elara, you're okay. He won't touch you."

I hear him, feel his hands on me, yet I'm not here. I'm there, back when I was Jerry's.

The world around me starts to spin.

I can't let him find me. I can't let him hurt Brody or Tynan. I have to run again. There's no other choice.

"Elara? Do you hear me?" He still sounds distant, yet growing nearer. "Elara." His hand cups my face.

"Hmm?" I pant, focusing on his face as I blink faster. "Yeah, sorry." I swallow down my fear as everyone stares at me.

"I'm gonna take her inside. She's shaken up. I'll catch up with you guys later."

"Alright, son," Patrick says. "You call us if you need anything."

"Yeah, thanks, Dad."

He hooks his arm through mine and leads us inside the home. My pulse slams in my ears, the start of a headache forming in my temples.

With a gentle hold, he takes me up the stairs and to our bedroom, carefully settling me on the edge of the bed. "I'm gonna get you some water."

He leaves me for a moment, and I repeatedly draw air into my lungs, hating that I have to drag him into my hell.

This is why I wanted to be alone. I didn't want to involve anyone else in my past. But here we are, and there's no hiding any longer.

He returns a moment later, a bottle of water in his outstretched hand. "Drink, baby."

I take the cold liquid from him, already opened, and consume half the bottle, not realizing how dry my mouth was.

He takes it from me and places it on the nightstand, clasping both my hands in his. "Look at me, Elara."

My lashes flutter, fresh tears gathering in my eyes.

"I'm sorry," I cry. "I really am. You didn't ask for this. Neither did Brody. I think—"

"You think *what*?" He searches my gaze, and I find it hard to say the rest out loud, wanting so badly to stay here with him and the boy I love.

"I think it's better if I go. Today. I don't want you or—"

"If you think…" His jaw clenches like he finds it hard to finish. "If you think I'd let you leave us, you don't know me." He clasps the back of my head and stares down into my eyes, and it's like he's seeing into my soul. "I'm never letting you go, Elara Quinn." He lowers to his knees, his mouth nearing until his lips brush mine. "Ever. And if you try to run, I'm gonna find you, and I'll bring you right back to me."

I let out a sob and throw my arms around him, smashing my lips to his.

He lets out a low growl, pushing me down on the bed, his body climbing over mine. His kisses turn deeper, more urgent and demanding, like he's reminding me that I'm his.

A hand sinks into my hair as he gives me every ounce of passion and affection that's been growing between us day by day, hiding between words trapped in our withered hearts.

And in this moment is when I know that all I want…

All I really want…

Is to stay.

Breathlessly, he rears back and pins his forehead to mine, not saying anything for a few seconds.

"I want to know everything, Elara. I promise, he won't ever hurt you again."

I believe him. I believe he wants to protect me. But I know there's no way he can ever keep that promise. Sometimes our best is just not good enough.

He slides off me, helping me sit up while I try to find the courage to dig into my past and give him that ugly part of myself.

"It all started when my father owed money to Isaac, Jerry's dad. When he couldn't pay it back, he told them they could have me in exchange."

He holds my hand in his large one, his thumb rolling reassuringly over my skin. "What did they do to you, baby? How did you get that scar?"

Tears burst from my eyes as the memories overtake me.

He's there to wipe them away, his face contorting with his own wretched pain. "I'm sorry for doing this to you."

"It's okay." I grab his wrist and stare right at him. "Though you should know, you might hate me for it."

"That'll never happen."

He sounds so sure.

I let out a breath of a laugh. "We'll see."

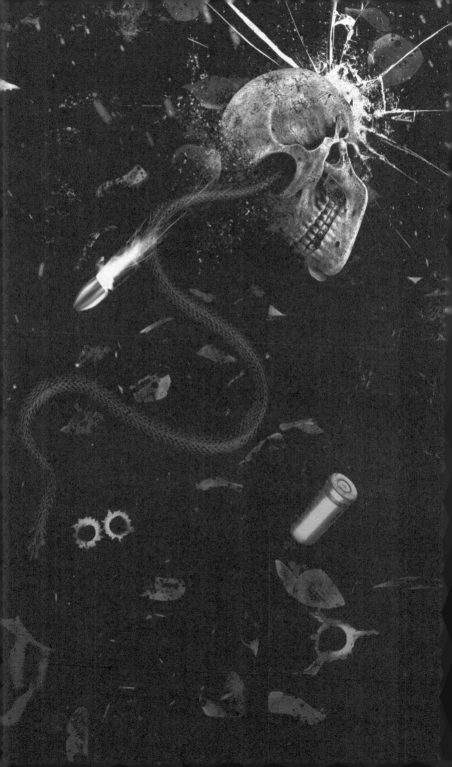

# THIRTY

## ELARA
### ABOUT A YEAR AGO

Three girls and I stand beside one another, all of us trembling, knowing what's coming next. It's not the first time, yet every time they make us do this, it feels like it'll be the last.

A girl named Carly stands inches away, her fingers close to mine, grabbing my hand with her shaky one as she tries hard not to cry. Her eyes overflow with tears, but she keeps quiet. They don't like it when we cry.

"I can't do this again," she whispers.

"Shh. They'll hear us," I warn her, not wanting her to end up like the girl last week who was shot for talking back.

"Shut up!" Ludwig, one of Jerry's guys, hollers, a canister of anesthesia in his hand.

Another man with gloves on rolls a metal cart toward him, and Ludwig brings it the rest of the way toward us.

*"Open your mouth," he tells me.*

*The tightness in my glare only makes him angrier. But I don't want to do this anymore.*

*His palm whips out, and he strikes me hard across the face. "If I tell Jerry you're not doing your job, he's gonna do far worse to you." He grabs my jaw and squeezes. "Open your fucking mouth!"*

*I shut my eyes and open wide, knowing I don't have a choice. The cool liquid coats my throat as he sprays all the way down.*

*I know what comes next before he even shoves the first condom filled with cocaine into my throat.*

*"Swallow."*

*And I do.*

*I barely feel it go down. I barely feel any of the seventy he makes me take inside my body, each one with about ten grams of pure coke.*

*That's what they do to us. Spray our throats with anesthesia and force drugs into our bodies before hoarding us off on planes.*

*The other girls have it worse, though. Jerry also sells their bodies for profit, and they don't get a dime.*

*Me? He keeps for himself. So nice of him.*

*Ludwig forces the rest of the girls to swallow the drugs, then hands us each two laxatives for the trip.*

*We're then shoved into a van and taken to a private airstrip in Colombia.*

*Once we arrive, I see Jerry, and my stomach fills with disgust.*

*"Hey, Ev." His cunning smirk has me wishing I could shoot him.*

*The closer he gets, the more the nausea crawls up my throat.*

*His arm around my hips makes my body feel as though tiny spiders are crawling all around it.*

*"You better not cry on that fucking plane like last time," he whispers into my ear. "I swear to God, I will kill you."*

*"Ready?" Ludwig asks.*

*"Yeah, let's go." He thrusts me up the steps of the small plane and*

*pushes me into the first seat, lowering beside me.*

*My head spins, knowing there are drugs inside my body. Drugs that could seep out of a ruptured balloon at any given moment.*

*I'd die within minutes.*

*That's what happened to a few girls who used to be here. We watched them go from dropping to the floor and foaming at the mouth to dead in a flash.*

*Maybe that'd be a better outcome than this life. I don't know how much more I can take.*

*But Jerry has me hostage. He has proof that I killed my father, and he plans to use it against me if I don't do what he says. And worse, he swore he'd kill my grandparents. I already lost my mom and Kennedy. I can't lose them too.*

*The plane takes off, and I force my eyes closed for the rest of the flight, hoping Jerry doesn't talk to me or look at me. It's enough that he's sitting right beside me.*

*The plane starts to dip, and when I look down, I realize we're landing. We still have to go through customs, but it's private and takes less time than commercial flights. Nothing I haven't done before. Jerry's men curl an arm around each one of the girls, pretending they're together so the customs officers don't get suspicious.*

*As always, the officers check our passports, check the plane, and we're on our merry way. Once we get to the drop-off, that's when the real fun begins.*

*We arrive in the middle of nowhere at one of the huge homes belonging to Jerry's father. One that they don't use, except for their drug business.*

*"Come on, keep it moving." Ludwig shoves Carly past the door, us following them.*

*"Let's go, Evelyn. You know what to do." Jerry pushes me into the bathroom.*

*Swallowing down the anxiety, I force myself to get the drugs out.*

*It takes half an hour, and after I'm done, someone goes in there and counts all the balloons.*

*I start toward Carly, but a voice stops me.*

*"We're two short."*

Nonono!

*My heart beats louder.*

*I didn't count them.*

*I should've counted!*

*How could I be so stupid, especially after what happened to Kennedy!*

*"I—I can take more meds."*

*"Fuck! It's probably stuck." Jerry runs a frustrated hand through his hair. "We need it out now. They're coming to pick it up in less than an hour."*

*I shake my head, tears filling my eyes because I know what he'll do. "Please, let me try more meds!"*

*I can't let him do this!*

*"Cut it out of her." Jerry's eyes lock with mine, his snarl sending terror running down my spine.*

*"Please, no! I beg you!"*

*Kennedy flashes before my eyes. Bleeding in the back of the car.*

*Dying.*

*I can't let that happen to me.*

*"Jerry, let's get the doctor," Brevin says, the one who notified him of the missing balloons. "Remember what happened last time to that other one? We can't keep losing girls."*

*"We'll find new ones. I said get it out of her!"*

*Carly lets out a sob behind me while fat tears trickle down my face.*

*Whenever this happened in the past, they had their doctor come in and get the drugs out. Except with Kennedy.*

*And now me.*

*I want to run. Yet there's nowhere to go.*

*"I can't do it." Brevin looks as though he's gonna be sick.*

*Jerry growls. "Get me a fucking knife and I'll do it."*

*"P-p-please," I beg him through my sobs.*

*I beg the devil for an ounce of compassion, and he doesn't give it to me. Grabbing my arm, he shoves me onto a gurney while I fight and scream and claw for him to stop.*

*"I'm begging you, please don't do this. Jerry, please!"*

*"Shut. Up."*

*When I stare up, I realize there's no humanity within him. None at all. He calls over two of his men.*

*"You hold her legs, and you get her arms. Brevin, get a rag for her mouth. Bitch is about to scream, and I'm not in the mood to hear it."*

*"No, no! Please!"*

*The girls cry in the background, and when I turn my face to the side, my gaze connects with Carly's broken one.*

*Jerry moves to the metal cart and picks up a thin scalpel a surgeon would use.*

*Placing it against my lower abdomen, he slices into me, and I scream with the most horrifying pain.*

*Until my world turns black.*

*Until everything vanishes.*

*And I pray I'm already dead.*

When I stare back at Tynan, I don't find repulsion. Instead, his eyes have grown with fury. His expression softens for a moment as he brushes my cheek with the back of his hand.

"I'm gonna tear him apart. And I'm gonna do it for you."

Tears blanket my vision, and he's there, wiping them away, kissing the side of my face, my lips, my eyes. His arms circle me before he tucks my body tightly against his, letting me cry while he holds me.

"I'm here, Elara. You never have to run anymore. From anyone."

"You don't hate me?" I peer up at him through my murky vision.

"Why would I hate you, baby? You did nothing wrong."

I shake my head. "I feel responsible for the lives I probably ruined by helping them bring the drugs here."

"My God, Elara. That's not your fault." He holds my face in both palms, staring intently at me. "You're a good person who was made to do bad things. That's all."

My eyes pinch shut, memories of my mother storming in. "I'm not a good person." I shake my head. "I killed my father."

I look at him then, but he doesn't even flinch.

"Why? What did he do?" His thumb rolls over my tear, brushing it away.

"He murdered my mother."

A muscle in his jaw pulses. "Then he deserved it."

I shake my head with a scoff. "I know it's probably nothing to you, but I killed him. I killed my father. Me!"

"You did what had to be done. You hear me? He killed your mother, and you took him out. Be proud of that."

I try to believe him. Though one bad act doesn't excuse another.

"Did he tell you why he did it? Why he killed her?"

"No…" I release a sigh. "But he was always smacking her around. Always belittling her. I begged her to leave him, and she wouldn't. When I saw her like that, all bloody, him crouching down and apologizing as he sobbed, all I felt was anger. Once he dropped the knife, I just grabbed it." I pin my eyes shut, my stomach churning, remembering all that blood. "Before I knew what was happening, I was stabbing him in the chest over and over until I was almost paralyzed with rage."

He kisses my forehead reassuringly. "It's okay, mo ghrá. It's okay."

"I sat there for a while, with my clothes soaked, numb from what had just happened. Then it hit me. My mother was truly gone and I was a murderer."

"When my mother was killed…" he says. "All I wanted was blood. It's okay to want to avenge those we love. It doesn't make you a bad person."

"I'm sorry you lost your mom too." The back of my hand strokes his jaw, and his eyes grow heavy.

I want to ask how she was killed, but I don't think my heart can take any more pain.

With a sigh, I finish my story, so he knows everything.

"After what I did, I had no one to call for help. So I called Jerry. Of course, he offered to help me bury the bodies. Little did I know, he collected proof of my father's death and all the evidence of me smuggling drugs and used it to blackmail me into staying."

"Motherfucker," he snaps. "I'll help you get it all back and destroy it."

"Really?" My eyes widen. "You'd do that for me?"

He clasps my nape and brings his face close to mine. "You're my wife, Elara. There's nothing I wouldn't do for you."

Emotions punch through my chest until I'm crying again, throwing my arms around him and holding on to him tight.

"Where does he keep it?" Fingertips trace up and down my spine. "Do you know?"

I look back at him. "Last time I checked, it was on his laptop. He had two, but one is where he keeps all the personal stuff. If he has it anywhere else, I don't know."

"I'll find it." He stares at me with absolute sincerity, and my body rocks with a sob.

Because for the first time, I'm not fighting this alone.

"You don't have to put yourself at risk for me, Tynan." I grip his heavy bicep, and it jerks under my touch. "You have Brody to live for, and if anything happens to you, I won't forgive myself."

He quirks a brow and gives me one of his tiny crooked smirks. "Is my wife starting to care about me?"

A finger reaches up to tuck a piece of my hair behind my ear, and my heart literally beats right out of my chest.

"Eh." I can't help my own smile. "Maybe a little."

He chuckles. "I'll take it."

We talk a little more, and I tell him about my life back home. How I found out that my father was knee-deep in criminal activities and that I had no idea, nor if my mom knew either. I thought about opening up to my grandma about it, but what's the use? How will her knowing the truth help?

"I'm sorry," he whispers with a pained tone.

"Not your fault."

With his knuckles, he traces the outline of my face. "Yet I still am."

Grabbing his hand, I kiss the top of it, and he holds me in his arms, both of us content in the stillness.

"I want to see Brody," I tell him. "He needs to know that everything will be okay."

"Yeah, let's go talk to him."

With a rough exhale, I get to my feet, stretching out my hand for his. "Coming?"

His eyes shine brightly. "Always, mo chuisle."

Tears brim my eyes, and together, we make it downstairs to find Brody in the kitchen with Ruby, eating spaghetti.

As soon as she sees us, she's rushing over. "You okay, honey?"

"I am now." I glance up at Tynan, who's staring down at me sweetly.

"I made dinner." Ruby squeezes my forearm. "If you need me, I'll be in the den."

She somehow knows exactly why we came down.

"Hey, buddy…" My gaze lands on Brody's teary eyes.

He lets out a small snivel, and as soon as he does, he hops off the chair and rushes toward both of us.

One of his arms holds on to my hip, while the other holds on to Tynan.

And with my overwhelming emotions, I look at him. The man who changed my life for better or worse—I don't yet know—but I'm happy he found me. Happy Brody has him.

Because underneath everything, there's a man with a heart of gold.

A smile slopes up the corner of his mouth, and my belly flips.

Because that's what his smiles always seem to do to me: ignite my world and set it on fire.

Yet with him, the flames no longer burn.

# THIRTY-ONE

## TYNAN
### THREE DAYS LATER

I had her take off work the past few days because I couldn't handle the thought of something happening to her. She fought me on it. She loves her kids and didn't want Jerry to ruin this for them—or her, for that matter.

Teaching is her passion, and I didn't want to be the one to crush it. Protecting her doesn't mean shattering her dreams. So we compromised. In the form of four bodyguards, around the clock. For her and Brody.

More men means more eyes.

But we're still looking for that asshole and his father. If they wanna hide like rats, then so be it. We'll find their people and take them out one by one until they have no choice but to face us.

Sometimes, to cut the head, you have to cut the arms first. Isaac and Jerry have no idea who they're fucking with.

There's a soft knock on the door of my office, and it's Elara, all dressed up. Her hair's curled at the ends, and she's in a tight white dress with beige heels.

Stalking over to her, I wind an arm around her back. "Where are you going dressed like that?"

"Like how?" Her mouth curls. She knows exactly what I mean.

"Like you're about to leave a trail of dead bodies behind you."

"And why is that, Mr. Quinn?" She throws her arms around my neck.

"Because I'd have to kill every man for looking at you the way I am right now, mo chuisle."

She giggles all sexy, leaning in for a kiss, and with a growl, I grab the back of her head and kiss her right back.

She's been different since she told me about her past. She gives her affection more freely now, and I like it.

Very much.

I've been careful with her since the car chase, knowing how much it all affected her. I haven't pushed for anything, merely content with holding her every night.

But her kissing me like this, it just broke my damn self-control altogether.

I throw her body up against the wall, a hand sinking into her hair, the other gripping her hip as I slide my tongue into her willing mouth.

"Mm," she groans, scratching her nails up and down my back. "You're gonna make me late for my date."

My mouth drops to her jaw, nipping and biting down the column of her neck. "A date, huh? Tell me his name so I can eliminate the problem."

She sucks in a gasp when my fingers slink up her inner thigh, tracing her pussy, covered in a pair of thin panties.

"*Her* name…" she breathes when my palm drives into her core, forcing her to ride it.

"Her? Who's her?"

"Elara, are you ready?" a voice I recognize booms from the other side of the house.

"You're going out with my sister?"

She laughs at my shock. I hadn't even realized they were talking, which of course makes me happy. I want her to get close to my family. But Iseult? Mm…debatable.

Elara clears her throat and tousles her hair with her fingers in an attempt to fix it. So much I could do to that hair while I fuck her. Maybe bent over my desk. I think it's time I christen it. Maybe get her pregnant like that.

Fuck, the thought makes my dick throb.

"Yes, I am. Is that a problem?" She curves a brow. "Iseult called me this morning and asked if I wanted to go shopping with her, so I said yes."

Now, normally I'd say no, even with four of my men tailing her. But knowing she's going to be with my sister, one of the best assassins I know, makes the situation a lot easier to process.

"No problem at all, baby." I kiss her forehead, inhaling her fragrant perfume. "Have a good time. And please spend our money. I want you to spoil the shit out of yourself."

"Okay, Mr. Quinn." Her flirtatious smirk makes me ravenous. "I'll make you proud."

"That's my girl." I grab a fistful of her ass and drag her body into mine, kissing her one last time, her red lipstick already completely ruined.

She notices me looking there. "Ugh, it's my lipstick, isn't it? Is it that bad?"

"I mean, define bad."

She groans, rushing into the bathroom attached to my office. "Tell Iseult I'll be right out and that it's all your fault."

"Take your time. She can wait."

While she fixes herself, I go to greet my sister, who has the patience of a toddler.

Her over-the-knee stiletto boots clack on the ceramic as she paces, talking to someone on the phone. Probably Gio.

"I've gotta go, babe. Gio says hi," she says to me.

I nod to return the same.

"He says hi too. Glad everyone loves each other. I'll see you later," she tells him. "Don't kill anyone until I'm back."

He must say something to that because she rolls her eyes, but her face flushes.

Don't wanna know.

She ends the call and places the phone in her bag.

"So, you and Elara are friends now?"

"Yes, we bonded over our mutual disdain for you." She flips her hair back. "And our mild affection too."

"Watch out for her." I squeeze my temple, unable to stop worrying while Jerry's still out there. "I can't let that prick get to her."

She grips my shoulder. "Not gonna happen with me around. I'd never let it."

Pinching the bridge of my nose, I force my eyes to a close, taking a deep breath and telling myself that Elara will be okay. She has to be.

"Shit, you're in love with her."

I immediately stare back at her. "What? No, I'm not."

She drops her hand to her side. "Oh my God. You are! You can lie to yourself, but not to me." She lets out a short laugh. "It's okay. It happens to the best of us. I won't tell anyone," she whispers. "Especially Devlin, since you'd owe him a million dollars."

"Shut up about it. Stupid fucking bet," I mutter.

"I know how much you hate to lose. But this time you're done for, brother."

"I don't know," I tell her honestly, and her face grows serious. "I can't explain it."

"Explain what?"

"The things I'm feeling."

"What sort of things?"

"Like the fact that I hate not knowing if she's okay when I'm at work. If she's upset or crying thinking about that piece-of-shit ex. I want to be near her all the damn time, to a maddening level. And I like her laugh. I even like it when she's pissed at me. But all I really want is to take care of her and make her happy. Every damn time."

"Aww." Her face drops to the side, her lips tightening. "Time to face the facts. You're stupid in love." She slaps me on the back. "Mazal tov."

"Nah, I don't think so."

She rolls her eyes. "Denial doesn't look good on you, brother."

I let her words sink in, marinating in my head. But I can't think about that. Of falling in love with her. Of losing her…

Images of my mother burning to death come barreling in. If she hadn't married my father, she would still be alive. I know I can't rationalize it all this way, but it's all I've got. I don't want what happened to my mother to happen to Elara. It'd kill me.

"Well, this is as much emotion as I can handle." My sister starts to walk away. "I'll wait for her in my car."

"Thanks, Iseult. She really needed a normal day. As much as I want to, I know I can't keep her prisoner in the house until we find Jerry and his father. We need to find them, though, because I can't handle knowing they're still alive."

"We'll find them, and we'll kill them. And everyone who works for them. But for now, you're right. You can't keep her prisoner here. She needs to live her life."

"Have fun today. Please make sure she spends money. I constantly have to remind her that it's not just mine, but ours."

She winks, flinging her red hair behind her shoulder. "Don't you worry, I'll make sure she spends the shit out of it. Oh, and we're taking your jet. Have your pilot on standby."

"Just make sure she comes back to me in one piece."

Her face softens, and that's something for Iseult. She feels everything, but hates showing it.

Her younger years weren't easy. Losing our mother at fourteen, having to take care of our baby sister, who was five at the time. My father was too busy enacting revenge for my mother's death to worry about how much the loss hurt Iseult. Then throw in everything else she endured because of Konstantin's father, and I'm surprised she's even here at all.

I admire her.

She's made herself into a weapon, and no one can fuck with her now.

"I promise, Tynan. She'll be okay."

And I believe her.

# ELARA

My eyes grow as soon as we step foot inside Dolce & Gabbana. I can't get over the fact that we took a jet here. This is all wild. People actually live like this.

*It's your life now too.*

I don't think I'll ever get used to it.

Iseult made sure the store was only open to us. That way I won't worry about looking over my shoulder every second.

I've been keeping a good front for Tynan and Brody and my grandma, but I'm petrified. Because if Tynan and his people still can't find him, that's not good. I thought by now Jerry would be found.

But I can't keep hiding from him. I want to go back to teaching, to living my life. I want to go visit my grandpa.

I've begged Grandma to come stay with me and Tynan in the

meantime, but she refuses, wanting her independence. I don't fault her for that. It's what I want too.

Tomorrow, I'm finally going back to work, and I'll get to see Grandpa after I'm done. He may not know who I am, but I know him, and I miss him terribly.

Things with Tynan have been good. Fun, in fact. Every day, it gets harder to remember why I'm not supposed to want this. He's a good man, and I can see how easy it would be to fall head over heels for him. And some days, it feels as though I'm already there. Yet at the end of the day, this marriage isn't real.

When I get married, I want it to be my choice. And I want the man I marry to actually love me.

"Are you ready to do some damage?" Iseult throws her arm around my shoulders, moving toward a rack of clothes.

I like her. She's got an edge. Definitely don't want to be the one to ever piss her off, though.

"I guess."

She picks up some red leather pants while I examine a green pencil dress, the shade reminding me of Tynan's eyes, and I instantly know I want it. It has a faux belt and a deep V-neck. But when I look at the price tag…

"Oh my God."

Iseult appears beside me. "We're getting that one."

"It's ten thousand dollars, Iz!"

"So?"

"I can't keep buying things that cost this much! It's crazy!"

"Hello! My brother is loaded, and now so are you." She smirks. "And I promised Tynan you'd shop your heart out, so shop. Or else I'll have to call him and tell him how difficult you're being," she teases with a quirk of her brow.

I know she's right, that this is our money now, but it still feels weird to me.

We continue shopping, both of us trying things on and showing them to the other. I'm forcing myself to ignore all the price tags, even though it's quite difficult.

Iseult picks up a black-and-gold embroidered one-piece swimsuit with the center cut open.

"This would look amazing on you." She hands it to the sales associate. "She's going to try this on."

As I attempt to pick up the price tag, she swats my hand away.

"I'm gonna have them rip off all the tags if you don't stop."

"Okay, just for my curiosity, can you just tell me what it costs?"

"Fine." She huffs. "Thirty-three hundred. Now, can we find more things to try on?"

My eyes fly open. "Jesus, for a scrap of material?"

She shakes her head, treading toward the men's section. "Oh my God." She holds out a canary-yellow suit. "Can you imagine Tynan ever wearing this?"

I break out in a fit of laughter. Picturing that man, who only wears neutral colors, wearing something like this is comical. It's like Big Bird and Tweety Bird had a baby.

"He'd die before he'd ever wear this," she says. "You should buy it for him."

"Pretty sure he wouldn't appreciate that."

"I know. That's why you should do it." Her wicked grin is deadly.

"Oh, you're bad." I examine the suit, unable to hide my own smile. "You know, maybe you're right. He *has* been telling me to spend money. Maybe it's time I really did."

"Phyllis," Iz calls the sales associate. "We're gonna take a bunch of these suits. Which colors do you think he'd like?"

"Hmm…" I purse my lips to stop from laughing. "I think the yellow, the green, and that bright purple would really make his eyes pop. Don't you think?"

"I think I do."

"Phyllis, we want all the colors. You have my brother's size on file, yes?"

"Yes, ma'am." She nods, not even a bit fazed.

"I think Tynan will approve of your lavish spending habits, sister-in-law." She bumps my hip with hers.

"I think you're right."

"I wish I could see the look on his face. Any chance you can record it?"

"I'll see what I can do."

He's gonna hate this, and I'm giddy with excitement.

I never realized how exhilarating torturing one's husband could be.

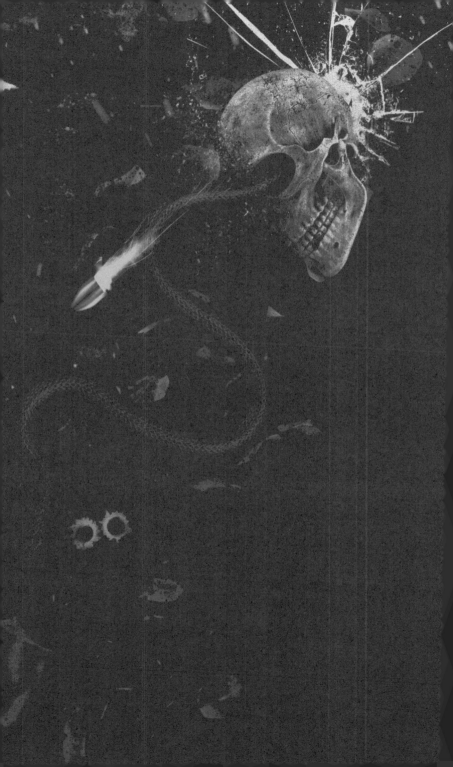

# THIRTY-TWO

## TYNAN

While the girls are out shopping, I spend the day with Brody and my brothers, playing basketball, ordering takeout, and hanging out by the pool while Bubbles runs around the lounge chairs, stealing my damn leather sandals.

I've given up on her tolerating me. I thought Elara would be the last to break, but it seems like the dog is stronger than I thought.

At least Elara has warmed up to me. She doesn't look like she wants to kill me anymore, which is quite the turnaround.

The conversation with Iseult plays in my head. Could I really be in love with Elara? I'm crazy about her. She has to know that by now.

But love? I don't know what that looks like. I've never experienced these feelings I have for her. Not with anyone. And I wish I could say they're not terrifying, but they're scaring the shit out of me.

Brody grins, rushing up to me holding a book Fionn gifted him when he got here. I don't know much about books since I don't read, but the kid loves them, and I love that he does.

"That looks cool, bud. Is that from the same series Elara got you that other book from?"

He nods, stars in his eyes. He smiles so freely now, I'm afraid to say it out loud so as not to jinx it. Feels like at any given moment, the rug will be pulled from under my feet.

If he can smile, then maybe there's a chance he'll talk soon. I just have to be patient. Though patience has never been my strength.

"You look like you need a beer." Cillian hands me one as Brody leaves the book on the lounger and joins Ruby in the pool, Bubbles jumping in after him.

"Thanks."

Fionn joins us, his face tense as he places his cell in his shorts pocket. "Heard back from our guys just now. They killed six of Jerry and Isaac's men. Left their headless corpses at Jerry's doorstep."

A grin spreads on my face. "Any of them talk?"

"Nah. They were loyal."

"That's too bad. But this should get them to make contact. If they don't in the next couple of days, we'll kill more of their guys until there's none left."

"We should expect a war with them," Cillian adds. "It's their style, though we'd squash them easily."

"Let them come." I keep watching Brody play. "We'll be ready."

Silence falls for a few moments before he speaks again.

"The kid looks different. Happier." Fionn folds his arms over his chest, looking out at the pool.

"Yeah." I nod. "I knew Elara would be good for him."

"You look better too." His face breaks with amusement.

"Mm-hmm. Don't make me toss you in the water."

But a crack of a smile appears on my face, because I *am* happier. With her.

My phone rings on the lounge chair, and when I pick it up, I find my banker on the other end.

"What's up, Ed?"

"Sir, I'm sorry to bother you, and I wouldn't if we didn't have a rather worrisome problem."

"And what's that?"

"Well, uh…it seems there's a rather large pending transaction at the Dolce & Gabbana store that I wasn't sure if you wanted me to approve."

*Ah, Elara has finally listened.*

"Approve it."

"But you don't even know how much it's for."

"Doesn't matter. It's just my wife, and she can spend whatever she wants."

Can't wait to get my hands on her just to show her how proud I am.

"Okay, but, sir, it's for almost three-quarters of a million," he whispers.

I let out a big laugh, and both my brothers stare at me, wondering why.

"Wow. I'm really impressed. Approve it, and from now on, I want you to approve them all. She has no limit."

"Okay, sir, thank—"

I end the call and throw my phone back down.

"What was that about?" Fionn asks.

"Elara's finally learning to spend our money."

He chuckles. "You know that's probably our sister's influence, right?"

"I know. I told her to make sure of it. It's not every day Iseult actually listens to a goddamn word I say."

"Truth." Cillian lets out a snicker.

"Oh, I forgot to tell you guys, Konstantin called this morning. His new associate wants to meet us before he decides if he wants to work with us. We meet at my place in two days at three p.m. sharp. Make sure you're both there."

"Yeah. No problem. Who the fuck is he? Do we know?" Cillian asks.

"Some big shot."

"Alright. We'll be there. Just want this shit done. Hate working with the Russians."

"We all do, but we need them," I tell him. "They're a good connect. Without them, we wouldn't get this deal."

"Did you know he invited us to his fortieth birthday?" Fionn snickers.

"Shit." I run a hand down my face. "I was hoping the invitation got lost in the mail."

He chuckles. "No such luck. We all have to go. Would be taken as an insult if we missed it."

"Yeah, I know."

I just hope he doesn't insist on one of my brothers marrying a member of his family. It may help mend bridges, but the last thing we want is to tie ourselves to that family for life.

Hours later, and Elara returns, bags of clothes all over our bedroom.

I shut the door with my foot and wrap an arm around her, kissing her softly against the corner of her mouth. "Had fun?"

"The best." Her eyes practically twinkle, her hand sinking into my hair and massaging my scalp as I groan.

"I want you to see all the stuff I got." She seems excited about it, and that only makes me happier.

"I see you had no problems spending money today."

"Nope." Her pretty mouth curves when she pulls away, her hips swaying as she moves toward the bags to grab one off the floor. "I did buy you some stuff too." She peeks up at me for a moment, picking up a vivid green dress. "Didn't want you to feel left out."

I prowl closer, my hand snapping her jaw with a growl, kissing her hard. "What a thoughtful wife."

She melts into me.

"I try." Her raspy voice makes my dick jerk.

"How about I help you put all the clothes away?" Fucking her in the closet plays on repeat in my head.

Never said my offer was altruistic.

"How very kind of you, husband."

"Mm, I like you calling me your husband."

"Do you now?" She works her hands up and down my back, her nails digging into my skin and muscle.

I want her to carve them into my flesh. Want to hurt. Want to feel it all with her.

As I look into her eyes, I start to wonder if Iseult could be right. If I am falling in love with her, and if I'll truly ever know for sure.

"You okay?" she asks, her brows furrowing.

"Yeah, baby. Just thinking."

"Oh. Well, don't think too hard. You wouldn't want to hurt that little brain of yours."

I groan with a laugh. "Oh, little serpent, you wanna play, don't you?"

She lets out a giggle and slides out of my grasp, biting her bottom lip with a grin as she starts to run.

"You know what happens when I catch you, right?" My gaze narrows, a smirk pulling at my mouth as I start uncuffing my shirt and dragging it up my arms.

"No. What?" Her voice grows wispy, eyes leaden.

"When I catch you, I will fuck you."

She gasps, her breasts climbing higher with each breath. Then she's running across the bedroom, rushing into the closet, and closing the door behind her.

But her attempt at holding the door shut is futile. I force it open

LILIAN HARRIS

easily, finding her body trembling as I stalk closer, shutting it behind me.

My gaze skims down her body—so fucking perfect, I ache for her.

As I draw closer, she advances backward.

"Nowhere else to go, baby." I'm on her in a flash, palms on her hips, lifting her in the air and pushing her up against the wall.

"You're trapped." I run my palm up from between her breasts until my fingers are wrapped around her throat. "I'm gonna fuck you just like this. Naked and spread open, pummeling inside you, making you come over and over until you can't move."

"Tynan…" She grasps my hair, circling her hips right into my throbbing dick.

"Fuuuck, Elara." I squeeze her throat. "You're killing me. Wanna fill you up and get you pregnant. I swear, I never in my life thought I'd say that to a woman."

"Thank you?" Her cheeks grow crimson right before I smash her mouth to mine, ravishing her with every emotion she's made me feel.

My every desire come to life.

A dream I didn't even know I had.

Until I met *her*.

I don't know if she feels what I do. Fuck, I don't even know what it is I'm feeling anymore. But I know one thing: there's no one else for me except her.

Snapping her head back, I leave a trail of rough kisses down her neck, dragging her dress down and sucking a nipple into my mouth.

Her feminine sounds of pleasure only inflame my desire. But I want her begging and quivering. I love it when she begs.

She gasps in protest when I lower her back down. Breathlessly, she narrows her eyes up at me with confusion, her lipstick a mess, her eyes watery.

So sexy.

"If you want it…" I grab her jaw. "Ask for it."

She fixes her dress, a challenge in her eyes. "Eh, think I'm good."

"Is that right?" My smirk deepens.

"Have so much to unpack. Fucking you doesn't seem as important right now."

She's playing games, and I love games.

"Okay, then. Show me what you bought. I hope there's some lingerie in there."

She scoffs. "You wish."

I chuckle, gazing down at her lips. "It's okay, sweetheart. Don't need anything special to get hard for you."

Her shy little smile makes me wanna kiss her all over again.

She starts toward the dozens of bags on the floor, and I follow her as she removes her clothes and places them on the bed. I never realized how good it would feel to have someone to spend money on.

When she grabs another bag and takes out some really bright suits, I try to hide my grimace. "Those are…uh, colorful."

"So you like them?" Her eyes brighten as she peeks at me from behind her shoulder.

"Of course."

I'm not about to tell her how hideous they are. If she wants to wear them, then who am I to stop her? Though they do look quite big…

"I'm glad you think so!" She grins. "They're for you."

I cough, trying to keep a straight face. "Is that so?"

"That's right." She arches a brow. "I thought your closet could use some color. Want to try one on?"

I chuckle, advancing closer, clasping her hips.

She throws her arms over my shoulders, grinning like a tempestuous devil.

My lips brush hers. "Having a little fun?"

I palm her ass and squeeze hard, pulling her into my body.

"You *did* tell me to spend your money." There's a sultry edge to her tone.

"*Our* money, mo chuisle. Remember that." I kiss her, just barely, teasing her until she groans.

"I thought maybe I'd get under your skin long enough for you to divorce me."

I let out a low growl against her ear. "Is that what you thought? That I would let you go for some little prank?"

She grabs fistfuls of my hair. "Mm-hmm."

"Do your worst, baby. There's nothing you can do to make me let you go."

"Is that a bet?" She pushes me back, gazing straight into my eyes, and my heart flinches.

*I'm obsessed with you...*

"Bring it on."

"*Really* wish you hadn't said that." She scrunches her nose in the most adorable way.

*What could she really do to me?*

My hand curls around the base of her jaw.

"I can play dirty too," I remind her, staring deep into her eyes. "Just hope you come prepared, little serpent, because you're not the only one who can bite."

She grips my wrist. "I like it when you bite."

With a growl, I crush my lips to hers, kissing her with blistering fury, wanting to get lost inside her.

Her fingers slip under my shirt, and her hands on my skin make me lose my fucking mind. With a grunt, I throw her onto the bed face-first, roughly dragging her dress up. I slap her bare ass, needing that thong off of her.

"Stay just like that." I work my belt, yanking it out, before my pants and boxers come next.

My damn pulse batters in my ears, needing her so badly, I'm willing to beg her for it.

She pops out her ass, gyrating her hips, teasing the fuck out of me as she catches my eye from over her shoulder.

With my cock free, I fist it, squeezing the head, my precum seeping out as she watches.

"Want it inside you?"

She reaches into her panties and starts touching herself, smirking at me like she knows she's not allowed to do that.

"Get that hand out. You don't get to play with that pussy until I allow it."

But she doesn't listen, her mouth parting, brows snapping with pleasure as she continues to touch herself.

"Fuck, you drive me insane." In a split second, I'm tugging her fingers out and sucking them into my mouth, groaning from the taste of her.

With a fistful of her hair, I arch her back until my mouth is level to her ear. "I think it's time I taught you a lesson."

"Is that so, Mr. Quinn?" She bows her ass into my cock.

"That's right. When I tell you something, you do it."

"Seems like I'm not much of a listener."

I spank her hard, and she cries out.

"I think it's time I fixed that." In a flash, I'm seated on the edge of the bed, her ass over my knee.

Her desperate, quivering moans make it harder for me not to just fuck her.

My fingertips roll over the slit of her ass, descending until I trace her pussy, yanking her panties to the side. "Shall I examine how soaked you are?"

"Tynan, please." She squirms, her eyes full of lust, her toes curling on the floor.

"So damn hot when you're begging." I thrust two fingers inside her as she cries out, sliding them out of her to show her the evidence of her arousal. "Look at it. So wet. So desperate for your husband's cock."

"Please, Tynan, I need this."

"I know you do, but I think I wanna play with my toy first." I shove my fingers into her mouth, grinding my molars as she moans. "Good girl. Keep sucking."

Dragging my fingers out, I spread her ass open with both palms. "Gonna fill that hole too. Gonna fill every desperate hole in your body."

She begs for it, unable to stop herself. I spank her again, her skin growing pink from my heavy touch.

When she tries to fight me, I catch her wrists and pin them to the small of her back. "Not done having my fill of you just yet." Another spank, and her body jolts. "Want you red and sore before I fill you up. Gonna watch me dripping out of your cunt."

"Oh fuck, I'm gonna come."

"Don't you dare." I ram my fingers deeper and she cries out. "You come, and I'll punish you again."

She quivers, whimpering something unintelligible.

I use her slick arousal and bring it up to her other hole, filling her up with my thumb while two fingers thrust into her pussy at the same time.

"Oh my God, I feel so full." Her walls squeeze me from both ends, and I'm about to come myself.

"On your knees, little serpent. I think it's time I watched you gagging on it."

She stares at me all wild-eyed, and I revel in it. Been wanting her to suck me off so damn bad.

I grab her jaw and kiss her hard before forcing her onto her knees.

With unsteady hands, she fists me, lowering her mouth until her tongue traces the tip.

"Oh, shit…" I clutch the top of her head. "Need you to take all of it, baby."

She lets out a breathy moan, and with her eyes on mine, she

swallows the tip into her mouth, grabbing my balls and squeezing them as she takes more of my erection.

"That's it. That's a good wife. Take it all."

I force her head down even more, and she starts to gag.

"Damn, you sound good choking on it."

She takes me whole, touching her pussy while she bobs her head. I'm ready to release it all into her pretty throat, but all I want is to fill her cunt with it.

I wrap her hair around my fist and tug, dragging my cock out of her. "My God, you're perfect."

"Tynan…" She attempts to control her erratic breathing, rising until she's straddling me, clasping my face with her warm hands.

These feelings inside me.

This want.

This *need* for a woman who appeared in my life as though out of nowhere.

I can't handle it.

Yet she consumes me further with every single moment.

Unable to wait another second, I toss her onto the bed, bending her over the edge. That dress is around her hips, her ass and pussy mine for the taking.

My body lowers over hers, my cock at her entrance.

"You're undoing me, Elara." I slide in just a little, stretching her just enough. "Inch by inch, I'm unraveling."

I force more of myself inside her, until my first piercing enters her.

"Oh, God! More, please…"

"Say it. Tell me you want me to come inside you. Tell me you want it all with me."

"Yes, please. I want it. I really want it." Her eyes fuse with mine from over her shoulder.

And when I find that desperation piercing within them, that's all it takes for me to break.

The bed creaks as I slam myself deeper, sliding all the way out, then giving it to her harder, over and over again.

She grabs the comforter, her body quivering, tiny tremors of her walls milking my cock until she comes, squirting all over the damn place.

"That's it, baby." I spank her ass, her high-pitched cries loud enough to crack the walls.

Yet I don't stop, giving it to her harder. Her eyes lock with mine, her breaths as wild as her gaze while I continue to take what belongs to me, chasing my own release.

With a growl, I let her have all of me, hot spurts shooting into her. And I pray like hell it gets her pregnant.

She releases a huff, laughing with tortured breaths. "If I knew getting you a bunch of silly suits would make you fuck me like that, I'd have done it sooner."

I lie on top of her body, biting into her lobe. "I wanted to. I just didn't wanna push you after everything."

Her eyes swim with emotion. "That's so sweet."

"Yeah, that's me." I arch my hips into her ass. "Sweet."

Flipping onto my back, I pull her onto my chest.

We lie in each other's arms for a while, my fingers lazily rolling up and down her back.

*This is nice.*

"What do you wanna do today?" I ask.

"Well, I was kinda hoping to shower, then watch a movie with Brody. Wanna join us?"

I kiss her temple. "Of course I do."

"I really don't wanna get up, though." She groans.

I nudge her chin with a finger. "Promise to make it worth your while."

Her teeth nip at her bottom lip, making a low growl emanate from deep in my chest.

"Come on, let's take a shower together so I can fuck you up against the wall."

Her gaze turns fiery.

I get to my feet, pulling her up and stripping off her clothes until she's bare and beautiful. My ravenous gaze takes her in, and her nipples bead in the wake of it.

When I lock eyes with her, those cheeks of hers turn pink, and a smirk falls to my lips.

"Being shy on me?" I grab her jaw.

"A little."

"Don't be. I've already seen every inch of you, and I'm not going anywhere."

# ELARA

I don't think I can physically get off this sofa after what we did earlier.

Sitting between Brody and Tynan is exactly where I want to be.

I won't lie and say I'm not scared that I'm starting to feel things for Tynan. Things I want to deny. But that's becoming harder with each passing day.

He's a surprise—one I'm afraid to welcome. Yet I want to at the same time.

Brody looks up at me and grins, moving the bucket of popcorn in my direction. When I return the sentiment, he leans his head against my shoulder, moving the bucket toward Tynan.

"Thanks, bud." He grabs some, tossing it into his mouth. And when his eyes catch mine, his lips curl, sending my stomach soaring with butterflies.

He reaches for my hand and holds it behind Brody, and we remain that way.

Lost in each other.
Lost in these feelings I'm still wrestling with.
Unsure how long I can deny them.

# THIRTY-THREE

## TYNAN

The Russians arrive at my home with their associate for our scheduled meeting at exactly three p.m.

"Welcome." I shake hands with Sloan, the man they say can facilitate the weapons deal.

Once he greets my brothers, I'm ready to get this show on the road.

"Your home is beautiful. So is your land." Sloan removes his sunglasses and settles on one of the sofas in my office, the Marinovs joining him.

"Thank you. Shall we get down to business?"

He runs his fingers over his goatee, slowly nodding.

"Konstantin has given me all the details, but I'm a careful man, you see, so I wanted to meet you and your family face-to-face. Just so I know who I'm dealing with."

"We understand." I purposely make myself seem casual as he studies me.

The man looks to be in his fifties, maybe late forties. And though he doesn't appear to be familiar, there's something about him that isn't settling right with me, and I can't figure out why.

A sudden knock on the door interrupts my thoughts. Who the hell could be bothering me during the damn meeting?

"Come in."

When the door opens, all eyes land on my gorgeous wife.

And I instantly want to tear each one from their sockets.

I grind my teeth as my gaze takes her in. She's in one of those see-through bikini cover-ups, and I don't miss the way every damn man shifts when their attention falls to her body.

A flush rises up my neck, fingers curling. It probably wouldn't be smart going on a killing spree right now, but it sounds fucking tempting.

"What can I do for you?" Didn't mean to sound homicidal, but fuck, do I wanna punish her for walking into my meeting barely dressed.

"Oh, gosh. I'm so sorry to bother you. I can come back." She looks embarrassed, and I'm feeling bad about it.

"It's alright." My voice softens. "Is something wrong?"

Concern gnaws at me. Why else would she interrupt my meeting?

"No. Just…uh, needed to tell you something." She clears her throat and shyly looks at the men. "Hello there."

"Is this your wife?" Konstantin rises.

"I am the wife," she says, popping a brow. "And I can answer for myself."

He lets out a short laugh. "Ah, I can see he picked a good one."

He approaches, taking her hand in his and kissing the top of it. She politely removes it from his grasp when she notices my white-knuckled fist on my desk.

Can just imagine what my face looks like. But I don't want another man's lips on my wife, especially when she's barely wearing any clothes.

I swear, if Konstantin doesn't sit back down, I won't be able to stop myself from killing him.

"It's a pleasure to meet you, Mrs. Quinn. I'm Konstantin. I hope it's not the last time we are in each other's company."

"I'm sure it won't be."

Fionn drops a palm to my shoulder. Didn't even notice him getting up, my attention zeroed in on Elara, her ass and chest almost all out in the black one-piece swimsuit she's wearing.

Shit, wanna lay her on my desk, slide the swimsuit to the side and fuck her senseless.

Sloan looks her up and down. "You look familiar."

Her demeanor instantly shifts, her eyes assessing him. She throws on a fabricated smile, one I know too well.

"Sorry, don't think we've met before." Her eyes lock to mine. "Anyway, sweetheart…" She moves toward my desk, my cock growing harder the closer she gets. "I just wanted you to know, I made that donation to the charity we talked about the other day."

I peer up at her with confusion.

"Oh, you know…" Her voice grows small, a little smirk growing. "To Firm Belief. For, uh…" She glances around. "Erectile dysfunction."

Konstantin bursts with a chuckle. "Problems, Tynan?"

I grind my jaw so hard, my teeth ache.

She thins her lips to stop from laughing.

*Oh, she's gonna pay for this.*

She places the paper on the table, and in small print, it says:

You told me to bring it on. So I did.

I snatch the paper and ball it in my grip before tossing it in the garbage.

"They were so happy about our donation of two hundred thousand. I mean, it is a worthy cause, right, gentlemen?"

She gazes around the room, and all but Konstantin grumble in agreement, because he's too busy laughing again.

"Hey." She turns sternly toward him. "I'll have you know many men suffer with that problem. It isn't a laughing matter."

She pats my hand, and I yank it away, too proud and pissed at the same time. She got me good, which means I'll have to get her better.

"That's great, baby. You're always on top of things. Glad I married you." I grab her wrist and throw her onto my lap, wrapping her hair around my wrist.

My mouth drops to her ear. "You're gonna pay so hard for this, baby girl."

"I can't wait," she whispers, a challenge in her eyes.

She leaves a sweet kiss on my cheek, and I almost forget I'm supposed to be mad at her.

Almost.

"Anyway, have a great meeting. Brody and I are off for a swim. If you need me, just let me know. Love you."

My pulse instantly quickens. *What did she just say?*

She's already out the door, and I'm left wondering if she meant that.

I'm sure she was just putting on a show, though my heart hasn't caught up to my mind. Or how good it was to hear her say that.

"Well, your wife is some woman." Sloan shakes his head, like he's clearing dirty thoughts of her.

The meeting continues without interruption. But as soon as Sloan gets to his feet, he glances out the window...at the perfect view of Elara swimming with my son.

Rage simmers in my blood.

"What the *fuck* are you doing?" I'm right behind him, my hand gripping the nine at my waistband.

"Just enjoying the view." His tone is indifferent and that only enrages me. "You're lucky you get to fuck that." When he faces me, a single brow curves. "Yet I'm wondering if you actually know who your wife truly is."

My fingers round the grip of my gun. If this fucker says one more word, I'm gonna kill him.

"I suggest you stop talking right now," Fionn says from behind me.

"Yes, let's all relax, gentlemen," Konstantin throws in. "Before one of us does something we can't undo."

But I ignore them all, my body pulsing, needing to rip Sloan's goddamn throat out.

"I don't mean any offense." Sloan raises his palms in the air. "I just remembered where I've seen her before. Don't you wanna know where?"

Blood rushes to my head, and I grit my teeth for control.

"In Colombia, getting drugs shoved down her throat."

I'm on him before anyone can stop me, fighting my brothers as they try to tear me off from the ground.

My fists are in his face, and I don't even know how many times I've hit the bastard.

I remove my gun, forcing the barrel into his mouth, and his eyes widen with deafening fear.

"Say something now, you fucker." The blood from my knuckles drips over his face.

"Do not kill him," Konstantin warns.

I don't give a shit. He'd do worse.

"Now isn't the time," Cillian warns as he attempts to pull me off.

But it is. He deserves to die for what he just said about her.

Fionn helps Cillian drag me up.

"Not here," he whispers.

My breaths rage out of me as Kirill helps Sloan up.

The motherfucker still manages to grin, wiping the blood from his mouth. "All I wanted was for you to know who you married."

I rush for him again, breaking from my brothers.

But Konstantin appears between us, palms against both of our chests. "I am truly disappointed." He sighs with a shake of his head. "This is not the way to do business."

"I agree." Sloan's nostrils flare, his one eye starting to swell. "We're done here." He looks at Konstantin. "And if you think I'll ever do business with your family if you continue to associate with these barbarians, then you have another think coming."

He heads for the door.

Konstantin sighs. "What a pity."

Before we know it, he whips out his gun and shoots Sloan in the back of the head.

He falls to the ground with a thud.

"What the hell was that? Thought you told me not to kill him."

"I did." He smirks. "Though only because I was looking forward to doing it myself. He was really starting to piss me off."

Fionn chuckles, while Konstantin returns the weapon back to his holster.

"Well, now we need another contact." I run a frustrated hand down my face. "Got anyone else in mind?"

More blood leaks from Sloan's head, and I hope it doesn't ruin my floor.

"I do, actually. Someone with a lot more integrity and respect, which is very important in our business." He stares contemplatively. "But he's skittish. Really doesn't like new people. However, I will convince him." He walks over to Sloan's body and spits at his face. "Suka. We, of course, know never to mess with each other's women. He clearly never learned that lesson."

"Let me know about the new contact. We really need this done."

"Everything in due time, my friend. Once I arrange a sit-down, I will let you know."

I nod.

"Do you need our help cleaning this up?" He peers down at Sloan in disgust once again.

"Nah, we have our own people for that."

"Very good, then. Let's go, boys." His brothers start following him out, shoving the body away with their loafers so they can get past.

"And tell your lovely wife we said goodbye," Konstantin adds. "I do hope you both can make it to my party."

*Shit. His birthday.*

"We'll all be there."

"Wonderful."

Then he's out the door.

What a fucking day.

# ELARA

My pulse batters in my temples as I scold myself for being so stupid. Why did I think it was a good idea to interrupt his meeting? A meeting I knew was with people like him.

Dangerous people. Men who could very well know Jerry.

I've gotten too comfortable and let my guard down. Now that could cost me everything.

That man who said he knew me didn't look familiar at all, but Jerry had many contacts, and some could've even seen a photo of me. He could be just about anyone in Jerry's circle.

Tynan is still in his meeting, and it's been over an hour since I left. I really need to see him and find out if that guy said anything else about me.

I should've never played that stupid prank. It sounded a lot better in my head.

What if that guy was sent by Jerry to see if I was really here with Tynan? Now he'll know!

"Ugh!" I yank my hair, pacing in the laundry room, not wanting Ruby or Brody to see me this way.

I jolt when my cell beeps with an incoming text. Staring down at the screen, I find that it's from Tynan.

**TYNAN**

> Come up to our bedroom. We need to talk.

That doesn't sound good.

I rush out of the laundry room and straight for the stairs.

He's probably mad at me for being stupid too. Maybe I've finally overstepped my boundaries. Then I had to go and throw "love you" at him, trying to act like we're truly married.

It was stupid. I shouldn't have said that. He clearly told me what to expect from this marriage. And love isn't an option for us.

Not that I love him or anything. Those were just words. They didn't mean anything.

*Didn't they?*

I shake off that thought as I enter our bedroom, finding him pacing with his back to me, the same clothes he had on at the meeting.

When he turns, his expression is tense.

But that's not what stops me dead in my tracks.

Blood.

So much blood.

I rush toward him, grabbing his bruised-up knuckles, crimson covering them too. "Are you okay? Are you hurt?"

Frantically, I look him up and down. That gets a small crack of a smile to burst through.

"If I knew almost killing someone would get you to be concerned about me, I'd have done it sooner."

I suck in a harsh breath. "What? Who? Why?"

He cups my face, his brows snapping, emotions riddled in every crevice of his features. And I'm lost to it. Lost to him. Lost to the utter and beautiful way he consumes me.

He lowers his mouth a fraction at a time until he's kissing me. Invading my heart and my soul. So much so, I don't even care that he's touching me with bloody hands.

This kiss is slow, yet deeper somehow. In meaning and intention. I can feel it pulsing between us, like it's alive.

He pulls me closer, pinning his forehead to mine.

"Tell me what happened," I whisper. "Was it that man? The one who said he knew me?"

He snaps back, anger radiating in his gaze. "Did you remember him?"

I shake my head. "But what if he does know me through Jerry's family?" Panic sucks me whole, my inhales and exhales battling for space. "What if he tells everyone about me?" I move past him, grabbing my hair. "I'm so sorry…"

My body grows shaky until I'm close to collapsing.

But his strong arms hold me from behind, his soft voice lulling me. "Shh, relax. No one will hurt you anymore, Elara. That's over now."

I want to believe him. I really do.

But I can't.

Not until I see Jerry and his father dead for myself.

"Take a shower with me, baby." His palms splay across my abdomen, like he's cradling a child that isn't yet there.

"What?" I drop my head against his chest and take deep, calming breaths.

"I need to get cleaned up, and you need help relaxing."

"Okay."

His mouth finds my neck before he starts stripping all my clothes, taking his time, until I'm bare before him. As he turns me, his eyes drift down my body, and I don't feel an ounce of shame like I once would've.

I like it when he looks at me.

And I realize somewhere between the time he forced me to show him my scar to this very moment, I stopped feeling uncomfortable with him looking at my body. It's freeing. This feeling of letting all that go.

He runs a hand down his face and mutters something in Gaelic before he's stripping his own clothes, bringing them to the bathroom with us.

Taking my hand in his, he brings us into the shower, the water sluicing down our bodies. With the back of his hand, he tugs my chin up, his eyes lost to mine.

"I'll always keep you safe. I need you to know that."

"I do," I tell him.

But he can't protect me from everything.

His mouth drops to my neck, his lips kissing me hotly, palms across my hips.

"Let me clean your hands," I whisper, grabbing a bar of soap.

He watches intently as I wash the blood from his hands, my fingers slicing through his, the water dripping down our bodies.

Picking up my sponge from behind me, he works up a lather, washing me gently, spreading my thighs open to make sure I'm clean everywhere.

He pours some shampoo into his palms and works the pads of his fingers through my scalp as I let out a sigh, leaning back into his chest.

"I like taking care of you, mo chuisle." His voice is sinful, yet sweet, making me crave him with every passing moment.

"Mm," I groan as he lets the water run the suds out, using his hands to clean me off before pouring conditioner into his palm and working it through my ends, fingers massaging up through the strands.

My body grows languid.

Enjoying the way he touches me.

I allow the conditioner to remain while I pick up a bar of soap, cleaning him with care the way he did me.

He groans when my palm runs down his abs, and his cock jerks from the feeling of it.

"What happened to that man?" I ask, my heart beating faster. "The one who asked about me. Did he say anything else? Did you let him go?"

Rage sizzles in his green irises. "I was gonna kill him anyway, but someone did it for me."

My heart gives a thump. I'm secretly glad that the man is dead, even though I hate thinking that way. But if he was connected to Jerry, then he can't go back and tell him anything.

"Is he still in the house?"

He shakes his head. "We got rid of him."

"How?"

He grasps the back of my head, his gaze searching. "You don't need to worry about that. That's my job."

"Okay," I whisper.

He tugs my face to his chest, holding me firmly while I start to wonder if Jerry and his father will ever truly be gone, and if I'll ever feel safe again.

# THIRTY-FOUR

## TYNAN

When I wake up the following morning, she isn't in our bed. I hated seeing her upset yesterday and in fear for her life.

All I've been thinking about is ways I'll kill Jerry and his father. The things I'll do to them before I finally let them die. It satiates the possessive beast in me. The one who needs to keep Elara safe.

She barely said much last night after everything that happened with Sloan.

I tried to talk to her about it, but she said she was tired and wanted to go to bed. I didn't push. It wouldn't help. It would only further destroy what we've started to build.

It's like we've stepped backward, and it fucking destroys me. I want to return to how it was before Sloan ruined it all.

Too bad I can't bring him back to life just to kill him again. Just when she was finally starting to ease into this marriage, it all blew up in my face. Now I don't know where her head is at.

I take a quick shower, needing to see her, to try to talk to her.

Getting dressed for work, I head down to the kitchen, registering Ruby and Elara talking.

As soon as they see me, they both stop.

"There he is, Mister Sleepy," Ruby teases, pouring me a cup of coffee and handing it to me.

"Wife kept me up all night." I wink at her, but Elara's mouth only slightly thins into a barely there smile.

Fuck. That kills me.

"Good morning, bud." I kiss the top of Brody's head, and he doesn't recoil anymore like he once used to.

Things are finally starting to get better with him. I just hope things between Elara and me aren't ruined for good.

"Can we talk?" I whisper, pulling up a stool beside her while Ruby washes a pan in the sink.

She exhales a sigh. "Maybe later. Just a lot for me to process right now."

She's closing off again.

*Fuck!*

Grabbing her hand, I bring it to my mouth for a kiss.

"Eat." I gesture my chin toward her pancakes.

She picks at her food like she once did when we first met. But her appetite has returned recently, and I need it to stay that way.

She forces a small piece into her mouth.

If she withdraws any further, we might never go back.

So I make a promise to myself that I'm gonna fix this, no matter what it takes.

"Where are you going?" she asks, seated on the edge of our bed as I come out of the shower after work.

Her eyes fall toward the towel wrapped around my hips.

"I have a meeting with Konstantin. I'll be home late."

He called hours ago to tell me I have to hop on a plane to Jersey to meet the new contact at one of the clubs the Marinovs own.

"Oh." Her eyes go downcast. "How late?"

"I don't know. I'll call you, though."

"Okay."

She plays with her fingers, an obvious wedge between us, but I have no time to fix it. Not properly anyway. I have to go and make this deal happen. I don't want to rush the conversation she and I definitely have to have.

I head into the closet and take out one of my suits and a dress shirt.

As soon as she sees me walking back out, her face contorts with horror.

"Please tell me you're not wearing *that*."

"What's wrong with it?" I let a smirk fall to my face. "My wife bought it for me, so I plan to let the world see it."

She slaps a hand to her forehead. "Oh, come on, Tynan. I was playing. I didn't actually expect you to wear them."

I fling my towel off, my smirk only deepening when she stares right at my cock, swallowing thickly.

"Can't keep looking at it like that, love. You're gonna make me late."

Her fingers run up and down her neck as she clears her throat, making sure to look at my face this time. But she just can't seem to help herself, stealing small glances, and that only makes the blood rush to my dick.

"Please, Tynan. You don't have to wear that yellow suit. I can return them all. It was stupid of me."

I start slipping into my black shirt, buttoning it up before sitting on the bed and putting on the ugly-as-hell pants. "Don't you dare return a thing. I'm gonna make sure everyone sees what great taste you have."

"Ugh…" She groans, dropping her face in her palm for a moment.

"Just promise you're not gonna kill anyone for making fun of you."

I tug her hand in mine, my gaze growing with affection. "For you, I promise."

She sighs, and I don't think she believes me.

We start down the stairs, and when Brody sees me from the foot of the staircase, his eyes bug out. Before I can make a joke about my appearance, he bursts into a laugh.

And in that instant, all the air stills in my lungs.

I remain motionless, not believing what I just heard.

My pulse pounds endlessly because he just laughed.

He just laughed for the first time since his parents died.

Emotions cling to the back of my throat.

And Elara's eyes? They're on mine, filled with tears as we experience this moment together.

I'd wear every goddamn suit in the rainbow if I could make him laugh like that again.

"Oh, you think that's funny, huh?"

His laughter continues, and I rush down the rest of the way and flip him upside down in the air.

"Not laughing now, are you?"

But he continues to giggle, punching me in the stomach.

"Geez, you're strong. What have I been feeding you?"

Elara sniffles, wiping under her lashes.

I still, my gaze on hers.

My heart beats frantically. This is all I'll ever want.

Her.

Brody.

My family.

This need to tell her how much she means to me overtakes me completely.

But I don't have the right words.

I arrive at Konstantin's club. I didn't exactly know it was a strip club.

It isn't my scene, but it's something I have to do if I want this damn deal to finally happen.

I'm ushered into a private room, where the Marinovs all wait with a man I assume is the new contact.

He's around my age, hair as dark as his skin. Never seen him before.

"Ah, there you are, Quinn." Konstantin drops his cigar into the ashtray. "I want you to meet my friend Darnell. Darnell, this is Tynan."

The stranger outstretches his hand for mine, and we shake before I'm offered a seat across from him.

"Nice suit." Darnell grins.

"Thanks. The wife got it for me."

Konstantin chuckles. "Another one of her jokes?"

I nod.

"Funny woman."

"She's that, alright."

And more. A lot more.

"So…" Darnell picks up a crystal cut glass filled with amber-gold liquid. "I hear you're looking to get strapped and need a connect to bring the metal to the States."

Darnell gets right to the point, and I respect that in a man.

I nod. "Think you can help with that?"

He looks me up and down. "It's gonna cost you extra. I don't come cheap."

"How much more?" I fold my arms over my chest.

"Another two hundred grand for security. My route is secure." He tips the glass to his mouth, finishing his liquor.

Konstantin gestures for one of his men to come near, whispering something into his ear.

Before I have to wonder what, six women dressed in nothing but G-strings walk in.

*Fucking great. Just what I need.*

"Thought we'd have a little fun while we talk business. And bring us the best bottle," he tells his guy, who immediately retrieves some shot glasses and a bottle of Russian vodka.

He starts to pour while the women dance on the three poles in the room, the music low so we can still hear ourselves.

I definitely need to get the hell out of here.

One of the women approaches me, bending over, rubbing her hands on my chest. "Want a dance, pretty boy?"

I fling her palms away.

"Or more? I do more too." She straightens, squeezing her tits together.

But my dick doesn't even move.

"No. I'm married." I stare right at her. "Happily."

She politely moves on.

Darnell whistles. "Damn. You're one loyal son of a bitch, aren't you?"

"Can we return to business?" I'm trying hard to remain calm, but I just wanna get the hell out of here.

I can't even text Elara because there's no damn service. Pretty sure Konstantin did that on purpose.

"Of course." Darnell brings another drink to his mouth. "But look, I don't like problems, and new people? They cause problems. Konstantin did vouch for you, and that means something to me, but I want to hear it from you. That this will go smoothly."

"I promise to do my part. We don't like problems either."

His foot bounces as he stares at me for what feels like minutes. "Okay." He flips a hand. "I'm good with working with you, as long as my price tag is acceptable."

I reach out my palm for his. "Got yourself a deal."

He shakes my hand, and that's it.

It's finally done.

"Now we celebrate!" Konstantin gestures with a hand toward one of his men, and the music turns louder.

"I've gotta go home." I start to get to my feet, but he stops me.

"Come on, brother. Not yet. Stay and have a few drinks with us before you go crawling into your wife's bed."

"Fine. But just one drink. Then I'm going."

"Horosho."

Shit. I'm not getting out of here, am I?

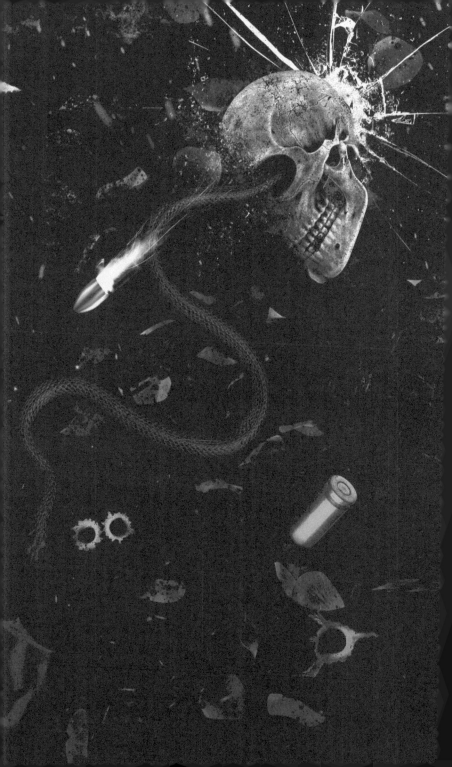

# THIRTY-FIVE

## ELARA

I t's way past midnight, and he's not home. Not only is he not home, but he hasn't even answered my texts. And every time I call, it goes straight to voicemail.

Worry gnaws at me.

What if he was killed?

What if the plane crashed?

What if he was arrested?

What if, what if, what if?

Every bad scenario plays in my head over and over until I'm a basket case. I just need to know that he's okay.

I keep pacing by the front door, just hoping he walks through it.

Maybe his battery died. I mean, I'm sure even mobsters lose phone battery, right?

Getting tired, I head for the den to watch some mindless television when the door finally opens.

I jump to my feet, dropping the remote and rushing for the door.

The foyer is pitch black, and I find his looming shadow there, my heart racing, unable to contain my emotions.

Relief hits me. He's alive.

"Tynan?" I whisper.

"Elara. You're still up."

The moment I hear his voice, tears blanket my vision, and my relief turns to anger.

"Where have you been?" I march forward until I'm standing right before him, unable to really see his eyes. "I've been calling and texting, and you didn't even have the decency to respond?"

Emotions plague me. So many of them hitting me at once, I'm overwhelmed.

I want to kiss him. Yell at him. Then kiss him some more.

"Come here, baby." He clasps the back of my head with a palm, his mouth stroking mine.

And in the dark, all the sensations are enhanced, igniting me.

"I'm sorry I worried you."

My fingers sink into his hair and as I try to kiss him back, I gasp.

"What the hell?" I force myself backward, insane rage radiating through me.

That was perfume I smelled on him.

He was with a woman.

And that instant thought is like a blade to my heart, slicing it in half.

I didn't think he could do that to me, but I was foolish, wasn't I?

It's what the Mafia men are known for, right? Whoring around on their significant others. Why would Tynan be any different?

"Elara?" he calls my name, yet I barely hear it. "What's wrong?"

My chin trembles. So while I was worried sick, he was fucking someone. My heart is as heavy as a ton of bricks, and I just want to run. Or smack him. Or both, actually.

I swear I wanna kill him, and I hate myself for even getting this worked up!

I shouldn't care. He's not my husband, not really. It's not like we met and fell in love and then got married.

He doesn't love me.

He'll *never* love me.

It's what he said.

Of course he'd go out and fuck someone else while I was here, worrying about whether he was dead.

His palm falls to my waist, but I roughly push him away.

"Don't fucking touch me!" I whisper-shout, not wanting to wake Ruby or Brody.

I step back even farther, needing to be far away from him.

"Elara! Tell me what the hell just happened!" The lights suddenly turn on, and he's there, still handsome, concern fitting his eyes as he marches forward.

But nausea hits my gut when I imagine what he could've been doing tonight.

"What's wrong? Did I do something?" A crease forms between his brows, and when his gaze prances down my body, wearing nothing but one of his white t-shirts, he grunts, clenching his jaw.

"Don't you look at me like that!" I snap. "Who the fuck were you with tonight?" I stare at him accusingly, unable to control my tone or the tears spiraling down my cheeks. "And don't you dare lie to me!"

"You think I *cheated* on you?" His eyes flare.

I nod.

"Mo chuisle…" His voice softens. "I would never. Ever. I swear."

I sniffle. "Says every man who's ever cheated on a woman."

Blinking back tears, I swipe them away, wanting for once to believe that I could be loved. That I could be treated with respect and loyalty.

But it's never been that way for me. Jerry would be out sleeping with everything that walked, not that I cared much about that. It was the fact that he was touching me at all that made me sick. And my boyfriend before him slept with a friend of mine and wasn't even sorry about it. I don't have the best track record for loyal men.

I just hoped that maybe, just maybe, Tynan was different.

I'm always wrong about people, aren't I?

"It's fine if you did." I clear my throat, fighting the ache in my chest. "This was never real, right?" I force a smile, straightening my back. "Just don't expect me to be faithful to you either."

I turn on my heels and march out of the room, breaking into a silent sob, pinching my eyes closed from the pain in my chest.

But I don't get far.

He grabs my wrist and yanks me against him, my front pressed to his. He cups my chin, searching my gaze with the raw emotions painted across every line of his face, like he's hurting too.

"Don't you *dare* walk away from me, love. Not when you just accused me of doing something that despicable."

I let out a sob, unable to contain the pain etched inside me from the images of him with another woman. "You smell like perfume. And it's not mine."

His features turn brooding and intense, and in an instant, he's grabbing my jaw, pushing me up against the foyer wall.

"You think I came home late because I was out fucking someone?" He tilts my chin up with his thumb, his eyes dropping to my lips. "That I would do that to you? That I could ever replace you like that?"

My bottom lip quivers, and I look down.

"Look at me, baby."

When I do, I let out a cry, my resolve breaking, wanting so badly to believe he's different.

"Never, Elara. There were women there, yes, and one tried to touch me and I immediately pushed her away. I didn't touch anyone. I would never do that to you."

He smirks.

"Why the hell are you smiling?" Confusion settles on my face.

"Because…" He slides his free palm up my thigh, his voice thick and raspy. "It's clear you were jealous, which also means you care."

The tips of his fingers softly roll higher until they're tracing my bikini line. My lips part on a throaty moan, his touch making me forget why I was upset to begin with.

"Did it make you crazy to imagine me with someone else? Tasting her? Filling her cunt with my cock?"

"Stop it!"

And I don't mean what he's doing, but what he's saying. Because it does make me crazy. I can't handle the imagery.

A single finger feathers over my bare pussy. "Then say it. Tell me it made you jealous."

His touch rolls against my clit, and I buck and groan, yanking his hair. His mouth drops to the underside of my jaw, teeth sinking, biting into my sensitive flesh. Every inch of me comes alive, dying for his touch.

"Because the thought of you with someone else…fuck, Elara, you have no idea what I'd do to him," he grits through clenched teeth, his breath warm, skimming over my skin.

His gaze zeroes on mine, dark and hungry and almost possessed.

"You're mine," I tell him with conviction, holding his face between my hands. "All mine. I will never share you, Tynan Quinn."

He inhales deep, pinning me further into the wall, his lips drawing near. "I am yours, mo ghrá."

Then he crushes my mouth with his.

My God, he devours me.

His tongue roughly enters my mouth while my fingers unbutton his jacket, ripping his shirt open, buttons scattering everywhere, and he slips my shirt over my head. With hurried fingers, I start undoing his belt, but something instantly catches my eye, my hands slowing in my state of confusion.

"What's that?" I whisper, staring at my name in the middle of his chest.

My heartbeats quicken, and I slowly reach out to hover a fingertip above each letter, his skin red and raw.

"It's a tattoo." He laughs. "Do you like it?"

"Yes…"

Paralyzing emotions overtake me. And the more I look into his eyes, softening for me, the more I wanna hold on to him and never let go.

"H-h-how…when did you get it?" My tone is low, my gaze returning to the beautiful artwork.

Thorny vines wrap around each letter, black roses on both sides of the tattoo.

He feathers his thumb across my lips, his eyes on mine. "There was a guy at the club. He was a tattoo artist. I asked him to create something worthy of you. I wanted to wear you on my skin. I wanted it so fucking badly, I couldn't wait."

"Why?" I ask again. "It's so permanent."

Yet I can't help the way my stomach clenches at the sentiment. Why would he get it if he swore that he'd never love me? Why do that to himself if all we're supposed to be is married friends who sleep together? People can care about one another and still not be in love with each other.

But this? The tattoo? Why would he need it if he doesn't love me? Doesn't want to love me.

"Because…" He cups my face, his brows furrowing. "You fucking own me, Elara Quinn. Never felt a damn thing like this before."

Tears fill my eyes, until they overflow.

*What does it mean?*

I desperately want to ask him, yet I'm afraid of the answer. Because if he was falling in love with me, he'd say it.

"I'm crazy about you." His eyes grow heavy-lidded. "I've been crazy about you from the moment I met you at the café. I wanted you right then."

My heartbeats thunder at the confession.

"But it wasn't until tonight while I was at this meeting, wanting to come home to you, that I truly realized how insane I am for you."

He shakes his head like he himself can't fully grasp what he's saying. That he too doesn't know what this all means.

"I'm sorry I couldn't call you, baby. There was no reception at the club, then some drunk Russian broke my phone." He chuckles dryly. "I didn't want to be there longer than I had to, but Konstantin is... well, Konstantin. Yet all I could think about was seeing you."

He touches his forehead to mine, kissing the tip of my nose, while I stand there, a complete mess for this man.

"You promise you didn't touch anyone?" I swallow the thick ball of nerves in my throat, needing to hear him say he didn't one more time.

He cradles my cheek, his face contorted with his emotions. "Never. I swear on my mother. I would never cheat on you."

I let out a small snivel, and he takes that moment to kiss me again, slower, like he's savoring the taste and feeling of me.

He gathers me into his arms, looking into my eyes as he takes us up the stairs.

That's what I need right now, to feel connected to him that way.

Once we reach our bedroom, he lays me on the mattress, stripping off his pants and boxers until his skin is as bare as mine.

His eyes take me in from above, breaths heavy. And as he longingly stares down at me, I can't handle the overflowing feelings it brings out.

He crawls over me, and the heaviness of his body on top of mine makes me more aroused.

"You're all I want," he rasps, sliding a hand between us, his fingers nudging inside me, until he's thrusting them with ease.

I buck every time his palm presses against my clit. The sensation is incredible. He thrusts deeper, making me moan and gyrate my hips into the mattress, my eyes on his.

"Please, Tynan…I need you. Just you, nothing else."

"Need you too," he growls low, removing his fingers and replacing them with the crown of his cock.

His gaze aligns with mine while he keeps himself there at my entrance. Those eyes of his soften, and the look he gives…it's as though he's crawling into the very depths of my soul and asking to stay.

And I'd let him.

"Just sex, right?" he whispers, brushing his lips with mine.

*No.* My heart beats faster. *It doesn't feel that way.*

"Yes." I grab the back of his head. "Just sex."

And with his gaze still on mine, he enters me with one single thrust.

"Fuuuck…" he grunts, while I'm gasping in pleasure.

His mouth hovers just above my lips, his breath warm and intoxicating, and all I want is to feel his mouth on me.

"You feel too good, mo chuisle."

Then he's kissing me, smashing his mouth to mine, driving his full length all the way out and then thrusting back in, sending my body and my heart into a wild crescendo.

We quickly turn into a twisted mess of legs and arms, our moans and the sound of skin on skin filling the space around us. He snaps my head to the side, deepening our kiss, wanting it to last just as much as I do. I'd give anything to be like this forever.

To be his forever.

And that thought? It no longer terrifies me, and that's terrifying on its own.

But with Tynan, it feels as though every part of me is finally alive. Wanting to feel something real for the first time. It's like I've been asleep all this time and Tynan woke me up.

His hips move with intention, yet slow and unhurried at the same time. Like quiet waves of an ocean, powerful and deep.

Our gazes lock, and that only heightens every sensation.

Every breath.

Every growl.

Every touch of his skin on mine.

His hand wraps around my throat, lips brushing my mouth until he's kissing me again. And it's a kiss filled with yearning and longing and deep-seated passion.

My body melts for him, and I crave more. I crave everything with him.

His tongue rolls with mine, his hips pummeling me with deep, punishing strokes until we're eternally connected—bodies and souls twined into one being.

I've never felt anything more powerful.

My legs round his hips, my heels pressing into his back, needing him deeper. My nails sink into his shoulders, digging into his muscled flesh as his mouth lowers to my jaw, biting and sucking down to my throat.

My neck arches, unable to contain the series of moans escaping from my chest. His cock drives harder into me, and my walls pulse and throb, my need spiraling until I crash with a cry.

"Oh God, Tynan!"

He squeezes my throat, his fingers spanning the entire length of it.

"Look at me when you come." His voice…it's so thick with need, it only makes my release more intense.

I don't know how long it lasts, but it feels like forever, though not enough at the same time.

As soon as I come down from the high, he flips me over, his body pressed to mine from behind. His cock is at my pussy, hand sinking into my hair as he pulls my head back, and with one swift move, he's back inside me.

He takes me harder and deeper, until I'm coming again. And before I know what's happening, he's forcing me on all fours, fucking me so roughly my eyes are rolling back once more.

And when my release hits me this time, I scream out his name.

Because this feeling? It's like no other, and I never want it to end.

# THIRTY-SIX

## ELARA

"So, how's married life?" Gran asks as we head to see Grandpa after work the next day.

"Oh, you know…"

She laughs. "Well, you're smiling a lot more. That's a good sign."

My cheeks warm. "I feel more myself these days."

Her brows gather and she pats my knee. "I did tell you he was the one."

"Pretty sure that's not exactly what you said." I give her a playful look.

All the while, memories of Tynan and me from yesterday fill my mind. The possessive way he took me. The way I sounded. How hard I came.

Those things alone are not enough to sustain a marriage, though. But Tynan…he's given me more than that, hasn't he?

He comforted me when I cried. Didn't push to have sex with me after the car chase because he worried more about my well-being than his own needs. That counts for something.

But can I stay married to a man who so adamantly told me he'd never love me? Those words hurt more now than they did then.

Because there's something between us now that didn't exist before. And I want to unravel that to discover what we can truly be.

Lately, we've been having fun too. And I've missed that—having fun with someone again. The way I did with friends before my life was turned upside down.

A grin spreads when I think about him.

"Ah, there's that smile again."

I scoff while still grinning. "Did I tell you I played a joke on him and bought him all these obnoxious-colored suits?"

"No! Do tell." She arches a mischievous brow.

"When I brought them home…you had to see his face, Gran." I burst with a laugh, causing her to follow suit. "I swear, I did not think he'd wear them, but he wore this bright yellow one to some important meeting."

Her mouth pops. "The man's clearly crazy about you."

I shrug. "Eh."

"Don't 'eh' me! It's true."

I don't tell her he was very specific when he told me he'd never fall in love with me, and how badly I wish he would.

And that sudden realization—that I want him to love me—both shocks me and hurts me at the same time.

I never meant to fall for him. I never thought I could or would. Or maybe I was just in deep denial. But all I want is to be with him. To make this marriage work.

Yet telling Gran any of this won't help matters. She'll just try to convince me that he's just a man, scared of feelings, yada, yada. I've heard this talk from her before when I was dating my one boyfriend.

It won't change anything. Tynan has made up his mind, and he doesn't seem like the kind of man who changes his mind too much.

Though I want this relationship to be real, I can't read too much into how he's been with me. It won't do me any good.

I clear my throat. "Anyway, it's just been nice, you know. To have some fun. After everything."

She nods. "You deserve happiness, sweetheart. It wasn't good for you to keep yourself so closed off the way you were. I'm glad to see some of that spark back in your eyes."

Gran pats my knee as we pull up into the parking lot of the nursing home. "Come on, let's go tell your grandpa all about your new husband."

I shake my head with a laugh, following her out. As we step into the reception area and I start to sign in, the secretary greets us.

"Hi, guys! Are you here to collect the rest of Mr. Hill's things?"

I jump back a step in confusion.

Then panic sets in.

My heart races like mad. "Wh-what do you mean, collect his things? Is—is…"

No…he can't be gone.

Gran grabs my arm before I burst into tears. "Where is my husband?"

"Oh, I'm so sorry!" Fear and alarm grip her young face.

He can't be dead. He can't be!

"Um, your husband was moved." Her forehead creases. "I thought someone told you already."

The hammering in my head intensifies. "What do you mean, moved? Who moved him, and where? I don't understand what you're saying right now."

What if Jerry's people took him out to lure me? Or to punish me?

Dread hits me again, and when I look at Grandma's eyes, I know she's worried too.

The secretary glances at her computer, pressing a few keys. "Let me get the address of where he was relocated. He was just taken there a few hours ago." She hits a few more keys, peering at us. "I'm so sorry."

I clasp a hand over my mouth. "Just tell me where he is. We didn't approve this."

Her face turns ashen. "I…I can get Ms. Davis to speak to you. But here's the address."

She writes it on a yellow Post-it and hands it to me.

At first, I don't understand what I'm seeing. How can this be? It makes no sense.

"Are you sure?" I pass the Post-it to Gran.

"Yes, that's what's in our system."

"Okay. Uh, thanks."

We start rushing back to the car, Gran keeping up pace beside me. As soon as we've got our seat belts on, I start the engine.

"Still not sure if he's the one?" Gran smiles.

I glance at her as we enter the highway, tears pricking my eyes.

It was Tynan.

He brought Grandpa to his home.

*Our* home.

Emotions clog my throat. "I don't understand. How could he bring Grandpa to the house without saying anything to me?"

She shrugs, not the least bit worried anymore. "I'm sure he just thought he would surprise you. I think it's lovely."

My pulse still beats from the fear I just experienced. Yet with every second, that fear melts away, and in its place is absolute happiness.

I need to see Grandpa. I need to make sure he's okay.

But after that, I need to see my husband.

Half an hour later, and we're back on the estate, me jumping out of the car and rushing inside to make sure Grandpa is really there.

Brody greets me and Gran with a wave.

"Hey, sweetheart." I give him a tight hug, and Gran does too. "Weird question. Did you by any chance see an old man here today?"

He nods and takes my hand, leading me.

My heart lurches.

Grandpa is really here. Where I can take care of him anytime.

It's what I told Tynan I wished I could do and how much I hated sending him to a home. Is that why he did this?

I blink back tears as Brody leads me to a long corridor, and on the left, there's a single door. When he opens it, I find Grandpa in his wheelchair, three nurses there fiddling around the room.

My breaths still, and I swipe a hand under my lower lashes, emotions making it hard to speak.

The room is luxurious and spacious with a king-sized bed, and even a small kitchen on the left. There's everything Grandpa would need right here.

The women look up at me, one of them coming toward us.

"Hi there. You must be Mrs. Quinn, and you must be Nora." She shakes our hands. "I'm Betty, and this is Morgan and Stacey."

They both say hello.

"We'll be your grandfather's live-in nurses and will take different shifts so that all his needs are met."

"I—" I sniffle, unable to speak.

I need to see Tynan right now so I can thank him for this over and over and over again.

"Uh, thank you." Tears start leaking down my cheeks. "I need to go," I whisper.

Gran grabs my hand and gives it a tight squeeze. "Go find him and thank him for the both of us."

I nod, hurrying out of there, almost running into Ruby.

"Oh, there you are! I'm sorry I didn't tell you about your grandpa." She grimaces playfully. "I'm terrible at keeping secrets, but Mr. Quinn swore me to secrecy, and I couldn't ruin such a lovely surprise."

"He's been planning this?" My voice grows smaller, unable to keep my emotions at bay.

"Oh, yes! He wanted to make sure all the ducks were in a row before he brought him here. And we're so happy to have him!"

I let out a small cry until the dam breaks and a sob punches through.

"Oh, you sweet thing!" She holds me as I cry on her shoulder.

How can I stop myself from falling in love with him? Even if he never returns the sentiment.

"Is he home?" I wrench back.

"No, he's in the office today. Though if you want to go see him, I might know the address." She smirks.

"Please. I would love that."

She shoots off his location, and I'm in the car in no time, unable to bear another second without kissing him.

# TYNAN

I despise board meetings.

But being that I'm now the head of the family, it falls on me to be here. With owning the farms and different businesses, we have investors and people to please like anyone else.

One of the associates presents data on the growing revenue we've had in agriculture over the past year, while I pretend to listen.

My mind is on her, though.

It always is.

I wonder if she's realized I had her grandpa moved by now. She would've called, wouldn't she?

I know how much he means to her, and I know she hated having him in a home, so I figured it'd make her happy if he was with us and cared for.

My sister's words play in my head again.

Fuck. I never wanted to fall in love. It seemed more like a curse at the time.

Love and death, they're tied in our world.

But what if I am in love with her?

What if I'm just in denial?

What the hell do I do with that? Do I tell her? Or do I wait until I know for sure? Or maybe I don't say anything because she might not want to hear it.

I run a frustrated hand through my hair.

"Ma'am, you can't go in there!" my secretary hollers.

My attention instantly snaps to whatever is going on.

I'm about to get to my feet when the doors fly open.

And when I see Elara there—glassy eyes, rosy cheeks—everyone else disappears.

In this moment, I remember when Aiden first met Willow. He was so damn happy, constantly grinning like a fool every time she'd walk into the room. I'd tease the hell out of him for that, and he'd tell me I'd understand one day.

I finally do.

"Get out."

Her face falls, and I realize she must think I'm speaking to her.

"All of you, out. Now."

And that gets their attention, scrambling to get their things as they hurry out right past her.

"What are you doing here, Elara?"

I just want to hear her say she came for me. To see me because she missed me.

She shuts the door and sniffles. "You stupid, sweet man."

She rushes for me, and I immediately rise, grabbing her hips as soon as she's before me. Her eyes grow tender, and her hand cups my cheek. I groan from the feeling of her on me, lowering back into the seat and forcing her to straddle me.

Her gaze searches mine.

Needing.

Feeling.

And fuck, do I feel everything with her right now.

"Why did you do that? Why did you bring him to live with us?"

I take her fingers to my mouth and kiss each one. "Because, like I told you from the very first day, I want to make you happy. So, are you happy, baby?"

Tears begin falling down her cheeks and she nods right before she leans in and smashes her mouth to mine, and nothing has ever felt better. She leads this kiss, and I welcome it, needing to know she wants me just as much as I want her.

Her tongue slides against mine.

Hungry.

Sucking and moaning. Tempting me with everything she is.

I throw her onto the table, not separating our kiss, lowering my body over hers. My hips circle between her thighs as she claws my back, yanking my shirt up from beneath my dress pants.

Her fingers fumble with the buttons, and I help her out before tossing it behind me.

I stare down at her in awe, this beautiful creature offering herself to me like this. I've always led everything between us, but she's the one who came here. Who kissed me. Who wanted me. It means something.

I pop open her jeans and pull them down with our eyes locked, yanking her cotton thong along the way.

She spreads her legs, her pussy glistening for me. A low growl emanates from my lungs; I need to taste her.

"Take off your shirt," I demand.

She does in an instant, bare on the table, ready for me to make her my meal.

"Now what?" Her chest flies up and down desperately, and I draw closer, grabbing her ankles until her ass is on the edge of the table.

"Now I get to show you what you mean to me."

Her emotions return as my body crawls over hers, grabbing her jaw and kissing her once as I stare down at her.

"I'm losing myself in you, Elara."

"I'm sorry?" A smile breaks through her tears.

"Don't be. You're the best thing that ever happened to me." Then I capture her mouth, my hand drifting down her body, thrusting two fingers inside her as I kiss her to the same slow, yet passionate rhythm.

Her palm lands on the back of my head, drawing me deeper into our kiss, her whimpers shuddering against my mouth.

My lips drop lower, peppering kisses down her neck, between her breasts, until I'm grabbing under her thighs, bending her knees to her shoulders.

My tongue swirls around her clit, tasting her before I latch on and have all of her.

"Oh, God!" One hand grabs my hair while she rises on an elbow and watches me eat her sweet cunt.

I lick and thrust and suck, unable to peel my eyes from hers, the connection between us deepening, making everything better. Her mouth parts, legs trembling until her walls squeeze around my tongue and I taste her release.

"Tynan, yesyesyes! Oh, God!"

"Mm." My groan against her sensitive pussy makes her jolt, and I chuckle, circling my tongue around her clit until she's begging me to stop. "I'd make you come around my mouth again, except I can't wait to be inside you, mo chuisle. I fucking need you right now," I hiss through gritted teeth.

She stares at me with renewed arousal, squeezing her breasts together.

In seconds, my pants are off and my hard-on is in my fist. I scoot her to the edge a little more, the crown of my erection at her entrance.

LILIAN HARRIS

I keep it there, staring at her, and everything in me coils and pulses. This—whatever it is between us—feels unbreakable.

*Fuck. I really think I'm falling in love with you.*

"Just sex, right?"

I want her to deny it like she never has before. I want to know I'm not the only one with these feelings growing inside me.

She shakes her head, tears brimming. "No, Tynan. It's so much more than that."

*I know.*

With a growl, I pummel inside her until she screams my name. I can't control the crazed way I take her. And the way she sounds, the way she takes all of me, only fuels my desperate desire.

"Watching you take my cock like this…shit, baby, you're beautiful."

She claws my forearms, crying out for more.

"You're so damn tight," I hiss.

"Yes, please stretch me out."

"Fuuuck!" I snap, needing this to last, but she's making it damn difficult.

"Yes, just like that!"

I take her slower, an arm sliding under her back, my eyes on hers, watching her face twist in pleasure.

No one will ever touch her like this.

No one will dare.

Elara is mine for the rest of her life.

I bring her body up until she's almost seated on the edge, my arm supporting her back as I take her deeper, hitting that spot inside that has her losing her mind, moaning things I can't make out.

I give her more, harder and faster with each thrust, until she cries out with her release.

"Yes, that's it, let me feel it all." I fist her hair and groan, enjoying the sight of her falling apart.

Her nails sink into my shoulders as she comes in ripples, tightening around me until she's finally through. Her body sags, and that's when I allow myself to come, pounding inside her and filling her up.

I growl out a curse, clutching the back of her head, both of us breathless.

Letting out a short chuckle, my lips stroke hers. "You here... This was a nice surprise. You can surprise me like that any time."

She shoots me a dreamy, wistful smile. "I might consider that."

"Mm." I grab a fistful of her ass. "You make me crazy."

"We've established that already." She throws her arms around me. "Think I could somehow climb through your window so no one has to see me do the walk of shame?"

I brush my thumb over her rosy lips. "I can always kill them. They've been pissing me off anyway."

She rolls her eyes playfully and swats my chest. "I don't need you to kill anyone for looking at me funny."

"You married the boss of the Irish Mob, baby. It's what we do." I grin. "Don't worry, though. I try my best to only kill the really bad ones. The other ones, I just maim."

"Aww." She pouts. "You're so thoughtful."

"Aren't I?" I give her a quick kiss, groaning as I do.

My arms curl around her, not wanting her to go. She doesn't fight it, melting right into me.

And I swear right here and now that I'll destroy anyone who tries to take this away from me.

This family we have now, it's forever.

And I won't let anyone break us.

# THIRTY-SEVEN

## ELARA

He bought me a beautiful gown for tonight's birthday party for Konstantin. Apparently Konstantin is not just anyone. He's the head of the Russian Mafia. The Bratva, as he told me it's called.

I stare at myself in the bloodred sweetheart gown, a small train sweeping the floor.

The door creaks behind me and he whistles, causing me to turn with a wide grin. I don't miss the small black box he's holding, curious to see what's inside.

"You look beautiful." His hooded gaze takes me in, making my nipples pebble beneath the silk.

"Thank you. And you look insanely handsome." My face flushes when I take him in.

His dark hair is coiffed back, eyes appearing even more emerald than normal. His large frame is hugged tight in his black tux.

"I'm so glad you're not wearing one of those colorful suits," I tease, remembering that awful yellow one he wore.

"Keep talking and I might just change." He leans over to kiss me on my temple, and my heart skips a beat.

I'd return the favor, except I know I'd smear my burgundy lipstick all over him.

"What's inside?" I glance down at the box. "Got me a diamond necklace to go along with these diamond studs?"

I finger one. The four-carat earrings he got me earlier today complement this dress nicely.

"Even better." He smirks devilishly, and I instantly know he's up to something.

I play with my hair, twirling it around my finger, a fluttery feeling weighing in my stomach.

"Nervous?" His thumb rolls over the outline of my jaw.

"Nope." I raise my chin.

*Just keep a brave face, Elara. Whatever is inside that box can't be that bad.*

I'm sure he's not trying to pay me back for my little pranks. I mean, he hasn't tried yet. He probably forgot all about that whole erectile dysfunction fiasco…

"You should be a little afraid." He grazes his knuckles down the side of my throat, my pulse speeding up from his touch. "I warned you, remember?" His fingertips roll down my chest, stopping right above my breasts. "I told you I'd pay you back for that little prank you played."

*Crap.*

*Crap!*

"I would've let the suits slide." His palm rolls back up, until he's got his hand wrapped around my throat. "But the other thing…." He shakes his head, mouth tugging on one side.

"Oh…that…" I shiver with a nervous laugh, my stomach turning to knots. "I was hoping you forgot." I throw my arms over his shoulders.

"Aren't we past all that? I mean, you did kidnap me. Maybe you can forgive me?"

He chuckles deep in his chest, lips drawing nearer, hovering right before mine. "I see what you're trying to do, Mrs. Quinn."

He uses his free palm to cup my behind and squeeze my body to his. And it's then I feel him hard and heavy.

"Is it working?" I whisper, growing aroused at the feel of his cock.

He shakes his head, his mouth curving playfully.

I love seeing this side of him. Fun and carefree. Though right now, I'm a tad terrified of what this "fun" entails.

He moves back. "Ready to see what I bought you?"

"Not exactly." I grimace with a shaky voice.

He laughs, opening the box, and when I stare down into it, I grow confused.

"You got me panties?" A black lace thong lies inside.

"Not just any panties." He picks it up, and beneath it is a small egg-shaped…toy.

*Oh, fuck…*

My eyes widen, backing up a step. "Tynan, please. I mean, this looks fun, but not tonight. Not while we're at the party."

I know vibrating panties when I see them. He's going to drive me insane all night long.

What have I done? If only I could go back to Elara from days ago so I could warn her of this.

Alas, I cannot.

His gaze narrows, mouth curling as he drops the box on the bed, the panties in his grasp. "When we met, I distinctly remember how fond you were of toys. Consider this my wedding present. One of many."

"That's *not* exactly what I was thinking."

"Lift up the dress, Elara."

That rough, demanding voice has every hair on my body standing up.

When I don't move, he grasps my jaw. "Now, Mrs. Quinn. Before I do it for you."

My breath stutters when he forces me into his gaze as I gather the silk and lift up the gown.

With concentrated attention, he inspects me, and I feel even more exposed.

"No panties again, huh?" He drops to his knees, grabbing my ass with both hands, his nose pressed to my core.

"Tynan!" I cry, grabbing his head, working my nails through his scalp.

The warmth of his breath on me there, the tip of his tongue snaking out for a taste, it's all too much. Running a fingertip through my slit, he hungrily stares up at me.

"I'm gonna enjoy torturing the shit out of you tonight." He smirks salaciously, and I almost come just from this sight of him alone.

He slips the panties up my thighs, and once they're secure around my hips, he rises to full height, reaching for the box and picking up the toy.

"They say this is the best one on the market. Can't wait to get your feedback." He teases me with it, rolling it around my pebbled nipple that's poking through the material. "You're gonna wear this all night, understand?"

I nod, throat going dry as I squeeze my thighs.

He slides a hand into the panties, finding the special slot for the toy. "Perfect." Fixing my dress, he moves back so he can look me up and down. "How does that feel?"

His jaw clenches when I let out a low moan, the toy already pushing into my clit.

My hands tingle, the excitement and nerves pulsing through me. "Fine."

"Fine, huh?" He grins, picking up a small remote from the box, and when he presses a button…

"Oh my God! Fuck!" I gasp, almost tripping on my heels.

The vibration is so intense, my whole body quivers.

"Tynan, please don't do this."

I don't tell him I'm already throbbing and ready to come. There's no way I'll last if he plans to do this to me all night.

He captures my chin. "Promise to be my good girl tonight?"

"I promise no such thing."

His grin spreads. "Well, then, I'll have to see if I can fix that."

Another vibration hits between my thighs—slow, then fast—and I almost collapse.

Then, it instantly stops, while I'm left reeling.

He clasps his palm around my nape, his lips stroking mine. "This is just as hard for me as it is for you."

My heart races, nails clasping his huge biceps. "Doubtful."

With another throaty laugh, he tugs me out the door, and I know it's gonna be a night to remember.

# THIRTY-EIGHT

## ELARA

We enter through a guarded metal gate on Konstantin's estate, driving down a private double road with trees on both sides, as though hiding something sinister beyond them.

"How big is his property?" I ask Tynan.

"I don't know exactly, but it's pretty substantial. We have to drive down to another gate, and then his home is about a quarter mile from there."

"Wow." I stare out the window.

I should've realized Konstantin is filthy rich too.

As we arrive at the tall iron fence, two men with black hoodies and rifles on their backs greet us.

"What's your name?" one of them asks in a thick Russian accent.

"Tynan Quinn." He looks at me, waiting for me to give the guard my name.

"Elara Qu—OH!"

A powerful vibration hits my center, and it becomes impossible to breathe. My eyes widen at my husband, because the bastard doesn't stop it.

My core throbs and pulses, while he fights his amusement.

"What?" the guard asks with an annoyed tone.

"U-u-u-h—mmm." My nails dig into the leather beneath me.

"Her name is Elara Quinn," Tynan offers, glancing at me with a glint in his eyes. "Excuse my wife. She's not herself today."

The man looks at the tablet he's holding, then peers at us before the gate slowly parts, allowing us entry. As soon as it does, the vibrations stop, my heartbeats thumping in my ribs.

"Tynan, I swear to God, you better not do that to me again!"

A smile spreads on his face while my entire body thrums with need. This is gonna be worse than I thought.

He clasps my thigh, his fingertips squeezing tight. "You better not be giving me any demands or else I'll keep it on all night, edging you slowly until you're coming in a room full of people."

"You're such a bastard." I let out a sigh, loving yet hating the sweet torture.

When he smirks at me, I *really* wanna punch him in the face.

He continues down a long, winding road that ends with a gray towering mansion.

We pull up to the side of the estate, since the driveway is already filled with various sports cars, with more vehicles parked around the property.

Getting out first, Tynan opens my door and helps me up, sliding his hand through mine. "You ready?"

"To attend a birthday party for the head of the Russian Mob?" I crinkle my nose. "Maybe a little."

He chuckles as he takes us up the cobblestone steps, where tall white columns sculpted into angels greet us. A guard lets us through the doors, and music instantly surrounds us, soft and classical, which is odd for a man in the Mob. Then again, I've learned not to judge.

I squeeze Tynan's arm with my free hand and burrow myself to his side.

"What's that for?" he whispers as he leads us past the foyer with its white marble flooring and large sparkling crystal chandelier.

I shrug. "Just hugging my husband."

Stopping in place, he stares down at me through narrowed, suspicious eyes. "If you think that's gonna stop the way I'm gonna torture you all night…" He grasps my jaw. "You'd be mistaken."

A shiver runs down my spine from his husky tone.

"Ah, there you two are." Konstantin appears from behind us as though out of nowhere, and I jolt, separating from Tynan.

He's a good few inches taller than Tynan, probably six-six or even six-seven. And with those dark, cunning eyes, he's intimidating to look at.

"Mrs. Quinn." He nods in greeting, picking up my hand and kissing the top of it. "What a pleasure it is to see you again, and looking so radiant I might add."

"Thank—oh, God!" I moan, squeezing my eyes. "Fuuuck…"

My hands tremble.

My toes curl.

*I'm gonna kill him!*

Konstantin's brows squeeze in confusion. "Are you alright? Should I get my doctor?"

"Mm…no, no." I shake my head, forcing a smile, fighting through the frustration. "I'm fiiiine!" My voice goes shrill, and I swear I hear Tynan laugh.

That dirty bastard!

"Haaaapy birthday!" Okay, if my voice gets any higher, I'm gonna sound like one of those people who has swallowed up helium.

He increases the speed.

*Oh my God! I'm gonna come!*

"Tynan!" I look back at him, widening my eyes.

His mouth tilts, and suddenly I breathe a sigh of relief.

Clearing my throat, I look back at the confused man before me. "Sorry about that." I smooth out my dress. "You have a beautiful home."

"Why, thank you." His thick, dark brows furrow before he smirks at Tynan.

My face burns. Oh my God. Does he know?

"Thanks for having us," Tynan adds, walking up beside me and grabbing my hand.

"Of course. It's not a party without friends. Your whole family is here already. Shall we go join them?"

I nod, needing to sit down so I can get some reprieve from the way I'm turned on right now. With one touch, I could go off.

We start toward the back of the home, past a dining room with a table for twelve. "You know, I own some clubs around the world..." His eyes swivel to mine. "Lots of married couples go. Maybe it's something you two would be interested in."

He smirks, but Tynan shoots him a glare.

"It was just a suggestion." He chuckles as we head into a modern white kitchen, where cooks and waiters busy themselves with trays.

"What kind of club do you mean?" I glance between them.

Konstantin grins, right before Tynan pulls me close and whispers, "He owns a bunch of sex clubs."

"Oh!" My face twists in shock. "Wow. Yeah, I...uh, will have to think about that."

"Nothing to think about," Tynan snaps. "Will never happen."

"You should ask your brothers how much fun they can be."

"Don't care what they do and with whom. I'd never fuck my wife for your cameras to capture it."

Konstantin laughs, slapping a palm on Tynan's back.

We head past double glass doors and into a lavish yard decorated with white tents and tables, LED lighting coming from the DJ booth. One of his men pulls him aside, and Konstantin gives us a dismissive glance.

"You two have fun. I'll be around."

"He's a lot," I whisper as we head for the tables.

"Yeah, his whole family is. Stay away from them."

"Pretty sure that won't be a problem. Not like we hang out in the same circles."

He shoots me an intense gaze. "You do now. Things have changed for you, Elara, if you couldn't tell. You have to be careful all the time."

My heart lurches. I guess I really didn't think about it all that much.

We step past a dance floor, people already having a great time while the DJ plays some upbeat songs.

When I spot Iseult waving to us, I wave back, and we start in her direction, the entire Quinn family already seated there.

"Nice of you to finally join us." Devlin pulls Eriu into his side, tilting his chin up in greeting.

"You look beautiful," Eriu tells me.

"You too."

Her emerald-green gown matches her eyes with perfection.

"How about we go dance?" Iseult glances between Eriu and me.

"Sure." In a flash, my eyes roll back. "Oh fuuu…dge… No."

My pulse beats in my ears, my heart drumming.

I'm gonna cut his dick off.

"Wait, what?" Iseult's forehead creases. "You okay?"

I purse my lips and nod, fisting my hands, my breaths stilling in my chest.

I can't believe he's doing this to me again! In the middle of a conversation with his family!

"So, when are you two having some little ones?" Fernanda asks, while I fight not to moan or beg or scream.

"Oh my God!" I grit my teeth, groaning as I squeeze my legs.

"I'm sorry, that was rude of me." Her face turns crimson.

"Uh, no, no, I…just remembered…I…um…" My words tremble out of me. "F-f-f-forgot something for work."

*Please make it stop.*

My whole body feels like I've been zapped by electricity. I grab Tynan's thigh, turning toward him, my nails sinking into the brick he calls a leg. I bet this doesn't even hurt him, so I carve my nails in deeper.

He only smirks. "Hopefully soon. There's nothing I want more than to see Elara pregnant with our child."

"Wow!" Iseult huffs a laugh. "Look at you. I quite remember the time you told me you'd rather be thrown into a volcano than get married."

"My God, son," Patrick chuckles. "You really didn't wanna get married, did ya?"

"Aww, now look at them," Fernanda gushes, while I grit my teeth and smile like an idiot.

*Oh my God, they all need to stop talking!*

"Tynan, please," I whisper into his ear. "I'll do anything, just please…"

"I'm having too much fun watching you squirm," he husks, his lips brushing past my quaking pulse. "I can just imagine how wet you are. How easy it would be to thrust inside you."

"This isn't fair." I grip his leg tighter and tighter.

"Need I remind you, I've never been a fair man?"

"What are you two whispering about?" Fionn chuckles. "Seems like something we'd all want to know."

*Pretty sure you don't.*

The vibrations instantly stop, and Tynan tugs me to him, kissing my temple. I sag against him, the desperate need still clinging to me. But at least I don't feel like I'm gonna explode.

He drops his mouth against my ear. "You don't know how badly I wanna fuck you. Bet your clit is all swollen, waiting for me to suck it into my mouth."

I quiver, my eyes on his, the desire for him spiraling.

As I get lost in his eyes, he switches the vibration back on and I choke on a cry, biting the inside of my cheek.

"U-u-m-mm…." I stutter on a cry. "Please excuse us." I grab Tynan's bicep, eyeing him intently. "Let's go. Now."

He fights a smile, getting to his feet, a hand in his pocket where he's got that tiny remote.

"Ooh, someone's pussy-whipped," Iseult teases.

"Shut up, Iz," he mutters, her laughter echoing as I grab his hand, barely able to walk.

"Turn that off!" I whisper-shout when we find a corner to speak. "If you ever want to get laid again, I suggest you throw that thing away."

He draws nearer, his eyes hooded and equally filled with yearning. "I have a better idea." His knuckles draw down my cheek. "How about we find a room so I can take that ache away?"

The vibrations stop, and he's thrusting his hips into me, his rock-hard erection causing my body to coil with unparalleled lust.

"Been throbbing for you." His lips brush mine. "And I won't last until we get home."

Discreetly, he pushes a finger between my thighs.

"Please…" I beg, needing him just as badly.

He grabs my hand and kisses my knuckles. "I want you bent over the nearest sofa so I can use your body any way I damn well please."

The pounding in my ears quickens, the unquenchable desire to be filled and stretched overwhelming me. "Okay, yeah…let's do that."

He drags me out of the yard and past the doors, taking me farther into the house.

"Do you know where we're going?" I ask as we walk toward the right, opposite from where we first came in.

"No clue."

My stomach clenches. This is kind of exciting. Or I'm just a feral cat who needs to get laid.

A maid passes me by, softly smiling. "Hello."

Tynan nods, while my face grows hot. He takes me to the end of the hall and opens the last door to our left.

When he switches the lights on, my eyes adjust to my surroundings, finding multiple rows of seats and a large screen before them.

A theater room.

"Do the doors lock?" I'm terrified someone could walk in on us.

"No. Is that gonna be a problem, Mrs. Quinn?" He stalks closer, unbuttoning his tuxedo jacket, causing my blood to hum, literally burning for him from the inside out.

*Fuck it.*

"Not at all." I squeeze my breasts together, leaning back against the row of seating.

My pulse races, skin growing heated and sensitive under this dress.

His jaw tightens, his molten gaze drawing a path down my body while he's tossing the jacket over one of the seats and starting on his cuffs.

I shuffle on my heels, unable to wait another moment. But of course, he's taking his time on purpose.

He lifts up the sleeves, the veins of his forearms thick, like they're pulsing. "Bend over and hold on."

I feel the dominance in his voice, feel it in every crevice of my body. Waiting and willing to be his however he wants me to be.

Doing as I'm told, I face away from him, clutching the back of the seat tightly, my nails clinging to the black leather. I register him behind me, and the closer he gets, the more rapid the flicker of my heartbeats becomes.

The instant he fists my hair, I cry out in pleasure from the vibrations against my clit.

"Oh f-f-f-fuck!" I quiver. "Please, please, I can't!" My whimpered tone grows, and his grunting, the way he tightens his grasp around my hair, only makes me want this more.

"I'm gonna fuck you hard, Mrs. Quinn." He lowers his mouth to my ear. "Gonna take whatever I want from this tight little body, and if you say please, maybe I'll even let you come."

I don't even recognize my own voice. The way I beg and plead for him to give me what I need.

He runs a palm down my back. "Look how fucking sexy you are, turned on and needy for it."

"Please. I need you, Tynan. So badly."

"Mm," he growls, sucking my earlobe into his mouth before he's grabbing the back of my neck, forcing me down until I'm completely bent over. "Stay just like that."

I register him working his belt, and the sound of metal reverberating through the large space only heightens my desire.

"Please!"

He chuckles, lifting up my dress, and cool air hits my ass before he slaps it hard. My skin aches, but it's nothing compared to the pulsing in my center. I've never wanted to be fucked this badly before.

He removes the toy and slides my panties down, leaving them across my ankles as he pushes his palm between my thighs and works me against his hand.

"Such a needy wife." He thrusts a finger inside me, using his thumb to rub my clit.

"Oh God, yes, just like that. I need to come."

He hisses, then the crown of his cock pushes inside me.

"Never wanted anything more." His tone is heated and desperate.

When he clutches my hair this time, he thrusts all the way deep, each one of his piercings pushing into me, making me feel even fuller. My eyes roll back, and I let out a scream, not caring who can hear me.

He drives into me with fervor.

With demanding possession.

And it's exactly what I need.

"Yes, yes, so good…" I arch my hips back, wanting him deeper.

He slaps my ass. "My fucking little whore."

Those words only fuel my lust.

His pace increases, my body almost there.

I reach between my thighs and touch myself. "Yes, Tynan, I'm—"

"Oh, excuse me." Konstantin's voice startles us both.

I gasp, my face burning with humiliation as he gives us a wicked smirk.

"My cameras detected some movement here, so I came to investigate, but do go on. I'm glad someone is making such use of this room."

"Get out, Konstantin," Tynan grits.

He chuckles, walking over to the wall and pressing a button. Suddenly, the room is filled with a soft romantic melody coming from the speakers.

"Some mood music for you two." He looks us up and down. "Though I don't think either of you need much help."

"Get the fuck out, Konstantin."

He raises his palms. "Don't worry. Your wife's dignity is intact. I haven't seen a thing." He glances at Tynan's ass. "Though I've now seen more of you than I bargained for."

Tynan growls, but Konstantin finds it all amusing.

"Alright, alright, my friend. I will leave you to fuck your wife in peace. And feel free to use the game room right next door. There's a sturdy pool table you may want to take advantage of." He winks before he walks right out.

I release my breath. "Oh my God! I can't believe that just happened."

"Forget him." His lips drop to my neck and he nudges into my

G-spot, making me forget the interruption.

Then we're lost once more. Lost in each other. In the way he makes me feel.

His hand snakes around my front, grabbing my throat and squeezing tight as he gives me everything.

I rub myself as he groans.

"That's it, baby. Touch yourself while I fuck your pretty cunt. Gonna leave a mess on the floor like a good girl."

He pounds fiercely, not giving me much reprieve.

My mouth falls open with a soundless cry, needing the release like I need air. Nothing has ever felt this good. Nothing ever will. The swell of my orgasm grows within me, so close I can taste it.

And the rougher he takes me, the more I chase it.

Until I fall, screaming his name.

"Tynan, oh God!"

His grasp around my throat tightens, his movements more urgent until his body locks and I feel his warm spurts inside me, like he's marking me as his.

But I already am.

Body and heart both forever tied to this man, no matter what happens after.

"That's it, mo ghrá, take every drop."

I'll take everything he gives, over and over again.

His body slows, and he's shifting my face to the side, his gaze wild and possessive, right before he's capturing my lips with his. He remains inside me, kissing me with insistence. With passion and want and all the things I once desperately craved.

And as he does, he takes small pieces of my soul with him.

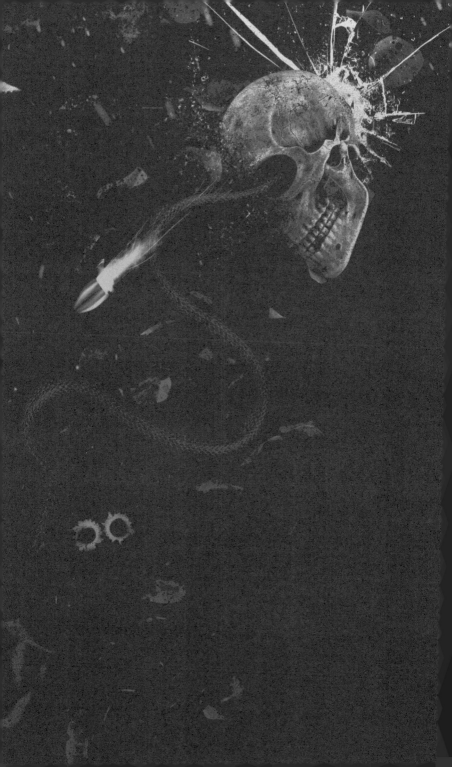

# THIRTY-NINE

## TYNAN
### ONE WEEK LATER

The day has finally arrived. The weapons the Russians promised to deliver are getting here shortly.

I made sure the delivery point was far enough on our land away from the house so that this doesn't touch Brody or Elara.

All I told her was that I have an important meeting with the Russians. I don't want her to know all the details of what I do. I want to shield her from it, even though she knows by now what she married into.

I'm not afraid of her running, because I will always find her. But I don't want to give her more reasons to go, not when things between us have been good.

This past week, we've gotten closer, and my infatuation for her only grows.

And Brody? Well, he's always loved her, and with every day, with every smile and laugh he gifts us, I believe in my heart that he will talk again. When he's ready.

Love....

That word, it sits in my head. And I want to say it, but I can't seem to get it out.

But the fact that I even want to? That's the first step, isn't it?

And that scares the shit out of me.

It's like I'll be sending a signal out into the damn universe. Like a calling card to all my enemies so they can use my love for her against me.

But ignoring my feelings, that isn't fair to her or myself.

If something were to ever happen to me and I never got to tell her, I'd regret it. I don't want her to ever wonder if I did love her. If all this was just about sex, when it wasn't.

Elara means more to me than even I realized.

She's the air I breathe.

The blood in my marrow.

The reason I want to wake up every morning.

Before her, my life was all about work or worrying about Brody. Now, it feels like I'm actually damn happy for once.

Damn.

I'm a goner, aren't I?

If Aiden were to see me now…

My walkie-talkie chirps.

"They're coming through," one of my men informs me.

"Alright. Let them know where to go."

"Ten-four."

Fionn and Cillian wait with me, and about five minutes later, the sound of the truck grows nearer. My brothers and I all have our weapons on us just in case. I don't anticipate anything going wrong. It's more as a precaution. The Russians aren't known for breaking their word or short-changing anyone. They're all about business and respect.

A white truck pulls up, a black SUV right behind. Konstantin and Kirill hop out, greeting us with a shake of their hands.

"We have your entire shipment here." Konstantin orders one of his men to open the back of the truck.

The metal pulls up, revealing cases of armor and ammo.

He takes one of the suitcases and unzips it, exposing over a dozen pistols. "You may inspect them all if you'd like."

I look him dead in the eyes. "I trust you."

His mouth cracks with a cold smile, which only makes him appear more predatory.

"Very good." He reaches out his palm, slapping mine hard. "I appreciate that show of respect. It means a lot to me." He stares at the driver of the truck. "Alright. Come on, Dimitriy, let's go."

As Konstantin and his brother head back toward the SUV, the young kid opens his door, but as he does, two other SUVs come barreling down the dirt road.

Right for us.

"What the fuck?" Fionn reaches for his gun, and in a flash we all have our weapons out, pointing at the incoming vehicles.

My immediate thought is that it's either Jerry or one of the other organized factions, trying to undermine us.

That never works.

We always win.

Cillian radios our men at the gate, but there's no answer. "Fuck!"

"So they're not with you either, I presume?" Konstantin glances behind his shoulder at me.

I shake my head.

"Very good, then. Let's kill the bastards." With a growl, he lets a few rounds rip from his nine.

My brothers and I join him, while Kirill grabs a few rifles from the truck, giving one to each of us. One of the men from the vehicles slips his head out from the window, a ski mask covering his face and a pistol in his grip.

He fires a few shots at us, and we return the favor, missing his fucking head.

"Now it's a party." Konstantin's sinister chuckle only fuels my rage as he shoots his way through the windshield, killing the driver and causing the SUV to swerve off its path before it lurches to a sudden stop.

Fionn takes that moment to finish off the passenger while the rest of us fire at the other car.

I don't know how many men they have. But before I can wonder, four men in ski masks jump out of the second SUV, hiding behind the doors as they pop out their weapons, firing right at us.

"Take cover!" I holler at my brothers.

"Blyat! I'm gonna kill these sons of bitches!" Konstantin roars, firing a hole into one guy as bullets fly right past him.

The fucker has a death wish.

Or he thinks he's invincible.

I'd guess it's the latter.

How did these fucks get through the fence? They must've killed our men at the gate. That's the only explanation.

"Fuuuck!" Worry instantly gnaws at me.

What if there are men coming for Elara? What if they're already at the house?

I need to get the fuck out of here just to make sure she's okay.

"Get down, Konstantin!" I shout, killing a man who was about to put a hole through the back of his head.

As soon as the guy goes down, he stalks toward him, eyes widening.

"Suka!" He shoots off into the dead body, over and over, his face turning crimson with his fury.

Three men remain.

There are too many of us. They have to know they won't win. But they refuse to back down, firing off more bullets in our direction while we all hit them back.

The engine of the truck suddenly comes to life, and before any of us realize what the hell is going on, it starts gunning down the road.

"I'm going after him!" Fionn rushes for his car, but before he can get in, one of the assholes fires into his windshield, shards of glass splintering through the air.

"Okay, you fuck with my Royce? Now I'm pissed." He shoots two into the guy's head, and he goes down with a thud.

Konstantin raises his rifle in the air and empties three bullets into the truck, taking out two of the tires.

With a snarl, he charges toward the driver's side, harshly pulling the door and dragging the man out until he hits the concrete with a loud thump.

He kneels, ripping off the man's ski mask, while gunfire still rings in the air. "Who sent you?" He straightens. "Tell me now and I won't come after your mama."

The man raises both palms in the air. "Please, man, don't kill me."

I can't see the asshole's face, too busy trying to take out the last two men. I get one in the chest, and soon there's only one left.

He starts to retreat, throwing his weapon down and raising his palms in the air.

Kirill takes him out without hesitation.

Now there's no one left except the kid on the ground who's no more than twenty, maybe even younger. Terror fills his eyes as he stares at each of us.

Pressing the heel of my shoe into his throat, I repeat the same question Konstantin asked. "Tell us who sent you."

"I—I…"

"Are you stupid?" Kirill asks. "Or you want to get your whole family killed? Because I promise on my mama's grave, we'll find your family and cut each one of their throats."

"Nozh." Konstantin reaches a hand toward Kirill.

Before I can wonder what the hell he said, Kirill is removing a knife from the holster around his waist and handing it to him.

"Oh, God…" the kid cries. "Please don't do that, man! I'll talk! I'll talk! I swear."

"What a good boy." Konstantin pats his cheek, but it's more like a slap. "So, who was it?"

"His—his name is Jerry. His father is Isaac."

Blood floods my veins. He sent his people to our property. After our weapons. If he comes after my wife too, I'll rip him to pieces.

"Jerry is a crazy motherfucker!" the kid continues. "He runs the Eight crew with his pops."

"That's very good." Konstantin peers over at me. "You know them, yes?"

I nod, dropping the rifle and removing my phone to call Elara.

"We find them and we kill them together. We in agreement?" Konstantin wants blood as much as I do now.

"Yes." I nod once, dialing Elara's number, needing to know she's okay.

"Please! Please just let me go. Don't wanna die, man." The kid trembles, fear filling his eyes.

"No, no." Konstantin shakes his head. "We don't kill you."

"Oh? You have a better suggestion," I ask just as her phone rings.

"We send a message, my friend." He grins, and before the kid knows what's happening, Kirill is holding him down while Konstantin is chopping off his finger.

"Ahhh!" His scream is deafening.

Moving away, I wait for her to answer, but her phone just rings and rings.

"Come on, baby. Pick up the phone."

I glance back and there's blood oozing from the kid's hand.

"Now, you will go back to your boss and tell him Konstantin Marinov is coming for him. Yes?"

But the kid's screaming only gets louder.

"Did you hear what I said? Or should I take another finger?"

"N-n-n-no please…I—I—I will tell him. Just don't. Please!" he chokes out.

"That's very good. You're a good boy. I bet you make Mama proud. Let me help you up." He yanks the boy to his feet and straightens out his t-shirt, pulling it down at the hem.

The guy's eyes widen with terror as he holds on to his bloody hand, waiting for further instructions.

"Now you may go." Konstantin pats him on the cheek. "Better find something to tie that hand with, or you will bleed out before you send our message."

As the kid runs toward one of the SUVs, Konstantin chuckles wryly, peering over at me. "Did the wife answer yet?"

I shake my head, something heavy hitting my stomach. "We're going to the house."

"Pashli." Konstantin waves over his brother.

I jump into my car and turn it on in a split second, speeding down the road. She has to be safe. I can't lose her.

I won't.

As I continue toward the house, I call one of the men stationed at the front of my home. As soon as he answers, relief hits me. It means they didn't attack the house.

"Sir?"

"Is everything okay over there? Did anyone come?"

"No, sir. All is quiet. Should we be on the lookout?"

"Yeah. We've just been hit. More could be coming. Make sure Elara and Ruby don't leave the house."

"Shit," he mutters.

My heart instantly stops. "What is it?"

"Sir, she already left."

"Who?" I spit out.

"Your wife."

Cold dread pummels through my body.

"God damn it!" My fist connects with the steering wheel over and over. "When?"

"Over an hour ago. But Rogue is with her. He wouldn't let anything happen to her."

I want to believe that. Rogue would lay down his life for hers, though if he's dead, she's unprotected.

Fuck, I hope she's wearing the damn bracelet. It's the only way I can track her.

"Call Rogue."

"Yes, sir."

"Did she say where she went?"

"Not to me."

"I'm about to pull up. Call him. Now!"

He hangs up, and I swear I will kill all my fucking men if she's dead. What good are they if they can't protect her?

The tires screech as I park in my driveway, entering the app on my phone that can give me her whereabouts. Every cell in me buzzes, hoping like hell Jerry doesn't have her. That he hasn't killed her already.

The tracker keeps spinning, like it's trying to find her location.

This is one of Grant Westfield's inventions. It works globally. If it isn't showing up, it's because it was tampered with.

"Come on, come on!" My teeth snap until my jaw aches.

My door flies open, and my brothers are there, the Russians behind them.

"What happened?" Fionn's face grows tight. "Is she here?"

I shake my head. "She left and I can't track her." My chest seizes. "They have her. They have my Elara. I can feel it."

And as I say the words out loud, it's as though my damn heart is being ripped apart, the pain like nothing I've ever felt before.

Because if I lose her, I won't survive it.

And the blood I will shed in her name will be written in the history books.

# FORTY

## ELARA
### A COUPLE OF HOURS EARLIER

While Tynan is out at his meeting, Brody and I watch a movie, sharing popcorn, giggling at characters on screen who play practical jokes on each other. Kinda reminds me of Tynan and me, except a lot less inappropriate.

I wonder when he'll be done with his meeting. I was hoping we could take Brody to get some ice cream at the café in town.

Curling my arms around him, I kiss the top of his head. He laughs when one of the characters falls. I love hearing his laughter. It's a beautiful sound, one I'll never get sick of.

"Elara?" Ruby calls as she approaches from the kitchen. "You just got a delivery. Looks like a wedding present."

She holds out a white shimmery box with a big white bow on top.

"Does it say who it's from?"

She glances at the tag. "Just says from friends. Wish you a happy marriage, Ev."

A hand flies to my chest.

*Jerry.*

*Oh, God.*

Her brows crease. "That's a weird nickname for Elara. Is that something your friends call you?"

I rush to my feet, taking the box from her. Brody glances at me but I feign a smile.

"Yeah," I tell her, laughing nervously, hoping she doesn't suspect anything. "I had this friend who liked to call me that on purpose. Anyway, thank you."

I start back toward Brody, hoping she leaves so I can open this somewhere private.

"Sure. I'll be in the kitchen if you two need me."

Curiously, she peers at me over her shoulder before she disappears.

I attempt to keep my cool, all the while terrified of what could be in this box.

"Hey, buddy?" I call to Brody. "I'll be right back, okay? Just need to put this box away."

He nods, throwing some popcorn into his mouth, while I head toward an empty den.

Placing the box down, my hands tingle as I pop it open, and when I do, nausea fills my gut.

An icy shiver races down my arms, my expression of shock frozen for a moment until tears spring in my eyes.

"No, no, no!" With shaky hands, I grab the small white envelope beside the severed finger.

Gran's finger.

"Please, please, it can't be."

He must be messing with me.

But it's hers. I know it.

Staring at the black sapphire ring still attached to Gran, I start to sob silently. It's the ring Grandpa gave her on their fiftieth anniversary. She never takes it off.

Is she alive? Did Jerry kill her to punish me?

*Not Gran. Please not her. I can't lose another person.*

A guttural sob falls silently from my lips.

*They took her finger!*

*I'm gonna be sick!*

I rush for the small garbage pail in the corner and hurl into it, my pulse beating in my temples.

When I return, I don't feel any better.

I choke on a silent cry, covering my mouth with my palm. I knew they would find me. I knew they would hurt my grandparents.

I start tearing open the envelope, blinking back tears as I read the note, recognizing Jerry's handwriting immediately.

*I have her. And you know I'll kill her. I'll take you instead.*

*But come alone. If you tell him or tip anyone off, she dies.*

*I've got eyes everywhere. 666 Main Street. Lake Tavern.*

Covering the box back up, I stuff the note inside and rush toward the door, needing to get to that address before Jerry kills one of the last living relatives I have.

I can't let him do this. I won't.

I want to call Tynan, but I'm afraid that Jerry will find out and kill Gran. When I glance down at the bracelet he gave me, I'm immediately thankful for it. He'll find me. It'll be okay. Everything will be okay. Jerry doesn't know it tracks my location.

I act casual as I get to the back of the house, smiling at the guards. I don't yet know how I'll make it past them. Other than Rogue, Tynan still has three other guards on me. I can't have any of them following me.

"Ma'am." One of them nods in greeting and opens the door, probably thinking I'm going to the garden or the pool to relax.

Every cell in my body wants to break out in a sprint toward my car, but I don't. I take my time, acting like nothing is going on.

When I'm out of view, I start rushing toward the one side of the gate that normally has no one stationed there because it's got a hidden lock. Tynan once showed it to me in case of emergencies and gave me the code. I enter it into the keypad, and the door instantly opens.

I notice some guards on the far right, but no one is paying attention to me. I quickly head for my car, parked a short distance away. If I can just get out of the main gate, I'll be able to help Gran. But I don't even know if those guys will let me go.

My pulse pummels in my temples as I approach my car. Just a little more, and I'm almost there.

"Please, Gran, just hold on."

"Elara?"

*Oh, no.*

My eyes grow when I register Rogue's voice behind me. I stay rooted while gravel crunches beneath his feet.

"Why didn't you tell me you were leaving?"

"Um…"

*Think, damn it!*

He comes around to face me. "What's wrong? Are you crying?"

"Um…I, uh…I have to go see my grandma. She's not feeling well, so she asked me to come."

"Okay, I'll follow you."

If he follows me, so will the other three bodyguards.

"No, that…that's okay. I mean, I'm not going far."

"It doesn't matter. I'm instructed to go wherever you do."

"Rogue, please! Not today!" I plead, tears leaking from the corners of my eyes.

His eyes lower to what I'm holding. "What's in the box?"

I shut my eyes, knowing there's no way out of this. He's gonna insist on calling Tynan, and my grandma is as good as dead.

Letting out a heavy exhale, I give it one last-ditch effort to save her life. "Look, some bad people from my past are after my family and me. They sent me this."

I open the box and he stares at it with a tight jaw. As he picks up the note and reads it, I continue.

"If I don't show up—alone—they're gonna kill her. I can't let that happen." My bottom lip quivers. "Don't you have family you'd do anything for? That's what my grandparents are. They're all I have left. Please just let me go."

He returns the note, and I shut the box, growing sick at the sight of her finger. The pain she must be going through. Nausea rocks me.

"I'll help you. But I can't just let you go alone. They could easily kill you and your grandma."

I run a hand down my face.

"Look, it's gonna be fine," he tries to reassure me, yet all I feel is more anxiety. "I'll text the other guys that we're just heading to grab coffee and they can stay at the house. Once we get there, I'll let you out and take cover where the people who have your grandma can't see me. But…" He stares at me intently. "I've gotta tell Tynan and the other guys once we get there. They'll back us up and get you two out."

What he says makes sense. At least I think so.

"Okay. Fine. Let's go."

"It isn't far." He starts for his SUV. "It's just a couple of towns over."

I nod, getting into the passenger side while he jumps into the spot beside me, and we're off toward the gate.

My foot bounces as I think about what Gran could be going through.

Rogue speeds down the road, zooming past other vehicles.

"How long?" I ask.

"Maybe another fifteen."

*Gran may not have fifteen minutes…*

As we make another turn, I notice an SUV behind us doing the same. I saw it earlier, but thought it was just heading down the same street.

"I think that car is following us."

"Shit," he mutters, increasing his speed.

But so does the car.

It grows closer.

I gasp as tires screech, another SUV coming right for us.

They must've followed us from the house.

Rogue tries to pass them, but they block his way.

"Nonono!" I cry when a man in a ski mask jumps out and marches right for us, a gun in his hand.

"Get us out of here!" I scream at Rogue.

But when he looks at me…a shudder runs down my spine.

I've never seen him look at me this way before.

Fear grips around my throat, and I grab the door handle, pulling, shoving. But it's locked.

"Open it! What are you doing?"

He removes his own weapon and holds it on his lap.

"No…" I whisper, staring at him in disbelief as the man in the mask opens the door and gets into the back.

"Hi, Ev. It's been a long time."

"Where is she?" I holler from the floor of the living room in some broken-down abandoned home they took me to.

I don't know how long we drove for, but it wasn't too far. Maybe another town some miles away.

"Where's my grandmother? What did you do to her?"

I don't know how many men Jerry has with him, though I saw three standing guard outside the door, and one is inside with us.

There could very well be more. They all had guns. Even if I could escape, they'd shoot me down. My best chance at survival is to draw this out and hope like hell that Tynan's coming for me.

My icy glare flays Rogue where he stands, not even appearing ashamed at his own betrayal. He's been lying this whole time.

But why? Why hurt Tynan or me?

"How could you do this to Tynan? To his family!" I shake my head with utter disgust. "I expect Jerry to be a backstabber, but you? He trusted you, and you betrayed him. Why?"

He stares at me with narrowed slits of his eyes, refusing to utter a word.

"Answer me!"

Jerry marches forward, slapping me hard across my face. "Shut your mouth, bitch. You don't ask questions."

My cheek burns, and I want to rub at it, but my wrists are tied behind my back, throbbing from the zip ties.

Rogue brushes past Jerry, kneeling down so we're eye level.

"Do you know how it feels to work for the man who killed your father?" Anger pours from his eyes.

"Wh-what? Tynan killed your dad?"

"No." His features grow tight. "Patrick did. I was ten when he came into our home and tortured my father until he bled on the floor. I watched it happen from the closet. Watched my own father die. Had to get my mother off the floor as she sobbed."

My heart truly hurts for him and the child he was, though that excuses nothing.

"I'm sorry. I really am. But that doesn't mean you have to do *this*." I glance at Jerry, hatred winding its way through my skin. "Do you know who you've aligned yourself with? They've killed children. Do you wanna be a part of that?"

He inhales long and deep, getting to his feet. "I'm not a part of anything. My job was to get you here, and I did that."

"And the rest of it? What they'll do to my grandma? Me? It doesn't matter to you?"

He stares indifferently, and I realize I'll never get through to him. Revenge is all he knows, and he'll get it any way possible.

"Enough talking!" Jerry snaps, rushing forward and pressing a gun to my forehead. "If you don't shut up, I will kill you."

I shut my eyes, fear settling deep in my stomach. If this is how I die, then so be it.

It's then I see Tynan and Brody. The days we've spent together. How happy I've been. How much I'll miss them.

It flashes before me, and tears start to fall.

Drop by drop, like all the days we'll no longer have.

Jerry nudges the barrel deeper, and just when I think he's going to pull the trigger, a door creaks from somewhere in the house.

"Now, now, Jerry. We didn't agree to that."

My eyes widen in horror.

Heartbeats batter painfully in my chest.

"G-G-Gran?" My pulse hammers, confusion causing my brain to fog. "But you… I—I don't understand…"

My throat's closing in. Oh, God, I can't breathe. I don't yet see her, though it was her voice. I know it was. It wasn't a hallucination.

Did she escape? Did she agree with Jerry to let me go?

That has to be it. Gran came to save me.

But in the back of my head, this feeling—this sinister feeling—just won't go away.

Her soft footfalls draw nearer.

Jerry sighs dramatically, dropping his gun to his side. "Nice of you to finally show up."

Then she's right there in front of me.

My gran.

And her fingers?

They're all intact.

Every last one of them.

Her ring is still there too.

"Oh my God," I sob as she advances forward. "Gran? Gran, please, what's happening?"

I gasp for air, needing her to tell me she's here to save me. That she has a plan. Yet that doesn't make sense either.

Not anymore.

"Your finger. He…he told me to come here to save you."

She nods, her face softening. "I know, sweetheart. You must be so confused. I'm sorry about that." She glares at Jerry. "Why the hell did you tie her up? I told your father to treat her well. This is not what I had in mind."

"And what did you expect? For us to all sit around a table and chat about long-lost times?" he scoffs. "Get lost, lady. You have her. It's what you wanted, right?"

*What? What does that even mean?*

"Gran, please tell me what's happening. What are you involved in?"

I can't even fathom my grandma being involved in anything with Jerry or his family.

She sighs, grabbing a chair and settling into it. "This is gonna shock you, but just hear me out, okay?"

My unsteady pulse ricochets in my ears, and with shaky breaths I nod, needing answers.

"Before I was born, my father ran a business. Then after he died, he passed it on to me."

"Business? You mean the textile company?"

Jerry laughs, like I've said something stupid. "Get to the fucking point already!" His cold, dead eyes shoot her a scowl. "Your gran ran a gang, Evelyn. She's been running that gang since before you were even born."

"Wh-wh-what?" I whisper, shaking my head frantically. "No. You're lying. Right, Gran?"

She blows a tired breath. "You don't know how long I've wanted to tell you. I came close a few times, but it never felt like the right time."

"Oh my God." My vision grows blurry from the moisture there.

"I ran it well with no problems, then grew tired of it, so I passed it to your idiot father, which was a huge mistake." Her mouth twitches with annoyance. "He decided to cause problems with the Eights." She jerks her head at Jerry. "And once I found out, it was too late. He'd already agreed to sell you to them, and I couldn't stop it." She presses two fingers into her temple. "I wanted to get you out from the drug-muling, but Isaac wouldn't have it. We were at war and people were dying, and soon it would have been me. So I needed us to go. I made you think it was your idea. But it was the only way we could get away."

I can't process what I'm hearing. I don't...how? I...

Silently, I sob, unable to handle hearing anymore yet she continues to break my heart.

"My brother took over the business when we left, but the war continued. I was sick of people dying. So I called Isaac to stop all this."

"H-h-how? How did you try to stop it?"

"By fucking your husband over." Jerry grins. "Can't wait to see the look on his face when my guys take all his weapons right from under him."

"What? Gran? You didn't! Please tell me he's lying."

She peers down for a moment and blows out a breath. "I had to give the Eights something big, and I knew how badly they needed new weapons. So once Rogue told me about the shipment arriving, I knew that was the thing to get the war to stop."

"Rogue? He helped you?" My voice is so low, I barely recognize it. "H-h-how did you even know to approach him?"

"I knew his dad." She glances at him fondly. "I knew who he was the moment I saw him, and he knew me. So we met and talked, and I realized he was looking for the perfect opportunity to get back at the Quinns for what they did. And here we are."

She flits a hand in the air while I burn in agony.

Not only did my father betray me, but so did one of the most important people in my life.

How did I not know that my family was a bunch of criminals?

"Why did you need them to kidnap me? I don't understand."

"Because…" The crease between her brows deepens. "I wanted to keep you safe from the fallout when Tynan finds out what I did. He'd kill us both. You know that, right?"

"No!" Angry tears stream down my face. "Tynan would never do that to me."

Her lips thin. "Oh, sweetheart. When it comes to money, anyone could kill anyone."

Suddenly, thoughts of my mother come storming in. Does she know what my father did? Does she know why?

"And Mom? Is that why she died?"

She drags in a long breath and stares at the ceiling for a nanosecond.

"Oh, God," I whisper. "You knew the whole time! You knew Dad killed her!"

"Elara…I'm sorry. I know how close you two were."

"So you know what I did too?" My eyes expand.

She nods. "I knew from the start. Isaac told me."

Nausea returns to my gut, swirling and crawling up my throat until all I want is to dig a hole and die in it.

My heart…how much more can it break? I want to scream. Want to tear everything apart, the way my whole life has been torn into pieces.

Jerry snickers. "You don't know what really happened to your mother, do you?"

Gran jumps from her seat. "Shut up, Jerry!"

"Why the hell would I do that? I thought we were all being open and honest, *Gran*. So tell her. Go ahead."

"Tell me what?" My heartbeats rap wildly against my ribs, the room spinning faster and faster with every second I wait for an answer.

"Don't you dare!" Gran flares him with a venomous glare, but he's too busy leering at me to care.

"Your grandmother. She ordered the hit."

# FORTY-ONE

"You're lying!" I shout at Jerry. "Gran, please tell him!"

I stare at her.

Waiting.

And waiting.

And waiting for her to deny it.

But it never comes.

And my world? It comes barreling down, and there's no way to come back from that.

No way at all.

"No! No! Why!"

She couldn't have done that. She loved Mom!

I can't be here. I…I need to get away.

My snivels wrack me and my fingers curl at my back, wanting to rip through the zip ties and run from here. From her. From him.

I just want Tynan. I want my husband. I just want to crawl into his arms where it's safe. Where I've always been safe. The people I trusted were the ones who were lying to me. He's the only one who was actually honest with me. He never hid his intentions. He told me who he was. While my own family kept their true identities hidden my entire damn life!

"How?" I sob. "How could you do that to her? Why?" I shout with a deafening cry. "Tell me what she could've done to make you hate her this much!"

"Elara…"

She tries to reach for my face, but I flinch, anger radiating from my every pore.

"Very well." She sighs dramatically, returning to her seat. "Your mother was going to turn us in to the feds when she found out that your father sold you to the Eights. She was a mess." She tsks. "I tried to reason with her. I told her I would get you out of it, but she wouldn't listen." She stares absently, as though remembering, before she looks back at me. "I had no choice. I ordered your father to do it. And once I found out you killed him in retribution, that was when I realized that one day you'd be ready to take over for me."

I laugh wildly. Like one of those insane laughs, because what she just said was the craziest thing I've heard. Or maybe not the craziest. Maybe tied with everything else she's told me.

I swallow the bitter taste in my mouth. "You're insane, Gran. If you think that I'd ever run your gang or want anything to do with you after this, you're crazy."

"Elara, sweetheart, your grandpa and I love you. This is just who we are."

"Don't bring Grandpa into this!"

She's the one laughing now. "You think he wasn't in the business with me? Honey, come on."

"I don't care. He's not well anymore. You need to stay away from him!"

She rolls her eyes. "Don't be ridiculous. He's my husband. I'll see him when I want."

"No you won't, Gran. When Tynan finds out what you did, you'll have to run, or he will kill you."

"And you're just going to let him do that?"

"You make it sound like I have a choice." I look at her with revulsion. "You had Mom killed for betraying you, and she was family. You're nothing to the Quinns. Once they find out what you did, they'll want payback. And right now, I wouldn't object." Bile rises up my throat. "I will *never* forgive you."

"See, this is why I didn't want you to find out." She narrows her gaze at Jerry, and he shrugs nonchalantly.

Of course he doesn't care. He lives to tear people apart, physically and emotionally. But as much as it hurts, I'm glad I finally know the truth.

"What was your plan, Gran? Keep me here until Jerry's guys are done screwing Tynan over? Then what? We run? Do you think Tynan would just let me go?"

"Once Jerry's men tell him that they have the weapons, Rogue is gonna feel out the situation and figure out if Tynan suspects me. If not, we return like nothing happened. Jerry won't talk, because if he does, he will die." Her mouth curls as she gives him a quick glance. "I have it all figured out. This plan benefits both Isaac and us."

"And what makes you think Jerry's people could overpower Tynan and his family?"

Jerry marches forward, pointing his gun in my face again. "Are you trying to say we're weaker?"

"That's exactly what I'm saying."

"You little—"

"Enough!" Gran shouts. "Lower that gun before I shove it up your ass."

Her face turns icy. I've never seen her this way.

"Tynan is calling." Rogue stares at the phone.

"Answer it." Gran places a palm on his arm. "Just like we practiced."

He nods. "One word from you…" he says to me. "And I kill you."

Gran tsks. "She won't say anything. She's smarter than that."

I ball my hands as he answers the call, but I have to keep the faith that Tynan is tracking me and maybe already here.

"Sir?" Rogue answers, pausing as he listens to whatever Tynan says. "Elara is fine. She went to visit her grandma, and I'm right outside."

He stares at me without blinking, his mouth twisting.

Tynan won't believe it. He'll go searching for me and realize I'm not there.

"Fuck… Okay, yeah, I'll bring her back when she's done. Bye, sir." He drops the call and looks over at Jerry. "Bad news. Your guys are dead."

"What?" he snaps, barreling toward him.

"That's what he said. He knows you tried to rob him, and he's coming after you with the Russians."

"The Russians!" Jerry starts scrambling, pulling at his hair. "My father is going to lose his mind!" He aims his gun at Gran. "You told me this would be easy! That all we had to do was take the truck and go. You never told me we were stealing from the Russians too!"

"Didn't I?" She grimaces. "You know, I'm getting old. Sometimes I'm a little forgetful."

Before I can take my next breath, she whips out her own gun from her handbag, aiming it at him. And seeing her like this, I don't even recognize her.

Who is this woman?

Did I ever really know her?

Was she pretending the entire time?

"Gran, don't!" I shout, realizing I don't want her to die. Not even after what she did.

But she ignores me, both of them staring each other down.

"Your time is coming to an end, you old bat." Jerry laughs.

And just as they're about to shoot each other, there's a knock on the door.

His eyes widen, and he gestures for one of his men to go see what's going on.

My heart punches in my chest. I hope it's Tynan coming to save me. But when I register the door opening, it's a woman's voice that I hear.

"I'm sorry. Can you help me? My tire is flat, and my boyfriend just broke up with me." She starts to cry.

"Wrong house. Leave now," the guy tells her.

"Please. I'll do anything if you could just change my tire. I can pay you a grand. I have one in the trunk. I just don't know how to do it myself."

Rogue's vision connects with mine.

He knows. Of course he knows.

He's gonna ruin everything.

"For fuck's sake!" Jerry hollers, rushing for the door, Rogue on his tail. "Get the fuck out of—"

But his words die in his throat, and the rest happens in a blur.

Gunshots fire off, and Gran frantically rushes out of the room for a few seconds. When she returns, she's hurrying toward me, cutting off my zip ties with a knife.

"We need to go! Now!" She tries to grab my arm, but I fling it away, knowing help has arrived.

Because the woman at the door was Iseult.

"I'm not going anywhere with you! Get away from me!"

"Elara, we have to—"

"You heard her, Gran." Iseult comes marching toward us, dragging a bloody Jerry by his shirt.

But he's still very much alive.

Though Rogue? He's not with her…

She gives me a little wink, her red-painted lips curling, not a single red hair out of place. "You hurt?"

I shake my head. "Is he here?"

Every cell in my body craves to see him. To throw my arms around him and never let go.

"He's here." She grins wider, just as a few more shots fire. "He's just taking care of some loose ends outside."

She drops Jerry on the floor and presses her foot over his chest, digging her high-heeled boot into his sternum.

"You know…" she tells Gran. "I admire a woman boss. Running her own shit. It's too bad we're gonna have to kill you. You know, for fucking us over." She shrugs a shoulder. "No hard feelings, right?"

Gran's eyes narrow. "It doesn't have to be this way."

"Oh?" Iseult grabs a chair and settles into it, folding her arms across her chest. "Do tell."

When Jerry groans, she digs her heel in deeper. "Shut up down there. Women are talking." She slices a hand through the air. "Please, do go on. Can't wait to hear all about how we shouldn't kill you."

The thought of them killing Gran makes me physically ill. Yet when I think of what she did to Mom, I want her to suffer. Does that make me a monster?

Gran sighs. "Who told you I was involved?"

"There's always someone who squeals. You should know that from your line of work."

"You have to understand," Gran says. "I only gave them the information about the deal because I knew there was no way they could win. I wanted you guys to kill them and get rid of the problem. You all certainly stood a better chance than I did."

Iseult chuckles, throwing one long leg over the other. "So you were doing us a favor? Is that it?"

"In a way, yes. I wanted to ensure Elara's safety and mine. Your family's too. The Eights, they're unstable and rash. They don't think logically. So I knew if I presented them with a chance to get the weapons from you, they'd jump at the chance."

"Wow!" Iseult slow claps. "You have some balls. But I'll be honest, you're still gonna die."

My stomach drops.

"Elara?" Tynan calls. "Elara, baby, where are you?"

He comes barreling in, breathing heavy, hair a mess.

My mess.

Tears fill my eyes as soon as I see him, and I'm running toward him with all the strength I can muster.

"Tynan!" I cry, throwing my arms over his shoulders as he lifts me up in the air, my legs twining around his hips, his palm clasping the back of my head.

Everyone else disappears. All I focus on is him.

"Fuck," he whispers into the crook of my neck, emotions wafting through his voice. "I thought I'd lost you."

He pitches back, brows drawn in pure anguish.

"I'm okay." I hold his face with both hands. "I'm okay now."

With a rough breath, he clasps my cheek to his chest, and we stay that way for a minute, ignoring everything around us.

My arms grasp tighter around him—this man who feels like my home. The only place I belong. The only place I want to be.

He wrenches back, searching my gaze before he captures my mouth with his, hands in my hair, clinging like he never wants to let me go.

I melt into him, my heart beating right out of my chest.

"Fuck, Elara. I'm so sorry," he breathes, lips skimming mine.

"No." I shake my head. "This isn't your fault. It's mine. You didn't do anything."

His jaw clenches, his glare sliding behind me, and I know he's looking at Gran. He kisses me one more time before he's putting me down, clasping his hand with mine.

Fionn and Cillian walk in, dragging Rogue, his wrists zip-tied in front of him, face bloody.

Is this really over? Will I finally be done with the Eights for good?

"What are you gonna do with them?"

In his eyes, I find a hungered beast. "*Everything*."

And I feel that word. I feel it in my marrow, knowing that's his oath to me. For all the wrongs I've endured.

"Take her away," he tells Iseult.

"No!" He doesn't understand how badly I need to see Jerry dead.

"Elara…" His eyes soften. "I don't want you to have to watch this."

"I don't care. I need to see it."

"If that's what you want, I won't deny you."

More footfalls draw closer. When we look in that direction, we find Konstantin and another guy who looks very much like him walking in.

Konstantin drops someone on the floor.

*Isaac.*

"Guess who my men found hiding in one of the cars outside." He smirks.

My heartbeats quicken as I stare at the men who ruined my life, neither one saying a word.

Isaac's one eye is swollen and his mouth bloodied. And from the appearance of Konstantin's knuckles, it's likely he's the one who did it.

"Sit them up," Tynan tells his siblings, and they pull the men to a seated position.

Jerry grins wryly, and I find that one of his teeth is missing.

Tynan removes a knife from his ankle holster and nears the tip to Rogue's throat. "I trusted you. *We* trusted you…" His body reverberates with rage. "And you betray us? You put my wife at risk? Why?"

Rogue drags his face up and stares at him. "What would you do if my father killed yours?"

Tynan grabs the back of his neck, nearing his face toward him. "This."

With one quick jerk, he sinks the blade into his eye.

I gasp, looking away while Rogue roars in pain…

Tears burn behind my eyes. This is all too much.

"I'm not done with you yet. I'll drag this out. Each one of you will suffer." He kneels in front of Jerry. "I will enjoy every fucking second of watching you die."

Jerry's upper lip curls. "Fuck you, you cock-sucking bastard."

"You really shouldn't have said that." He glances at Cillian. "Give me another knife."

For a brief second, real fear flashes before Jerry's eyes, and before I know what's happening, Tynan pushes him down flat on the floor while Fionn and Cillian hold him down.

"What the fuck are you doing?" Jerry tries to fight them, but it's no use.

"Let my son go! You can have me."

Tynan ignores Isaac's plea, prying Jerry's mouth open. And when he slices his tongue off, I cover my mouth to stop from hurling, squeezing my eyes shut.

Muffled cries fill the air while Isaac curses, swearing to kill him. Though that's laughable, really. He won't get away.

"Load them all in the trunks. We're bringing them to the barn."

"I'd be more than happy to dispose of them for you," Konstantin offers. "My pigs get very hungry." His vicious sneer makes me shiver.

His pigs? He feeds them human remains? Is that what he meant? I'm gonna be sick.

"I may take you up on it." Tynan isn't even fazed.

I forget that Gran is here for a moment…until she tries to sneak away, backing up slowly, planning her escape. Our eyes connect, and the part of me that still loves her wants her to get away. But the other part, the one that can't reconcile the fact that she was the reason Mom died? Well, that part wants her dead.

"Now, where do you think you're going, Gran?" Iseult grabs her arm just as Tynan zeroes his attention on her too. Iseult points a weapon at her chest. "You're coming with us."

Gran grunts, knowing she has no other choice.

Fionn and Cillian grab Jerry and Rogue, pulling them up and dragging them out the door, while Konstantin removes Isaac.

"What were you thinking, coming without me?" Tynan turns to me, his brows knitted. "I could've lost you."

His eyes, they swim with pain. So much of it, I ache.

Tears pierce my vision, and I sniffle back, everything hitting me at once. That I could've died. That Gran betrayed me. That Mom died because of her.

"I'm sorry." I throw my arms around him, holding on to him with every fiber of my being.

He inhales deep, his palm gripping the back of my head. "It's okay, baby. Don't cry. It breaks my heart when you cry."

He lets me anyway, holding me as I do. And for a moment, all that worry and fear slips away. Because he's here and he's got me. But when he perches back, the look of vengeance in his gaze returns.

"I wanna get you home."

"What are you gonna do with them? With her…" I whisper, needing Jerry and Isaac dead.

I need that closure. Need to know they'll never come after me again. But Gran? That hurts. I don't think I can watch him do that.

"I'm gonna do what I promised. I'm gonna make them all suffer. Then I'm gonna kill them."

Tears trace my cheeks.

"I'm an old woman," Gran interrupts. "Are you really going to do that to me?"

Tynan's breaths howl out of him. "You're the worst of them. You were her family, and you betrayed her."

He grabs my hand and squeezes it while I fall apart inside, knowing that I'm gonna lose another family member. Grandpa will be all I have left, and he doesn't even know me.

Was he just as bad as her? Did he know about Gran ordering Mom's death? He had to know. But how can I be mad at him now that he's someone else? What would be the purpose?

"Get her out of here," Tynan tells Iseult, and she grabs her arm, shuffling Gran out of the room until we're alone. "Come on, babe. We've gotta go."

I'm grateful to finally get out of here. Grateful that I'm alive.

He walks us out of the house.

Gran looks back at me, her expression pained. "Let me say goodbye to her. Please."

His jaw clamps, and he looks at me as I nod, letting him know I need this. I need to let her go. I need closure, no matter how I get it.

"I'll be right next to you." With his hand still clasped to mine, we take a few steps toward her, Iseult not leaving Gran's side.

"I'm sorry, Elara. I'm sorry I took your mom from you." Tears fill her eyes, her words sincere. "I'm sorry about all of it. I never meant for it to come to this."

I don't know what to say except that I don't forgive her, so I say nothing at all. How can I after what she's done? My mother's death. Betraying me and Tynan. It would take time, and even then, I don't know if I can trust her ever again.

Her eyes press shut, and for a second it seems like she's going to cry.

But she gives me a hug instead, and as she does, she whispers, "I'll see you on the other side, sweetheart."

Tynan lets out a groan. "Fuck."

I jump back, eyes wide when I find blood.

So much blood.

On his hands.

His stomach.

"T-T-Tynan? Oh my God! Help!"

My heartbeats explode in my chest, unable to comprehend what just happened. That Gran's holding the knife with his blood on it.

Her mouth curls.

His men come rushing.

"How could you?" I shout. "How could you do this?"

But she doesn't respond.

"You bitch!" Iseult whips out a gun and shoots her right in the head.

She falls on the ground.

*Oh, God. Gran's dead.*

I can't process it all right now.

"Tynan!" My heart is literally breaking as the men pick him up. It's all too much.

"Move!" Iseult screams at the guys. "Get him in the car and let the doc know we're on our way!"

I'm right by his side, grabbing his hand, looking into his eyes and praying that he doesn't die.

"I'll be fine, mo chuisle. Don't worry about me." His voice...it's low. Tired.

*Please, please don't let him die.*

"Of course you'll be fine." A silent cry slips from my mouth.

Because I don't know if that's true.

I don't know if he'll make it through this.

And I wonder if this is it.

If our story is going to end before it ever truly had a chance to begin.

# FORTY-TWO

## ELARA

**B**rody sits in my lap, sobbing against my chest as I try my best to reassure him that Tynan will be okay. That he'll pull through the surgery.

But me? I'm dying inside. Dying slowly, trying my best to keep it together for this little boy. My boy. My arms hold him tighter while I stare at the doors of the hospital, waiting for someone to tell us something.

I haven't even come to terms that Gran is gone. My mind hasn't fully grasped it all. Who she really was. That she ran a gang for most of her life. That she knew Jerry and his family. That she had Mom killed.

My stomach forms tight knots. Can't think about that now. I have to focus on Tynan and Brody.

"I can't fucking wait another second!" Iseult's hands curl as she paces, shoving away Gio's arm as he tries to hold her.

"Babe, it's Tynan," he says. "He's gonna be fine."

Though Gio fails to convince me, let alone Iseult. She loves her brother. It's easy to see how much by the look on her face. She doesn't cry. But she's hurting.

"Yeah," Patrick says this time. "Our boy is gonna be fine, darling. You'll see."

Eriu, though? She's quietly sobbing against Devlin, while he appears tense himself.

His brothers look worried too. They're a close family, and I love that about them. I know in my heart none of them would ever betray each other like my family has.

We wait for what feels like hours until an older man walks out, removing his green plastic cap.

Brody and I jump off our seats, everyone approaching the doctor.

His pale blue eyes bounce between us.

Why isn't he saying anything?

"Tell us how he is, Doc." Patrick is the first to break the silence.

"Well, he lost a lot of blood and—"

"Oh, no!" I snivel. "Please…"

Eriu comes to my side and wraps an arm around me, while I grip Brody's hand.

"He's alive, Mrs. Quinn. Tynan is alive."

"Oh, thank God!" I slap a hand to my chest, my heart beating so fast I grow lightheaded.

"The surgery went well. The wound was shallow. The knife just missed his spleen. He's very lucky."

"Thanks, Doc. I owe ya." Patrick slaps a hand to the man's shoulder.

"When can we see him?" I ask.

"As soon as he wakes up, one of the nurses will let you know."

"Thank you." I wipe the tears fogging my vision, relief hitting me like a ton of bricks.

He's gonna be okay.

We're gonna be okay.

Brody cries, circling his arms around me, and I hold on to him even tighter than before.

# TYNAN

It takes me a moment to realize where I am. The smell—like disinfectant. The lights blaring in my eyes from above.

The hospital.

I groan, trying to sit up, but throbbing pain in my abdomen causes me to lie back down.

"Elara," I call for her, yet as my eyes adjust to the room and I look around, I find myself alone.

The memories hit me then. Her fucking grandma. That bitch stabbed me.

I grab the call button, pressing it five times, needing to see Elara desperately.

A nurse walks in. "Mr. Quinn, we're so happy to see you up."

"My wife. My son. I need to see them. Now."

Her eyes expand at my harsh tone.

I've got no time for pleasantries. I want my family here.

"Alright, not to worry. I will go get them for you."

She rushes out, and I stare at the ceiling, wondering if Elara will be the one in the hospital next. It could've easily been her. It could happen at any time.

How the hell do I reconcile these feelings? The fear for her safety, the love for her that I can no longer deny.

Is it wrong to tell her now? Do I wait until I'm home? What if I don't make it home? What if I die here?

The door flies open, and Brody is there, his eyes stricken with tears. Elara is behind him, her gaze bloodshot.

*I love you.*

The instant thought hits me so hard, my breaths still.

Brody rushes to me, and I sit up, fighting the pain just as he crawls up on the bed, pressing his head to my shoulder and crying against me.

Elara appears beside him, her tears falling freely.

"Tynan…" The rest of her words die in her throat.

"I know." My voice is croaky, and I hate it. "I'm alright now." I take her hand and kiss the top of it. "Never gonna leave you."

"Pl—"

That voice…

It wasn't hers. And it wasn't mine.

Was I imagining it?

But one look into Elara's widened eyes, and I know it was real.

"Brody?" I tilt his chin up. "Did you say something?"

Elara stays in place like she's afraid to move.

"Talk to me," I beg him.

"Please…"

Oh, fuck. He's doing it. A throb clings to my throat.

"Please don't leave me too."

Elara sniffles, cupping her mouth.

"Never, Brody. I'm never gonna leave you." Blinking past my own emotions, I hold him tightly to me, ignoring the stabbing pain, focusing on the fact that he talked again.

He fucking talked.

"I've missed your voice, kid." I kiss the top of his head, squeezing my eyes shut for a moment. "You know, maybe I'll get stabbed more often if that's what finally gets you talking again."

He cracks a smile, swiping under his lashes. "Not funny."

I shrug, my mouth tipping up. "It's a little funny."

"Yeah, no." Elara wrinkles her nose as she shakes her head. "Not even close to funny."

I let out a chuckle right before my face grows serious when I stare into her gorgeous cerulean gaze.

"Elara…" My chest squeezes. "Sit by me."

Brody slips a little lower on the bed, staying by my knees to give her room beside me.

She places a palm around my face. "I'm glad you didn't die."

I laugh. "Me too. It'd be much harder to tell you how much I love you."

Her chest swells with a quick inhale, lips parting with the shock weaving through her features.

"You don't have to say anything," I tell her. "But I've wanted to tell you for a while now. I just… I didn't know how to. Never said it to a woman before, but you…" I take her hand in mine and kiss the center of her palm. "When I woke up, all I wanted was to see you and tell you that I love you. That I want you. That I *need* you, Elara. With all my damn heart."

Her tears streak silently as I go on, needing to get it all out.

"And I know I forced you into this and that wasn't right. But I need you to know I'm not sorry about it. I'd do it again if I could. Because you were meant to be mine, Mrs. Quinn. And with every single day you wear my ring, I'm gonna prove to you that I'm worthy of you."

I stare deep into her eyes.

Waiting.

Hoping for her to say that she loves me right back.

Yet it never comes.

# ELARA

I can't make my mouth move, rendered speechless. He was adamant about not falling in love with me, and a part of me accepted that I might never hear him say those words. But now, actually hearing them, my heart's ready to explode.

"It's okay if you don't feel the same." His gaze grows pained. "I understand. But it will never change how I feel."

I place my hand over his chest, searching his gaze, knowing what I feel is too powerful to ignore. There's no way I can allow him to think I don't feel the same.

"I don't know how it happened, Mr. Quinn, but I'm crazy in love with you too."

His grin, it lights up the room and my soul right along with it. "Never said I was *crazy* in love with you."

His teasing has me laughing. Brody's chuckling too.

"Kiss me, mo ghrá," he whispers. "Kiss me and tell me you love me again. I need to hear it."

And those words, the way he says them—so raw and full of passion—they warm me from the inside out.

I let my lips fall closer, feathering them against his as I whisper the words I've longed to say. "I love you, Tynan. I love you so much it hurts."

He inhales deep and captures my mouth with his, growling low just as Brody groans.

We both laugh, and he kisses me one more time before we separate. He stares into my eyes, and I swear I could stare at this man for hours.

"I'm gonna try to get out of here today."

I scoff. "Be reasonable. You have to take care of yourself. They said you were lucky to be alive, so lie here and get better."

He shakes his head with an exhale. "I'm not good at this. Doing nothing."

"Well, too bad. Your wife says you have to."

His brows rise. "Oh, I like you bossy."

"Mm-hmm, get used to it. There's gonna be a lot of that while you're recovering."

"Yes, ma'am." Then he grabs the back of my head and kisses me some more.

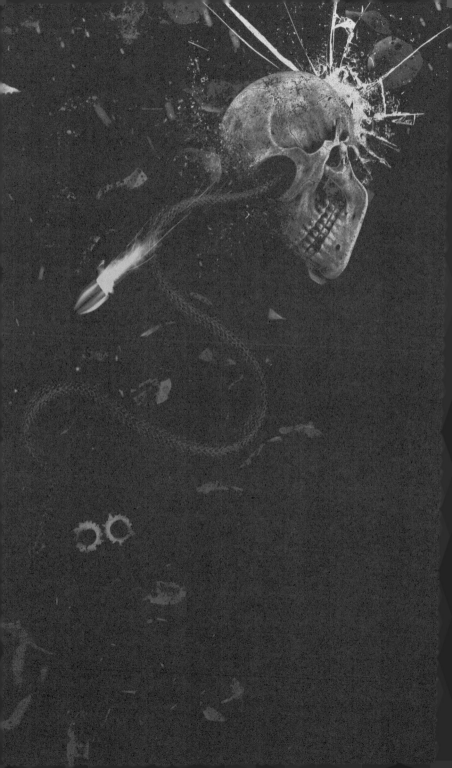

# FORTY-THREE

## TYNAN
### THREE WEEKS LATER

"Give me those bags!" Elara demands. "The doctor said you can't do anything strenuous for four to six weeks."

She grabs the groceries from me while I laugh, taking them right back.

"I love you for taking care of me, but I'm okay." I tug her jaw and kiss her, enjoying the feeling of her lips on mine.

She shoves me away and stares disapprovingly. "Go sit down and let me get you some food. You haven't eaten lunch yet."

She's taken the whole bossing-me-around thing seriously, making sure I don't open my wound. It's actually adorable, and I let her, even though it's been killing me doing less than I'm used to. But I know she was afraid something would happen to me. I feel fine, though, and I have to get back to work.

And most importantly, I have to kill them.

"Alright, baby." I slap her ass, and she yelps. "I'm a little hungry for something else, though."

Arousal paints her gaze, and I take this moment to force the front of her body to mine.

"It's been too long. I need you, mo chuisle."

"The doctor was specific," she breathes as my mouth strokes hers. "No sex for four to six weeks."

"Close enough." My fingers slide through her hair, tugging her strands in my fist, kissing the underside of her jaw.

I slip the thin strap of her tank down, needing her bare.

"Eww!" Brody's voice has me stopping just as Elara backs away, her face flushing. "Can you guys stop kissing like every minute? It's so gross! Right, Uncle Fionn?"

"Totally gross!" He makes a gagging face, then winks at me.

"What are you two doing back?" I ask. "I thought you were off to the park to play baseball."

"We are, but I left my cell." He points to the counter, grabbing it and stuffing it into his pocket.

"Okay, well, you two have fun." Elara kisses the top of Brody's head.

"I will. Love you guys."

That has her features straining with emotion while my pulse pounds in my ears, still not believing the fact that he's actually talking to us. Telling us he loves us, no less.

"Love you too, kid."

"I love you," she says as we both watch him walk away. "I can't get over it."

Her head falls against my chest.

"Me either. I keep thinking he'll just stop one day. That I'll do something to mess it up."

"No." She shakes her head, turning to face me. "Stop thinking any of that was your fault."

"Yeah, I know." A deep exhale falls out of me.

"Come on, go sit down. I'll warm you up some shepherd's pie."

"Whatever you say, boss."

She tugs me toward the empty chair, and I'll gladly sit here and stare at her ass all day if she lets me.

Hours later, I make my escape to the barn, where I've held them prisoner all this time.

I've never enjoyed torturing someone as much as them.

My brothers, of course, helped.

"Have you had enough yet?" I glare at Rogue as Cillian beats him, kicking his stomach, his face. He's barely recognizable. "Wanna die?"

We've fed them just enough to survive, so we can torture them all over again.

Every *fucking* day.

I warned them that their deaths would come slowly, and I'm always a man of my word.

Rogue groans, looking up, and I'd be surprised if he sees anything from his one eye that's almost swollen shut.

"Pick him up."

My brothers drag him to his feet while I grab thick rope, taking it to one of our horses.

She lifts her forelegs once she sees me approach, her harness already on her. "Good girl." I glide my hand down her mane, then tie the rope securely around her saddle, tugging it to make sure it's secure.

Cillian pushes Rogue onto the ground, while Fionn grabs the other end of the rope and starts tying it around both of his wrists.

"Is he good?" I ask.

Fionn nods.

"Come on, girl." I pull on her lead rope, applying enough pressure until she runs. And she can run forever.

She drags Rogue through the mud, past rocks, his body hitting them hard, and I know he won't last long.

"Let's go," I tell my brothers, needing to take care of Isaac and Jerry next.

We march toward the two separate stalls where we've kept them. Fionn pulls a bloody Isaac out of the barn, while I have the pleasure of dragging Jerry by his foot, making damn sure his face greets the hay and dirt as I take him to join his father.

They've been in the same clothes since they got here. We've hosed them down to clean them off, of course. But that's all they got, and that's only 'cause I don't wanna smell them.

"Sit him up." I gesture my head to Isaac, and Fionn forces him up as he groans in protest.

I kneel before him, tilting his chin so he's looking at me. He snarls, his nostrils widening.

"Nothing to say? Not even to beg for your lives?"

His mouth curls. "Go f-f-fuck yourself."

I inhale a calming breath as I straighten to full height. "I'm gonna make you watch your son die. Then I'm gonna kill you."

Cillian hands me a knife, and I fall to my knees before Jerry's body. The tip of the knife nears his throat, and he trembles.

He should be scared.

"You remember what you did to her? Because I will never forget."

Before he can bother saying a word, I rip his stomach open, fucking blood everywhere. His screaming only makes this more satisfying. Reaching into my pocket, I retrieve ten grams of coke, fitting it into his abdomen.

His father gasps, knowing fear for the first time, I'm sure. I slice the baggies open and let the drugs seep into his veins.

He will die slowly. Painfully.

I can't fix what's been done to her. But I can do this. And even this doesn't feel like enough.

Grabbing Isaac's wrists, I slice open his arteries and lay him next to his son. When they're dead, we'll cut them up and take them to Jersey and let Konstantin's pigs have at 'em.

"Let's go home," I tell my brothers. "We'll take care of the bodies tomorrow."

"Shit. I need a shower." Fionn sniffs himself.

"I need food," Cillian throws in. "Got any at home?"

"Yeah, actually, I do." I laugh. "Elara made enough for an army."

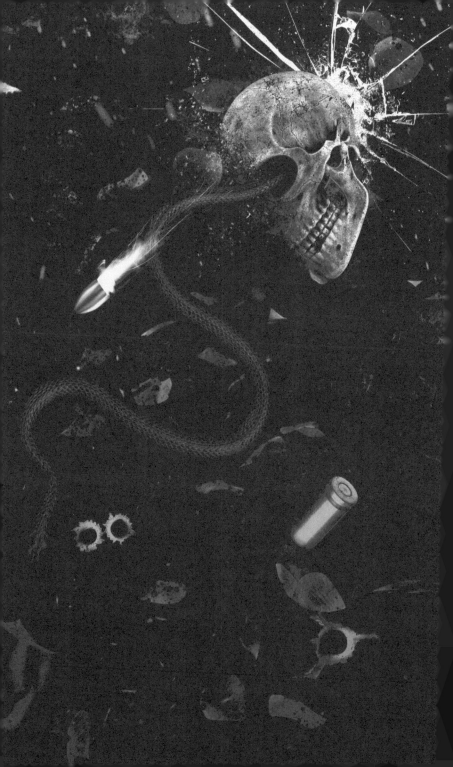

# FORTY-FOUR

## ELARA
### ONE WEEK LATER

It's been a month since Gran's death, and I've slowly come to terms with who she was to me and who she was to everyone else who really knew her.

I don't think I ever truly did. Didn't know Grandpa either, I suppose. But I can't allow those things to eat away at me.

I don't know if I'll ever forgive her for Mom or what she did to Tynan. I could've forgiven almost anything else, but not that.

She took Mom from me, and she wanted to take Tynan. She knew she'd die for it, but she wanted to make him suffer too. In turn, making me suffer. How do I forgive a woman like that?

Grandpa still lives with us, and I don't want him to go. I can't do that to him, not when he's like this.

Tynan has been amazing through it all, giving me everything I need: someone to listen, someone whose shoulder I can cry on. He's always there for me.

My throat tightens as I clear it, laying red poppies on my mother's tombstone while Brody and Tynan wait for me a few feet away. My heart still misses her. Still aches for her. Still wishes she was here to meet my family.

The stabbing pain in my chest will never go away, but I'm at peace now. As much as I can be. Tynan not only killed Jerry and his father, but he found the evidence Jerry held over me and made sure all traces were destroyed.

And as far as who I am—Evelyn or Elara—I've decided to keep my name. My new name. I need to stay Elara. Because Evelyn? She was someone else entirely.

"I love you, Mom. I'm sorry. I wish I'd been there to stop him." I wipe tears from my eyes. "I'll come back next week. I promise."

Tynan told me we could fly here whenever I wanted, that I could see her anytime I please, and that gives me some comfort.

With one last look, I turn around to join my husband and my son. Though I don't ever expect Brody to call me Mom, I will always love him like one.

Tynan and I told him he can call us his aunt and uncle, that we're both okay with that, and he seemed to like that idea.

"You ready to go home?" Tynan gazes at me through adoring eyes.

"Yeah, I am."

In these past few weeks, it feels as though I've shed a part of me and replaced it with something stronger. That *I'm* stronger than I ever was before. I hate that it was because of all this tragedy, but if it makes me stronger instead of weaker, I guess that's all I can ask for.

"I love you," Tynan whispers, knuckles brushing down my cheek, completely undoing me. "I love you so damn much, and I'm sorry you're hurting."

"I love you too, Tynan. But I'm okay now. I swear."

Brody hugs me tight. "It's okay to cry. I miss my mommy and

daddy all the time."

His own tears gather, and I kneel before him. "I want you to know you can talk about them any time you feel like it. Because there's nothing I want more than to get to know the people who made such an amazing little boy."

He throws his arms around me and sniffles.

As I close my eyes and hold him close to my heart, I make a promise to myself to always love him unconditionally.

Because that's what love truly is.

# TYNAN

Fionn offered to have Brody over for a sleepover at his place so Elara and I have a night to ourselves. He didn't mind. He's good with kids. They all seem to gravitate toward him. But I'm still grateful for his help.

I even gave Ruby the day off, and the nurse on duty is in a different wing of the house.

I wanted everything to be perfect and without distraction.

Elara sits at our dining table, votive candles glistening in the center, the room dimly lit as I bring out a tray of saffron rice and curry chicken that I made.

"My God, Tynan, this looks amazing. I can't get over how well you can cook."

I smirk, placing the food down before cupping her chin and kissing her softly. She melts into me, moaning into my mouth, her nails raking up the back of my head.

Damn, does that feel good.

My lips stroke hers. "If you keep kissing me like that, we may not get through dinner."

She peppers kisses across the outline of my jaw. "That'd be a shame."

I clench my teeth, reluctantly separating from her, needing it all to go as planned. "Let me bring out the rest of the food so we can get to dessert quickly."

"And by dessert, do you mean…" She pops a mischievous brow.

"No, I actually meant dessert. I made a souffle. But wow, Mrs. Quinn, what a dirty mind you have."

"I learned from the best." She tips up her jaw. "Now hurry up…"

Her fingernails roll between her breasts, the slinky black dress she's wearing so thin and tight, I can make out every line and curve of her body.

My cock strains. Muttering a curse, I hurry off into the kitchen, grabbing the salad and honey-glazed carrots I also prepared.

Except for Iseult and Fionn, we all know how to cook. Those two are hopeless. It's a good thing for Iseult that Gio knows his way around the kitchen, or they'd be surviving on takeout.

When I'm finally seated and filling her plate, I watch her take the first bite. As she does, her eyes shut and she groans.

"Wow, this chicken is so tender. Please cook for me anytime."

Her compliment hits me right in the chest. "Always, baby. I love feeding you."

A grin spreads on her face. And soon after, I'm replacing dinner with dessert while my heart hammers in my chest.

Fuck, why the hell am I so nervous? We've done this before.

Not like this, though.

Holding her plate in a tight grasp, I take this moment to stare at her, thankful I have her.

I still can't get over the fact that she loves me.

I didn't expect her to say it back. Hell, I thought she'd run when I did. But she hasn't. She's still here because she wants to be. And I'll always be thankful for that.

Shit. I'm gonna have to pay Devlin that million, aren't I?

I grin.

It's worth it.

She narrows a curious gaze. "Are you alright?"

*Yes. Because of you.*

"I love you, Elara." I tread closer. "I can't seem to want to stop saying it now."

She smiles sweetly, tilting her face to the side. "I love you too."

"That's good." I chuckle "Because this would be a bit awkward otherwise."

Before she can wonder what I mean, I place the plate before her. As I do, I lower to one knee, a small box in my hand.

She gapes at me. Completely in shock.

On the plate, written in chocolate, are the words, *Will you marry me again?*

May not be original or grand, but I know Elara by now, and she doesn't need those things. I wanted to do it the right way this time. The way she would remember and tell our children about. The way that I'll know if she truly loves me.

"Tynan?" Tears fill her eyes. "I—I don't understand. We—we—we're already married."

"I know, but last time you didn't have a choice. This time, I'm giving you one."

Her gaze lowers to the ring, similar in design to the original engagement ring I gave her. Slowly, she returns her eyes to mine.

She cups my cheek, and every time she does, her touch… It hits me right in the center of my chest.

"And if I say no?"

My pulse quickens. But when I find the crack of her smile, I know she's just teasing me.

"Do I really have to answer that, mo ghrá?"

"You know, you never told me what that meant."

"It means my love, which is what you are."

"You're mine too, Tynan." She leans in to kiss me and my heart swells. "Of course I'll marry you."

Her teeth sink around her bottom lip as I hurriedly get this ring out, replacing it with the old, still keeping the wedding band on her hand.

"Wait. Where are you putting my old ring?"

"I was going to put it in the box and give it to you."

Her face falls.

"What is it, Elara?"

"Is it weird if I wear both? Maybe one on the other hand? I'm kinda sentimental, and this was the first ring you gave me."

I let out a laugh.

"What's so funny?"

"Here I thought you wouldn't say yes, and you want to wear both of my rings. I guess I'm just surprised."

She rises to her feet, leading me up with her. "I know you were a real ass in the beginning—"

"Mm, debatable."

"Yeah, okay…" She rolls her eyes teasingly. "Anyway, as I was saying, you were a real ass back then, but you've kinda grown on me, like a wart you can't get rid of. So yes, I want to wear both of the rings because you gave them to me."

"Wow, Mrs. Quinn." I chuckle. "You're quite the romantic."

"I know." She sticks out her right hand. "Now please give me my ring back."

"Happily." I slip it back on her finger and she stares down at both her hands, her face lighting up like the sun at dawn.

My body warms seeing her this happy.

Her arms fall over my shoulders, and she stares up at me.

"I'm gonna marry you all over again." I tug her chin up between two fingers. "This time in front of everyone."

"I want that." Her eyes glisten like two bright stars. "I want to marry you. I want this to be real."

I drop my lips close to hers, brushing them slowly. "It's always been real to me, Elara."

Then I kiss her, unable to stop, because in her arms, I forget the rest of the world.

All I know is her.

# ELARA

He lowers me onto our bed, his body crawling over mine, forcing his weight into me. I love the feeling of his muscles, his strength, pinning me to the bed.

His eyes swim with affection, and I take this moment to really look at him, the back of my hand gliding across the stubble of his jaw.

He inhales a breath, his eyes leaden and full of the same desire coursing through me. I'm not sure how we got here—to this place where I'm happy. Where being his wife no longer scares me, but excites me.

I never dreamed I'd actually agree to marry him. But now there's nothing I want more. It was sweet of him to give me that choice. Though let's face it. Had I not, he wouldn't have let me go anyway.

"What's so funny, mo chuisle?" The back of his hand softly strokes my cheek.

"Just thinking about how insane you are and how I'll have to put up with it for the rest of my life."

He chuckles, all gravelly, setting fire to my already scorching limbs.

"That's right, you will." His lips feather over mine.

"No one has ever wanted me this badly before." I kiss him, and he groans.

"And no one ever will."

He slams his mouth to mine and takes me in a brutal kiss, practically ripping off my dress until we're both bare and hungry for one another.

His gaze holds mine as our heartbeats thunder, desire burning in our veins. "I'm gonna love you for the rest of my life."

The promise in his voice, it takes my breath away. And I know he means it. I know with him, I've found not only a home, but a forever I can hold on to.

He slides a hand between us, poising his cock at my entrance.

"Show me." My hand lands across his cheek. "Show me how much you love me."

In a single thrust, he's inside me.

Filling me.

Stretching me.

He's so deep. So damn deep.

But when he starts to move, I come alive, my body and heart both filled with affection. It's hard to even define what he's become to me.

He flips me over, taking me with him, until I'm on top, his hand clutching the back of my neck possessively. His eyes swim with aching passion as he bows his hips, forcing his erection deeper.

"I love you so much, Elara."

He pulls me in, lowering my face to his, and my heart lurches at the suddenness of his mouth on mine.

Taking me with demanding fury.

With forceful dominance.

Our bodies bringing each other pleasure.

I once wanted this so badly. Wanted to be loved. And I swear, I never thought I would ever get here. But Tynan, he proved it was possible. That *we're* possible, as crazy as that once seemed to be.

I grab his shoulders, needing to touch him, to feel him everywhere.

There's no one else in this world who can compete with the feelings he gives me. Like I'm floating.

My husband.

The man who wrecked my life, then built it back up into a world I never dreamed could be mine.

Marriage.

Falling in love.

It once seemed like a fantasy.

I thought I'd be on the run forever. Yet with him, I don't have to run anymore.

I slow my movements, searching his gaze, and the way I feel for him could move mountains. I never thought I could. Or would.

But falling in love with Tynan was the best thing I've ever done.

My soul is forever his. Forever clinging to the hope that nothing can break us.

Nothing can undo what we have.

I welcomed him into my body, but somehow, he stole my heart along the way.

# FORTY-FIVE

## TYNAN
### TWO MONTHS LATER

There was a time when I didn't think we'd ever get here. Sure, we were married legally already. But to have a wedding, my whole family here, her getting ready with my sisters, I never imagined it.

I didn't know what happiness was until now. Until her. Until forever became a possibility for someone like me.

Devlin and I sit around with my brothers at the outdoor patio bar at Necker Island. It's small and private. We own the hotel, so arranging a wedding here, especially with Fernanda's help, was easy.

I can't wait to see her. Bet she's gonna light up the whole place with how beautiful she is.

"So…" Devlin lifts a glass in the air. "This calls for a toast. He's finally in love and getting married. Told you it was gonna happen."

He smirks as my brothers lift up their own drinks.

"Yeah, yeah. Guess I owe you that million."

"Bloody right you do. But you keep it. Just glad you found what you didn't know you were looking for."

"Thanks, brother."

We toss our drinks back and ask for another.

From the corner of my eye, I see a couple arguing, and Fionn's eyes immediately land on them too.

His jaw clenches when the man grabs the woman's arm, angrily saying something to her while she's visibly shaken. The girl… She's no more than nineteen, her hazel eyes full of fear.

Before I can stop him, Fionn's on his feet, stalking toward them.

"Oh, fuck…" I mutter, getting up after him. "Elara won't forgive me if I get bloody before the wedding."

Cillian laughs, smacking a palm to my back as we all head after him. Yet he's already gripping the man's shirt, saying something we can't hear.

"If you touch her like that again, I'll kill you."

"Who the fuck do you think you are?" The man tries to fight my brother off, though doesn't stand a chance.

When he realizes we're all with him, fear passes through his eyes.

"I don't know what the hell you think you saw," he tells Fionn. "But that's my girl, and how I handle her is not your fucking business."

Fionn tips his face closer, looking down at the guy, who's a good six inches smaller. "I've made it my business. What are you gonna do about it?"

Fionn could crush him. The asshole has to know that.

"You're gonna leave. Now. You're gonna get your shit and get the fuck away from her before I permanently remove you."

"Is that a threat?"

"It is. Do you want a demonstration?"

"Whatever," he spits out, glaring at the young woman. "You want the whore, you can have her. She's boring in bed anyway. Half the time, I can't even get it up looking at her."

The woman sobs, frantically wiping her eyes and pushing her dark hair out of her face. She's small too. Maybe five feet. And I catch a bruise on her arm. An older bruise.

Jesus. What the hell did we walk into?

"Maybe it's your dick." Fionn's nostril's flare. "Because from looking at her, she's definitely not the problem."

He can't see her, but the woman's eyes widen and she blinks past her tears, like she can't believe he said that.

Fionn drops the man. "You have five minutes to get out of this fucking hotel. I don't care where you go, but you're not staying here."

He scoffs. "Yeah, okay."

"I guess you're hard of hearing." Fionn brings his face closer. "We own the place. So unless you want to see what happens to people who don't do what we say, I suggest you get lost before I lose more of my patience."

He shoots the woman a glare, muttering something unintelligible under his breath before marching off.

Fionn turns to the girl, and when he sees her bruise, his fist curls at his side. "He did that to you?"

She shrugs. "It's okay. It happened a while ago."

Her gaze falls to her feet.

With a finger, he tilts her chin up. "It's not okay. No one has a right to put their hands on you."

Her bottom lip quivers.

"How about I get you some food?"

"Ah, no…" She swipes under her eyes. "You don't have to do that."

"I know." He smirks. "I want to."

"Okay."

Her voice is so small. Poor thing. Can just imagine what she's been putting up with.

"Do you have the key to the room you two were sharing?"

She shakes her head, picking at her nails. "He kept everything."

"Alright, don't worry. What's your room number?"

"Sixty-six ninety-three."

"Okay, I'll get you a suite and move all your things to it."

Her eyes grow. "I don't have money."

"You don't need money."

She whimpers. "Why are you being so nice to me?"

"Because someone has to be."

Her bottom lip quivers. I can tell Fionn is affected.

"Come on, let's get you settled into a new room."

She nods, walking beside him, yet keeping a safe distance.

"Do you like weddings? Because one of my brothers is getting married in about three hours and I can use a date."

That gets her laughing a little, and I don't hear the rest of it as they disappear inside the hotel.

"Wow." Cillian chuckles. "That was…"

"Fionn?" I offer.

"Yeah." He shakes his head. "Jesus. I mean, he could break her."

"Or maybe he can make her stronger."

"Well, weirder things have happened," Devlin adds. "I mean, Elara did fall in love with you."

"Fuck off." I punch his shoulder, returning to the bar.

In a few hours, she's going to be walking down the aisle to me, and I can't wait until I see my wife again.

# ELARA

I stare at myself in the full-length mirror of the bridal suite, rolling my hands up and down the Chantilly lace of my mermaid gown.

My hair lies in perfectly styled Hollywood waves, the ends tickling my bare back. The dress was made just for me by Dolce & Gabbana, beautiful embroidered flowers all over the gown.

"You look so pretty!" Eriu dabs her eyes.

"You know you're too good for Tynan, right?" Iseult teases. "If you're thinking of running, I have a car ready for you."

I laugh. "There's no more running for me. This time I'd like to stay."

"Good." She tilts her face up with a smirk. "I was just testing you."

I shake my head. "I'm afraid to know what would happen if I failed."

Before she can respond, someone knocks at the door.

"Who could that be?" Iseult heads to open it while I stay where I am, just in case Tynan tries to sneak a peek again.

"Tynan!" she scolds. "I told you, you can't see her."

"Come on, just for a second."

"Nope. Can't see the bride before the wedding."

"You're terrible," he tells her, while I stifle a laugh.

It makes me so happy that he's so eager to see me.

"It's what they tell me. Now go! Oh, hey, Brody," she says. "You can come in."

"Why the hell is he allowed in?"

"Because we actually like him. Goodbye, brother."

The door shuts, and she's returning with Brody.

"Oh my goodness! Look at you." I grab his hands. "You look so handsome in your tux."

"Thank you. I have the rings." He holds a box.

"And I know you're going to take great care of them."

"I won't lose them, I promise."

*Please don't let him lose them.*

It's still hard to believe that Brody is talking again. That after all this time, he's finally found his voice. It's truly the greatest miracle, and we couldn't be happier.

As the clock winds down, it soon becomes time to walk down the aisle. Knots form in my stomach.

It just hit me now that I'm alone. No family here. No one to walk me down the aisle. It shouldn't bother me, yet it does.

"Hey, what's wrong?" Eriu's brows furrow. "You look upset."

Iseult takes my hand in hers. "What happened? Do I need to kill anyone?"

My laughter fills the room. "No, not today. I was just thinking how I have no family here. I don't know, it just sucks."

"You do have a family." Eriu smiles. "We're your sisters now."

That has me choking up, fanning my face so I don't cry.

"I know it's hard," Iseult says. "But we've got you."

"Thank you. That means a lot to me."

Another knock comes through.

This time, it's Patrick's voice I hear when Iseult opens the door. "May I come in?"

"Hey, Dad."

"Hey, darlings." His eyes go to mine, and he smiles wide.

"You look beautiful. My son is a lucky man to have met you. And right about now, he's out of his mind waiting eagerly for you."

My heartbeats pound in my chest, wanting to see him too.

"We know." Iseult rolls her eyes.

"Hey, Brody," Patrick calls him over. "They're ready for you out there."

"Oh God, is it time?" I ask.

"Looks like it." He takes a step closer to me. "I did come here to ask you something, and feel free to say no, but I was hoping I could maybe walk you down the aisle."

My eyes start to water.

"I know I'm not your da, but I'd like to think of you as my daughter now, so if it's alright with you, it'd be my honor to take you down.

What do you say?"

Emotions clog my throat, and tears roll down my cheeks. "I would love that."

He hugs me tight and kisses the top of my head.

"Dad." Iseult gives him a stern look. "You're ruining her makeup with your sappy shit." Though she's discreetly fingering under her lashes.

"I'm sorry!" he says. "Alright, alright, no crying."

Iseult quickly fixes my makeup, and before we know it, the girls are walking down the aisle, with Brody close behind.

When it's my turn, I take a deep breath, nerves hitting my stomach. Not because I don't want this, but because there's something else I need to tell him.

The soft melody starts, and we begin our descent down the aisle.

All the guests rise. But he's the only one I see.

It's why I didn't want the veil covering my face. I wanted to see him, and I wanted him to see me. To see how happy I am to be his.

Emotions cling to his eyes, and he swallows harshly when I grow near.

"You'd better take care of her, you hear?" his father says as he places my hand in Tynan's.

"I promise," he whispers, his eyes filled with longing and love—so much of it, I feel it whispering in the air around us. He holds my cheeks firmly, yet with softness too. "You're the most beautiful woman I have ever seen."

"Thank you. You're looking very handsome too."

"I've been dying to see you all day."

I laugh under my breath. "I heard. You're pretty persistent."

"You should know that about me already." He picks up my hand and kisses it.

Leaning in toward his ear, I whisper, "You're so persistent, you've finally knocked me up."

He jerks back, the swell of his emotions lighting up his eyes. "Are you serious?"

I nod, my eyes watering. I love seeing him so happy.

He cups my belly, his brows furrowing.

"What are you two bloody talking about? Care to share with the rest of us folks?" Patrick hollers from his seat.

Tynan waits for me to give him permission to reveal the happy news, and I nod. We're all family, and I want us to have some good news after everything we've been through.

"Well, it looks like I'm gonna be a father." He chuckles. "Fuck."

"Language!" Ruby tsks before she grins from ear to ear, coming over to hug us both, giddy with excitement. "Ah, a baby!"

Then everyone's on their feet, congratulating us, telling us how happy they are.

I might have lost a family, but I've gained one too.

"Should I go ahead with the vows or…" The wedding officiant glances between us while everyone returns to their seat.

"Please do." Tynan grabs my hand, and pulls me up against him, body-to-body, soul-to-soul.

And as he looks deep into my eyes, he clasps my chin between two fingers.

"Just get to the good part," he whispers, nearing his lips to mine, repeating what he told the priest on the day we were first married.

But that feels like a century ago.

My heart fills with so much love, I could burst.

"By the power vested in me by the State of Massachusetts, I now pronounce you husband and wife. You may kiss the bride."

With that, he pulls me in and seals his lips to mine.

And though we've been through so much already, our journey has just begun.

# BONUS EPILOGUE

## ELARA
### EIGHT MONTHS LATER

"Tynan, you know I love you, but I'm pregnant, not injured."

He tightens his grip around me, holding me against his chest as he carries me through the door of our home.

In one hand, he holds bags of groceries, and I'm not sure how he can handle that much weight on his poor arms.

Brody laughs as he gazes up, carrying one of the grocery bags. It still amazes me that he talks and laughs. I don't take it for granted one bit.

"I know," Tynan says. "But you're nine months pregnant, mo ghrá, and your feet swell when you walk."

My face warms at the adoring way he says that, the way he looks at me. It still makes my stomach flip.

He's not wrong. My feet have been killing me. It's nice to have someone take care of me the way he has. Doting on me and the baby any chance he gets. It's sweet, really.

"I love you." My lips press to his, and his eyes shut, a smile forming.

"Hearing you say that still makes me insane." He kisses my temple before lowering me onto the sofa, opening the recliner so I can rest my legs. "You stay here while Brody and I cook."

We're supposed to have the Quinns over in a few hours for family dinner, and I'm excited to see them all. They usually rotate who hosts dinners every month, and this month is our turn.

"Are you sure you guys don't want my help?"

"Nope," Brody says, popping his chin. "We can do it."

Tynan throws an arm over his shoulders. "That's right. You stay here and look pretty and let the boys take care of dinner."

I let out a sigh, my heart swelling as I stare up at their faces. It's hard to contain my love for them. These months have been everything I could've dreamed of.

My pregnancy was rough at first, lots of morning sickness, and that had Tynan worrying. I swear I've never seen a man that scared in my life. Even the doctor telling him it was normal didn't quell his nerves.

I can just imagine how worried he'll become every time the baby has a sniffle.

Brody has been excited for the baby too. He keeps picking out books he's going to read to her.

My hands cup my protruding belly, tears growing in my eyes.

*Can't wait to meet you, Adora.*

Tynan's gaze seizes the thrumming muscle in my chest, a smirk growing on my face. Because I know he feels it too: the magic in the air.

Brody settles beside me, hugging my midsection and lowering his face against it. "Will the baby be my sister?"

Tynan quirks a brow at me, and I fight a grin. Brody hasn't brought this up yet. But we want him to be comfortable with whatever he chooses. This has never been about us.

"If you want her to be." I stroke his hair as he sighs.

"I do. I want her to be my sister."

As though my heart hadn't already burst, he had to go on and say that.

"Then that's what she'll be." My arms squeeze him tighter.

"Does that mean…" His words are lost in thought.

My eyes grow as I stare up at Tynan, wondering if maybe he's trying to say what I've been dying to hear.

"What is it, bud?" Tynan asks, settling beside him.

Brody sits up straighter, his vision bouncing between us. "Well, if Adora is gonna be my sister, does that mean you guys will be my mom and dad?"

Emotions stitch up my throat. "We'll be whatever you want us to be, Brody."

From behind him, Tynan grabs my hand and holds it tight.

"I think I want that." Brody's little mouth twists. "I don't think Mommy and Daddy would be upset."

Oh, my goodness. Is that what he's been thinking? I can't imagine them ever being upset at him for that.

"Of course they wouldn't be." Tynan grasps the back of his head, his gaze intense as he goes on. "Your mother and father only want to see you happy, and so do we. Elara and I both love you like you're our son, and that will never change, no matter what."

That has his gaze glistening. "Okay…Dad."

Tynan visibly swallows and tears continue to fill my eyes.

Brody turns to me, hugging me tightly. "I love you, Mom."

I choke on a silent sob, unable to contain how full my heart is in this moment. "I love you too, sweetheart. Always will."

We stay this way for a while, this beautiful little family we've created. Hearing him calling me Mom, it fulfills me, because he's always been my son.

I hate that I had to be because he lost his mother, but I'm glad they trusted Tynan with their baby. And I hope wherever she is, Willow's looking down at us and is filled with happiness too.

"Alright, you guys, go do your thing in the kitchen and I'll put on a movie or something."

That has Tynan smirking, and my body warms every time he does. "Good. Call us if you need anything."

"Thanks, babe."

They head into the kitchen, leaving me here to do nothing but stare at the TV, unsure what to watch.

Thirty minutes later, and I'm bored out of my mind, getting up to wander into the kitchen. They don't notice me at first, their backs to me as Tynan shows Brody how to cut tomatoes. I love that he can cook. That he will teach Adora how to cook too.

I hold tight to my belly, thinking about my mother and how much I wish she were here to see this. To see me and the child we've created. A pang hits my chest, and I close my eyes, fighting my aching emotions.

I'd be lying if I said I have forgiven my grandmother for what she'd done. For what she took from me. Maybe one day I will, but that's not today and it won't be tomorrow. Quite honestly, it may never happen, and I'm okay with that. I think we put too much into forgiveness, like we need that to move on. But we don't. Because some things are unforgivable, and that's okay too.

My grandpa still lives with us. He has some good days, but unfortunately, the bad ones outweigh the good. When he has moments of clarity, he remembers me, and I wonder if he remembers what they did to Mom. And though it hurts, I can't stay mad at him for long. Not when he's in such a state.

"I thought I told you to go rest." Tynan appears before me as I open my eyes to find him tilting a brow.

"Well…" I throw my arms around his shoulders, leaning my mouth up toward his ear. "I thought it'd be a lot more fun to watch my sexy husband cook instead."

He growls low, dropping his mouth to my throat, my pulse racing the closer he gets.

"Is that right?" His strong hands grip my ass.

"That's right." I go breathless, his body pressed to mine.

"You're not supposed to make me hard right now, wife."

"I'm sorry?" My lips stroke his while Brody continues to cut tomatoes.

"Don't be. Just means I get to punish you later."

"Good," I whisper. "Make sure you punish me extra hard, because I need this baby out of me."

He chuckles, all hoarse and croaky. "My pleasure, Mrs. Quinn." His palm lands on my stomach. "I love you both so damn much."

"She's gonna love her daddy."

He runs a hand down his face and laughs. "Still can't believe I'm having a girl."

"You'll be amazing."

"I hope so, mo chuisle." His eyes bore into mine, his mouth growing closer until he lays claim to mine, kissing me with undulated passion and yearning.

"Ew!" Brody says. "Less kissing, more cooking."

We both burst with laughter, staring into each other's eyes, realizing how lucky we are to have this life. To have each other.

And knowing that each day isn't guaranteed makes me cherish every moment we have like it's the last.

"Go on," I tell him. "Our son needs you."

He cups my face, his eyes never leaving mine until he kisses me once more and I hold on to him just a little tighter, like I never want to let go.

# THANKS FOR READING!

Up next is Fionn Quinn and Amara Edwards. *Filthy Savage* will be an age gap, forced marriage, single mom story. It will be the first time I've ever written a breeding kink before!

Wondering if Iseult & Gio have a story? They do in *Twisted Promises*!

Want to know how Aiden died? Jump into the Messina Crime Family to discover what happened.

# PLAYLIST

- "Escape" by Vincent Lima
- "Can You Escape the Devil" by Kendra Dantes feat. Eyla Rae
- "Truth Comes Out" by Willyecho
- "Know" by SAYSH feat. Anderson Rocio
- "Beautiful Creature" by MIIA
- "Known" by Tauren Wells
- "Let It Rain" by Kendra Dantes feat. Pei Pei Chung
- "Dead Man" by David Kushner
- "Morally Grey – Nation Haven Edition" by April Jai feat. Nation Haven
- "Where Do You Go" by Jessie Murph
- "How Could You" by Jessie Murph
- "Lose Control" by Teddy Swims
- "Sweet and Dark" by Miles Hardt
- "Hurt Me" by Suriel Hess
- "You Put a Spell on Me" by Austin Giorgio
- "No Mercy" by Austin Giorgio
- "Something Real" by Roses & Revolutions
- "Beautiful Things" by Benson Boone
- "Home" by Good Neighbours
- "Deed Is Done" by Six Black Skulls
- "Holding On" by Shaya Zamora
- "Is It Alright?" by James Arthur
- "Daydreams" by We Three
- "In the Cold" by Vincent Lima
- "Hearts" by Roses & Revolutions
- "Sinner" by DEZI

- "It Is What It Is" by Abe Parker
- "Some Things I'll Never Know" by Teddy Swims
- "If You Love Her" by Forest Blakk
- "Trouble" by Camylio
- "High, High, High" by Camylio
- "Drip Off" by Austin Giorgio
- "Fetish" by Selena Gomez feat. Gucci Mane
- "What You Do to Me" by John Legend

LISTEN ON SPOTIFY!

# ALSO BY LILIAN HARRIS

## *Fragile Hearts* Series

1. *Fragile Scars* (Damian & Lilah)
2. *Fragile Lies* (Jax & Lexi Part 1)
3. *Fragile Truths* (Jax & Lexi Part 2)
4. *Fragile Pieces* (Gabe & Mia)

## *Cavaleri Brothers* Series

1. *The Devil's Deal* (Dominic & Chiara)
2. *The Devil's Pawn* (Dante & Raquel)
3. *The Devil's Secret* (Enzo & Jade)
4. *The Devil's Den* (Matteo & Aida)
5. *The Devil's Demise* (Extended Epilogue)

## *Messina Crime Family* Series

1. *Sinful Vows* (Michael & Elsie)
2. *Cruel Lies* (Raph & Nicolette)
3. *Twisted Promises* (Gio & Iseult)
4. *Savage Wounds* (Adriel & Kayla)

## *Savage Kings* Series

1. *Ruthless Savage* (Devlin & Eriu)

2. *Brutal Savage* (Tynan & Elara)
3. *Wicked Savage* (Fionn & Amara - January 6th, 2025)
4. *Filthy Savage* (Cillian - May 5th, 2025)

# Standalone

1. *Shattered Secrets* (Husdon & Hadleigh)

WITHIN EVERY HEARTBEAT,
THERE'S A STORY.

For Lilian, a love of writing began with a love of books. From Goosebumps to romance novels with sexy men on the cover, she loved them all. It's no surprise that at the age of eight she started writing poetry and lyrics and hasn't stopped writing since.

She was born in Azerbaijan, and currently resides on Long Island, N.Y. with her husband, three kids, and lots of animals. Even though she has a law degree, she isn't currently practicing. When she isn't writing or reading, Lilian is baking or cooking up a storm. And once the kids are in bed, there's usually a glass of red in her hand. Can't just survive on coffee alone!

**FIND LILIAN ONLINE!**

Made in United States
Troutdale, OR
09/25/2024